Praise for
THE RETRIEVAL ARTIST SERIES

The SF thriller is alive and well, and today's leading practitioner is Kristine Kathryn Rusch.

—Analog

Readers of police procedurals as well as fans of SF should enjoy this mystery series.

—Kliatt

Instant addiction. You hear about it—maybe you even laugh it off—but you never think it could happen to you. Well, you just haven't run into Miles Flint and the other Retrieval Artists looking for The Disappeared. ...I am hopelessly hooked....

—Lisa DuMond
MEviews.com on *The Disappeared*

An inventive plot and complex, conflicted characters increases the appeal of Kristine Kathryn Rusch's *Extremes*. This futuristic tale breaks new ground as a space police procedural and should appeal to science fiction and mystery fans.

—RT Book Reveiws on *Extremes*

Part science fiction, part mystery, and pure enjoyment are the words to describe Kristine Kathryn Rusch's latest Retrieval Artist novel.... This is a strong murder mystery in an outer space storyline.

—The Best Reviews on *Consequences*

An exciting, intricately plotted, fast-paced novel. You'll find it difficult to put down.

—*SFRevu* on *Buried Deep*

A science fiction murder mystery by one of the genre's best.... A book with complex characters, an interesting and unpredictable plot, and timeless and universal things to say about the human condition.

—*The Panama News* on *Paloma*

Rusch continues her provocative interplanetary detective series with healthy doses of planet-hopping intrigue, heady legal dilemmas and well-drawn characters.

—*Publishers Weekly* on *Recovery Man*

...the mystery is unpredictable and absorbing and the characters are interesting and sympathetic.

—*Blastr* on *Duplicate Effort*

Anniversary Day is an edge-of-the-seat thriller that will keep you turning pages late into the night and it's also really good science fiction. What's not to like?

—*Analog* on *Anniversary Day*

Set in the not too distant future, the latest entry in Rusch's popular sf thriller series (*The Disappeared; Duplicate Effort*) combines fast-paced action, beautifully conflicted protagonists, and a distinctly "sf noir" feel to tell a complex and far-reaching mystery. VERDICT Compulsively readable with canny plot twists, this should appeal to series fans as well as action-suspense readers.

—*Library Journal* on *Anniversary Day*

Rusch offers up a well-told mystery with interesting characters and a complex, riveting storyline that includes a healthy dose of suspense, all building toward an ending that may not be what it appears.

—*RT Book Reviews* on *Blowback*

We always like our intergalactic politics as truly alien, and Rusch delivers the goods. It's one thing to depict members of a Federation whining about treaties, quite another to depict motivations that are truly, well, alien.

—*Astroguyz* on *Blowback*

Fans of Rusch's Retrieval Artist universe will enjoy the expansion of the Anniversary Day story, with new characters providing more perspectives on its signature events, while newcomers will get a good introduction to the series.

—*Publishers Weekly* on *A Murder of Clones*

THE RETRIEVAL ARTIST SERIES:

The Disappeared
Extremes
Consequences
Buried Deep
Paloma
Recovery Man
The Recovery Man's Bargain (Novella)
Duplicate Effort
The Possession of Paavo Deshin (Novella)

The Anniversary Day Saga:

Anniversary Day
Blowback
A Murder of Clones
Search & Recovery
The Peyti Crisis
Vigilantes
Starbase Human
Masterminds

Other Stories:

The Retrieval Artist (Novella)
The Impossibles (A Retrieval Artist Universe Short Story)

A MURDER of CLONES

A RETRIEVAL ARTIST UNIVERSE NOVEL

KRISTINE KATHRYN RUSCH

WMG PUBLISHING

A Murder of Clones

Book Three of the Anniversary Day Saga

Copyright © 2015 by Kristine Kathryn Rusch

All rights reserved

Published 2015 by WMG Publishing
www.wmgpublishing.com
Parts of this novel appeared in different form as the novella
A Murder of Clones (*Fiction River: Moonscapes,* edited by Dean Wesley Smith,
WMG Publishing, February 2014)
Cover and Layout copyright © 2015 by WMG Publishing
Cover design by Allyson Longueira/WMG Publishing
Cover art copyright © Madartists/Dreamstime
ISBN-13: 978-1-56146-608-5
ISBN-10: 1-56146-608-5

For Kevin J. Anderson
because he and I have been navigating this writing stuff together
for more than thirty years now. I don't think I could've done it
without you, Kev.

Acknowledgements

Thanks to Paul B. Higginbotham for his help in designing the court system for the Retrieval Artist universe. I had stumbled along early, but he has come up with a way to make it work. Of course, any errors here in understanding common legal procedures are mine and mine alone.

Thanks also go to Allyson Longueira for figuring out how to make these projects work, to Annie Reed for making sure I get my facts straight, and to Dean Wesley Smith, who consistently says, "Just write it, Rusch, and then we'll worry about what to do next."

And finally, thanks to all you readers who have joined with me for ten books now. Each book is an experiment, the Retrieval Artist series more than most, and I appreciate your willingness to join me on the journey.

Author's Note

Dear Readers,

You have in your hands book three of The Anniversary Day Saga. However, if you bought this book thinking it's a standalone title, your reading experience should be just fine. If you enjoy the book, however, go back and read Anniversary Day *and* Blowback *before moving on to the next book in this saga,* Search & Recovery.

As for the rest of you who've faithfully read the Retrieval Artist books, yes, I'm using the word "saga." I did not intend for this saga to happen. When I started Anniversary Day, *I thought I was writing one novel. I was wrong.*

I wrote the opening sequence of A Murder of Clones *to explain a scene in* Blowback *to myself. I thought* A Murder of Clones *would be a standalone novella. Of course, it wasn't. It was a novel. At that point, I thought I could write the novel years from now, when I wasn't finishing what I thought was the Anniversary Day trilogy.*

The minute I made the decision to make the novella something bigger, I quit writing on the novella and went back to Blowback.

One year later, I came back to the novella with the idea of finishing it for the Fiction River *Kickstarter project that Dean Wesley Smith and I did in the summer of 2012. I thought finishing the novella would be easy—and it was.*

But, as I finished it, I realized that I couldn't move forward with the next book in the Anniversary Day trilogy without writing Judita Gomez's story. At first, I thought I could write her story for myself, and not publish it.

I soon realized, however, that if I followed that plan, the moment Gomez appeared in the book I was writing, she would seem like a deus ex machina. In other words, her appearance would feel both superficial and a cheat.

I was then faced with two problems: my trilogy had just become something bigger. And the next book I had to publish in the Anniversary Day saga would be a Retrieval Artist novel without our favorite Retrieval Artist showing up at all.

I knew many readers would wait for Miles Flint to appear, and he's not going to. Not in this novel. Which is why it's called a Retrieval Artist Universe novel. He'll be in some of the books in this remaining arc, I promise.

In fact, when you finish this saga, you'll see that the center of the books-long story is Miles Flint.

Honestly, the fact that my unruly brain served up Judita Gomez next shouldn't surprise me. When I first designed the Retrieval Artist universe, I wanted some books to focus on other characters besides Flint. My desire to write non-Flint books is modeled on the mystery genre, particularly two of my favorite writers in the genre—Elizabeth George and Ed McBain. Each of George's books focus on a different main character within her series. But I suspect McBain had a larger influence on the Retrieval Artist Universe.

I have always said that this series is my 87th Precinct. Ed McBain wrote dozens of books about the precinct, and rotated his characters in and out of the novels. Some books would focus on a few of the characters, others would focus on different characters.

This is the first full novel in which Miles Flint does not appear. There will be others. There have already been side stories without Miles Flint, like The Recovery Man's Bargain. There will be more of those as well.

Which is a long way of telling you why I'm starting this book with a letter to the readers.

What WMG Publishing and I decided is that the last six books of this saga will come out every month until this saga is finished. You're holding A Murder of Clones, which is a January 2015 release. The next book will appear in February of 2015. Then you'll get a book every month until June, when this saga ends.

The Retrieval Artist series won't end there, of course. I already have a lot of side stories sketched out (and started), and several future novels in mind. I will take a break from the universe after more than a year of writing in it. I have other series and stories to tend to.

I'm having a lot of fun writing this saga. It's a challenge, and I love challenges. However, I promise (as much as I can with my recalcitrant brain) that the next RA novel after I finish this mini-saga will standalone—like the first eight did.

Thanks for joining me on this journey.

—Kristine Kathryn Rusch
Lincoln City, Oregon
April 29, 2014

A MURDER of CLONES

A RETRIEVAL ARTIST UNIVERSE NOVEL

ANNIVERSARY DAY SAGA

RA

BOOK THREE

FIFTEEN YEARS AGO

1

THE STENCH MADE HER EYES WATER. MARSHAL JUDITA GOMEZ HAD A protect-strip over her mouth and nose, but the stench still got through. Something had died here. Something big, or many somethings big. The fact that the stench was so strong meant she would have to destroy her clothes. Nothing anyone had invented had been able to take the overpowering smell of corpses out of clothing.

At least nothing had done it to her satisfaction.

And perhaps nothing could have satisfied her. Every time she found a corpse, she felt the death viscerally. It became part of her. Perhaps it made sense, then, that it would seem to be part of her clothing as well.

She carefully moved several flat leaves, following the Eaufasse into the cluster of trees. She hadn't studied this culture at all, just responded to their call. So she touched what the Eaufasse touched and stepped where the Eaufasse stepped, which was hard, since the Eaufasse was the size of a thin twelve-year-old human child with extra-long legs and feet the size of fists.

Be extremely careful, she sent to her partners Kyle Washington and Shakir Rainger through their links. They'd been with the Earth Alliance Frontier Security Squad for years, but she wasn't sure they'd ever been in a situation like this before.

She wasn't sure *she* had ever been in a situation like this before.

The Eaufasse Emir had contacted the Earth Alliance about an enclave of humans hiding in the back country, near one of the Eaufasse's major cities. The Eaufasse was one of sixteen different sentient species on Epriccom, the habitable moon of an uninhabitable planet in a sector of space that the Earth Alliance dubbed the Frontier.

Ever since its formation, the Earth Alliance had given several sectors of space the Frontier designation. That meant most of the planets within the sector had applied for Earth Alliance membership—or were potential applicants for membership. Most sectors ended up becoming part of the Alliance, but every once in a while, the designation backfired, leaving the sector unapproved or with only a few Alliance planets, making it difficult for anyone from the Alliance to do business there.

And no matter what the Alliance said, what its propaganda dictated, the Alliance was always about business.

Gomez moved slowly. She loved her job, even at moments like this, moments when a single misplaced footstep could cause an interstellar incident. Her work was not the same from hour to hour, let alone day to day or week to week, and she saw parts of the known universe that most people never got to see.

She focused on the steps in the dirt before her, noting the strange plants that slid toward her feet. They seemed to move without wind or even being touched.

She'd been trained to watch for cues like that, things that might mean whatever she was looking at was sentient. She carefully avoided those plants, and she sent a message through the secured link to her deputies to do the same.

She didn't expect them to answer. One reason she had chosen Washington and Rainger for this mission was because they had the most experience of all her deputies in first-contact situations. Not that this was the first time humans had contact with the Eaufasse, but as far as she could tell, this was the first time that the Earth Alliance authorities—not diplomats—had in-person contact. And in-person contact was always different from contact through networks and links.

For one thing, it was infinitely more dangerous.

The Earth Alliance Frontier Security Squad had jurisdiction in any sector designated Frontier. But jurisdiction didn't mean they could override local laws. It simply meant that the FSS investigated, policed, and patrolled any Earth Alliance members who found their way to a Frontier planet.

And usually, the shadiest Earth Alliance members found their way to the outskirts of Earth Alliance territory, knowing that the FSS was underfunded and spread much too thin.

Gomez was deeply aware of that right now. She needed half a dozen deputies, not the two she always traveled with. The Emir believed that the human enclave was up to no good—at least that was how the translation program had filtered the Eaufasse's extremely complex language.

The relationship with the Eaufasse was so new that very few Eaufasse spoke Standard, and those who did didn't speak it very well.

One of those Standard-speaking Eaufasse was just outside the investigation area, listening in on a link hooked up to both Gomez and the Eaufasse tracker/police officer/military official who led the small group to the corpses.

The language barrier was still so complete that she wasn't sure what job the Eaufasse in front of her actually had.

Finally, the group reached a clearing. The ground dipped here in a bowl shape, and she knew without looking that the corpses were here. The nose never lied.

She held up a fist, so that her deputies stopped moving. They froze. They didn't dare do anything else. One wrong word, one wrong gesture, one wrong step, and the FSS officer could find herself on the wrong side of an alien judicial system.

There were exceptions for marshals. Exceptions were part of the agreements made with Frontier planets. But that didn't mean every single culture on those planets abided by the rules, nor did it mean that the Earth Alliance would always defend a marshal's behavior, particularly if some authority in the Alliance felt the marshal was out of line.

We would like to spread out along the rim of this small clearing, Gomez sent through the joint alien-marshal link. *Do we have your permission to do so? If not, where should we stand?*

The Eaufasse responded quickly. *Of course, permission.*

And she had no idea if that meant she had permission to stand wherever she wanted or if she had to wait while it translated her request to the Eaufasse leading her.

That Eaufasse turned its pointed head toward her. Its eyes, large and liquid, fixed on hers. Then it waved one of its extra-long limbs toward her, in what seemed like a very human gesture for *Continue.*

She knew better than to assume she knew what the Eaufasse meant by the gesture.

After a moment, it tilted its head away from her, and another message came through the link.

Of course. Permission. Stand you want. Okay.

She cursed silently. She hoped that meant it was okay to stand where she wanted. At least she had it on record.

She put down her fist, gestured for the others to join her, and moved near the Eaufasse. It hunched toward the bowl like a mangled question mark.

The two deputies fanned out beside her, moving as cautiously as she was.

The clearing had an open view to the sky. Epriccom's bright sun made the plants glow bluish green. Epriccom had the right oxygen mix for humans, which made it an enticing planet for development, but it was clearly an alien place.

So alien, in fact, that it took her a moment to recognize the bodies in the tangle of vines, leaves, and branches that passed for ground cover here.

The bodies were equidistant apart. They sprawled face down, heads turned toward her, arms outward, feet bent. They were so bloated she couldn't tell much about them—male, female, age. Nor could she quite comprehend what they were wearing; in most areas the bloating was so severe that they had burst through their clothes.

6

The identical positions, and the fact that they sprawled face down, however, led her to believe they had been killed. Whether or not they had been dumped here was another matter.

She suppressed a sigh. She also didn't know what kind of killings Eaufasse did, if any, and how they treated their dead.

May we approach the corpses? She sent through the links.

Of course. Permission. Stand you want. Okay.

"Okay," she muttered. Washington glanced at her, his mouth a thin line.

She started down the incline, leading the way. Washington and Rainger followed, doing their best to walk where she had. Branches clawed at her boots, and she had the impression that some of the stuff had scuttled away from her feet.

Her heart pounded. She hated this kind of thing. She always felt out of her depth in situations that involved killings in Frontier planets. She had no idea what the temperature ranges were, how the local flora and fauna interacted with rotting material, what kind of insects—if any—went after corpses, and on and on.

She could only guess at things, and she was terrified she would guess wrong. Not only did her future depend on the correct moves, but often so did the future relationship between the Earth Alliance and the Frontier planet.

When she was within a few meters of the bodies, she turned slightly toward the deputies.

Spread out, she sent through the private links. *Tell me if you can make any sense of this. Try to limit your guesses to the ones you're at least half certain of.*

Rainger gave her a grim smile. Washington nodded once. They picked their way around the other side, with Rainger continuing until he stopped above the corpses' heads. He crouched. So did Washington near one of the corpse's backs.

Gomez stood near the feet, gazing upward. As she'd been traveling here, she had downloaded all the information she could find on the Eaufasse. She'd stored a backup copy on a chip in her thumb. Not that there had been a lot of information, just the preliminary report, filled with the usual happy-shiny crap about what a great planet it was, how accommodating the locals were, and how happy they would be to cooperate with any Earth Alliance culture that wanted to set up a base here.

No initial cultural difficulties, not with the advance team, and no mention of crime at all. Now whether that meant that the Eaufasse didn't commit crimes against each other or whether it meant that the Eaufasse had a different conception of crime than the Alliance did was anyone's guess.

And search she did, but hadn't found anything on Eaufasse death rituals. So that meant the advance teams and the later observers weren't allowed to see what the Eaufasse did. But she had learned not to interpret that either. It might mean that they kept the rituals private like some cultures kept bathing private or it might mean that the teams simply hadn't been near a death so didn't get to see what the Eaufasse did in that circumstance.

Not that it mattered now. She couldn't find the answer she wanted. She had no idea if these corpses were arranged in an Eaufasse death position or one of the other fifteen species on this planet had been involved in any way or if she was looking at a human-on-human crime.

She sighed softly. She had hoped for a simple knife in the back of one of the deceased, with a note attached, explaining all the reasons for the crime—or at least something similar, something that was obvious and unambiguously human-on-human.

Something she could deal with.

"Rainger," she said out loud, knowing that the Eaufasse could hear her conversation and would do its best to translate it for the other Eaufasse. "Send for the collection team. Tell them you'll meet them here, and remind them of the delicacy of the recovery effort."

"Yes, sir," Rainger said. "Mind if I continue to examine the scene, sir?"

"Don't touch anything," she said. "In fact, make a secondary recording. Get up close. The more information we have the better."

He nodded.

"Washington," she said. "You're with me."

"Sir?" he said, looking startled.

"We came here to remove a human enclave," she said. "I think we should see what we're facing."

2

Two marshals couldn't remove a human enclave from anywhere. But they could investigate the enclave, see its layout, maybe get a guess as to how big it was.

The Eaufasse that brought them looked at her, then at Rainger, then back at her. This one she could interpret: It wasn't certain if it should stay with Rainger or go with her. Clearly someone had asked it to keep an eye on the team of humans that had arrived.

That was their mistake for not sending more than one Eaufasse on this little adventure.

Gomez settled it for the Eaufasse. She started out of the clearing, following the footsteps they had made on the way in. Spread across her left eye, she had a map of this area that she had downloaded from some database. The trail she needed to follow branched off the trail they had originally walked down.

The Eaufasse let out a small peep and scrambled after them, using its long limbs to pull itself through the branches. The branches would swing it forward just a bit until finally it arrived at Gomez's side.

Wait. Please. Me lead. The translator said for it.

It's okay, Gomez sent. *I have a map.*

No, no. The Eaufasse sounded distressed. Could Eaufasse sound distressed? Or was she anthropomorphizing again? *Colleagues yours. Know not. Secret us.*

Okay, she sent. *I didn't understand that. Try again.*

Colleagues yours. Think secret. Yes?

She sighed. She still didn't understand it.

"I think it's saying that the enclave has no idea that the Eaufasse know anything about them," Washington said, sounding tired. Or maybe he was overwhelmed. This was already shaping up into something bigger than either of them wanted it to be.

Is that correct? Gomez sent. *Do the humans know you are watching them?*

Humans know not us, the translator sent back. *We want not humans know.*

That one she got. They didn't want the humans to know that they had discovered the enclave. Which begged the question: how did the enclave get here without the Eaufasse knowing?

But Gomez wasn't going to ask. She wouldn't get an answer she understood anyway. She'd leave it to the diplomats, whom she was going to have to send for, given the three bodies.

I won't reveal your location, Gomez sent. *I don't want the enclave to know about us either.*

At least, not right now. Not when there were only two marshals standing here and an unknown number of people in the enclave.

I just want to see the property, Gomez sent. And in case they didn't understand that, she added, *I want to know how big it is.*

One hundred, the translator answered.

She hoped to hell that was 100 humans and not 100 buildings. But she didn't ask that question either. All would be answered soon enough. She simply sent a thank you and kept going.

The weird underbrush was thinning. She recognized this area. It took her back to the trail carved into the wilderness—or what she thought of as wilderness. She could cut across the trail and head directly to the enclave, or she could backtrack, and take a much larger trail that had forked from this one a click back.

She was about to take the long route when the Eaufasse peeped at her again. It made that same gesture with its arm (at least she thought of it as an arm), the gesture she had thought of as *Come on.*

Maybe that was actually what it meant.

If we stay off the trail, she sent to the translator, *are we in danger of walking in protected areas?*

That was probably too complicated for them, Washington sent her on their private link.

There was no answer, at least not immediately.

Of course. Permission. Walk you want. Okay.

"Or maybe not," Washington muttered, just loud enough for her to hear.

She smiled. They continued. As long as she had permission on the record—or something she understood to be permission—she was going to take the easier route.

The land was hilly here, with more thick underbrush. The Eaufasse would touch branches as it went by, probably wishing it could pull itself along with them like it had before. It would lose Gomez and Washington quickly if it did that.

As rough as the terrain was, the distance they had to cover was relatively short. They reached a hill. The hill wasn't that high, but the hillside was steep.

Down, down, the translator sent.

Gomez and Washington looked down, seeing nothing but ground cover. But the Eaufasse with them made that *Come on* gesture again, only its head was pointed toward the top of the hill.

Then it fell on its—stomach? front? Gomez wasn't certain what to call that part of its anatomy—and started pulling itself through the underbrush. So that was what the translator meant by *down.*

You gotta be kidding me, Washington sent her.

Something wrong? Rainger sent.

Not with us, Gomez sent. *Collection there yet?*

They say they're an hour out, Rainger sent. *I can join you.*

We're okay, she sent again.

Except for this stupid obstacle course, Washington sent, then promptly fell on his belly. It wasn't like they hadn't done this in training. They'd pull themselves forward by their elbows or their gun barrels or their knives, sometimes for hours.

But Washington was a lot closer to that training than Gomez was. She hadn't done this in nearly a decade. Plus she didn't know what this ground, and this ground cover, was composed of.

Still, she flopped down and pulled herself forward, using the branches. They actually moved with her, and she wondered if they were some kind of creature. She remembered that feeling she had earlier, that they had clawed at her boots. She wasn't sure if they were physically pulling her forward now.

The movement through the underbrush was a lot more quiet than she expected it to be. She could barely hear the rustle of Washington and the Eaufasse ahead of her. It took almost no time to reach the crest of the hill.

The branches formed a web in front of her, but she could see through the openings. She could have sworn that the branches weren't in that position when she had started up the hill, but she didn't say anything. She'd seen too many strange things throughout her career to doubt her impressions now.

She moved just a little closer to the edge. Washington was at her left, the Eaufasse was at her right. It almost flattened against the ground, looking like a pile of branches all by itself. The perfect camouflage.

She blinked a high-powered scope over her right eye. For the moment, she kept her left open. The red lines of the map converged before her, but she didn't need them.

The enclave looked like an eyesore against the landscape. Gray buildings, made with that weird self-grow permaplastic that colonists often used, rose from the underbrush like rectangular rocks.

She blinked the map away, and closed her left eye, letting the scope in her right eye magnify even further.

Seven buildings, six in a circle around a large main building of some kind. The underbrush had been destroyed here, and it looked like there was some kind of dome or force field around the enclave itself. The underbrush ended several meters away from the first two buildings.

The enclave looked like it had been here for a long time.

Do you have any idea what they do here? she sent to the translator.

No, it answered.

How long has this enclave been here? she asked.

Unknown. Long time. Guess.

That was clear enough. The fact that the enclave had been here a while complicated matters although not with the Earth Alliance. Earth Alliance law was clear on this point. In a Territory, Earth Alliance enclaves were guests at the whim of their hosts. If a guest offended its host, the guest had to leave, no matter how much it had invested or how long it had been there.

The problem wasn't the law. The problem was enforcing the law.

And that was the saga of her entire career.

She deactivated the scope and glanced at Washington. He looked at her, and she could see on his face the same frustration that she felt.

They were going to have to monitor these bastards, maybe for months, while they waited for the Earth Alliance Military Guard to arrive. Then it would take a small-scale war to get these idiots out of here. After, of course, someone—probably her—tried to talk them into leaving voluntarily.

The diplomats got the easy job in these situations. The diplomats got to talk to the locals who barely understood Standard and who probably didn't understand Earth Alliance customs at all.

She was going to have to talk with the humans who had been here for years, humans who didn't want to be found, humans who were probably doing something they believed to be ideologically pure or economically beneficial. Humans who would probably go to war—either for their beliefs or their fortune.

And she wasn't sure which one was worse.

Because they would both cost her months of her life—and, if she wasn't careful, her life itself.

Then she smiled to herself, keeping her head down. Moments like this were the reason she loved this job.

She glanced at Washington again. He was looking at the enclave with great concentration, probably through a scope of his own.

We need to set up surveillance, something as modern as we have, so that their monitors won't find it right away, she sent to him. *And we'll do something from orbit, of course.*

And maybe, if the diplomats did their job and got permission from the Eaufasse, they could fly little bug-like cameras around the enclave itself.

She was tempted to go down to the edge of the enclave and see if someone would let her in. But if they didn't—or even if they did—she would tip her hand. The enclave would know that the Eaufasse were aware of them, and would know that the Eaufasse had contacted the FSS.

She glanced at the Eaufasse. It looked like part of the ground cover. She'd never seen such effective camouflage. Only the glistening of its eyes and the fact that she knew it was there let her see it at all.

Let's go, she sent, and wondered how the hell they were going to back their way out of this mess. And by that, she meant both the branch ground cover, and the situation here on Epriccom.

3

GOMEZ'S SHIP, THE *EAFS STANLEY*, WAS ONE OF THE FLAGSHIPS IN THE FSS fleet. The ship had all of the bells and whistles the squad could ask for, from the latest weapons systems to the best forensic labs to several prisoner wings. Not to mention an entire section designed for non-standard passengers.

She had set up the non-standard section to Peyti normal. But she was less concerned with the non-standard section than she was with the forensic lab. She wanted to find out what the heck was going on with these corpses and why they caused the Emir to send for the FSS in the first place.

The bodies had proven difficult to move. It had taken nearly 24 hours to remove them from their resting place in the clearing and get them to the orbiting ship. Several of the branches had worked their way into the corpses and had to be dislodged. Of course, no one wanted to do that without the Eaufasse's permission, and no one quite knew how to ask for it.

Plus no one knew if it was possible to carry bodies out of the place where they had died. If this were a Disty-run area, the problems would be extreme. The Disty believed that bodies contaminated everything, and had elaborate rituals for dealing with them.

The Eaufasse didn't seem to have problems with bodies, but the translations weren't really clear on anything. Gomez was guessing, and sometimes not even guessing on much evidence.

She had managed to retrieve the bodies with her own squad, feeling uncomfortable the entire time. At least the shuttle landing points had been safe.

One of the first things the Alliance did with any Territory was negotiate landing points. The Eaufasse had a space traffic system, but no real port—not in the way that the Alliance thought of ports, anyway—so some diplomat somewhere had negotiated landing areas.

Gomez's team had used the one closest to the bodies for picking up the bodies. After she had done what negotiations she could, given the limitations of the language, she had assigned Rainger and the collection team the task of bagging and carrying the bodies back to the shuttle.

She had had more important things to negotiate: She needed to coordinate everything, from the diplomats to the arrival of the Earth Alliance Military Guards. She also needed someone who spoke both Standard and the Eaufasse's language well. Fortunately, that person wasn't too far away.

Unfortunately, that person wasn't really a person at all.

That person was Peyti, which was why she had set the non-standard section to Peyti normal. The Peyti had arrived quickly.

Its name was Uzven. She had no idea what its gender was. The Peyti were unusually reticent about gender. It was considered offensive to ask. The names certainly didn't give a clue either.

She wasn't a big fan of the Peyti, but she had to work with Uzven because there was no diplomatic unit anywhere near Epriccom. And she wasn't going to let the Earth Alliance Military Guards anywhere near Epriccom until she had diplomats and translators in place.

Which meant that she was on her own until she figured out what was going on here. She preferred it that way. Her experience had taught her that most things could be resolved with very little work, as long as the parties involved understood each other.

The first thing she had to understand was what happened to those corpses. And the first step toward figuring that out was determining what killed them. She knew no one better than Lashante Simiaar, the best forensic director in the entire FSS.

Simiaar ran the forensic lab on the *EAFS Stanley*. The lab was the most important part of the ship. In fact, a well-stocked forensic lab had become one of the most important parts of *all* FSS ships. Often the problems that marshals ran into could be resolved with the right kind of forensic analysis. Or they could at least be understood.

Uzven, the Peyti, was in the forensic lab, along with Simiaar. As Gomez entered the lab, she smiled at the two of them standing side by side, watching the last of the corpse removal on a gigantic flat screen. Uzven wore a human-style business suit, which had the effect of making it look like a child wearing its parents clothing.

The illusion wasn't helped by Simiaar's presence. She looked large next to the Peyti. She was a tall, broad woman with extra flesh that held a surprising amount of muscle. She could lift and move and carry better than almost anyone on the team, but she was no good in a fight, and she probably hadn't run anywhere in the past fifteen years.

"What a mess," she said to Gomez without looking at her.

"Yeah," Gomez said, knowing that neither of them was referring to the corpses. Both women knew that something was amiss here, something they didn't understand yet. "May I borrow Uzven now?"

Uzven looked at her. It looked like every other Peyti she'd ever known. It wore a mask over its face, because it couldn't breathe oxygen. Its eyes were huge, but the rest of it looked like it could easily fall into pieces.

The Peyti were fragile, and they tired easily. Plus, Gomez didn't like them on principle. Most of them had gone into the legal side of the Alliance justice system, and a startling number of Peyti had become defense attorneys.

She wasn't fond of defense attorneys. Every time she had had to testify about something they made her seem stupid.

She expected no less from a Peyti translator, since it did have the upper hand. After all, it knew the Eaufasse language, and she did not.

Simiaar sighed. "I guess you can borrow Uzven. But when those corpses get in here, I'm going to need Uzven back. I don't know what they got contaminated with, and so I need to ask the Eaufasse a lot of questions."

Simiaar had already set up part of the forensic wing as a quarantined area, just in case the dead had contracted something or been infected with something that wasn't obvious to the collection team.

Gomez beckoned Uzven to move with her to a different part of the lab. Gomez wanted to keep Uzven here in case Collection had more questions for it.

Uzven walked beside her on its spindly legs. It hadn't said more than a handful of words to her since its arrival. She didn't know if it was naturally reticent or if it disapproved of the *Stanley's* presence here.

"First," Gomez said, "I assume you understand the Eaufasse culture since you speak their language. Maybe you can answer a question for me."

Uzven put two fingers against the breathing mask that covered the lower part of its face. It adjusted the mask as if the mask were uncomfortable, then said, "The assumption isn't a good one. We have just begun to understand the Eaufasse. Our language is more compatible with theirs than yours is. That is why I am somewhat fluent."

"Somewhat fluent?" Gomez didn't like the sound of that. She had asked for someone fluent.

"I am as fluent as anyone in the Earth Alliance," Uzven said. "But that is not saying much. I understand quite a bit of Fasse, the Eaufasse language, but I do not have much jargon for technical details."

"Like murder?"

"Death is a universal," Uzven said. "However, I am not entirely sure of what constitutes murder to the Eaufasse. Not that it matters here. We do not have Eaufasse corpses. We have human ones. I will keep the discussion focused on the human side of things as much as I can."

"I don't want you to make unilateral decisions," Gomez said. "If I have a question that needs an answer, I expect you to ask it. And if you cannot get an answer from the Eaufasse, I don't want you trying to find a way to force one. I want to know that they didn't answer my question. This isn't a court of law, so I don't necessarily need something on the record. I need information, and if we can't get that information without a cadre of diplomats working the case, then I need to know that as well."

"I understand," Uzven said. "I am at your service."

Gomez thought she heard sarcasm. It wouldn't surprise her. Peyti always thought themselves superior to humans. Working with a human boss had to be difficult for a Peyti. But Uzven had signed up to work with the Earth Alliance, so it didn't get to choose who its boss was on any particular job.

"We will be speaking to my initial contact with the Eaufasse," Gomez said. "If we need to speak to someone of higher rank or with different knowledge, then we'll do that."

Uzven nodded, always a strange movement from a Peyti. The mask didn't really bend, so the head moved without any mask movement.

With Uzven's help, Gomez contacted the Eaufasse. She did not have this conversation through an audio-only link, but used both audio and visual, so that the Eaufasse could examine her body movements. She didn't move a lot, though, just in case some movement might be offensive.

Still, the Eaufasse had had interactions with humans before, so they were somewhat familiar with the way that humans did things. She stood as casually as she could when she began the conversation.

The Eaufasse had blacked out the area behind it, so she couldn't see where it was standing. The Eaufasse looked like it floated against a black background, unmoored by anything. Privacy concerns? An unwillingness to let humans or the Earth Alliance see what the interior of Eaufasse offices looked like? Or something else entirely?

It didn't matter, since the interior of an Eaufasse building or even the exterior of an Eaufasse street was not her concern. She didn't care where the Eaufasse was, so long as it talked with her.

She thanked the Eaufasse for the initial contact, and confirmed that she would be removing the enclave. She also told them that it would take time, since the enclave was so big she couldn't do it without a larger force. She asked for permission to bring a larger group of humans onto Epriccom for the sole purpose of removing the human enclave. She promised that the force would leave as soon as the enclave left.

The Eaufasse said it understood and had been expecting such a thing. It did not offer any help from its own people, which, Gomez knew, was a good thing. She had no idea what that enclave would do if it saw a group of Eaufasse approaching it. She certainly didn't want weaponry fired at the Eaufasse on their own land, which—she also knew—was a possibility.

She didn't want to be the person who inadvertently started a war between some humans and the Eaufasse.

After dancing around the topic for a while, she finally asked the question that had been the real point behind this conversation. She always began pointed and possibly offensive questions with an apology first, having learned the hard way that translators did not add politeness in the cultures that required it, but always subtracted politeness when it didn't serve the needed purpose.

"Please forgive the intrusive nature of the remainder of the conversation," she said. "But I need information to help my people understand what has happened here, so that we might remove this enclave quickly and easily."

Uzven translated, its fingers tapping against its suit jacket.

"It seems like the enclave has been on Epriccom for quite a while," Gomez said. "Did something recently bring it to your attention?"

Uzven continued to translate, then looked at Gomez, clearly waiting. Then the Uzven bowed its head and closed its eyes, listening.

It had not been doing a simultaneous translation from the beginning of the conversation. Uzven did not think itself fluent enough, which worried Gomez.

Uzven translated after the Eaufasse finished. Gomez wondered how much Uzven missed just by waiting. And Gomez didn't entirely trust a summary. Sometimes the Eaufasse said a lot, and Uzven translated it into very few words.

Gomez didn't know if that was because Fasse used more words than Standard or if Uzven felt the need to shorten long thoughts or if Uzven was actually leaving out important details.

"The ambassador said the enclave applied for permission to build on the land sixteen years ago. Permission was granted with minimal fuss. This is a remote part of the Eaufasse nation, and so the Eaufasse do not pay it much mind. In fact, they did not hear anything more from the enclave until it started attacking itself."

Gomez cursed silently. She wished she spoke Fasse. There were so many areas that could be misinterpreted in just that one little reply.

But she was a veteran at this. She'd had more first- or second- or third-contacts than most diplomats in the Earth Alliance.

"Okay," she said to Uzven. "Before you translate for me, answer me a few questions. Tell them that's what you'll be doing, for clarification."

Uzven spoke rapidly to the Eaufasse. The Eaufasse raised its arms and wrapped them over its shoulders, which made Gomez look away. She had no idea if that was a relaxed position or if it was the same as nodding in her culture.

"Proceed," Uzven said to her.

Proceed. She took a deep breath. She didn't like its tone, but Uzven was all she had. "The Eaufasse I'm speaking with is an ambassador?"

"That is how it identifies itself," Uzven said.

Crap. That created all kinds of problems for her. Technically, she was supposed to interact with a counterpart, someone of equal rank—if, of course, the alien/native culture had a ranked system. Conversations with ambassadors were supposed to be conducted by diplomats.

Still, this ambassador was her contact, so she could argue that she had no choice about who she talked to. And of course, the argument would be true.

"Do you understand the governmental rankings within the Eaufasse?" she asked.

"Not entirely, no," Uzven said. "If you are asking me if you are conducting an inquiry above your pay grade, then I cannot answer that. For all I know, all Eaufasse who deal with non-Eaufasse in minor matters are called 'ambassador.' Remember that we are filtering through two languages here, one imperfectly known."

Two?

It took her a moment to understand what Uzven meant. It meant that it was translating into Peytin first before translating into Standard. Just great. Yet another way to add in misunderstandings.

"I want to double-check the number," she said. "Sixteen years? Not six?"

"Sixteen," Uzven said in a tone that definitely showed it was insulted that she checked.

"Because Epriccom had just applied for Earth Alliance membership sixteen years ago. We hadn't had much contact with any of the species here before that," she said.

She knew this because she had investigated it before she had gotten here. It took a minimum of twenty-five years from application to approval to become a full Earth Alliance member. And that was if everything ran smoothly.

"Sixteen," Uzven said again.

"Damn," Gomez muttered. This group of humans was even more private than she imagined.

Uzven did not move, and neither did the Eaufasse on her screen. The ambassador. If it was a real, high-ranking ambassador, then she was screwing up by holding it up—at least under Earth Alliance protocol.

"All right," she said softly to Uzven. "Let's continue."

Uzven bowed a little, then turned slightly.

"Forgive me, Mr. Ambassador," she said. "Mister" and "Sir" in Standard had become gender-neutral. She hoped Uzven translated them that way. "I still need clarifications of some of what you've told me. Did the enclave predate your application to the Earth Alliance?"

Uzven dutifully translated. The Eaufasse's arms came down to the position they had been in before. Its eyes shone whitely for a moment. Gomez had no idea what that meant.

"Why is that important?" The Eaufasse asked. The question sounded defensive, but she wasn't sure if that was the Eaufasse's defensiveness or Uzven's.

She was going to act as if every emotion belonged to the Eaufasse. "Sir, I am trying to understand the enclave from a human-to-human

23

perspective. If the enclave's arrival predates our contact with you, this tells me that the enclave was looking for some place not affiliated with the Alliance to form its community."

That whiteness flared, then disappeared. The ambassador's arms flopped over its shoulders again, elbows—if that's what they were— pointing at her. She wasn't even going to try to understand the body language. It unsettled her, and she didn't want to be unsettled.

"Their arrival predates the application by six months," Uzven said. "And before you ask me, the ambassador is referring to months as the Earth Alliance calculates them."

"Thank you," Gomez said, and before she could ask her next question, the ambassador continued.

"It was their arrival that made the Eaufasse and the others on Epriccom aware of the Earth Alliance. It was in the researching of the humans that Epriccom decided that joining the Alliance would be a good idea."

That was interesting.

"Why?" she asked.

"The Earth Alliance is a trade and protection organization, facilitating business throughout several sectors. It would bring much-needed revenue to Epriccom while providing many opportunities to the various local groups here."

Gomez almost laughed in surprise and relief. The ambassador was selling her on Epriccom's final entry into the Earth Alliance. As she realized that, she relaxed slightly.

"So," she said, "the enclave have been good neighbors until they—as you said—started attacking themselves."

"Slang," Uzven muttered loud enough for her to hear. Then it tilted its head slightly—a Peyti sign of disgust—and translated for her. Apparently it didn't approve of "good neighbors," which she didn't consider slang at all.

The Eaufasse ambassador brought its arms down again. She wished now that she had left this on audio. The movements were distracting. It turned its head away from her for just a moment. She got a sense that it was not alone. She wondered if it had another translator or if it had someone of higher rank just off camera.

Then it turned toward her and spoke.

"They needed supervision in their first year as they built their enclave," Uzven translated. Then it added in a more confidential tone, "You should know that the ambassador may have used the word 'crafted' here. I chose 'built.'"

Gomez nodded.

Uzven continued its translation. "The supervision included monitoring the materials they brought to Epriccom, transporting them to their location, and overseeing their building. They have a dome, although they do not need one because Epriccom's atmosphere suits humans, but the Eaufasse appreciate the dome nonetheless."

She expected Uzven to continue, but it didn't. She glanced at it, then at the Eaufasse. Apparently that was all it had said.

"Why do you appreciate the dome?" she asked.

"Because the humans have landing ships. Those ships go into and out of their dome, and do not do anything except transverse our airspace."

Uzven started to explain all the words it changed, but she didn't care.

"You don't mind the ships?" she asked, feeling cold.

"They are small. They must be scanned for weaponry. They have none. We see no threat."

"Weaponry?" She turned toward Uzven. "Does the ambassador mean external or internal weapons?"

Uzven asked and received a quick answer. "The ships are weaponless. The interior scans, done in a cursory manner, do not show weapons either. But you know that part means nothing—"

"Was that 'means nothing' thing your editorial or the ambassador's?" she asked.

"Mine, of course," Uzven said.

Of course. She didn't like this. She knew more about weaponry than any Peyti translator could, and she knew that weapons could be built onsite of components that many governments thought harmless.

Once again, she was at a disadvantage. She didn't know enough about Eaufasse culture to know what they considered harmless.

"Do you use Earth Alliance protocols for ships that land on Epriccom?" she asked the ambassador.

"For Earth Alliance ships, yes," the ambassador said. "As best we understand the protocols."

"Do you consider all human ships to be Earth Alliance ships?" she asked.

"Are they not?" the ambassador responded.

She wasn't going to answer it directly. It was fishing for more information on humans, and she wasn't about to provide it. Sometimes, the Earth Alliance did not tell Frontier members that humans were scattered all over the sectors, and were not always members of the Alliance.

Some, in fact, were enemies of the Alliance.

It was better for the Frontier members to remain in the dark about such matters and to call the Earth Alliance when they had a human problem.

Like the Eaufasse had.

"Your ship protocol is correct," she said. "Thank you."

The Eaufasse moved one arm outward. Uzven did not comment on the gesture, either as a translation or as an opinion.

"Mr. Ambassador," she said, "these attacks the humans performed on each other. Is this the first time such a thing has happened?"

"We do not monitor the dome," the ambassador said.

"Again, sir," she said. "The information I am asking for is to allow me to deal with the enclave. If we need diplomats to discuss human-Eaufasse relations, I am happy to provide them. But my job here is strictly judicial, and concerns the humans in that enclave only."

Uzven translated that. Then the ambassador spoke, and Uzven answered.

She felt left out, which she most definitely did not want to be.

"I want you to translate everything," she snapped at Uzven. It put out an arm toward her, its branchlike fingers tilted upward at a 90-degree angle. Finally, a gesture she understood. It was a Peyti gesture for *shush* combined with *wait*.

After a moment, Uzven said, "The Ambassador wanted to know why the Multicultural Tribunal was involved. I assured him it was not. I told him that we have a law enforcement branch designed to take care of recalcitrant individuals. Apparently, the Eaufasse do not use the word 'judicial' the way that our two cultures do."

It was Gomez's turn to be sarcastic. "Good to know."

"I am not entirely sure it understands the concept of law enforcement, so I might have to do extra explaining," Uzven said. "I will inform you when I am doing so."

"Thank you," she said as dismissively as she could. "Mr. Ambassador, is this the first time, to your knowledge, that the enclave has attacked its own members?"

"We do not know about life inside the dome," the ambassador said. "We have only seen a few of the humans outside of the dome, and then only on rare occasions. Generally, they walk to the clearing, look around, and then return to the dome."

"In a group," she said, for clarification.

"Always in a group."

"Were they in a group on this trip?"

"No and yes," the ambassador said.

Great, she thought. More nitpicking.

"Four emerged," the ambassador said. "They moved quickly. A dozen more emerged. They moved even more quickly. They carried weapons."

Gomez remained still, but a tension filled her.

"I asked him what kind of weapons," Uzven added. "He did not know. Long ones, he said."

"Thank you, Uzven," Gomez said. "So, Mr. Ambassador, for my edification then. Four left the enclave, followed by twelve. The twelve had weapons and chased the four."

"Not quite," the ambassador said. "The four left some time before the dozen. The dozen tracked them, found them, and killed them."

"But we only found three bodies," Gomez said.

"Yes, that is correct," the ambassador said. "The fourth is with us."

She felt a surge of adrenalin. That explained a lot. The bodies were in a state of decay, so they'd been dead a while—in theory, anyway. And if the fourth human somehow found its way to the Eaufasse before dying, the human's death could have caused problems inside the Eaufasse culture. Gomez could think of dozens of cultures in which going from living to dead in the wrong location caused all kinds of interspecies squabbles.

"Humans are particular about their death rituals," she said. "We will have to request that the body be returned."

The ambassador peeped, like the Eaufasse in the clearing had. It was an odd and noticeable sound. Then the ambassador spoke.

"The ambassador says he's sorry," Uzven said. "He was not clear."

"Word for word, Uzven," Gomez said tiredly. She hoped that the diplomats ended up with a better translator than Uzven, although she suspected they wouldn't.

"The ambassador said," Uzven said with emphasis, "'I am sorry. I have spoken unclearly. The fourth human is with us. It lives and asks for asylum. That is why we contacted you.'"

It would have been good to know the entire translation the first time. Gomez bit back her irritation, and concentrated. So the reason the Eaufasse had contacted the Earth Alliance had been because of the fourth human, not because of the dead bodies in the clearing.

She had not expected this. "My understanding is that the Emir contacted us to remove the enclave."

"The Emir did that, yes," the ambassador said. "Our politicians believe that the enclave will now be a problem and want it gone. But we contacted you before the Emir. We do not know how to proceed with an asylum request while we are under consideration for membership in the Earth Alliance."

Neither did she. She had never heard of such a thing.

"And you are...separate...from the politicians?" she asked carefully. Then she remembered to couch the terms more carefully. "Forgive me for my failure to understand your culture. I was the Earth Alliance representative closest to Epriccom when you requested Alliance presence. They chose me for my proximity, not for my understanding of your culture."

"That's all right," the ambassador said. "We do not have a deep understanding of your culture either. This is why we are confused about the asylum request. We did not know that one member of a culture can become alienated from that culture. It is not our way."

Oh, but it's ours, she thought, but did not say.

"My clan are the functionaries," the ambassador was saying. "We maintain the systems of government. The Emir and his clan direct the government. In other words, we do not make policy. They do. But we enforce it."

"Ah," she said. "Our jobs are similar then."

"No," Uzven said. "They're more like—"

"Let me, Uzven," Gomez said. "Just translate."

Or she'd grab Uzven's scrawny little arm and snap it in half, just to hear if it sounded like the twig it resembled.

All right, she acknowledged to herself, her level of frustration was higher than it needed to be. At least she was directing her aggression toward the Peyti, and not toward the Eaufasse.

"I do believe our jobs are similar," the ambassador said and tossed its other arm outward. Then its eyes flared gold. She hoped that was a good thing.

"Well," Gomez said, "I will work with you to make sure we make things easier for our politicians. The less they have to do, the better."

The ambassador wheezed. She glanced at Uzven in panic. Uzven was leaning back slightly, then it tapped the bottom of its breathing mask, as if it were trying to improve the flow of whatever it was that they breathed.

"Do not worry," Uzven said to her. "That is the sound of an Eaufasse laughing."

"Forgive me," the ambassador said when it quit wheezing. "If your politicians are like ours, they do less anyway."

She smiled. "They are similar, then."

The ambassador wheezed again. "We shall do what we can together. What do you need from my clan?"

She let out a small sigh, hoping it was inaudible. "If you have surveillance material of the dome, I would like to see it, particularly of the incident itself. You will not offend us if you do have such material. We expect it. Also, if I might meet the fourth person, the one who wants asylum. You may continue to protect him, but I would like to talk with him about the incident."

The ambassador's arms dropped to its side. "You do not offend with your requests, although I am surprised that you approve of the surveillance. It heartens me, like our mutual jobs do."

She smiled. "It heartens me as well."

"We shall send you the materials within the hour," the ambassador said. "As for the fourth, we shall talk with it. We shall encourage it to talk with you. But that is all we can do."

"I understand," she said. "I do have one last request, however. Even if the fourth human won't speak with me, I would like the name, the gender, and the place of origin, so that I might forward the information to the Earth Alliance. It will expedite the asylum proceedings."

"Will it?" Uzven asked.

Damn translator. "Just translate," Gomez said, just for him.

Uzven did. Or at least, she hoped it did.

"I shall have that information to you along with the surveillance materials," the ambassador said. "And now, if you do not mind, I would like to ask you a personal question."

"I don't mind." She had learned over the years such questions were often the most interesting of any conversation in a first-, second-, or third-contact.

"This is my first time working with humans," the ambassador said. "Usually such matters are for a different clan."

"Yes," she said, mostly so that it would continue.

"I would like to ask if you are a separate gender than those in the enclave. Or are you in a different clan? Your appearance is quite different. I am told by my assistant that your entire team all looks quite different from what we expect."

"Humans are a diverse species," she said. "I can better answer you after I have seen the person asking for asylum. Do you mind the wait?"

"Not at all," the ambassador said. "And please forgive the personal nature of the question."

"It's quite all right," she said. "I suspect I shall be asking difficult questions as well over the course of the next few days. Thank you for your candor and your assistance, Mr. Ambassador."

"Thank you," the ambassador said, and severed the link.

Uzven started to speak, but she held up a hand. Then she disassembled the screen so that it couldn't be activated from the other side. She didn't want the Eaufasse to listen in.

"You acquitted yourself well for someone who is unfamiliar with the culture," Uzven said.

She hadn't expected the compliment. "We'll see," she said. "This is only the first step. There's a lot more ahead of us, and if experience is any guide, most of that will be filled with surprises."

She hoped the surprises would be pleasant ones, but experience also told her that such hopes were idle ones. She was in for a bumpy few days. The best she could do was avoid making an already strange situation worse.

4

As GOMEZ TURNED AWAY FROM THE SCREEN, LASHANTE SIMIAAR POKED her head out of a sealed-up corner of the large forensic area.

"Suit up," she said, "and come in here."

"Both of us?" Gomez asked, using her head to indicate Uzven.

"Just you," Simiaar said. "No offense, Uzven."

"I do not take offense at procedure," Uzven said. "If I am not needed, I should like to leave so that I might settle into my quarters."

"You're not needed at the moment," Gomez said.

Uzven nodded, adjusted its mask, and walked out of the room.

Simiaar watched it go. "You'd think, given my job, I'd know that individuals are all different, that a species shouldn't have an effect on me, but jeez, the Peyti."

"Maybe we've just met the wrong ones," Gomez said.

"Yeah, sure," Simiaar said. "Get in here."

"Okay," Gomez said, choosing not to express her surprise. In all the years they'd worked together, Simiaar had never ordered Gomez into the autopsy area. Gomez had often gone of her own accord, but she hadn't been required to go in.

She could do what so many others in her job did, and watch the holographic recording of the autopsy. All the mess without the smell. And sometimes she did that, particularly when Simiaar was pulling apart some alien to determine if it got killed by an Earth Alliance weapon.

But usually she watched. As Simiaar once told her, the smells told as much as the body itself. Besides, if she had it to do all over again, Gomez probably would have gone into forensic pathology inside the FSS. A lot of alien contact, a lot of travel to distant worlds, and none of the difficult conversations with a species she didn't understand.

Simiaar handed her a pathology suit. Gomez slipped it on. It was different than the suits the marshals used to go planetside. This suit was a thin version of a biohazard suit, one that kept the icky stuff out while allowing her—or whomever—to do delicate work.

She slipped the equally thin helmet over her face. It adhered to her skin, and would keep everything out—including smells.

So the fact that she was wearing a suit meant the problem wasn't scent-related. It was something else.

Gomez slipped inside the autopsy area. The light was bright, with even more lights on the tables. Some of the lights were on, others were off. Simiaar's workstation was also brightly lit, and there were petri dishes alongside filled slides alongside microchip dishes, all storing samples. She also saw vials of blood and other fluids.

Simiaar was doing a full autopsy, using all the tools at her disposal, preserving tissue and fluids. Eventually, she would use nanoprobes to examine the interior of the bodies, but the probes changed the ecology of the bodies—anything inserted inside did that—so they were used last.

Simiaar was wearing her suit too, but her helmet was off.

"What've you got?" Gomez asked.

"I was finding some very strange stuff," Simiaar said, "so I decided on a holographic recreate. You need to see it. And before you ask, yes, I did double- and triple-check this."

She hit a button alongside her workstation, and the lights dimmed. Above the bodies, intact bodies appeared, reconstructed whole from DNA combined with the remains.

The bodies belonged to young human males, not quite full grown, with very rare pale skin covered with equally rare light blond hair. They had long, athletic legs, well-formed torsos, and muscular arms. They also had the exact same face.

Gomez frowned.

"Triplets?" she asked, hoping that she was right.

"Clones," Simiaar said. "I checked the telomeres. Definitely clones."

Gomez walked around them. Clones, like twins, ended up looking slightly different from each other. No matter what they did, they ended up living different lives, and those lives had an impact on the skin.

But these boys were too young to have lived through much, and besides, she was looking at a recreation, not at the actual faces themselves. The actual faces had decomposed into unrecognizability.

"You checked the telomeres?" Gomez said, suddenly realizing that Simiaar had checked the DNA, an unusual—if accurate—procedure for clones. "Does that mean there were no clone tags?"

The Earth Alliance heavily regulated human clones after criminal syndicates used clones to take identity theft to a whole new level. All clones needed an obvious interior tag and a clone mark on the exterior of the skin, usually in a visible place like the back of the neck.

"No tags," Simiaar said. "Are you surprised, given how far we are from anywhere?"

Gomez wasn't surprised. Especially since the clones looked young. "They're not fast-grow clones, are they?"

Because that would show up in the telomeres. Telomeres were often shorter in clones, especially clones made from an adult original. However, if the clones were meant for a normal-length life, a lot of the cloning companies engineered longer telomeres. Fast-grow clones had strange, sometimes broken telomeres, usually caused by the fast-growth process.

"They're not fast-grow," Simiaar said, "but their telomeres are pretty short. They were made from an older adult, and it seems to me that they were being groomed for something. Still, they are fully human—or at least, as human as a clone can be."

"Can you guess at their ages?" Gomez asked.

"If these were girls, it would be easier," Simiaar said. "With boys, it's a bit harder to be precise, but I can tell you that they were still growing. They were probably in their mid-teens when they died, just a few years past the onset of puberty."

"Seventeen? Eighteen?" Gomez asked.

"Sixteen at the oldest," Simiaar said. "But I'd guess fourteen or fifteen."

Gomez let out a small breath. "The enclave has been here for sixteen years," she said.

Simiaar's eyes met hers. "These clones weren't made at any of the cloning companies, I can tell you that. Or at least, any of the ones associated with the Earth Alliance. Because if they were, they would have a tag, and if their telomeres had been repaired, those would have a tiny gold marker."

"The shorter telomeres couldn't have another cause?" Gomez asked.

Simiaar shook her head. "Not like this. Whoever made these clones was very careless about it. There are things that cloning companies do that ensure longer life and better health for clones. None of that was done here. In fact, some of the things I saw here could be considered serious mistakes."

"Serious how?" Gomez asked.

"Well," Simiaar said, "in human cultures outside of the Earth Alliance, clones get sold, but the person or companies selling the clones have to guarantee the clone's health and the fact that it will have a 'natural' lifespan."

Gomez had heard about clone sales, but she had never encountered one. She was glad she'd been spared that part of the Frontier—at least so far.

"So these clones weren't made for selling?" Gomez asked.

"I don't know what they were for," Simiaar said. "But I can tell you this. Whoever cloned them didn't really care about them. Or only knew enough science to make a clone. They didn't know much else."

"Enough science," Gomez said. "What do you mean by that?"

"It's not as hard to clone someone as the companies make it sound," Simiaar said. "I could do it with the technology in this room. You couldn't, though. You don't have the scientific skills."

"Such a vote of confidence," Gomez said with a smile.

"Well, you don't have the training—"

"It's all right," Gomez said. "I have to admit, though, that I'm surprised the process isn't hard. So, could the clones have been made here, on Epriccom?"

Simiaar's lips pursed. "I don't know how I could tell you that. There's nothing in the science or the bodies that would show where the clones were made if they weren't marked with some kind of company tag. It—"

"That's not what I'm asking, Lashante," Gomez said. "I'm asking if the science is easy enough that some half-assed scientist could have run a lab in that enclave and made their own clones."

Simiaar let out small sigh. "You don't ask easy questions, do you? You know I don't like speculating."

"I'm not asking you if they did it," Gomez said. "I'm asking you if they could."

Simiaar looked at the images of the intact bodies floating over the mess that the corpses had become.

She sighed. "These poor boys got created somewhere, under pretty primitive conditions. Or at least, with an inept scientist who only knew how to clone, not how to make a clone anything more than viable."

"So," Gomez said again, "the cloning could have happened on Epriccom in that enclave."

"Or on a ship on the way here or in a city a thousand light years away. I'm telling you, Judita, I don't know and I have no way of finding out."

Gomez stared at the bodies just like Simiaar was doing. Gomez had never understood why clones were treated differently under the law. People could argue that everyone got made, just using different methods.

But she knew that the laws she upheld—at least for now—made unlicensed cloning illegal.

"But," Gomez said, "you can't rule out the fact that they could have been made here."

"Good grief, Judita. Are you sure you weren't trained as a lawyer? Yes. Okay? I can't rule it out. But this isn't a damn court of law." Simiaar ran a hand through her thick, curly hair.

Gomez smiled at the backward compliment. Simiaar hated lawyers.

"I know it's not a court of law," Gomez said. "Still, I thank you for your answer."

"You shouldn't thank me," Simiaar snapped. "Because if these clones were created here, we stumbled onto something both big and dangerous."

"I know," Gomez said.

"An illegal cloning operation could be worth millions," Simiaar said.

"I'm aware," Gomez said.

"And they'll kill to defend it. Human life is cheap to people like that."

"I know that, too," Gomez said. Simiaar was about to start a rant, so Gomez had to retake control of the conversation. "So, do you know how they died?"

Simiaar sighed. She ran a hand across her mouth and then studied those intact images. The boys almost looked angelic. The imagery certainly seemed unreal, particularly considering the destroyed bodies below.

"There's a lot of damage here because of the decomposition," Simiaar said, "plus I'm not sure how those branches work, exactly, but they had some effect on the bodies."

"Enough that you can't say how the boys died?" Gomez asked.

"I'll have to run tests with some organic specimens that I grow," Simiaar said. "You wouldn't, by chance, be able to get some information from the Eaufasse on those plants?"

"I can barely understand the Eaufasse when they're giving me walking directions, and I'm pretty sure the Eaufasse have a similar problem with me."

"It didn't sound that way with the Peyti," Simiaar said.

"If it's translating things correcting," Gomez said.

"You have doubts?" Simiaar asked.

Gomez didn't answer. She raised her eyebrows, just so that she could claim that she had said nothing bad about the Peyti.

"I know you don't like to speculate," Gomez said, fending off that argument again. "But, the plants aside, what can you tell me about the bodies?"

"I can tell you what I don't like," Simiaar said. "I don't like the age of these boys. They're too young to die of natural causes, even for clones, and they shouldn't have died in a group."

Gomez nodded. She agreed with that.

"I don't like the fact that the shirts I pulled off them had laser burns in the back. I don't like the fact that the skin on their backs have laser burns as well. A cursory glance of their internal organs, particularly their hearts, show more laser burning."

"A laser pistol?" Gomez asked.

"A laser rifle, given the power of the shot or shots," Simiaar said. "But I don't know. I'm just telling you what I see and what I don't like."

"And the laser pattern looks familiar to you?" Gomez asked. "It's not something that the Eaufasse use?"

"How the hell should I know?" Simiaar said. "This culture is as new to me as it is to you."

"I mean—"

"I know what you mean. And here's my answer. The laser burns are consistent with human weapons. That doesn't mean they're inconsistent with Eaufasse weapons or that they might come from some weird laser source that I don't know about. I'm just telling you what I don't like."

Which was, apparently, different from speculating. Gomez didn't understand the distinction, but she appreciated the fact that Simiaar made such a distinction.

"What else can you tell me?" Gomez asked.

"Nothing," Simiaar said. "My likes and dislikes are accounted for. Now I need to get my hands dirty, do some real science, and then go through the DNA database to see if the source of these clones is registered somewhere."

Gomez had never heard of such a thing. "Why would you do that?"

"Because home-grown clones like these usually come from mega-lomaniacs who don't believe one of themselves is enough to satisfy the universe. They need to create more of themselves in their own image to satisfy their God complex."

For a moment, Gomez thought Simiaar was joking. Then she realized that Simiaar wasn't joking at all.

"You think that person might be in the enclave?" Gomez asked.

"I think that person might be *identifiable*," Simiaar said. "That's all. Now, get out. I have work to do."

Gomez didn't need to be told again. She left the forensics lab with more to think about than she had ever expected. Simiaar told her a lot without saying anything. And Simiaar's opinion coincided with what the Eaufasse said. A group from inside the enclave chased these boys into the clearing and killed them.

So why had one lived? Had he lived as a warning? If so, why was he outside the enclave instead of inside?

That surviving kid would have answers that Simiaar was just guessing at.

Gomez had to figure out the legalities. She had no idea if she could interview someone who requested asylum from humans. She wasn't even sure if "asylum from humans" was a proper request.

She headed back to her cabin to contact whatever idiot lawyer FSS managed to have on call.

5

THE IDIOT LAWYER HOVERING ON THE OTHER SIDE OF THE TABLE IN Gomez's office was older than she expected, and not as vain as some people his age. His holographic image shimmered, either as a result of the extreme encryption necessary to have this conversation or because of the distance between them. He was chubby, stuffed in a cheap suit, and had no obvious enhancements. His fleshy face showed signs of exhaustion.

She saw none of that as a good sign. If the idiot lawyer wasn't fresh out of law school and working in the prosecutor's office as a junior attorney attached to the FSS, then he was most likely a lifer who had given up on any ambitions or creativity long ago. Or he was a supervisor.

She was praying for supervisor.

In fact, she was going to be blunt about a supervisor.

Before she even said hello, she said, "No offense, but I need a ranking prosecutor who has worked on Frontier issues his entire career. Are you that person?"

To her surprise, he smiled slowly and it softened his features. "And if I said I was and I was lying, do you have a way to check?"

She did. She had hundreds of databases at her fingertips in this office attached to her private suite. Some of those databases were what she liked to call extra-legal. Others were sanctioned.

40

The only problem she had was that the official FSS database she carried was about a year old. She hadn't updated in a long time, because her secure connections out here on the Frontier were as good as the one she had with him.

Which was to say, unreliable at best.

But she didn't want to look him up. She'd have to terminate the conversation, investigate, and then request him (or not) when she contacted the judicial branch attached to the FSS a second time.

"So this is the kind of conversation we're going to have?" she asked him. "Defensive and territorial? Because I've got big issues here, and I want someone not just experienced, but experienced with clout."

"Why?" he asked.

"Name, position, and for God's sake, tell me if you can help me, because if you can't, I'm going to find someone who can," she snapped.

He grinned. "Your reputation precedes you, Marshal. You never call in for legal help. You know more about the Frontier and its legal issues than most lifers here ever will. So when you pinged us, we knew it was important, and you got me."

She wanted to ask, *So I should be impressed?* but she didn't. Instead, she waited. Waiting had become part of her arsenal over her years as a marshal. Waiting protected her from blurting something stupid to an intelligent species she didn't understand; waiting helped her discover many crimes because humans generally couldn't remain silent; waiting made her seem mysterious and strong when, in reality, she was often just plain cautious.

The caution was why she was good at her job.

He tilted his head and gave her a half-smile, as if he were acknowledging that she had just won this part of the conversation.

"I'm Frank Mishra," he said. "I'm one of the chief litigators for the FSS. I'm also linked at the moment to one of our best legal researchers, just in case you have an issue we haven't heard of before."

So they really were worried about the issue she was bringing up. The respect surprised her. She hadn't experienced it in her early years with FSS, and after those early years, she hadn't really needed the judicial branch.

She'd made sure of that. She had hated dealing with officious bastards.

"All right," she said, making sure her tone wasn't quite as abrupt as it had been. She folded her hands on the tabletop and watched his chubby image flicker. "Let me explain my issue. I have a young man who survived an attack by humans in his own enclave. He has asked the Eaufasse for asylum. But his request was not for asylum from the Earth Alliance, but asylum 'from humans.' Realize that I got all of this from the Eaufasse through a Peyti translator, and that the Eaufasse do not know there are humans outside of the Earth Alliance. I'm not even certain that the word 'asylum' is the Eaufasse's or the Peyti's. But I do know if I do something wrong here, we will have repercussions for years."

Mishra ran a hand over his mouth. He tapped the table in front of him, so that it looked like his holographic image tapped the table Gomez's arms were resting on. Only her table didn't vibrate from his touch. His movement made him seem unreal, as if he were a figment of her imagination.

"Your fear of repercussion, is that why you haven't spoken to him directly?" Mishra asked.

"I'm not sure I'm allowed to," Gomez said. "In fact, I'm not sure I have any standing with the young man at all. Let me add that the Eaufasse are willing to let me speak to him, but they are also eager to become part of the Earth Alliance. They tried to sell me on Epriccom in the middle of our discussion about the enclave."

"You can't trust them," Mishra said.

"I honestly don't know what trust means in this circumstance," Gomez said.

Mishra sighed. He glanced sideways, maybe checking with that "best legal researcher" he said he was linked to. He looked grim.

"Do you know who this kid is?"

"We don't know anything," Gomez said. "We don't even know what the enclave is."

"What information have you received from the Eaufasse?" he asked.

"What I just gave you. Courtesy of the rather obnoxious Peyti translator, who admitted he was translating from Fasse to Peytin to Standard, which, as you can tell, is not the ideal way to talk with another species."

"Especially about something that turns on a word." Mishra held up a finger, and this time, he turned most of his body sideways. His lips moved, but Gomez couldn't hear anything. Then he nodded, as if he had just received an answer.

He turned back toward her, and for once, their link was solid. He stopped flickering.

"You were correct to contact us. I'd like about an hour to research your question. May I have it?"

"Yeah," she said. "I'd rather have you act on an educated guess instead of a hunch."

Mishra grinned again. "You think there's a difference?"

"Oh, maybe," she said. "To some of the Multicultural Tribunals, anyway."

"Good point," he said and signed off.

The room actually felt bigger and emptier without his image floating on the other side of the table. The muscles in her shoulders were tight. She felt more alone at this moment than she had in years.

There was a lot at stake in this one interaction. She could handle murder. She could handle an illegal enclave. She could handle a first- or second- or third-contact situation.

She wasn't sure she could handle a legal request from a government that her government didn't yet recognize.

She wasn't sure what would happen—to all of them—if she got it wrong.

6

She'd testified in front of most of the Multicultural Tribunals, usually by hololink, and always in cases that she had resolved rather than ones in which she was an accused. She did not ever want to go in front of that part of the legal system because she had done something wrong. There wasn't a lot of give in the Tribunal system. Most everyone she knew who went in front of the Tribunals accused of some heinous act were found guilty of that act—even if she knew for a fact that they were not. She'd heard rumors, ones she did not want to substantiate on her own, that if the accused had the backing of a large corporation and all of its wealth, the accused might go free. Or get off with a slap to the wrist.

She had the Earth Alliance behind her, but she also had a sense that the Alliance was willing to throw most of its underlings aside if it served a greater purpose.

She tapped into the FSS database to see if she could find Mishra. She had no trouble. He was not only a supervisor, but he was at the top of his division, with an impressive list of cases behind him.

She should have felt like she was in good hands—and she did—but that still didn't reassure her.

Much as she loved her job, much as she loved working on the Frontier, moments like this made her nervous. The legal risks were the ones she couldn't control with a laser pistol or a well-timed look. She couldn't smile her way out of this or slam a suspect into the cells on the lower deck.

She hated ceding control to someone else.

And she hated waiting.

So she tried to research the asylum information on her own. As she did, she got a notification on her links that the materials from the Eaufasse had arrived.

She asked that the information get forwarded to her here, and that it remain off her links. She had learned the hard way that material on private links was sometimes considered personal, and she didn't ever want to be accused of a crime because she had downloaded the wrong material onto her private links.

The Eaufasse materials showed up on the table's main screen. It popped up in front of her, complete with menu. The Eaufasse had sent surveillance recordings of the incident, the discovery of the bodies, and the messages they had sent to the Earth Alliance.

They also sent materials about the survivor.

She went to those first, in case she needed more information in her next discussion with Mishra.

The images showed up as small holograms. She left the holograms alone, but called up a two-dimensional image on another screen so that she could see the boy's face clearly.

And it was a boy's face—unlined and very young. He was blond and unusually pale, so rare as to be almost unheard of in the Earth Alliance. She had noticed this with the clones' bodies, but had not really thought about it much, figuring that Simiaar's reproduction was as much guess as it was accurate.

Faced with a truly pale-skinned human, though, Gomez felt a slight disbelief. She knew that there were groups of pale humans with blond hair and blue eyes, but usually they were the result of decades of genetic purity—none of them allowed to breed with anyone who did not have similar skin and eye color.

Occasionally, there would be a pale, blue-eyed throwback in a large family, but it was so unusual that she had never met anyone that light-skinned in her travels.

The boy stood at the center of four Eaufasse. They encircled him, apparently deliberately. He was as thin as they were. His clothing was ragged and filthy, and he looked tired.

One of the Eaufasse spoke. The boy gave it a wary look, and responded. In Fasse.

"What the hell?" Gomez asked.

She scanned forward on the recording the Eaufasse had sent. The five seemed to be having a discussion. She stopped the recording farther in. The discussion was happening in Fasse.

Which meant that the Eaufasse knew what the boy had asked for. Now the question was if the Peyti had translated correctly for her.

She tapped a corner of the desk. "Please translate this discussion into Standard," she said.

An error reading rose in front of her eyes. *Language insufficiently known for accurate translation* was the response she got.

Dammit. She would have to talk with Uzven after all.

7

WHILE SHE WAITED FOR UZVEN TO ARRIVE, SHE WATCHED THE SURVEILLANCE recordings of the enclave. She couldn't tell time from them; like Fasse, the way that the Eaufasse told time was unfamiliar to her. But she could guess at how much time passed while she watched the imagery unfold before her.

The surveillance recordings began as four young men left the enclave. They were all the same height, thin, and blond. They wore identical clothing. They stumbled outside as if they had been pushed. Then they stood for just a moment, as if they had never seen the area before.

A loud bang made them jump. Then they all ran in the same direction. The camera floated above them, keeping the same distance, following them as they moved. Another image bifurcated from the first, keeping a vigil on the enclave.

Gomez realized that the Eaufasse probably had years of footage from that enclave. She felt a mixture of relief and exasperation. Relief, because she would be able to see what had happened in this place from the very beginning. Exasperation, because she would have to investigate all of this with her team, and it would take time. No matter how sophisticated a computer program she set up to cope with all of this, she would still have to review some of the footage in person. She wouldn't know what she was looking for until she found it.

Then a third image split off from the other two. One of the boys left the group. Instead of running blindly through the underbrush, this boy stopped and surveyed his surroundings. He no longer seemed nervous.

She backed the images up, going to the moment he first appeared. He remained slightly behind the other three as they stumbled out of the enclave. She hadn't been able to see his facial expression. She had assumed he had reacted the same way the others had.

She moved the images forward to the moment he had left the other three boys. As he walked away—calmly, slowly—he touched the plants. They shivered into place, as if no one had passed through.

Her breath caught. How had he known to do that? The others seemed confused by the area away from the enclave, but he had a calm familiarity with it.

The others continued forward, eventually growing tired and beginning to walk. By then, the other boy had gone very far in a completely different direction. Gomez cursed herself. She should have opened another program so that she could see where, exactly, all four boys were on the map of Epriccom. But she hadn't done that. She could either go back and start over, or she could continue to watch.

A sound behind her made her start. The door opened. Uzven entered. It adjusted its mask.

"You have footage for me?" it asked.

She nodded, and stopped the visual she was watching. Uzven did not ask about the boys, and she was glad of that. It sat down next to her, folding its twig-like body into what seemed like an uncomfortable position.

She started up the images of the surviving boy and the four Eaufasse. She played the imagery with the sound until the boy answered the Eaufasse.

Then she paused it.

"Is he speaking Fasse?" she asked.

"Yes." Uzven's tone was flat, even for a Peyti. It put its long fingers against its mask, adjusting again. A nervous habit, then. She wouldn't have believed that the Peyti allowed themselves such gestures. She thought all Peyti too controlled for that.

48

"What's he saying?" she asked.

"I—he's asking for asylum," Uzven said.

"They spoke first," she said.

"They want to know his name."

"And he didn't tell them?"

"He asked for asylum first," Uzven said.

Her heart pounded. "That was his word? 'Asylum'? He specifically asked for asylum from what?"

Uzven did not move. She let the images run a bit more, the sounds surrounding her, then she stopped it again.

"Uzven," she said. "What did he ask for?"

Uzven sat still.

"Why aren't you telling me?" she asked.

Uzven's mask made a large sucking sound. She turned toward it, afraid that it was suffering from mask failure. Instead, its hand dropped and its fingers played along the edge of the table.

"He is fluent," Uzven said quietly. "I am not."

"What did he say?" she asked again.

"He asked for protection," Uzven said. "He needed a promise of protection and safety before he would tell them anything."

"Protection and safety," she said. "You're sure?'

"No, I'm not sure," Uzven said. "I would need to listen to the entire interchange."

"Protection and safety from what?" she asked.

"From the humans," Uzven said.

"Which humans?" she asked.

Uzven's large liquid eyes turned toward her. "Those that want to kill him."

"Not all humans?" she asked.

"I don't know," Uzven said. "I need to listen to the entire interchange."

Her stomach turned. She had a hunch, one she didn't like. "The words that this boy uses," she said, "are they the ones that the Eaufasse used with you when you said the boy wanted asylum?"

"Protection and safety," Uzven said, turning its gaze back to the images. "What is that, but asylum?"

She cursed and slammed her hand on the table. Uzven leaned back as if it thought she was going to hurt it.

"*You* inserted the word 'asylum'?"

"The boy needs protection. Others were killed, by humans. The others were clearly clones. Your barbaric attitudes toward—"

"Son of a bitch," she said. "Get out."

"You need me to listen to the entire interchange—"

"I don't need anything from you right now," she said. "Get out of this room before I kick you out."

It stood, adjusted its mask, and hurried toward the door. There Uzven stopped. "None of us understand the Eaufasse well. We don't speak the language as well as that boy does. There are nuances—"

"That some other translator will find," Gomez said. "Consider yourself fired. I'll take care of the documentation myself."

Uzven made a noise she had never heard before. Its eyes had become slits. Then it let itself out of the room.

She stood, her heart pounding, her mouth dry. It had taken all of her strength not to grab Uzven and slap that scrawny little superior creature silly. It had cost her hours, and it had cost the legal department hours. She had a feeling that those hours would prove precious, although at the moment she couldn't say why.

And she also knew that Uzven's politics had gotten in the way of a solution. She could have spoken to the boy shortly after learning about him. Because Uzven was wrong. Protection and safety from the humans was not the same as asylum from all humans.

The boy just wanted to make sure he wasn't assassinated like his three compatriots.

She paced the room for another moment, gathering herself before she contacted Mishra. She'd listen to what research he had finished—it wouldn't hurt to know asylum rules on the Frontier—but she would also tell him how Uzven had interfered.

She needed a good interpreter. She wasn't sure how to find one. But she would have to ask.

She could never trust Uzven again.

8

THE EAUFASSE WOULD NOT LET HER SEE THE BOY FOR ANOTHER TWELVE hours. Apparently there were private rituals she did not understand, Eaufasse traditions that happened after Epriccom moved into a position opposite one of the other moons.

She discovered, to her dismay, that she was not allowed to fire translators, so she sent Uzven back to its superiors with a reprimand. She requested two more translators qualified to work with the Eaufasse, and was told they wouldn't be available for a week. So, she found her own off-site translator from a group she had worked with before. She chose the only one who claimed he was fluent in Fasse. He swore he would be here shortly.

He was not Peyti. He was human, and of questionable character. He'd been arrested by the Earth Alliance for trafficking in stolen goods, but for once, the charge didn't entirely stick. He was doing community service, and that service entailed putting his sizeable linguistic talent to use.

His name was Ragnar Okani. He did not allow accurate visuals on a link, which she suspected was an old habit from his criminal days. Still, others had worked with him and found him to be excellent. And she had no choice. Even so she tested him through the link.

She had made a snippet of that early conversation between the Eaufasse and the boy. Okani confirmed what Uzven had told her: the boy would not answer anything until he had a guarantee of protection and safety from "other humans."

"Not all humans," she said.

"That's where it gets difficult." Okani's face was in shadow, his voice masked. "The Eaufasse believe that there is no distinction among humans."

"I don't care what the Eaufasse believe," she said. "I care what the boy believes. He should know the difference between 'all humans' and 'other humans.'"

"He should also not be fluent in Fasse," Okani said. "You are splitting hairs here."

"I am not," she said, "because he did not ask for asylum."

"To my knowledge," Okani said, "the Eaufasse do not have that word in their language."

"What about a comparable word?"

Okani sighed. "I know Fasse pretty well, but not that well. Let me listen to everything you have. I'll tell you the context when I arrive."

"I need context," she said, "but I can't send you the rest of the footage through an open link. We'll do the work after you arrive."

He agreed, and they signed off.

He wouldn't arrive for another ten hours. That gave her two hours to show him the rest of the interrogation footage. Even if she didn't like him after he arrived, his initial answers calmed some of her fears.

She had received two interpretations of the boy's words, and in both cases, she was told he wanted protection and safety. She understood why he would want that, given what she had seen on the other surveillance footage.

In fact, the surveillance footage had calmed even more of her concerns. *She* would have asked for "protection and safety" as well, after what happened.

While she waited, she went back to the footage.

The surveillance footage tracked all four boys from the moment they left the enclave. She assumed that tiny individual cameras followed all of the boys, but she did not know that for certain. She did know that a single camera had followed the surviving boy to an Eaufasse outpost. When the boy reached the outpost, he had stood as plants grew around him, rising upward, touching the door itself. He didn't seem to mind. Then the door opened and he went inside.

The other boys did not go with him. Nor did the plants help them like they seemed to help the first boy. The other boys ran in a group, slowing as the plants grabbed at them. She was convinced now that those plants were actual creatures, convinced that they were somehow impeding the boys' progress for reasons she didn't understand.

When the twelve other boys appeared outside the enclave hours later, she froze their images and enlarged them.

Her breath caught. Those boys, all twelve of them, looked the same as the four.

The only difference was the twelve had laser rifles.

They stalked the path left by the four boys, not noticing where the single boy had split off. The path left by the three was obvious. The same plants grabbed at the twelve, holding them and pushing them at the same time. But the twelve had weaponry, and when they reached the top of the ridge, she knew without looking that they could see the three.

And then all twelve shot at the same time, then shot again. She knew the pattern. She could even count it down.

It was an execution; all twelve shot together so none of them would get credit for the actual kill.

She was glad she had watched the footage alone; it had left her shaken.

She had met clones before. If they knew the other clones with whom they shared DNA, they called themselves siblings. The word was a little off. The clones she had met were closer than most siblings, often completing each other's thoughts. The only time she had ever seen clones raised together that didn't get along, the clones had been victims of a poor cloning process.

She was making assumptions here, and she knew it: she didn't know if these sixteen clones were raised together or even if they were from the same batch. Clearly, they had come from the same original, but how they were created was a mystery—and she couldn't assume anything yet. She couldn't even assume human involvement outside of the clones themselves.

One phrase that continued to go through her mind came from the Eaufasse ambassador. *Your appearance is quite different,* it had said (or at least, that was how Uzven translated its words). *Or are you in a different clan?*

It might have meant how she was dressed, but it had belabored this point. Initially, she had thought that she and her people weren't what the Eaufasse had expected. Now, though, she wondered if the only humans the Eaufasse had seen had been clones of the same man.

And she had no way to understand why the twelve had murdered the other three.

Genetic predisposition? Some kind of ritual? A hazing gone wrong?

She was beginning to think the Eaufasse were the least of her problems.

She needed to focus on the clones.

She needed to identify their original, and she needed to know who was running the enclave.

Fortunately, she had come to Epriccom fully staffed. That meant five deputy marshals and ten assistants, not counting the three-person team staffing the forensic lab. Usually the assistants didn't work a case like this, because it was too difficult. The assistants either handled the documentation on past cases, filing everything with the FSS, or they handled the incoming information on future cases.

She decided to take the three assistants monitoring future cases as well as two others, and have them work on the surveillance data. She wanted it broken down: she needed to know how the enclave got established; how many ships had come in and out of the enclave over the years; how many times the members of the enclave had left the enclave; and if anything like this killing had happened before. She assigned one assistant to each question.

The fifth assistant would view the footage in chronological order, with the assistance of a computer program designed to digest large chunks of data like this, seeing if there was anything she or the four missed.

It wasn't really enough, and she knew that, but it would have to do.

While they were working, she contacted the lab for word on the original. She had sent Simiaar footage of the clones in motion, hoping that she could use those to trace imagery of the original. Simiaar was also doing a DNA scan to see if anything came up.

So far, Simiaar had nothing.

It was beginning to look like Gomez would face the sole survivor on her own, with very little actual information. She wasn't sure if that was a good thing or not: she might ask the right questions; she might miss the important stuff entirely.

She knew she would be making mistakes—they were inevitable when she was operating on so little information—but she wanted to avoid making the *obvious* mistakes.

If only she could figure out what the obvious mistakes were.

9

OKANI ARRIVED HALF AN HOUR EARLY. WASHINGTON GREETED HIM FOR Gomez, and set Okani up with the feed of the interview between the boy and the Eaufasse. When Okani finished, he went to a conference room on the forensic wing of the *Stanley*. Gomez met him there.

He stood as she stepped into the room. He was broad-shouldered and a bit soft around the middle. His thick, black hair fell across his forehead and accented his dark brown eyes. His features were as broad as his shoulders, and his skin was an unusual golden brown. The entire package was even more attractive in person, and yet he managed to seem unassuming; two things that, in her experience, rarely went together.

He nodded his head in greeting. She smiled and extended her hand. He gripped her hand lightly, his skin warm and dry.

"I don't envy you," he said.

"Why?" she asked.

He raised his eyebrows, and she could suddenly see a fierce intelligence behind his eyes. "There are many issues in this one interview."

She let out a small sigh. He pulled a chair out for her, as if the room were his. She could have made a big deal about the fact that he was doing community service, was under her legal supervision, and could, in fact, imprison him at any time.

But she decided not to make any power plays and, at the moment, to ignore any he pulled—if he was pulling any right now. He could also simply be polite.

She sat.

"Here is my problem," Okani said. "I have done business with one Eaufasse clan which operates outside of Epriccom. I've always had the impression that this particular group of Eaufasse were exiles, but I could never confirm it."

She didn't want to hear about him, but she had learned long ago that people often prefaced what she wanted to hear about with something important; she ignored his words at her own peril.

"I speak Fasse," he said. "I'm good at it."

She tensed.

"But I speak a formal version of the language. I just want you to know that."

"Why is it important?" she asked.

"Because, at times," he said, "in this interview, your group lapsed into a dialect that I think I understand. I can't guarantee that I do understand it."

"Oh, great," she said. "Just great."

She tried not to be too upset. She already believed Okani was a better translator than Uzven. Okani told her his limitations. Uzven placed his own interpretation on everything.

"The other thing you need to know," Okani said, "is that the kid here, he's fluent."

"In Fasse?"

Okani nodded. "His Fasse is better than mine. Much better. I don't have the accent and I don't have his gift for idiom."

She let out another sigh. Every time she thought she had a handle on this case, the ground shifted beneath her. "I've got to meet with him in less than an hour. Tell me what you can."

Okani folded his hands. "First, the asylum question. The Eaufasse don't appear to have a word for 'asylum' because, as far as I can tell, they don't understand the concept, at least not in the sense of protection from a foreign government and immunity from extradition."

She folded her own hands together, mirroring Okani's posture. She did that on purpose to make sure he relaxed.

He didn't seem to notice. "Apparently, the Eaufasse don't understand extradition. I couldn't find it in a quick search of their laws."

"You found a database of their laws?" She'd been unable to find anything like that; it was the first thing she had checked for. It was always the first thing she checked for whenever she was encountering a new culture. The laws told her more than any cultural representative would.

Okani slipped his hands apart. One hand gripped the arm of his chair.

"Um, *I* have a database," he said. "It's not official. It's the things I and my old friends learned about that little clan of Eaufasse we'd encountered."

"Do you know of anything official?" she asked.

He shook his head. "Believe me, I've looked. There's nothing easily accessible. Which doesn't mean it doesn't exist. It just means that we can't find it."

She brought her hands up and tapped her chin with her thumbs. She was going to have to document Okani's claims, so that if (when) she did misstep, she could show that she had tried to do things the Eaufasse way.

"All right," she said. "The Eaufasse don't have a concept of extradition, so far as we know, which means that they don't have a concept of asylum or protection from prosecution from the outside."

"Prosecution or persecution," he said pointedly. She wondered if that was a reference to his own legal troubles. She decided to ignore that.

"So he couldn't have been asking for asylum," she said.

"Not in their language, no," Okani said. "Your previous translator got that wrong."

He seemed to speak with a great deal of relish about that. Had she told him Uzven's name? Or just that it was Peyti? Or had she simply said she hadn't trusted it?

She couldn't remember. Not that it mattered. Okani's reaction might have had nothing to do with Uzven and everything to do with his own ego.

"My earlier translation was correct," Okani said. "This boy asked for protection from the humans. Even though that is part of the cultural definition of asylum, it would be a stretch to think he was saying asylum here. From what he says, his life was in danger. Someone was actively trying to kill him, and he wanted to be safe from that."

"Someone *was* trying to kill him," she said. "Someone managed to kill three of his companions."

Okani's mouth thinned. He nodded. "This boy is scared. That much is clear."

"What else is clear?"

"This is his first encounter with the Eaufasse," Okani said.

"Even though he speaks their language?" she asked.

"Yes," he said. "He must have learned it through vids or holographic representation or something, because he seems alarmed when they move, as if he doesn't expect that."

"Could that simply be a reaction to his circumstances?" she asked. "After all, someone did just try to kill him."

Okani shrugged. "I can't speak to someone's state of mind, particularly someone I've never met. He just seemed uncomfortable with them, more than you'd expect from someone who was used to the culture."

She had other questions along this line, but she decided to hold on to them for a moment. "You said you didn't envy me, that there were many issues. Then you tell me that he isn't asking for asylum, which changes my legal position for the better. So I don't understand. What problems are you foreseeing here?"

Okani sat up straighter, like a man who was about to face trouble of his own making. He clearly thought for a moment, as if he were choosing his words carefully. Then he said,

"The Eaufasse have strict ideas about property. Essentially, they believe that if they have something in hand, it's theirs. Their idea of ownership is similar to that of a three-year-old child's."

She had a hunch she knew where he was going with this, but she wanted him to get there on his own.

"It's pretty clear to me from what the boy said in that room that he's a clone of some kind. I don't think the Eaufasse understood that. I don't know for certain however."

She frowned. She didn't know where Okani was going with this part of the analysis. "And the fact that he might be a clone is important why?"

"Because of his legal status," Okani said. "If he personally hasn't been declared human under Earth Alliance law, then he's property, and if he's property, the Eaufasse will claim him."

The Earth Alliance was very clear in its laws about clones. Clones were not considered human under the law. That was why clones could be bought and sold. Clones were only considered human if someone with human legal status adopted them and then went through the long process to get the clone declared human.

"Are the Eaufasse familiar with clones?" Gomez had encountered some cultures that had no understanding of cloning at all.

"I don't know," Okani said.

She nodded. "Did he tell them he was a clone?"

"Not in so many words," Okani said. "They kept asking him for his name. He kept repeating that he had no name. That if someone had to distinguish him from the others, they called him The Third."

She let out a small breath. Humans would think of that as a possible clone tag. But it could also be cultural. The Disty only allowed themselves to be referred to by number as well, at least by outsiders.

"He didn't call himself a clone, though, did he?"

"No," Okani said. "He just kept asking them to keep him safe, and they made no promises. If I were that boy, I'd be terrified."

"What will they do with him if we don't take him?" she asked.

"I don't know," Okani said. "Kill him, keep him, trade him, sell him. It's all possible, and so are probably a hundred things we haven't even thought of."

She pushed herself up, then extended her hand. "Thank you," she said. "You've been invaluable."

"Am I dismissed?" he asked.

She shook her head. "I might need you again."

She almost told him that she trusted him more than she trusted Uzven, but that wasn't really true. She trusted Okani on the translation because he had no personal interest in this case. She had no idea what game Uzven had been playing, and she didn't want to know. Not now.

"If you want," he said, "I can go over this again."

"I'd rather have you go over the footage of my conversations with the ambassador. Double-check my translator."

Okani smiled. "I can do that."

"Good," she said. "I hope you find nothing untoward."

But she doubted it. There was so much more going on here. She suspected most of it had nothing to do with her, but she wasn't certain of that. She wasn't certain of anything yet.

She could only hope that certainty would arrive soon.

She needed it. If only just a little.

10

BEFORE GOMEZ WENT TO THE SURFACE, SHE SUMMONED RAINGER TO THE meeting room. He arrived, looking as tired as she felt.

"I need you to do a few things while I'm gone," she said. "First, I need to know what happened to those twelve clones after they killed the three."

"I'm pretty sure we have that information," he said.

"I'll also need to know if there are any changes near the enclave. If anyone else emerges or if there are ships going in and out."

"I can tell you now that no one has left since we arrived, and that there have been no ships going anywhere."

"Good," she said. She had asked for that information before, but she was glad to have the confirmation.

"Finally," she said, "Tell Lashante that I need to know who these clones are based on. She needs to speed up that research somehow. I'm pretty sure it's as important as anything else we're doing here."

Rainger nodded. "I heard from the diplomats," he said. "The closest unit is a month out and they're Peyti."

"Do you get a sense that the Peyti have some kind of agenda here?"

"Yeah," Rainger said. "I double-checked the record. Uzven's never had a complaint lodged against it before. In fact, most marshals and diplomats talk about how accurate Uzven is. Its behavior here just seemed very odd and uncharacteristic."

She didn't like that. Just like she didn't like the month delay. "Can we ask for a mixed diplomatic unit or a human-only one? After all, this seems to be a human-Eaufasse issue."

Rainger grinned. "Or we can say that it is."

She nodded. She'd been thinking of that as well.

"I'll ask," he said. "Here's the other news. The Military Guard is two weeks away. Do you want them before the diplomats?"

She thought about that for a few minutes. Technically, the Military Guard would be under her control. They would be able to help her if something happened at the enclave. And they wouldn't have to do anything if the enclave were quiet while they waited for the diplomats.

"Yes," she said. "Let's get the Guard here. Make sure they know I'm in charge of the mission."

"It's policy," he said.

"Yeah, and translators are supposed to translate word for word, not interpret," she said.

"Point taken," he said.

"I'm leaving in a few minutes," she said. "I want two deputies with me, in case we have to bring the boy back here. I also want an armored suit for him, a prison suit, one without weapons."

"You think someone will try to harm him?" Rainger asked.

"You don't?" she asked.

11

GOMEZ BROUGHT A SINGLE SHUTTLE TO THE SURFACE. SHE KNEW THAT was a gamble: it was always best to have two. But she had an odd feeling that the enclave was keeping track of her movements. She couldn't know that for certain, and she had a hunch she would later learn it was just paranoia, but she wanted to be cautious all the same.

That caution led her to bring Washington on this mission as well. He had already dealt with the Eaufasse. While he might not be comfortable with them, he at least had a bit of experience. The second deputy that Gomez had brought along, Malia Norling, was next in the usual rotation. Norling was tall and powerful, easily twice the size of a typical Eaufasse.

Okani presented another problem. His shoulders were so broad that he would have to go sideways through the average Eaufasse doorway.

Once again, the team would have to walk wherever it was going, not just because the Eaufasse didn't allow foreign transports, but also because no one in her group would fit in an Eaufasse ship.

At least this walk was shorter than the one to the clearing. None of those strange plants were around either. There was an actual path to the back of the outpost. It wasn't until the path started going uphill that it disappeared into overgrowth and tall trees.

As the party got closer to the outpost building, Gomez noted an increase in those strange plants. She kept an eye on them. She didn't like them; they made her very nervous.

This entire trip made her nervous. Her people were flanked by two Eaufasse. Another ran the Eaufasse-human communication link from a location near their ship. The setup was similar to the one she had used when she went to the clearing, except that this time, she had her own translator as well.

She didn't know the names or the gender of the two Eaufasse who led her group to the outpost. These Eaufasse seemed smaller than the others, and thinner, if that were possible. They also wore a greenish-grayish outfit that she had never seen before.

She took it for some kind of uniform.

The walk only took about half an hour, and seemed pretty straightforward. She didn't have to ask for any clarifications. This time, one of the Eaufasse led while the other brought up the rear.

It wasn't until she was nearly to the outpost that she realized the boy might not speak Standard. She had planned to speak to the boy alone. She didn't want Okani in the room—or anyone else, for that matter. If the boy didn't speak Standard, she could try a few other languages that she was fluent in. After that, she would need the help, even though she didn't want it.

The outpost was a brown building that appeared to be made of some kind of mud plaster. She followed the Eaufasse and stepped where it stepped, touched what it touched. Before she left the ship, she had activated a small camera chip in her lapel and another on her right ear. She wanted a record of everything that was taking place.

She didn't feel the need to tell the Eaufasse that they were being recorded.

As the first Eaufasse approached the door, those strange plants rose up along the walls as they had done for the boy. The tips of the plants seemed to be searching for something on the building's surface. They gave off the faint odor of vanilla mixed with sweat.

She hadn't noticed the scent before because of the overwhelming stench of decay near those bodies.

The Eaufasse stepped through the plants. Gomez hesitated as the plants moved. Their tips turned outward, as if they were looking at her, even though she didn't see eyes. Then the plants leaned back, their edges folding the way that the ambassador had folded its arm over its back during their earlier conversation.

Gomez swallowed hard, trying to at least pretend not to be nervous. She didn't want anyone to know just how much those plants unnerved her.

She stepped past them and through the open door. She did not look back to see if the others had trouble following. She assumed if they had trouble, they would say something.

The interior was significantly darker than the outdoors. It took a few moments for her eyes to adjust. The entry area was larger than she expected. The vanilla-sweat scent was gone, replaced by the smell of baked dirt. There were no windows here and no obvious screens built into the walls.

The outpost seemed primitive, even though she had a hunch it was not. She suspected most everything in here had been removed or shut down in anticipation of her visit.

Something brushed against her back, making her jump. She didn't like how on edge she had been since she arrived on Epriccom. She looked over her shoulder, saw Norling closer than she should have been. Norling's brown eyes were wide, but she dropped her gaze and stepped back just a bit.

Had Gomez seen fear in those eyes? She didn't want to think about it. She didn't want to guess at anyone's emotions, not even her own.

Stay here, she sent to Norling through the FSS's private channel. *I want to know if anyone else enters.*

Should I be outside? Norling asked.

Gomez thought of those plants. They had sent feelers through the skin of the dead bodies. She had a hunch those tips could go through living human flesh as well.

No, she sent. *Inside is fine for now.*

Norling moved away from the group and stayed by the door.

Approve this? That question came through the joint alien-marshal link. Gomez wasn't certain if the question was to her or to the other Eaufasse. Then she remembered that the other Eaufasse did not speak Standard at all.

It is our custom to protect entrances and exits, Gomez sent on the link. *I'm sorry. I should have checked. Is this all right?*

The two Eaufasse who were with the group looked at each other. One wrapped an arm around its head. The other leaned back like a branch in a strong wind.

This approve, sent the Eaufasse on the joint alien-marshal link.

Gomez took that as approval. If it wasn't, someone could stop her.

Thank you, she sent.

She didn't even think to have Okani handle the interaction until the interaction was over. He wasn't on the joint alien-marshal link. He wasn't part of the FSS.

Besides, he had enough trouble getting through the hallway. As she had suspected, his shoulders were too wide for him to move comfortably.

The first Eaufasse moved the group forward, leading them past rectangles carved into the walls. It took her a moment to realize that those rectangles indicated doors or windows.

As the group approached what seemed like the end of the hallway, a vertical rectangle slid back, revealing more corridors and a ramp that led downward. She thought she saw more plants poking their tips over the edge of the ramp, but she couldn't be certain.

A dim, brownish light illuminated the new area. The first Eaufasse waited half-in and half-out of the entry. When Gomez got close, the Eaufasse stepped all the way inside.

She followed, Okani directly behind her, and Washington near the second Eaufasse. Everyone seemed calm, which was a good thing. Norling had been too nervous for her tastes.

The Eaufasse led them down a side hallway, and Gomez realized they had made a U and were now going back toward the main door through a different corridor. She wondered if there had been an easier way to get to this part of the outpost, something that cut through those walls, going from one corridor to the other quicker. She suspected there was an easier way, but that it revealed more than the Eaufasse wanted her to know, at least at this point.

A single horizontal rectangle slid open in a wave of brownish dust. Through it, she could see the boy. He was in the same room she had seen from the surveillance footage the Eaufasse had sent her. He was pacing the back part of the room. A clear door led into an area she couldn't quite see.

A table filled the room. Around the table were three Eaufasse chairs, which looked a bit like cones that had risen out of the ground. On the far side of the table, near the boy, were two regular human chairs. They seemed shiny, new, and out of place.

The boy kept looking at them as if he didn't know what to make of them.

The first Eaufasse stood next to the window. *Go. Private*, the Eaufasse sent through the joint alien-marshal link. *No watch.*

She glanced at Okani. He looked back at her, and raised his eyebrows. She should have asked him to check on what was being said, but she found that she was reluctant to do so.

You in, the Eaufasse sent to Gomez. *You.*

As the Eaufasse voice spoke through the joint alien-marshal link, the first Eaufasse nodded to her.

"Are they speaking to you?" Okani asked.

She didn't answer that directly. "I'm going in alone."

I wouldn't advise that, Washington sent through their private links. *Let me go with you.*

The boy has asked for protection from humans, she sent. *One human's going to be hard for him. Two or three will be even harder.*

I don't like this, Washington sent.

He didn't have to like it. No one did.

You two stay with the Eaufasse, she sent. *I'll be fine.*

Then she sent to the Eaufasse through the joint link. *I'm ready. I'll talk to the boy alone.*

A door opened. She hadn't even seen the outline of the door in the wall. That door opening made her rethink her assumptions about the rectangles.

The boy looked up. When he saw that she was human, he backed away, hitting the wall behind him.

He started beeping in Fasse.

"He's saying he didn't want to see any humans," Okani said softly. "He's saying he asked for protection."

She figured as much. She didn't answer Okani. Instead, she stepped all the way into the room. The door closed behind her, and as it did, her external links shut off.

Great. She should have expected that, but she hadn't.

The silence inside her head without her external links always seemed to echo. She hated that. But it did make her concentrate.

"Do you speak Standard?" she asked the boy in that language.

He was as tall as she was, but very thin. His blue eyes had shadows beneath them. She could see the veins in his pale skin, except where his cheeks had reddened. His lower lip trembled.

He was clearly terrified.

She held up her hands, revealing her palms to him, in what she always thought of as a non-threatening gesture. "I'm not here to hurt you. I just want to talk. Do you speak Standard?"

"Get out, get out, get out!" the boy said.

"So you do speak Standard," she said, letting her hands drop. "That's a good place to start."

"I can't talk to you. Please. I want the Eaufasse. Please! Getoutgetout-getout! Please! Leave me alone!"

His terror made her heart rate increase. She'd never quite seen anything like it.

"I'm not here to hurt you," she said again.

"You *lie!*" He screamed that last word.

"No," she said. "I don't. I'm with the FSS. The Eaufasse called me here. I'm just going to talk to you."

"They…called you?" He closed his eyes and leaned his head against the wall, as if his last hope was gone.

She felt sorry for him. But she had to keep that emotion in check. She had misrepresented her presence just enough; the Eaufasse hadn't called her for him, although she let him think that.

Still, the idea that they might have betrayed him seemed to devastate him.

"I'm not part of the enclave," she said. "I don't even know what it is. I'm part of the Earth Alliance. Are you familiar with that?"

His lips were pressed together as if he were holding back a scream.

"The Eaufasse want to join the Alliance. That's why they called us. They don't know how to handle human interactions."

His eyes opened. "There wouldn't be a human interaction if you weren't here," he snapped.

His argument was better than she expected. He was clearly intelligent, and clearly willing to use that intelligence.

"The Eaufasse saw what happened to your friends outside the enclave," she said. "They've never seen anything like that before. They called us to interpret that."

His head turned slightly, his eyes still on her. "What happened to my friends?" he repeated, as if he wasn't sure he wanted to know.

She hadn't thought it through: Maybe he didn't know.

She took a deep breath. "You four left together," she said. "Then twelve others came out of the enclave."

He hadn't moved. He was watching her so closely that she thought he could see right through her.

"They followed the other three. They never came after you."

He let out a small breath. "They sent you?"

"The twelve?" she asked.

"No," he said. "The ones in charge."

If she hadn't been paying attention, if she hadn't been thinking about each word, she could have said the wrong thing. Because she *was* sent by the ones in charge—the ones in charge of the Eaufasse, the ones in charge of the FSS, the ones in charge of the Earth Alliance, if she wanted to be technical about it.

She wondered if Uzven would have been technical, if its answer to that one question would have ruined this entire interview.

"No," she said softly. "The ones in charge did not send me."

The boy continued to stare at her with that awful intensity. He seemed to have no idea about the FSS or the Earth Alliance, and he clearly did not trust her.

"I don't look like anyone you know, do I?" Her question was a gamble: he was a clone, so she figured his contact with adult humans was limited to a small set of people, some of whom might also be clones. She could be wrong as easily as she could be right.

But interviews were a gamble sometimes, particularly in her profession.

"No," he said, the word short and reluctant. "I've never seen anyone like you before."

"There are a lot of humans in this universe," she said, and stopped herself from explaining further. She didn't want the Eaufasse to know that their assumptions about the Earth Alliance were wrong. "The people who run the enclave have broken off from the rest of us. They want nothing to do with us."

That too could be an untruth. She had no idea what the truth was. But she suspected this boy didn't either.

"You say enclave," he said. "I didn't leave an enclave. I left the dome."

"All right," she said. "I didn't know what you called that structure. My people call it an enclave because that's what the Eaufasse call it."

The fact that he had offered up that detail was a good sign; it meant that in his mind, he was arguing about whether or not she was right.

He didn't say anything else, clearly thinking about that last interchange. So she kept the conversation going.

"I don't know what you're called either," she said.

"I told the Eaufasse," he said.

"I don't speak Fasse," she said.

His eyes narrowed. "Then how did they contact you?"

"Through others who speak their language. How did you learn it?"

His head moved slightly, almost as if he considered shaking it and then changed his mind.

"They call me Third of the Second." His voice shook. "Thirds if they don't want to say the whole name."

So Okani's translation was wrong. "Thirds" not "Third."

That would be easy to mishear.

"And your friends call you that too?" she asked.

His mouth moved, but nothing came out. Then he bit his lower lip, drawing blood. "What happened to the others?"

Her gaze met his. It was time to be honest with him, in more than one way.

"I wasn't called to see you," she said. "I didn't find out about you until several hours after I arrived."

She hoped he would understand the subtlety. She hoped he would know what she meant.

His eyes narrowed a little. He seemed to have an idea what she was talking about. He frowned.

"What happened?" he asked again.

She rather liked the fact that he wasn't going to assume. She liked that he needed confirmation.

"The twelve killed the three who left with you," she said as calmly as she could.

"How?" he asked.

She was surprised by that. She figured he would know they had used their laser rifles.

"They were shot," she said.

He turned his head to the side, quickly, and closed his eyes, as if denying the news. Then his face crumpled. He slid down the wall and brought his hands up.

She remained standing for a minute. Then she took one of the nearby human chairs, as much to prevent herself from going to him as to wait for him to calm a little.

He folded his arms on his knees and buried his head. His shoulders shook.

She watched. She'd seen similar reactions before, usually from parents who had lost children or people who had lost lovers. Sometimes it took quite a while for the person to calm down.

She didn't have quite a while. She was going to have to interrupt him eventually. Just not yet.

After about five minutes, he raised his head slightly, and wiped his face with his sleeve. He didn't apologize for his reaction like some people would have done. He didn't seem to care what she thought at all.

"You're going to give me to them now?" he asked, voice trembling.

"To whom?" she asked.

"The *enclave*." He used her word, as if it were forbidden.

"Of course not," she said. "They tried to kill you."

He bit his lower lip again, but he couldn't seem to stop it from shaking. He took a deep breath.

"You'll let me stay with the Eaufasse?"

How to explain the politics of this situation to this boy, who didn't even seem to know what the Earth Alliance was? Treaties, agreements, preliminary negotiations, all of that would have an impact on him if he stayed here.

Not to mention the fact that he was probably a clone, the third of the second—whatever that meant—which made him not human. If Okani was right, and the Eaufasse understood that the boy was property, then they might fight for him in a different way.

"You need to clarify some things for me before I can decide what to do." She had to tread lightly because she didn't want him to accidentally reveal his origins. "Can you explain the twelve coming after you four?"

His expression hardened. "It's a training exercise."

"So you were what? Running from them and those who survived got higher marks in the training?"

"I wasn't supposed to survive," he said. "They weren't supposed to go back until we were all dead."

She froze. She had asked Rainger to locate the twelve, but he hadn't gotten back to her on them yet. She had no idea if they had gone back into the enclave.

"What happens if one of you escapes?" she asked.

"We won't escape," he said. "They're supposed to kill us."

But you all look the same, she wanted to say. *How will they know if they missed you?* But she didn't say any of that. She had to be careful, with the Eaufasse involved.

"And if they don't kill you?" she asked.

"They will die too," he said flatly.

So much death. What was the point of that?

"Why would they die?" she asked.

"They failed," he said in that same flat voice.

"Does everyone die if they fail?" she asked. If so, how many clones lived inside that dome?

"On training, yes," he said. "You can't have a failure in a unit."

Again the voice was flat. As if he were telling her something normal but painful. Something he didn't want to think about because he didn't want to know exactly how it made him feel.

"Training," she repeated. "What are you training for?"

He looked at her like she were crazy. "Not for anything. For training."

"But training is for something. You train for something," she said.

"We have a job. The best of us will do it." Then he looked at his hands. "The best of *them* will do it."

He filled the word "them" with anger. All of the emotion he had felt but hadn't expressed so far.

He saw himself as a failure. Or someone as a failure. And it had made him disposable. Useless. Something worse than a failure.

"You can't do the job? Even though you've survived?" she asked, wanting to know what all of this was about.

"*I cannot survive,*" he said. "Don't you understand? That's why I need to stay here."

She let out a small sigh. "You can't stay here."

His mouth tightened and his eyes flashed. "So, you'll send me out to die, just like the others. You *lied*. You said you didn't want to hurt me."

She held up her hands again in that I-don't-mean-harm position. "I will not send you out to die. I will make sure you stay here until we can get you safely away."

"Then what?" he asked. "Where will I be if not with the Eaufasse or in the dome?"

"I'll take you somewhere else in the Alliance," she said.

"How can you? There is nowhere else." He spoke with great conviction. This little stretch of Epriccom was his whole universe. He had no idea that any place else existed.

His ignorance took her breath away.

"Oh," she said, sounding odd, because she couldn't bring herself to say his name, "there are so many places. You'll be happily surprised."

"Surprise is bad," he said.

She supposed in his world, it would be. "Do you know what a universe is?"

He shook his head.

"A world?"

He shook his head again.

"A city?"

"No." He sounded sullen.

"What do you call the dome?" she asked.

"The dome," he said as if she were stupid.

"There are thousands of domes," she said. "Millions. Tens of millions."

"I've never seen another," he said in a tone that implied *you lie*.

"You'll see many if you come with me," she said.

He studied her for a moment. "You are female."

"Yes," she said, wondering if he'd ever seen a woman in the flesh before.

"You have dark skin," he said.

"Yes," she said, resisting the urge to add, *Like almost everyone else.*

"Brown eyes."

"Yes," she said.

76

"Brown hair."

"Yes," she said, wondering where he was going with this.

"I've only read about creatures like you," he said. "In the Forbidden Documents."

He said that like she should know what those documents were. She didn't. She would have to find out.

"I'm not supposed to talk to you," he said.

"No," she said, trying to sound calm. "You're supposed to let twelve of your siblings find you and kill you."

He closed his eyes. A tear ran down his cheek.

"The rules of the dome no longer apply to you," she said. "Either you die following them or you come with me."

"I can't stay with the Eaufasse?" he asked.

"They don't know what to do with you," she said.

"Tell them what to do." He opened his eyes.

She let out a small involuntary chuckle. As if she knew what to do with him.

"I can't," she said. "Their choice was to call me and ask me to take you away from here."

"If I leave, they'll kill me."

"The Eaufasse?" she asked.

"The ones you call the twelve," he said.

His use of language was fascinating.

"Don't worry," she said. "We'll protect you."

She used that word on purpose. Protect.

He heard it. He looked up at her, his eyes wide. "We?"

"I have an entire crew of people," she said. "Dark-haired, dark-eyed, dark-skinned people."

"Not from the dome?" he asked.

"None of us has even been near your dome," she said.

"And you can keep me safe?" he asked.

"Yes," she said. "We can keep you safe."

12

IN THE END, THE BOY DECIDED TO TRUST HER. GOMEZ WASN'T SURE IF HE trusted her because she had used the word "protect" or because she looked nothing like the people he was used to or because he was smart enough to realize he had no other choice.

The result was the same. He was coming with her.

Once the boy decided what he would do, Gomez opened the door just a little and asked for Washington. Okani stood near the window, swaying slightly, as if he were worried. The Eaufasse watched. She couldn't tell what it thought.

For that brief moment the door was open, her links clicked on, filling her mind with familiar static, the sound of possibility. Then Washington entered, carrying the body suit, and she closed the door. The links shut out.

Except Washington's. She could sense it more than hear it.

First the boy looked at Washington, who stood near the door, the suit draped over his right arm. His weapon was half hidden beneath it. She should have had him remove the weapon.

She had no idea how trustworthy the boy was.

The boy looked from Washington to her. "He's darker," the boy said.

He hadn't learned social skills, or at least, acceptable social skills.

"We're all different," she said, wondering as she spoke the words if the boy knew that.

"I know you're different," he snapped. "Everyone's different. But your skin is different."

She glanced at Washington, and saw a look of compassion on his broad face. This poor boy had a lot to learn, and much of it, he wouldn't like. Not as long as he was a clone.

"Yes," Gomez said. "Our skin is different."

"Was that a deliberate design choice?" the boy asked. "Was there a purpose for it?"

Her breath caught. It seemed the boy had no end of ways to surprise her.

"We'll answer the questions as best we can once we leave here," she said. "Let's get you out first. This is my deputy, Kyle Washington. He brought you a protective suit."

"Why?" the boy asked her. Yeah, no social skills. He didn't even acknowledge Washington's existence beyond his appearance.

"We want to make sure you're safe as you leave here," she said.

"And that will do it?" the boy asked, nodding his head toward the suit.

"It will help," she said.

Washington set the suit on the table between them. The boy looked at it, then looked at Washington.

"I can't wear this," the boy said, his voice trembling.

"It should fit," Washington said.

"It's for an Elder," the boy said.

"It's for someone we need to keep safe," Gomez said. "Remember, the rules here are different from the dome rules. We decide who gets to wear the good suit."

The boy reached out with his right hand. He touched the suit ever so lightly. Then he glanced up at her.

"This is a trick," he said.

"No trick," she said.

"You do not wear a suit," he said.

"My clothing gives me protection," she said, instead of the thing she originally thought: *No one's trying to kill me.*

His eyes narrowed. She could see him weighing his options, trying to figure out what to do next.

Maybe we should explain that we're on his side? Washington sent through the links.

Are we? She sent back. *We have no idea who he is or why they tried to kill him. For all we know, he's defective and they were just protecting their enclave.*

Damn strange way to protect it, Washington sent.

She agreed. But she wasn't going to make any assumptions. Not yet.

Finally, the boy took the suit. He held it in front of himself as if he didn't know what to do with it.

"Just step into it," Washington said. "It'll do the rest."

The boy looked up, startled that Washington had spoken to him. Then the boy touched the interior of the suit, sniffed it, and rubbed his fingers against the edge. He glanced at Washington again, as if he worried that Washington was lying to him just by speaking.

Finally, the boy put one foot inside the suit, and then the other. His face registered panic for just an instant, and then the suit closed around him.

Gomez half expected to see him flail. He didn't. He didn't do anything for a long moment after the suit assembled itself on him. Slowly he raised a hand and looked at it.

She knew how he was feeling. The suit was heavier than expected, and it had information running along the bottom of the visor: temperature, oxygen levels, even danger fields—if it were programmed that way. She wasn't sure this one was.

Finally the boy lowered his arm. "Do I get a weapon?" he asked. He nodded toward Washington's laser pistol.

Gomez cursed silently. She had hoped he wouldn't notice it.

"No," she said. Then she sent an override command to the boy's suit. It would be under her direction. The boy could make it do minimal things—move, walk, change the information on the visor. But she could stop it at any point, shut it down, or make any part of it buckle.

In other words, she could send it tumbling to the ground if need be—with the boy in it.

"I am a good shot," the boy said.

"I'm sure you are," she said. "But for now, you'll have the suit."

"They're not supposed to go back until I'm dead," he said.

"You told me that," she said.

We're searching for the twelve, Washington sent.

I know, she sent, disappointed that Washington couldn't tell her that the twelve had been found. *We'll worry about them when we have to. Let's just concentrate on getting out of here.*

And keeping an eye on that kid, Washington sent.

That too, she replied, and glanced at the boy, who looked very uncomfortable. *That too.*

13

Gomez led him out of the room. Washington followed him. The Eaufasse said nothing, just stepped in with them. Okani looked at the boy in the suit, raised his eyebrows, and widened his eyes on purpose, as if to say, *Jeez, how come I don't get one?*

She wanted to reassure him that he would be safe. But she couldn't reassure anyone. Through her private link, she contacted Rainger.

Any news of the twelve?

He sent, *They didn't return to the enclave. We caught glimpses of them in the area around it. I think they're looking for the boy.*

Send us some backup. I'm bringing him to the Stanley.

Already have, Rainger sent. *I arranged a few more guides too. The Eaufasse should be bringing them soon.*

Any way to know if the twelve are near this building? She sent.

They haven't been sighted anywhere near you, he sent back.

Then we'll leave. The boy has armor. We should be all right.

The backup will meet you about halfway, Rainger sent.

She figured that would be enough. She sent her plan through the links to Washington. He nodded.

"We'll surround you as we walk," she said to the boy.

He glanced at the Eaufasse. Then he said something to it.

The Eaufasse responded quickly, putting its arms on top of its head.

He's asking if they know anything about a ship. The Eaufasse said they do, and they approve, Okani sent to her.

She nodded slightly. "Everything all right?" she asked the boy.

"Do I have a choice?" he asked.

She sighed. They could wait, she supposed. She wasn't sure what it would cost them, if anything.

Hey, Gomez, another voice chirruped on her links. *Got a minute?*

She recognized the identification. It was Simiaar. Gomez put a hand to her ear, the universal sign of an activated link.

"Give me one second," she said to the group and walked a little way down the corridor.

I'm about to take the boy to our ship, she sent. *Can this wait?*

I dunno, Simiaar sent. *That's why I figured you'd get to choose. We identified the original.*

The source of the clone.

And I need to know this now?

Well, it's creepy, if nothing else, Lashante sent. *Your original is Pier-Luigi Frémont.*

The name sounded familiar. Gomez frowned. Why would she know that name?

Before you dismiss this information or try to look it up on your own, just listen, Lashante sent. *PierLuigi Frémont committed genocide in three different colonies. When he got caught, he killed himself. That was more than forty years ago.*

She remembered now. Something about one of humanity's worst offenders. Lots of discussion in school about ways that naturally bred humans could go wrong. Whether such creatures as Frémont were human at all, even though they looked and sounded human. Even though he was born rather than grown.

And he left no orders for clones? Gomez asked, feeling a little unsettled.

I'd have to research it, Simiaar sent. *I'm guessing not.*

Damn. That meant they were dealing with True Believers in that enclave, True Believers who—it looked like—were trying to recreate a mass murderer.

Gomez shivered. She would wait to contact the enclave until the Military Guards arrived. This wasn't something she would handle on her own.

She thanked Simiaar and contacted Rainger. *Backup land yet?*

Yeah. They're not far from you, he sent.

Good. The sooner she got off this planet, the better. This boy was going to be a wealth of knowledge about something the Earth Alliance clearly needed to know. Why breed clones from someone like Frémont? There had to be a reason, and the boy might hold the key.

She made her way back down the hall. The boy had been talking with the Eaufasse. It looked at her, and she thought she saw guilt. She had no idea how she would know that.

Everything all right? she sent Okani.

Thirds is still trying to make sure the Eaufasse don't want him.

Do they want him? She sent.

Not at all, Okani sent.

Good. She smiled at the boy. "We're leaving."

He swallowed. She knew what his reaction was. It was fear.

"We'll protect you," she said, emphasizing the word "protect."

Washington looked at her.

The others are nearly here, she sent.

I think we should have weapons out just in case, he sent.

I think we should keep as much of an eye on this boy as we have on the area around us, she sent, but she didn't dissuade him.

She arranged the group. First the Eaufasse. Then Washington. Then the boy and Okani. She would follow, along with Norling and the last Eaufasse. It wasn't quite the perfect formation, but it would do until the backup arrived.

The Eaufasse led them down yet another corridor she hadn't seen before. This outpost was much bigger than she had expected.

Finally, the Eaufasse reached the main door. Using both hands, it pushed the door open. Washington peered out, made certain the area was clear, and then signaled the others to follow.

The boy stepped out, hand over his visor as the light changed. Apparently, he hadn't yet figured out how to handle the visuals.

She stepped out as well. The plants were rustling. They gave off a stinkweed stench, very different from the vanilla and sweat from earlier. She wondered what caused the things to change. She wished she understood them better.

The final Eaufasse closed the doors behind them. The first Eaufasse headed toward the path as the rustling got louder.

Then twelve boys popped up out of the plants.

Twelve boys who looked just like the boy she had in custody.

That boy—Thirds—reached for Washington's pistol, but Washington elbowed him backward. Gomez had her pistol out as well.

Need backup now, she sent on all FSS channels. *Double-time.*

She got chatter in response. The boys all had laser rifles, and they were all aimed at the boy behind Washington.

"Let him go," one of the boys said. "He belongs to us."

Thirds was silent. Okani had moved back toward Gomez, nearly knocking her aside. She pushed him against the outpost's exterior.

The plants waved.

"We're taking him with us," Gomez said. "Why don't you join us?"

"Forbidden ones," the first boy sneered. "We would never go with you."

He waved his laser rifle at Thirds. Thirds grabbed his helmet and yanked it off. Idiot. He would die if they shot him now.

He made a chittering sound as she overrode his removal command. The gloves of his suit forced his arms upward and replaced the helmet. He chittered loudly, until the helmet went on. Then the sound got blocked.

"Fire," the first boy said to the others.

Washington pivoted so that he could shoot the boys' leader, and Gomez leaned to one side so that she had a clear shot of the others.

But before the boys could shoot, their laser rifles bent sideways. The plants wrapped around them and pulled the laser rifles aside. Then the plants enveloped the boys.

The Eaufasse were chittering as well. The boys started screaming. The tips of those plants were burrowing into their skin.

"Are they doing that?" she asked Okani.

"How the hell should I know?" he said.

"Make them stop. We need those boys alive."

Not that they would live much longer. The tips of the plants were burrowing deep.

Okani spoke quickly in Fasse. Washington kept pivoting, moving his pistol as if he were looking for a target. She pivoted as well.

Boy command. Boy command, the translator Eaufasse sent through the joint foreign-marshal link.

What does that mean? She sent.

Boy must no say, the translator sent.

Somehow the words connected. *The boy sent the command?*

Yes, the translator sent. *Boy must no say.*

She got that too. She cursed, then overrode the command for the helmet. She kept her pistol in one hand, but with the other, she yanked off the boy's helmet.

"You started this," she said. "You stop it."

"They must die," he said calmly. How could he be so calm? "They tried to kill me."

"And now they won't," she said. "I need them alive."

"Why?" he asked.

She couldn't answer that in less than five seconds. "Stop it or I'll make your damn suit strangle you just like they're being strangled."

Now, she saw fear. He knew she could do it.

He chittered. The plants stopped moving.

"Tell the plants to listen to the Eaufasse," she said.

He frowned.

"Tell them, or I will hurt you," she said.

"They're not plants," he said, confirming what she had suspected.

"Do it anyway," she said.

He chittered again. The plants—or whatever they were—turned some of their tips toward the Eaufasse.

"Okani," she snapped. "You tell the Eaufasse to tell these plants or creatures or whatever the hell they are to hold the boys, but not burrow into them. And give the rifles to Washington."

Okani began to speak rapidly in Fasse. He looked terrified, the color on his cheeks high. The Eaufasse bobbed, then chittered. The plants pulled their tips out of the boys and wrapped them gently like loose ropes.

The boys did not move.

Blood flowed along the dry ground and past Washington, running into Thirds' feet. He just looked down at it, as if it didn't bother him.

Gomez shuddered.

The rustling had stopped, but she still heard something. She finally realized what it was. The backup had arrived.

I need medics and restraints, she sent. *Quickly*.

She knew what was happening down that trail. Those assistants with medical training would move to the front of the lines. The rest would pull out their restraints as they moved.

She took the boy's hands and pulled them behind him. She put him in restraints, even though she had his suit on lock-down. He wouldn't get any more control of the suit.

"You planned this," she said to him.

He looked at her sideways. "Not this," he said.

"Yes, you did," she said. "You taught yourself Fasse, you learned how to control the plants. You planned to kill them."

"That is true," he said. "I planned to kill them. All of them. When I became part of the twelve. I never expected to be the hunted. Now I can go back. I am still the victor."

His blue eyes were flat, his expression calm. All that empathy she had felt for him, all of that concern. Gone, in an instant.

"You're never going back," she said. "I can promise you that."

14

IT TOOK MOST OF HER TEAM TO CLEAN UP THE MESS. SEVEN BOYS DIED, and the other five were so badly injured that no one was certain if they would survive. She had placed Thirds in the most powerful holding cell she had, and she kept the sound off.

The Eaufasse were relieved she had handled him. They had no idea he had learned how to manipulate the plants. Which weren't plants, but weaponry that the Eaufasse had created. They looked like undergrowth, but they weren't. They operated as protective shields throughout Eaufasse territory.

Somehow Thirds had taught himself to override them.

Thirds would not tell her what happened in the dome. He wouldn't talk to her at all. The only way he would speak to her was if she allowed him to return, the triumphant warrior, to his home.

So they had a stalemate.

Hours after the battle outside the outpost, if anyone could call that a battle, Washington called her into one of the conference rooms. There, on the table, he had visuals of what was happening on the planet below.

The dome glowed from within.

"What is that?" she asked him.

"Laser rifle fire," he said. "I think they're killing each other."

She wanted to order him to bring a team in, but both of them knew they couldn't. They had no idea how many people were there, or what kind of weapons they had.

With the help of Okani, she contacted the Eaufasse ambassador.

"They're killing each other inside the dome," she said. "Can you stop them?"

"They are yours," the ambassador said. "We can do nothing."

As they spoke, the dome's glow increased.

"We have to do something," she said.

"You must," the ambassador said. "We leave it to you."

Then it severed the connection.

She watched as the glowing dome grew brighter. "That's a fire," she said to Washington.

"Or worse," he said.

They'd seen images of this before. Domes were vulnerable to internal attack.

The dome had turned bright red.

Washington looked away. He knew, as she did, what was happening inside. The people in there were actually cooking. Burning up. Disintegrating.

She didn't have the equipment to stop this.

She couldn't turn away. She watched as the dome grew brighter and brighter, until it blew.

She couldn't hear it, but she knew that on Epriccom, it must have sounded like a million bombs went off. The ground would shake; there would be other damage throughout the various settlements.

If the Eaufasse blamed her, she would use that contact she made with the ambassador as proof that she had done all she could.

"Why would they do that?" Washington asked.

The air was black with smoke. Bits of the dome flew like shards into the trees. She shut off the hologram. She couldn't look any more.

"They knew we were here," she said.

"So?" he asked. "We'd been here for days. Why now?"

She stared at the empty tabletop. Then shook her head. "The experiment failed. They lost all sixteen boys."

"I still don't understand."

She raised her gaze to his. "Success or failure," she said, "what do you do at the end of an experiment?"

"I'm not a scientist," he snapped.

"You disassemble it. You take it apart. You make your notes and you start over."

"No one left," he said. "No one made notes. No one survived."

"No one survived in the dome," she said. "But you don't know if they sent their results elsewhere. You don't know what kind of recordings they made."

"We've been monitoring communications," he said. "We would know."

"Would we?" she asked. "We didn't even know those things were weapons. We thought they were plants."

He stared at her, his skin gray and bloodless. "How have you done this for so long?" he asked.

The question so many of her deputies had asked over the years. The way that the deputy answered for himself determined his career.

She took a deep breath. She had answered this one for herself a long time ago.

She had to believe in what she was doing, believe that the Alliance was important, that the groups it finally accepted into the Alliance would be worthy of that Alliance.

Some wouldn't be. Some would.

And tragedies would happen along the way.

Even—especially?—tragedies caused by humans.

Gomez gave Washington a small smile. "You have to realize when you've done your job well."

"What?" he asked. "We didn't do this well. People died."

"Yes, they did," she said. "And people will always die. We can't stop that."

His eyes widened. He looked at her as if she had just said something horrible. Maybe, to him, she had.

She put a hand on his arm. "Our mission—our *job*—was to remove the enclave," she said. "We did that, and found out something along the way. And we've managed to keep a good relationship with the Eaufasse. All in all, we've done well."

He shook his head. "We just watched hundreds of people die."

"Did we?" she asked. "For all we know, there had been no one but sixteen clones in that enclave."

"You don't believe that," he said, and let himself out of the room.

He was right; she didn't believe that there had been only sixteen clones in that enclave. She did believe that her team had done their job.

She also believed that they had stumbled on something big, something the diplomats and the Military Guard would have to deal with, something she no longer had to concern herself with.

She was glad of that. The boy, Thirds, unnerved her. The other five probably would as well.

She ran a hand along the tabletop. One mission done. She would go talk to the assistants next, make sure they were again focused on possible future missions.

She didn't want to think about this one any more.

She had a hunch no one else did either.

ANNIVERSARY DAY

15

TORKILD ZHU ADJUSTED HIS SEAT IN THE FIRST CLASS SUITE ON THE MIDWEEK shuttle heading to Athena Base. He'd charged the suite to Schnable, Shishani, & Salehi, even though the bulk of the work he'd been doing on the Moon had been personal. Still, he was a junior partner at S3, as everyone called the firm, and they liked their partners to impress wherever they went.

He was new enough to the partner business that he almost felt like he was stealing from his employer to travel in such luxury.

The suite had two rooms—a living/office area, and a sleeping area barely big enough for his lanky, six-foot frame. The real thing that recommended this suite was the private bathroom, complete with private shower. Sure, he had to cram himself into it, but he didn't have to share it with his floor-mates, like he'd had to do on every shuttle to the Moon before his promotion.

The trip took more than three days, even on the fastest shuttle, and by the end of it, he would always know the bathroom habits of strangers, something he absolutely hated.

At least he was cleared to ride human-only shuttles. He'd taken shuttles that had mixed species; those were a real eye-opener—and not in a way that he wanted.

Maybe someday he would rate one of the corporate space yachts, although he'd been told when he became partner that he would only be able to use those to go to court outside of the Tenth District.

Most of the cases he handled were inside Earth Alliance IntraSpecies Court Human Division for the Tenth District, although he hoped to handle some larger cases in front of the Multicultural Tribunal for the Tenth District soon. Or for any district. He was licensed for all of them, just like every lawyer working in the Earth Alliance court system.

He was doing well, but he could do better.

He had surrounded his seat with a dozen holoscreens, building a circle of information around him. He would have to sit here while the shuttle awaited takeoff from Armstrong's port. The actual amount of time he needed to be strapped in would be about three minutes, but the space around Armstrong was so crowded that the port required every commercial ship to harness its passengers until the ship traveled outside of the Moon's space.

He hated this part of the trip. The shuttles were sophisticated enough to maintain gravity and attitude controls, so that no passenger ever felt the differences between being on the Moon proper and being in space, yet some of these old-fashioned rules still applied.

Although he'd once been irritated enough to see if the precaution was completely stupid, and that was when he learned that the accident rate inside the Moon's space traffic area, particularly around the major port of Armstrong, was twenty-five times higher than it was anywhere else in the Earth Alliance.

The Moon, which was a relatively small body in comparison to most other populated places in this solar system, was the gateway to Earth. Most ships weren't cleared for direct Earth travel, so passengers heading to Earth stopped on the Moon and got an Earth transport. If, of course, they could get through Earth Alliance customs.

Many, many, many people—alien and human—never made it to Earth, and had to be sent back to wherever they were from.

The system wasn't perfect—if it were, the gateway to Earth would be a lot bigger—but it was better than other places Zhu had been in the Alliance. Many major planets, filled with diverse cultures, had no gateway at all and were subject to all kinds of attacks, terror or otherwise.

Earth had not suffered a direct attack from outside its borders in centuries. Somehow the Earth had made herself both the center of the Alliance and the safest place inside the Alliance.

Given Earth's history, he would never have predicted that.

So while he was trapped in one spot, he would catch up on some entertainment—anything to keep his mind off what had just happened inside the port.

He'd been an idiot. A *cowardly* idiot. He'd assumed intelligence, which, one of his law professors had told him, would always get him in trouble.

He had volunteered to conduct some continuing education classes for the Armstrong bar, so that they would know which criminal cases belonged in the Alliance systems and which cases remained strictly local. He loved the intricacies of Earth Alliance law, as big as it was, and if he didn't like going to court so much, he might have become a legal scholar. Instead, he hoped he was on the track toward a judgeship—even though most of the Alliance judges were chosen from the prosecutor's bench, not the defense bench.

He was making enough political connections that he might become one of the token defense nominees. They always went through the Alliance system faster than the prosecutorial nominees, only because so few defense attorneys ever had success records that put them in the public eye.

The classes had kept him busier than he expected or, if he were honest with himself, as busy as he wanted to be. He had managed to avoid Berhane most of the time.

Berhane Magalhães, his now-former fiancée. Whom he had just left sobbing outside of Terminal 20.

Zhu rubbed a hand over his face. He could have handled the break-up better. He could have handled it *years* ago, when he knew a marriage wouldn't work. He had never expected her to wait for him. He stopped setting dates for the wedding a long time ago. She'd set the first two, and he'd missed them, mostly by failing to tell her that one date was the bar exam that would license him for Interspecies Court, and the other was the date he had to report to work at the Impossibles, which was where all defense attorneys got their start, just so they could see how hopeless the Earth Alliance court system truly was. At least he hadn't been indentured there, like some lawyers who couldn't afford law school. He'd paid for his own schooling, so he only had to serve six months in that hell.

Then he went on to S3 and his real career. He kept telling Berhane she didn't have to wait for him, that she *shouldn't* wait for him, and she never seemed to get the hint. One drunken evening, he'd even confessed to sleeping with other women, and still Berhane had held on.

He had no idea why, which he had just screamed at her an hour ago. Then she'd threatened to contact Daddy, just like she always did. Daddy—or Bernard Magalhães, one of the richest men on the Moon, who somehow managed to maintain all his wealth through investments that seemed shady to Zhu.

Not that Zhu knew much about financial crimes. They mostly fell outside his jurisdiction. He specialized in human-on-human crimes— the violent, nasty kind—that occurred in the darker regions of the Earth Alliance, often in places that preferred humans take their interpersonal problems outside of the non-human jurisdiction.

The moment Berhane had told him she had let Daddy listen in on her links was the moment that Zhu was done. Completely, totally, irrevocably done.

Instead of reminding her that his shuttle was about to leave, which was what he would have done in the past, he had shaken his head and said for both of their benefits, "*This* is why I'm walking away. *This*. I'm not going to marry your father, Berhane. And it seems like you two are a package deal. I've been running from the package for years. Let's just make it official, shall we?"

And then he walked away, actually resisting the urge to run in his dress shoes and suit. He felt free. He felt guilty. He felt stupid—because he should have done this years ago.

And he should have, for both of their sakes.

Then he smiled to himself. For *all three* of their sakes.

He was having trouble choosing what kind of entertainment he wanted for his thirty-minute confinement. Most everything had touches of romance in it, and the last thing he wanted was even a hint of romance. He had just settled on some virtual battlefield game, which seemed to be all about killing and scoring points from mayhem—something he usually avoided—when the imagery cut out.

He cursed. The last thing he needed was something short-circuiting his imagination, especially right now. He also knew that the staff of the shuttle wouldn't fix any problems in the entertainment system until the damn thing was outside the purview of the space traffic cops.

Then a face appeared on all of Zhu's screens. The face was male, older, with the pockmarked skin of someone who didn't give a damn about enhancements. It was attached to a neck and shoulders that were encased in a uniform Zhu didn't really recognize.

"Forgive me for the interruption," the man said. "I'm the senior pilot of this shuttle. We've been ordered to abort our scheduled flight. We're told this might only be temporary, but at the moment I don't know. All space traffic has been grounded until further notice."

Zhu groaned. He'd never heard of anything like this happening anywhere in the Alliance.

They'd be hearing from him. After, of course, he checked Armstrong Port regulations to see if they could actually do this.

"Everyone is to disembark. We will be going back inside, where you will have to be screened, for what, I don't know. Why, I don't know. I hope they'll explain this to us when we get inside. Please accept a small link to the shuttle before disembarking so that we can let you know when the trip will be rescheduled. I hope it'll be within the hour."

The pilot winked out.

"It better be," Zhu said to no one in particular. The last thing he wanted to do was go back inside Armstrong's port. There was no guarantee that Berhane had left yet.

He sighed and shoved the screens out of his way. Then he unhooked himself from the chair.

He was already downloading Port of Armstrong Regulations, plus all of the City of Armstrong's legal codes.

Someone would answer for this delay.

He would make certain of it.

16

Zhu trudged up the ramps out of Terminal 20. Along the way, dozens, if not hundreds, of other passengers from other luxury ships joined him. None of them were arrivals. All were departures, and all were talking in their various languages about their postponed trips.

Images floated on the screens in front of them, directing them back to the lounges. People separated out by class. Those who worked on the ships followed one row of lights. Those who paid less for their transport followed another. And those who either paid for a luxury berth or were frequent travelers followed the green light that lit up the floor for Zhu.

Because Terminal 20 was the luxury departure area, most everyone went that way. Even though he was taller than most of the humans, he wasn't able to shove his way past the group of Sequev who were galumphing their way toward the main door. Sequev had eight legs and resembled spiders. Even though they were the size of small dogs, they still managed to get in his way.

He resigned himself to getting nowhere fast.

Nowhere. That's where he was heading. As soon as he had word from the Port of Armstrong as to what was going on, he would contact S3 and let them know what his new itinerary was.

Just his luck that he would be going back to the departure lounge so soon after leaving it. He hoped—no, he prayed—that Berhane had already run off to cry in Daddy's arms.

Not that there was a huge chance of that. Her father was at some meeting with the governor-general, doing all those important things that a man of his station did. If Berhane had wanted to join him, she would have had to leave immediately.

Zhu wasn't even sure Berhane knew exactly where her father was.

Zhu shrugged his night-travel kit over his shoulder. He had brought that back out because the pilot had sounded uncertain about the future of the flight. Often, it was better to book another ship than try to work around some recalcitrant pilot who seemed to believe rules were meant to be followed.

When Zhu reached a series of doors leading to various departure sites in Terminal 20, he noted with relief that the Sequev moved to the right while he was heading left. He sped up and was the first through the door back into the luxury lounge.

It looked strange. Everyone was standing and all were looking at various screens. The humans had their hands over their mouths. There weren't a lot of non-humans in the lounge, which had become common since the bombing four years ago. Zhu had a private belief that the Port was separating its various customers by species, but he had no way to prove that.

His links filled with noise. Something about Arek Soseki, Armstrong's Mayor. Something about assassins and murders and shutting down the Port to make sure no "bad guys" escaped. Something about horrors and how terrible all of this was to happen on Anniversary Day.

He looked up at a nearby screen. Someone stumbled into him, and he realized he was blocking traffic. Not that there were a lot of places to go. All of the aisles were filled with people and aliens standing, staring at the imagery coming on the floating screens.

He moved as far away from the path of the incoming travelers as he could and found another screen. The images took a moment to process: the mayor, sprawled; the police, talking, moving, unable to figure anything out. Reporters were trying to update everyone with very little information.

But the images of Soseki—they were clear. The man looked like a statue of himself, gray and broken, and very obviously dead.

Zhu felt nauseous. Through his links he heard more whispers, something about other targets. He scanned the lounge, looking past the people clogging the aisles.

Some passengers sat in their comfortable chairs, hands pressed against their ears the way that humans did when they were trying to focus on information inside their links. A few Peyti lingered near the doorways, heads tilted as they got information, their masks elongating their faces, their sticklike hands at their sides.

He had to actually peer at people to see if Berhane was still here. She was a small woman, with dark, curly hair and very soft, chocolate skin. Her skin attracted him most. He had always loved it, even when he was getting frustrated with her.

But she would be hard to see in this crowd.

He scanned his links for word of the governor-general—surely someone would ask her for a statement in this time of crisis—and instead got some conflicting messages that something had gone wrong at her location as well.

Then he saw Berhane. Hand on her ear as if she were concentrating on links, head tilted upward as she looked at screens, she seemed like an island in a sea of trouble. His heart lifted when he saw her, and he didn't want that.

He wanted to be angry at her or hate her or feel something other than relief that he found her. He had treated her so badly, and he was starting to feel guilty. That was the last thing he wanted; as one law school professor of his said, *Lawyers should never feel guilty. If they do, they can't do the job.*

Berhane twirled slowly, looking up at various screens, most of which showed the same images—the mayor, down; the chaos near O'Malley's, of all places. What a place to die in front of.

Her face was blotchy. She'd been crying, but she wasn't crying now. Instead, her mouth was in a set line, as if she were trying to get information.

He knew that look. She was scared and determined and trying to ignore how she felt.

He threaded his way toward her, knowing he should probably stay away, knowing he was probably the last person she wanted to see, but going toward her anyway.

He reached her side, and lightly touched her back. "Berhane?"

She started. She hadn't seen him, or if she had, she wasn't processing it.

He said quickly, so she wouldn't move away, "If you don't want to talk to me, I understand, but I'm hearing something about the governor-general…?"

He half expected her to burst into tears. Instead she glanced at the screens and then back at him, that little frown line appearing between her eyes.

"I can't reach Daddy." She sounded a lot calmer than Zhu expected her to.

"So he is with the governor-general," Zhu said. "I thought you'd mentioned that. Tell me what's happening."

"No one knows." Another glance at the screens. She needed information, *he* needed information, and there was no way to get it here. No one knew anything in this lounge.

He made a decision. They had to get out of here. "Let's go somewhere else."

"We can't," she said. "The Port's in lockdown."

"I mean, inside the Port. Somewhere better than this."

"What could be better than this?" she asked.

Somewhere that the people in power went. Somewhere with better access. Somewhere he might be able to find answers.

He took her elbow, like he would have two days ago. Her lips thinned, but she didn't pull away.

So he smiled, just a little.

"Come on," he said in his most comforting voice. "Let's find out what's really going on."

17

THE EARTH ALLIANCE LOUNGE AT TERMINAL 20 WAS FILLED WITH diplomats, lawyers, and specialists of all ages and races, watching the images on the various screens while simultaneously leaning into their links. Some were subvocalizing. Others had that glazed look that humans got when they were concentrating on their links and not paying attention to anything around them.

An inordinate number of Peyti sat around tables, tapping on small screens, while pairs of Nyyzen hovered near the private chambers, obviously waiting to get in.

The Nyyzen unnerved Zhu. They worked in pairs, and when they did, they created a third, somewhat ghostly creature that was visible in outline.

That wasn't the hardest part of dealing with them, though. The hardest part was the fact that their heads were isosceles triangles. Their mouths were on the equal sides of the triangle, and their eyes on the short part. If looked at from one direction, it seemed like they had eyes on one side of their face and a mouth on the other. Zhu had no idea where their nose was—if they had a nose.

He had to pull his gaze away from the Nyyzen. A few Disty sat on top of tiny tables, their small bodies hunched, their arms busy while their feet pressed together. They could be mean when interrupted. He didn't want to stand by them either.

The chairs were full, but one table remained open with a few seats. The problem was that it was near a group of Rev. They were huge, and always took up twice the space of humans. Plus, the Rev were pear-shaped and hard to get around. They had extra arms, which retracted or something (Zhu never really understood how their anatomy worked), and the younger Rev sometimes pulled out their arms at odd moments to trick or harass humans.

Zhu had handled more than one case involving Rev, and he never really wanted to again.

"What is this place?" Berhane asked.

He had almost forgotten she was with him. He put a hand on the small of her back, partly to keep her steady and partly to make sure she didn't go to the wrong part of the gigantic room.

"I told you. It's the Earth Alliance lounge."

"It smells weird," she said.

It did. Any grouping of different species had weird, unduplicatable smells. Some species smelled horrible to humans, and others had no real scent at all. Combine all those smells, plus the smells of frightened and worried human, and you got—well, this miasma of low-level stink.

"You get used to it," he lied.

She nodded and seemed even more subdued than she had in the luxury lounge.

He had told her that they would be able to find out what was going on once they got here, but he wasn't sure that was true now. Everyone seemed preoccupied, nervous, and terrified.

He led her deep inside before he saw someone he recognized, a lawyer formerly at the Impossibles, now some sort of researcher in the Human Justice Division of the Earth Alliance.

"Hey, Barry!" Zhu's voice carried. Half the humans in the room turned toward him.

Barry Pliska wasn't one of them. He leaned against the wall, one foot braced against it, face gray. He looked almost ill. He had one hand against his ear and his head bowed.

Berhane grabbed Zhu's arm. "Look," she said, pointing at one of the images.

Zhu squinted. It appeared to be the exterior of a hospital.

"I think the governor-general is there," she said.

"Check your links," he said.

"I have been," she said. "They're working all right, except I still can't reach my dad."

"Keep trying," Zhu said, primarily because he wanted to keep her busy. He threaded his way through the crowd to get to Pliska.

Zhu didn't really care if Berhane followed. She wasn't going to leave the lounge without him, and he didn't want to be near her if she found out that her father was collateral damage in whatever had happened to the governor-general.

Zhu had made the mistake of talking to her shortly after her mother died in the actual bombing four years ago. He'd been calling to set up a time when he could do the right thing and break up with her then, but the moment he spoke to her, he had known that it would be wrong.

He felt relieved he had broken off the engagement before all of this started, and then he felt guilty for the relief. He had a hunch his timing was going to be awful, as usual. He had a hunch her father wouldn't be answering his links again.

"Barry," Zhu said as he got closer.

Pliska looked up, his expression as close to terrified as a man's expression could be. He held up one finger, then subvocalized something while maintaining eye contact with Zhu.

Then Pliska let his hand drop away from his ear. He wasn't on links anymore. He said, "Brace yourself—"

And then the entire Port shook. Disty fell off the tables. The Revs' extra arms came out, bracing the creatures against the wall. Humans staggered on their feet.

Zhu grabbed a nearby chair, which skittered under the force of whatever was happening. He heard the same words repeated in Standard and the other languages he half understood.

"Sectioning…"

"Dome…"

"Protection…?"

And then cursing, lots of cursing. The shaking lasted only a few minutes, maybe not even that, but half of the officials in the room had either fallen or lost their balance. Dust rained from the ceiling. Chairs had toppled, tables had bounced away from their usual positions, and on the screens—

On the screens, images of explosions. Blood against Dome sections, burning buildings, black air.

Zhu thought he could hear screaming, but he knew it didn't come from anyone in the room. Everyone in the room was trying to get up, making sure someone else was all right, or mesmerized by those images. The screaming seemed to come from his links.

His public links. Voices rode over the screams. Those were reporters—not screaming, trying to make sense of it. The screams were like a music bed beneath the news.

"What the hell?" he said. The question was rhetorical, or maybe it wasn't even a question, maybe it was just a statement, or a curse, but Pliska responded.

"We sectioned the domes," he said. "All of them."

Zhu frowned at him. "Everywhere?"

There were millions of domes in the Alliance. *Millions.*

"On the Moon." Pliska didn't seem to think Zhu's question was out of line. Pliska didn't seem to be thinking about Zhu at all. "There're explosions everywhere, but we might have gotten them contained."

"We?" Zhu asked.

"They were asking—the security office was asking—if the Alliance had the authority to order a dome sectioning because the Moon is, you know, city states, and I was trying to answer it when the order just came through. It just came through, and God, what if they destroyed Armstrong Dome again?"

Again. Zhu blinked, suddenly remembering Berhane. He scanned for her. She was standing in the middle of the room, arms wrapped around her torso, staring blinding at the screens.

This was worse, this was a thousand times worse than her mother. It brought everything back, and it might actually destroy her. He did care about her, maybe even loved her still, and he couldn't watch that happening; he didn't want it to happen.

He made his way through the half-standing people, the Disty trying to pull themselves up, the Peyti holding their masks, and somehow got to Berhane's side. He was about to pull her close, hide her face in his shoulder, when he actually looked at her.

She was calm.

"My God," she said, speaking a truth that he would only later realize was prescient. "Nothing will ever be the same again."

ONE MONTH AFTER
ANNIVERSARY DAY

18

Gomez stood near the door for High Functionaries in the perfectly round room, hands clasped behind her back. Five of her deputy marshals were scattered around the large room, one in front of each of the remaining doors. The room was a neutral brown, with a brownish skylight open to Thaaraenegra's two distant suns.

The room's color came from the six Cean. They stood in a perfect semi-circle, facing the six human campers who had caused this mess. The campers were having a hell of a time maintaining their semi-circle, but at least they were trying.

They knew the importance of the next hour.

The Cean liked doing everything in sixes or twelves. They also worked in perfect circles, and any deviation from that caused all kinds of problems. The Cean were in full battle garb: hair teased and colored bright blue and pink, matching paint along their naked bodies, genitals deliberately dyed an angry red.

The human campers didn't know where to look, partly because the Cean were built similarly to humans. The Cean had brow ridges, beaks instead of mouths, hands on wings instead of arms, and birdlike legs that curved downward into three-toed feet.

But their torsos looked just like a human's. And the Cean never wore clothes. They did not believe in covering any part of their bodies with something artificial. Even their dye was made from raw materials found on Thaaraenegra.

Their reluctance to wear anything prevented space travel, even though they had the technology for it. Other cultures on Thaaraenegra used space travel, but the Cean did not, and probably never would.

Still, they were fairly tolerant of aliens unless the aliens violated a major cultural norm.

Which the campers had done by, of all things, placing their tents in a triangle near a beautiful lake on the far end of Ceanese land. The lake, apparently, was sacred, and the triangle called bad gods. Or maybe it invoked bad luck. Or possibly it was as offensive to the Cean as what the Cean wanted the humans to do to atone was to the humans.

Gomez felt a giggle threaten. She suppressed it. The giggle was a sign of sheer exhaustion. She rarely giggled—at least when she was working. Even when she wasn't. She always viewed an impending giggle as a sign that she needed to rest for a few hours. Not that she'd get the chance for a while.

She'd been on Thaaraenegra for three full weeks, handling negotiations after she arrested the human campers. She'd explained to the humans that the arrest was mostly for the Cean, although not entirely.

The campers—all Earth Alliance citizens—needed special permits to travel this far out into the Frontier. Not that the permits had anything to do with non-Alliance cultures like the Cean. The permits were more accurately termed "waivers," but the Frontier Security Service had learned that most people would not sign a waiver to travel outside the Alliance.

They would, however, fill out permits.

Most of the time, anyway.

These six had been traveling for nearly a year, stopping at all kinds of beautiful non-Alliance worlds, somehow avoiding trouble—until now. Probably because their destinations had been so remote that even the locals didn't notice them.

The Cean did. The Cean took affront to almost everything the campers did.

Gomez shifted slightly, almost imperceptibly. In her many years with the FSS, she had learned how to move without seeming to move at all. It was better that way, since even the smallest thing could be offensive to an unknown culture.

She was now watching the head of the Ceanese warriors. When he was ready, he would spread the feathers on his left wing to signal her.

Part of the agreement with the campers and the Ceanese was that the campers had to perform their apology without assistance from the FSS. This was the only part that worried her. The apology had been the sticking point from the beginning, and the reason she'd lost three weeks of her life dealing with the Ceanese and the campers.

The apology had to be performed in the Ceanese method, miming Ceanese rituals. And just thinking about it made that giggle threaten again.

Gomez would have performed the apology reluctantly but quickly, and then gotten the hell off Thaaraenegra. The campers balked from the beginning.

Because this was one of those instances where the apology performance, while respectful in Ceanese culture, was considered obscene in almost every single human culture—at least when performed in public. The FSS had verified the ritual as an apology, after working with nearly a dozen other native species to confirm. Then the FSS had urged the campers to perform their apology from the beginning. Gomez figured the apology should be relatively easy, since the campers were three different couples. Gomez had assumed they did such things in private.

Only she later learned that they did not (or at least, they did not admit to it in a group of their peers). These six campers refused, not just because the requested performance was sexual in nature, but also because it was something that the religion of this group of humans had banned.

Gomez wasn't that familiar with the religion, a sect of a sect of a traditional religion, and she really didn't care that the ritual made the campers uncomfortable.

As she explained to them, their choices were to perform the ritual and then ask their god (and each other) for forgiveness, or spend the next twenty years in some prison-like place that specialized in indoc-trination, run by the Cean for Cean. Who knew if the procedures they used worked on humans?

It wasn't something Gomez would have wanted to find out, espe-cially since the indoctrination process messed with the mind and what the Cean called "the soul." Or, at least, that was what the translators, working with several different locals, had termed the thing that needed to be changed. One translator had translated it as an *anima*, another as a *soul*, a third as *the subconscious*. Whatever it was—and whether or not it existed in humans—was subject to debate.

The campers shifted and tried hard not to look at each other. She had instructed them to maintain eye contact with their Ceanese delegate, and the campers were struggling with that.

Gomez hoped that the struggle would end inside this room. Because the Cean, who lived at the known edge of the Earth Alliance Frontier, had so far refused to join the Alliance—and this little incident had near-ly destroyed any hope that the Cean would ever join.

Humans could be so dumb sometimes.

The leader of the Cean lifted his left wing and spread the feathers. The campers didn't notice, or if they did, they didn't understand. She hadn't explained the signal to them, although she had said her people would leave at some point.

She nodded to her staff. They all pivoted, as they had practiced, and let themselves out the doors. She left with a sense of relief. She really didn't want to watch the campers debase themselves just so that they wouldn't go to prison.

The urge to giggle faded, and she wiped a hand over her face. The circular room was inside yet another gigantic circle. The Cean designed everything as a series of concentric rings. She walked around the outer ring to the one set of stairs. The Cean had designed the stairs for the other species on Thaaraenegra, because the other species couldn't fly.

Even the stairs were circular, although not the way that humans would design them. They were wide circles with small declines, and would take forever to walk down. In the center was an open space, wide enough for a Cean to float down to a lower level.

Gomez waited outside the door to the stairway. Two of her marshals had already arrived, with the remaining three on the way. Elián Nuuyoma stood closest to the door. He was shaking his hands and shoulders, probably stiff from the awkward position he'd been standing in.

He was tall and slender, his skin dark brown and deliberately scarred from some childhood ceremony. The scarification always made his eyes look bigger than they actually were.

"Think they'll do it?" he asked.

She shrugged. "If they don't, then let's hope we get to arrest them, not the Cean."

"I'd like to be done with this," he said. "We could use the break."

He'd been with her the longest, which meant that the FSS would probably take him from her soon. In the last seven years, the FSS had sent the best young human marshals to her for training, partly because she saw so much, but mostly because she settled most of her cases to the satisfaction of the humans and the natives that they encountered.

"To this day, I don't understand what their problem is," said Jenna Baans, one of the other deputies. She was as tall and slender as Nuuyoma. Her eyes were a vivid, startling green, which had unnerved more than one alien species that the FSS had encountered in the last year.

She was the newest deputy on Gomez's team. Initially, Gomez had given her the task of convincing the campers to apologize to the Cean. When it became clear that Baans had no empathy for the campers at all, Gomez had given the task to Nuuyoma. He, at least, could get it done.

"Logic doesn't play a part as much as we'd like," Nuuyoma said to Baans. He wasn't really looking at her, instead peering down the hall so that he could see the others as they arrived.

In the beginning, he had treated Baans warmly, thinking her new and untested. Over time, he told Gomez that he thought Baans lacked the compassion needed for the job.

Gomez wasn't sure if more was going on than a disagreement over style. At the start, Nuuyoma would hover close to Baans. But as their tour got longer, they stood farther apart, rarely even glancing at each other.

Fraternizing wasn't forbidden on FSS ships—if so, the crew would never have relationships—but it wasn't always a good idea either. Gomez didn't know if the two of them had had a relationship, but if she had to guess, she would have said that they had.

The other three marshals approached, all looking tired.

"Do we wait?" Baans asked, glancing at the closed doors.

"I don't want to," Nuuyoma said.

Gomez smiled at him. "We're not supposed to coach them in any way. Both the campers and the Cean know how to reach us."

"Oh, you're too trusting," Nuuyoma said, his smile matching hers.

"No," said a new voice, "she's just as tired as the rest of us."

Gomez turned, and felt a half second of panic before she quelled it. Simiaar stood in the open doorway. She was breathing hard from climbing all those stairs.

Simiaar wasn't young any more, and she'd let herself get out of shape. She didn't like nano-enhancements, having seen too many of them gone wrong, and so she had to make the effort on her own to stay healthy. Because she worked as hard, if not harder, than Gomez, Simiaar had lost the battle with weight and exercise over the past fifteen years.

"You can't be here," Gomez said and glanced at the doors. If the Cean saw her, they'd believe the balance was off, and they'd find some kind of offense.

"Relax," Simiaar said. "That so-called ceremony is going to take a while."

Her eyes should have twinkled when she said that, but they didn't. Something was bothering her.

"You need to see something," Simiaar said softly.

"You couldn't send it to me on the links?" Gomez asked.

"No," Simiaar said. "Something just for you and me."

Gomez frowned. Simiaar only spoke like this when they had a case together. And right now, if they didn't count the Cean situation, they had no case.

"What's going on?" Gomez asked.

"Can you come with me?" Simiaar asked.

"Yeah, I guess," Gomez said. They were all going to leave anyway. But the presence of a seventh was going to create problems, just like reducing the squad to five would.

"What do you want us to do?" Baans asked.

"Stay at the restaurant on the lower floor, just like we planned," Gomez said. "I'll send a sixth."

If she told the truth, she was happy to skip the restaurant. It smelled like dying flowers and didn't serve anything that humans could eat. But it had tables that suited both humans and Cean, provided everyone fit into the circular pits dug into the floor around the tables.

"You're not going to join us, are you?" Nuuyoma said quietly, as if he hoped no one would hear him.

"Do you think I'll be missed?" she asked, only half-seriously.

"I hope not," Nuuyoma said. "They like working with you."

"I'm not sure they know who I am exactly," Gomez said. "You handle anything that comes up, *if* something comes up. I'm trusting the apology is going to happen."

"You just don't want to deal with the campers when this is all over," Nuuyoma said.

Gomez grinned at him. "That's right."

Then she headed toward the stairs, walking as fast as she could. She could hear Simiaar struggling to keep up behind her.

"Hurry," Gomez said, "before the Cean come out and force me to stay."

"You think they'll do that?" Simiaar asked, looking over her shoulder.

"No," Gomez said, "but it sounded good."

She couldn't run down the stairs because Simiaar couldn't keep up. Still, she kept a good pace. Simiaar managed to match it so far.

Gomez waited until they were down one floor before asking, "What's really going on?"

"Remember Epriccom?" Simiaar asked.

Gomez frowned. Epriccom. She hadn't thought of it in years, although sometimes the dead bodies turned up in her nightmares.

"Are we having trouble with the Eaufasse? I thought they joined the Alliance."

"They did," Simiaar said. "They're not the problem."

Gomez stopped. They had dealt with three things on Epriccom. The Eaufasse, who wanted nothing more than to join the Earth Alliance, a dysfunctional Peyti translator, and a human colony that had destroyed itself.

"Don't tell me," Gomez said. "The clones showed back up."

"Yeah," Simiaar said softly. "And it's a lot worse than we ever could have imagined."

19

His office felt strange.

Zhu stood in the door to his inner sanctum, as he called the office he'd received after he'd been promoted to junior partner, and stared at the room. The multicolored art, constantly revolving images that showed Old Earth oil paintings, covered the purple and black walls. The gray carpet accented the black furniture, and the actual window—which he'd been so proud of when he first got the office—showed a never-ending view of the glimmering lights of incoming starships.

When he'd left, more than a month ago, he'd believed this office to be the pinnacle of his achievements so far.

Right now, he felt like a stranger.

He tugged the sleeves of his white silk shirt over his wrists, the cufflinks Berhane had given him when he graduated from law school glimmering in the grayish-gold light. The light always took some getting used to, particularly when he returned from the Moon, where everything was set according to Earth sunlight levels.

This far out, nothing resembled Earth, not even when something was advertised as Earth-like. It was almost as if the designers made up an Earth that could be anything they wanted it to be.

Zhu stepped inside the office before one of his clerks saw him hesitate. *He who hesitates is dead*, or whatever that ancient quote was. It had been a favorite of one of his law professors, and it had been stuck in Zhu's head since Anniversary Day.

He'd seen so many horrible images since then, including an image of some man trying to decide if he would jump the barrier as Moscow Dome started to section. The man had waited a half-second too long before starting his jump, and had gotten crushed.

Some of the news announcers on various feeds kept showing that as a warning: here's what would happen to anyone who tried to cross a sectioning dome.

Zhu had seen it as an example of bad timing, which was where his brain had gotten stuck. Bad timing—he'd suffered from it with anything to do with the Moon, including Berhane.

And he didn't want to think about her.

He stepped around the grouping he had once called the Most Comfortable Chairs in the Universe. He'd actually gone to all kinds of nearby furniture stores, tried all kinds of specialty chairs, and even some that claimed to have nanotech that would redesign the chairs to fit whoever sat in them. He'd seen the choice of chair for his office as an important moment in his life.

Now that quest seemed so damn ridiculous.

It all did.

He walked to his precious window, saw his own reflection superimposed over the unusually well-lit part of space around Athena Base. The largest space station in the sector. All the important people in his profession seemed to gravitate here. They had the ritziest clients, both personal and corporate. And the ratio of human to alien defendants was stunningly low.

His face was drawn, shadows under his eyes so deep that no short-term enhancements could make him look healthy. He hadn't slept much since Anniversary Day, and some of that was his own fault.

When it became clear that Berhane had untold reserves of strength, and she went off on some volunteer mission, she'd left Zhu at complete loose ends. He hadn't expected it. He had, before consulting with her, got an extension on his time in Armstrong, pleading Anniversary Day, and everyone at Schnable, Shishani, & Salehi understood.

In fact, the senior partners at S3 had made it clear that they wanted him to stay in Armstrong. They wanted him to represent the firm in any way possible, so that it would appear to S3's most important clients that the firm was doing everything it could in this time of crisis. The firm had even offered his services to some corporate defendants who looked like they might have liability in building collapses in the surviving sections of the ruined domes—buildings that had been built before the codes had changed to accommodate sectioning domes.

Zhu had done preliminary work, stomach churning—the churn so bad that sometimes he got physically ill—then handed the cases off to some of the associates that S3 had sent to the Moon to handle the upcoming caseload.

He couldn't bear to defend people who had caused even more deaths through their negligence. Not after what he'd seen.

Not with Berhane—scholarly, intellectual Berhane—in hospitals and morgues, helping to identify the dead.

He'd never thought he'd feel admiration for Berhane. He'd always felt a bit of contempt for her, or at least, he had after he graduated from law school and she went back for yet another degree, living off the money her father made, not really contributing anything to any type of society (even though she thought her great scholarly work—whatever that would be—would contribute some day).

Then, just after Anniversary Day, after Berhane's announcement that everything would change, her words came true. He was defending venal idiots, and she was doing her best to make lives better.

It helped that her father had survived. He hadn't even been hurt. He'd just been detained by the authorities, like everyone else at that speech the governor-general was giving when she collapsed.

Her father wasn't sure he approved of his daughter's newfound work, and for once she didn't listen to him. She had stood up to him, told him that the Alliance was in crisis, and he needed to do all he could to help.

Her father had listened.

So had Zhu, even though he hadn't wanted to. He hadn't had time to help with the injured or the wounded. He didn't have the skills to help with the rebuilding. He was supposed to prevent the plaintiffs from getting any money from the companies who had built the shoddy homes in various domes, so that those people would have even less money. They had lost loved ones, and they would now get no compensation for something that clearly was the fault of the corporations involved.

Zhu leaned his head against the warm window. Temperature controlled, like everything else on this station. He could set the temperature in his office for each item of furniture, have a warm chair if he wanted it, a cool window, a hot expanse of carpet. He could scent the air with chocolate if it suited his fancy, or he could tint the oxygen mix with a bit of purple to match the walls.

He'd worked for such luxury, believing it mattered, believing that people needed a defense in this universe.

And they did.

They did.

The problem was that the people who needed it the most couldn't pay for it, and those who were actually guilty, those who had offended *everyone*, including that strange thing called *human dignity*, could afford to buy their way out of most crimes.

You'll hit a point, said Rafael Salehi, the great-great-great grandson of one of the founders of this firm, and the partner who had championed Zhu, *when you'll wonder what's the point of defense. You'll feel tainted. You'll think you've sold your soul for a bit of wealth and privilege. That's why you do pro bono work. Or you volunteer for a few months back at the Impossibles. You'll see the need for defense then. You'll remember it's not just about the guilty. It's also about what's right.*

Zhu had thought that conversation a bit pretentious at the time. *The speech he gives everyone*, he'd said to the other new hires over drinks after hours. He'd promised himself he would forget it.

But he hadn't. Apparently, it had gone in on some deep level. Apparently, he had stored it away for the times when he needed it.

And one of those times was now.

He sighed and turned away from the window, not liking the look of his face any longer. It was just a reminder of the fact that he hadn't been sleeping.

He sat behind his desk and scrolled through the private firm files to see what had come up on his docket while he was away.

He did need to do some pro bono work, but it couldn't be just any work. It had to be work that would have real value, work that would be the legal equivalent of the work Berhane was doing on the Moon.

Zhu needed to clean up some kind of major mess, to be on the side of good for a change.

He also needed a case he could win.

Maybe he should return to the Impossibles, because that was what he was looking for. Something completely impossible in the Earth Alliance's legal system. A defense case that had a worthy defendant, and something worth winning.

Everyone broke the law these days, and most people claimed they had a good reason for doing so. But those reasons were usually ignorance or a desire to get away with violating an "unjust" law.

The Earth Alliance legal system was deeply flawed. The laws were primarily local—if a human broke a law on some alien planet, even if that law made something like singing completely illegal, that human would be subject to the legal system of the native culture. And by human standards, those laws were often barbaric.

The disappearance systems had arisen so that humans could escape the reach of non-human justice, and so many corporations encouraged just that kind of behavior. There was an entire division in this law firm dedicated to Disappearance Theory and Practice, trying to find legal loopholes that would enable human corporations to operate their own disappearance services. Right now, most of them operated illegally, paying disappearance services under the table to squire away employees who ran afoul with local laws.

As a young lawyer, he'd thought defending those people fun and worthwhile. Until he saw how many people actually went off to alien justice systems and how most of those people were simply too poor to pay for a disappearance service.

Worse, how many of them had to send their children to serve time for their crimes, because aliens like the Wygnin believed that punishment for crimes went through entire generations.

Zhu tilted his head back. He would search for the right pro bono case. He didn't need more frustration at the moment, which ruled out the Impossibles. Most cases brought before a judge there were decided long before the attorneys made their pleas.

No, he'd take a case he could actually win.

Something that would make a difference.

He just didn't know what that was.

20

GOMEZ AND SIMIAAR WENT TO THE FORENSIC LAB ON THE *STANLEY* ONLY because Simiaar insisted. Gomez still considered the lab the most important part of the large ship. When the *Stanley* had been retrofitted ten years before, she'd demanded that the lab increase in size and that Simiaar get more staff. The lab was one reason that Simiaar stayed on the *Stanley*, even though there were nicer berths for a woman of her age and experience.

Simiaar had two offices—a small one that no one entered, no exceptions, and a larger one where she held small meetings. That office had two extremely comfortable chairs that could re-form into one uncomfortable couch, a built-in desk with an elaborate computer system, and a small testing area.

It also had a rectangular space that Simiaar set aside for holoviewing, mostly because she hated having imagery superimposed on her existing furniture. Since most of what she viewed concerned dead bodies and/or some kind of alien goo, no one really blamed her for being unwilling to watch that on her desk.

Simiaar indicated the chairs. "You can sit if you want, but I'm going to stand."

Gomez had heard that before, and it never boded well. "What am I watching? A new case?"

"No." Simiaar put her hands on the back of the overstuffed chair. Her fingers dug into the fabric. "While you guys were onsite, negotiating your sex deal—"

"It's not a sex deal," Gomez said.

"I don't know what else you'd call it," Simiaar said.

"An apology," Gomez said, "and I don't want to hear you call it anything else."

"I'd love to have someone apologize to me like that someday," Simiaar muttered.

Gomez resisted the urge to roll her eyes. She'd already had this discussion with Simiaar. They'd talked about the impropriety, the level of coercion involved, the discomfort and the religious side, and still Simiaar joked about it.

Of course, both she and Simiaar had learned over the years that sometimes an inappropriate joke was the only way to deal with a difficult situation. Usually they joked together.

"You wouldn't find this one funny if it were you," Gomez said, simply because she couldn't keep quiet.

"If it were me, I wouldn't have camped on that godforsaken lake in the first place." Simiaar raised a hand to stop Gomez from speaking, as if she knew that Gomez was going to say she missed the point. "If I *had* been stupid enough to come this far out to camp on some stupid lake that looks like one of a hundred-thousand lakes on Earth, except for the dueling sunsets, I would have apologized the minute I realized I screwed up. Don't these people know what can happen when you cross another culture?"

That was a question Gomez asked herself almost every day. With all of the troubles constantly in the news about people charged with crimes in the Earth Alliance for doing things in alien cultures that were everyday human activities in human-centered cities, she would have thought that sane people would be careful when they traveled to a non-human environment.

But most humans never researched where they were traveling to, expecting someone—maybe someone like Gomez—to take care of them.

They were always shocked when she informed them that, legally, she was obligated to abide by local laws and customs, just like she would be inside of the Alliance.

Maybe more than she would be inside of the Alliance, since no treaties governed the interactions humans had with others outside of Alliance space.

Gomez didn't want to think about this anymore. She actually wanted to plan some time off. But she wouldn't get that until she was done with whatever Simiaar wanted her to see.

"What are we going to watch?" Gomez asked.

Simiaar sighed.

Gomez then realized that Simiaar had instigated the old argument about the Ceanese situation because what they were about to watch made her extremely uncomfortable.

Simiaar glanced at the rectangular space, even though nothing was happening in it.

"While you guys were dealing with the apology, I decided to catch up on the news. I hadn't paid any attention to what's been going on in the Alliance for nearly two months now—"

"Me, either," Gomez said, not liking where this was heading.

"—and I selected for human stuff only, the biggest stories, just so that I could—you know—converse about current events when we got back into Alliance space."

Simiaar's fingers were still digging into the top of that chair.

"We missed..." her voice trailed off. She raised her head, her eyes red-rimmed. In all their years together, Gomez couldn't remember seeing that before. "We nearly lost the Moon, Judita."

Gomez didn't understand. What moon? When? How could someone lose a moon? "What do you mean, nearly lost the moon?"

"I'm not staying for this part," Simiaar said. "I'll get us something to drink. You want tea or something? If it weren't for the damn apology, I'd offer you something stronger."

"What part?" Gomez asked.

"I found an overview. It compressed a few days of information into an hour. I'll be back."

She toggled the program on, then left the office before Gomez could complain.

A flat, gender-neutral voice recited the facts of something everyone was now calling Anniversary Day, which confused Gomez enough right there. She knew about Anniversary Day because she had family on the Moon. Anniversary Day commemorated the deaths in a bombing in Armstrong four years ago that could have destroyed the entire city, but didn't.

It took her a few moments to reconcile the images that she saw with what happened. And that whatever happened had happened recently, not four years ago.

The voice narrated as the images bled from one scene of destruction to another. Apparently someone or someones hijacked this year's anniversary commemorations. Out of nineteen major domed cities on the Moon—Earth's Moon, *the* Moon to most human-centered societies— out of those nineteen domes, twelve had holes blown through them.

The destruction when a dome blew open was extreme. Buildings fell apart, people died horribly—and that was only in the outer areas. Nearer to the bombs themselves, actual craters appeared. The destruction was the worst that Gomez had ever seen.

She leaned into the chair, glad that Simiaar had warned her not to sit down. Gomez wanted to pace, but she also didn't want to take her eyes off the imagery playing out on the floor in front of her. Bombings, destroyed cityscapes, blackened and broken domes, people lurching through rubble searching for loved ones—devastation on a scale she couldn't quite comprehend, on a scale she couldn't entirely ignore.

She couldn't recognize most of the places involved, although she'd visited several of them. And even though everything happened weeks ago, she felt panic rise within her.

Surely someone would have contacted her if she lost family. Surely she would have known by now.

But she didn't know. She checked her links as she watched, and found nothing.

That wasn't unusual. Sometimes it took forever for information to reach the Frontier.

Her mouth was dry. She wanted to look up her family, but she also wanted detail, and this overview was not about detail.

Instead, it gave her statistics.

Hundreds of thousands—maybe a million—people died that day. More would have died if it weren't for the quick thinking of the Moon's chief of security, Noelle DeRicci. She had ordered the domes to be sectioned, limiting the damage to the areas where bombs went off.

Among the hundreds of thousands dead were most of the influential mayors of those cities, and Celia Alfreda, the visionary leader who had been trying to unite the domes into a single government.

Important people and people whose names never would have registered on any news site. More people than anyone could count. Hundreds of thousands, the gender-neutral voice had said, maybe a million or more.

Maybe.

Because no one knew.

Sometimes in bombings, bodies evaporated. They became tiny pieces of blood and bone and brain matter, so small that it would take years of painstaking searches with nanobots to separate one drop of blood from another, to run the DNA, to identify the lost people.

Gomez leaned against the chair, hand to her mouth. She thought her job had trained her to accept bad news with relative calm, but this—this was nothing like anything she had ever faced.

Her family was in Armstrong, one of the only domes that wasn't attacked. Apparently the bombing there got thwarted; something— she didn't quite process how it all happened—interfered, got solved, got noticed.

Too much information, too much *shocking* information for her to understand all of it.

She wasn't sure she moved a muscle through the whole summary. And as it wound down, she realized that what she saw only covered the first three days of the disaster.

The overview ended. It had been compiled a month before, a week after the disaster—or the disasters.

The imagery froze on the remains of the Top of the Dome, a restaurant/hotel complex in Tycho Crater, a place she had actually visited on vacation the last time she had gone to the Moon—which had to be maybe twenty-five years ago now.

She leaned against the chair—wishing, *hoping* that this was all an elaborate ruse. But she'd been watching closely. She had seen familiar faces among the people interviewed, people she knew by name if not reputation, and she knew, she *knew*, it wasn't faked.

Still, she would double-check. Mostly because she didn't want to believe destruction on this scale was possible.

Not in a modern society. Not in the heart of the Earth Alliance, around 384,000 kilometers from the Earth herself. Earth's doorstep, the Alliance called the Moon. So close that they were often considered inseparable.

Simiaar pulled the door open, balancing a tray precariously on one hand. Two steaming mugs slid one way and then another, stopping only when they encountered bowls of finger food.

Gomez wasn't sure she could eat, but she'd known Simiaar long enough to understand that Simiaar thought food the solution to any serious problem.

"Need a break?" Simiaar asked.

Gomez needed to go back one hour and remain ignorant of the Anniversary Day bombings. Actually, she needed the entire universe to go back a month and stop the bombings before they happened.

"There's more?" Gomez asked.

"Oh, yeah," Simiaar said.

"They come back, do more damage? If so, why didn't you just show me the complete footage and not let me—"

"It's not that bad," Simiaar said, then corrected herself. "Afterward anyway. It's cleanup and stuff. But what I have to show you, it's upsetting. To us."

"To us," Gomez repeated. "You and me?"

"Yeah." Simiaar set the tray down on the built-in desk.

Gomez took her mug of tea, not because she wanted something to drink, but because she needed to warm her hands. They had grown cold. *She* had grown cold.

"Just show me." She couldn't handle the suspense. And she was usually the most patient person on the *Stanley*.

Simiaar shut off the imagery of the Top of the Dome. She flipped through several other stored images, things that she had clearly followed as she tried to piece together what occurred.

"I'm going to show you the raw footage," she said, "because the commentary is—well—let's say it's ignorant."

Gomez leaned over the chair, gripping the hot mug of tea. It smelled faintly of perfume. Not Earl Grey, which she found too strong, but less pungent Lady Grey, which usually soothed her. She hoped that she wouldn't come to associate her favorite tea with this moment.

She concentrated, so that the smell wouldn't become linked.

Suddenly security footage appeared on the floor. The security footage was less condensed than the overview, easier to manipulate. She immediately recognized Armstrong's port. She'd arrived at it dozens of times. Armstrong's port, judging by the footage, hadn't updated its interior in nearly twenty years.

But she stopped looking at the structure of the port. Armstrong hadn't been bombed—at least on what they were calling Anniversary Day.

She frowned, not sure what she should be looking at. All she saw was a group of passengers leaving the arrivals area and laughing as they made their way into the wider crowds. She started scanning the crowds, and then stopped, gasped, and nearly dropped her tea.

"Go back and zoom in," she said.

Simiaar did.

The twenty faces—laughing faces—seemed so innocent. A group of family men, traveling together, cousins maybe, who looked a lot alike.

At least to the casual eye.

But Gomez's eye wasn't casual, and neither was Simiaar's. They'd seen these faces before, these *exact* faces.

The men, walking through Armstrong's ports, were clones.

"So what's the ignorance?" Gomez asked, not because she wanted to know so much as she wanted to think. She needed a moment to get rid of the spinning sensation the last hour or so had started within her.

"The stupid announcers all seem to believe that because these men are clones of PierLuigi Frémont, they're automatically mass murderers."

Gomez looked directly at Simiaar. Simiaar was staring at the tiny three-dimensional forms in front of her.

"But they *are* mass murderers," Gomez said. "They're the ones who bombed all the domes, right?"

"Yeah," Simiaar said. "But not because they're made from the same stuff as PierLuigi Frémont. They bombed the domes because they were *designed* for it. You know that. *We* know that."

Gomez did know it. She took a deep breath, remembering those faces—that whole incident. It had been—what?—fifteen, maybe sixteen years ago when the *Stanley* was called to Epriccom because of a problem that the Eaufasse couldn't handle.

"You mean to tell me that no one has any idea that someone cloned PierLuigi Frémont?" she asked.

Simiaar looked at the frozen image. She sighed. "Who knows what the press has been told and what the governments actually know."

Gomez recognized that tone. "You have a guess."

"Yeah," Simiaar said. "My guess is that someone wrote up the Epriccom incident, it got filed, and no one even noticed the link to Frémont. Or knows it now."

"What about Thirds?" Gomez asked.

"I don't know," Simiaar said. "We handed him to the lawyers, remember."

Gomez did remember, but that wasn't what she was asking. Thirds was supposed to talk with authorities about everything he knew. Then they would decide what to do with him.

"Did you look up Thirds?" Gomez asked Simiaar.

"I don't research well," Simiaar said. It was a bold-faced lie. She researched brilliantly, but only for cases that she had in front of her.

"You want me to do this," Gomez asked.

Simiaar grabbed a lemon cookie off the tray. She broke the cookie in half before taking a bite from it.

Simiaar clearly wasn't going to say a thing. Gomez didn't like that.

"So," Gomez said, "we just assume that the Alliance has known about the clones of PierLuigi Frémont for more than a decade and has chosen to ignore it, even now after some of those clones bombed the entire Moon. We'll just let the Alliance handle it."

"Dammit, Judita," Simiaar said around a mouthful of cookie. "You know no one in the Alliance has put Epriccom and the Moon bombings together."

"I don't know anything." Gomez glanced at those faces. Laughing. Apparently they arrived together. Why would that happen? It would make the attack obvious.

"You're curious," Simiaar said.

Gomez glanced at her. The cookie was gone.

"Yeah," Gomez said. "I am. And that doesn't surprise you."

Because they knew each other so well. They had become the best of friends partly because they both reacted the same way to something disturbing. They wanted to know why that something happened and how to resolve it.

But they also trusted that they were the first responders to some problem outside of the Alliance. They had to believe—they *had* to—that the Alliance would then take the information they had provided, and make sure everything would work out.

Gomez closed her eyes and leaned on that chair. Her legs were tired from standing in the same position for so long, but she didn't want to settle.

She didn't dare.

If she didn't find out how the information about the PierLuigi Frémont clones failed to get to the right people in the Alliance, then she would never trust the Alliance again.

21

THEY STARED AT HIM, EVERYONE IN THE RECREATION YARD OF THE PRISON. Only it wasn't a yard—not in the sense that he had known as a child. The prison was a space station, not planetside. He hadn't seen anything growing outside of the greenhouses in nearly fifteen years.

Trey wanted something to cover his face, a hood, a scarf, something to shield him. But of course, he had nothing here. So he kept his expression impassive. He stared at the holographic images playing out in the center of the recreation yard as if they had nothing to do with him.

And technically, they did have nothing to do with him.

He'd been in this prison longer than anyone else in the yard—almost half his life. He knew the system; he had been king of the cell block since he was twenty years old. He was thirty-one now, trapped here, forgotten.

But now the other inmates—all male, all human—stared at him, as if he had caused the explosions on Earth's Moon. Twelve explosions or more, hundreds of thousands dead, and the people who had committed the crimes, the men who had committed the crimes, the *clones* who had committed the crimes, all had his face.

Because, like them, he had been created from DNA provided by PierLuigi Frémont.

He wasn't the only one here who was a clone of PierLuigi Frémont, but he was the only one who was of an age with the Anniversary Day attackers, and he was the only one in this cell block.

And for the first time in a long time, the fact that he was the only one made him afraid.

The prison had been on edge since word of the bombings trickled in a month before. But the imagery didn't show up until two days ago, and even then it had only been of explosions. Those caused cheers throughout the block, but the new images, the ones that started running today, were the ones that unnerved him.

Because those images showing the faces of the bombers as they passed through the port on the Moon's largest city felt like something else.

Something new. Something that shoved the emotions building for the past month off that edge.

Those images finally gave the inmates something to do.

Trey realized that maybe a half second before they did. He managed to shout, "Lawyer!" just before the nearest inmate shoved Trey so hard that he stumbled backwards into two other inmates.

They pulled his arms back and held him tightly as the first inmate, his friends, and men who had wanted Trey dead—or at least, no longer in control—for a long time, punched that pretty face of his. Or what they used to call his pretty face.

His unusual face. Pale-skinned, blue-eyed. Rare and memorable, just like his progenitor, PierLuigi Frémont. Only Frémont had founded colonies with that face, claimed a special relationship with the people who followed him because of his unusual coloring, claimed he had descended as a pure example of the first men who left the Earth.

Trey wasn't pure and he technically hadn't descended from anyone. He hadn't even realized that there were people who looked different from him until he was sixteen years old. He hadn't even met a woman until that year, not that it had done him any good. The women he had met since had either run the prison or were upper-level guards.

His entire life was about being locked up somewhere—at first in a place he considered the entire world, which was just a small domed community, and then in ships, and finally here, the one place he'd believed he had conquered.

Until right now.

Fists in his face, knuckles against his skin. His nose shattered. His teeth bit through his cheeks. Blood filled his mouth. Someone punched him in the stomach, knocking whatever air he had left in his lungs out.

He gagged, then choked.

All of this happened in a kind of silence—the men didn't scream at him. They just hit him, the only sound flesh against flesh. Or the shattering of bones.

Something should have broken this fight up right away. There were androids on the yard, equipment that sensed a fight and stopped it.

The beating continued, not because the equipment failed, but because someone wanted it to continue.

And then the hold on his arms ceased. He toppled to his knees. Somehow he managed to put out his hands before he fell on his face.

He coughed up blood, spit blood, tried to wipe at his nose but nearly fell over, his balance gone. A door slammed, then another.

His eyes had swollen shut. He had to breathe through his mouth. He couldn't have asked for help if he tried.

Hands grabbed him and he flinched.

"Don't fight me, laddie," said a soft voice, a male voice, a vaguely familiar voice. It took him a moment to realize he heard the voice of the prison's doctor, someone he had barely interacted with, someone who had warned him once that the violence he had used to survive would swing back on him one day.

That day was now, apparently.

"You let me take you to the infirmary. We'll put a guard on you. A real one this time, not that you deserve it. You knew about those foul doings?"

Of course he hadn't known anything about the attack on the Moon. Because that was what the doctor was asking about, wasn't it? Hadn't the doctor thought this through?

Trey had been locked up here. He had had no visitors, he hadn't contacted anyone, not that there had been anyone to contact. Everyone he had known (everyone he had loved) was dead. No one even knew he was alive.

But he couldn't say that. He couldn't say anything from that injured mouth of his.

They had tested him after he arrived, found an intelligence so high they couldn't comfortably measure it. They figured he'd been artificially enhanced, but in his reading, he'd learned that PierLuigi Frémont had been unusually mentally gifted, apparently something encoded in his DNA.

Or so Trey had liked to believe.

Not that he had told anyone that, either. He hadn't wanted to call attention to his manufacture, or the fact that he had come from the DNA of a man who had murdered millions.

But that man, that DNA, had given Trey a prodigious brain, and Trey had trained that brain to anticipate things. (Not that he had foreseen this beating. How could he have known?)

He knew now that he would go from king of the cell block to the biggest pariah.

Everyone would try to hurt him, except maybe the damn doctor, who seemed to believe there was something redeemable in everyone.

Trey wasn't sure there was anything redeemable about himself. But he wanted to live, and that might not be possible here.

Unless he proved himself worthy of survival.

He couldn't just claim that he was innocent.

No one believed in innocence here.

He had to claim that he knew something. And maybe, deep down, he did. That shout for a lawyer might be what would save his life.

He let the doctor drag him out of the yard and into an enclosed plastic gurney with its own lock, its own air, and its own security shield. He would probably live in that damn thing until the lawyer arrived.

But that was okay. Because he would live.

Moment to moment, day to day, he would live.

And maybe, just maybe, they would move him from here. And maybe, just maybe, those damn prisoners had screwed up his face enough that no one else would gaze on him and see the Moon murderers.

Or PierLuigi Frémont.

Maybe, just maybe, this moment was the second luckiest moment of his life.

Maybe this moment would actually set him free.

22

IT TOOK A LOT TO SHAKE UP GOMEZ. SHE'D SEEN ALIENS DIE IN FRONT of her. She'd seen humans murdered in horrible ways. She'd seen negotiations that involved practices she didn't believe possible.

She'd had to eat foods that weren't really food for humans, sit in rooms that smelled so bad that she could barely breathe, touch furniture made from substances that made her stomach turn.

To do her job, she had become hardened. She was proud of that. She loved her work, and she was good at it. Part of being good came from being unflappable.

The attacks on the Moon—which happened more than a month ago—upset her. Not just because so many died. Not just because she never expected to see domes in the most settled part of the human universe shatter, but because she felt like she had a small hand in the attacks.

She hadn't followed up on the clones of PierLuigi Frémont. She had encountered sixteen of them, had an inkling there were many more, and she hadn't followed up.

Sure, she had reported it all to her superiors. She had flagged the incident as unusual. But she had done so because of the interactions with the Eaufasse and the Peyti, not because of the clones.

She sat in the office part of her suite on the *Stanley*. Early in her career, she had divided up the captain's quarters, feeling she had too much space. When the ship got retrofitted years ago, she'd had the captain's quarters reassembled and enlarged.

Part of her ability to survive in this job, part of her ability to do well, came because she had a quiet place to go, to think, and to recover.

She had designed an office in the very front of the cabin, where she met with staff or strangers who needed some kind of privacy. Two doors led to the living quarters: one door went directly into the small galley that the ship's chef used to prepare special meals for her dining room (another affectation she had initially removed and then later reinstated on the ship).

The second door went directly into the main relaxation area, away from the dining room, away from the kitchen, and away from the noise. She was the only one who could enter this area and the attached bedroom. She kept both spotless. She didn't even want help cleaning, although technically, she could have had some of the human staff scrub her quarters to complete perfection.

She didn't even use robot- or nano-cleaners. She wanted no one to see her when she relaxed. Usually she shut off everything except her emergency links. She didn't want recording, she didn't want tracking, she didn't want any record of what she did in her off time, not that she was doing anything wrong.

She just needed to be completely alone.

She valued the privacy more than she valued the assistance.

After seeing the holoimages of the Moon's destruction, she went to the private area and paced. She had to shake the unsettled feeling that she had. She couldn't think clearly when she was unnerved.

Emotions hurt her work; they didn't help it.

And the emotions rising inside her made her shake.

She needed answers.

She went into her small office and sat down. Here she had a dedicated computer that was networked with the EAFSS system. All the records, all the court cases, and all kinds of legal information about various species—aligned and non-aligned—filled this database. It grew by vast amounts of information every second, with reports from non-human marshals to interactions with non-aligned species to discoveries of yet another culture no one had interacted with.

Just sitting down and logging in made her hands stop shaking. She knew that five clones had survived the attack on Epriccom, although they'd been in terrible shape when they left the planet. And of course, Thirds had survived. He had disappeared into the system, and she had never checked up on him.

She wasn't sure she wanted to now.

First, she would find out what had happened to the five. Three had been hurt so badly no one thought they would live. The other two might have pulled through.

It took a while to dig through the database on a case this old. She found lots of legal jargon and lots of codes she didn't entirely recognize.

Each of the injured clones was treated separately, and each went to medical centers in different parts of the sector. She would trace them first, and figure out what happened to them. If all else failed, she could go to Thirds.

But she really didn't want to see him again. He hadn't lied to her, per se, but he had played her. And in her entire career, almost no one had played her.

Even now, just remembering him unnerved her.

This whole thing unnerved her.

She knew she was missing something. But for the life of her, she couldn't tell what it was.

She needed answers. She needed to know if, with a little more diligence, she could have stopped the attacks on the Moon. She also needed to know if she could help resolve those attacks—find the perpetrators, and maybe prevent another such attack.

Mostly, though, she needed to know what had gone wrong in the Alliance system of justice.

She needed to know that when she completed her job, other people in the system would do theirs.

Otherwise, there was no point in all the risks she took, all the meticulous care she used.

Otherwise, she had wasted not just her entire career, but her life as well.

23

ZHU MIGHT HAVE MISSED THE CASE, IF HE HADN'T FLAGGED EVERYTHING to do with Anniversary Day. Even then, he might still have missed it because the language was odd: *injured prisoner, beaten because of resemblance to Moon assassins, claims unfair imprisonment. Claim rejected. Will trade information for freedom. Requests attorney.*

Requests attorney.

Those weren't the words that Zhu stared at the longest. He stared at "resemblance to Moon assassins." No mention of Anniversary Day, no real mention of the attacks. The only reason his system flagged the case at all was because of the link between "Moon" and "assassins."

No other reason.

Yet the entire thing made his heart rate speed up.

Will trade information for freedom.

Zhu poked around the edges of the notice on the pro bono information board, but he couldn't find out any more about the case. Nor could he find where it hailed from.

He searched for "Moon assassin" "resemblance" "clone of PierLuigi Frémont." He found a lot on the latter listing, all of it inaccessible—case sensitive, and only available to an attorney with a legal interest in the subject.

In other words, the files were closed, and only an attorney certified by a court could get the proper information.

He spent two days doing his due diligence while working on other cases. Most of his caseload at the moment was light, partly because he had been gone so long. No one had known when he would get back, so his court cases were pushed back—not that he had many. He tried to settle whenever he could.

He had several negotiations this week between interested parties, but nothing that prevented the level of work he needed to do to figure out what was happening here.

He could have given the work to one of his clerks, but he hadn't. He wanted to handle this himself. It all felt...personal.

He didn't know any other word for it. This was the first case he had ever had that had real meaning to him. Not that he had this case. He didn't. He was just snooping around the edges of it.

He finally understood a few moments he'd experienced when he was serving in the Impossibles, where some family members in court cried when a client got remanded or his not-guilty plea was denied. It didn't matter how much Zhu had warned them such things could happen: they were still heartbroken when the worst occurred.

He would be heartbroken if no one was ever brought to justice in the Anniversary Day cases. He would be devastated, and he hadn't even lost anyone.

For the first time in his life, he truly understood Berhane. No one had been brought to justice in the first Moon bombing, in Armstrong. No one had even been accused of the crime.

Berhane's mother had died, and no one had ever gotten punished for it.

Maybe there was a reason his former fiancée had lost herself in scholarship. Maybe she preferred the life of the mind to what was actually happening in her real life.

Maybe he had been the worst kind of partner, the kind who hadn't even tried to understand.

These thoughts haunted him continually. He kept turning them over and over again in his head, unable to shake them free. A few times, he'd tried to contact Berhane, only to get a block on her links, saying that she didn't want to talk to him; he could leave a message.

He never did. He had nothing of importance to say.

Except maybe *I'm sorry*. And he should have said that—and acted on it—a long time ago.

Finally, after the second frustrating day in which he tried to find out more about the case, he realized the only way he would learn about it would be to actually become one of the attorneys involved.

A note in the file mentioned that the client would want a meet. Which meant that if Zhu took the case, he would have to leave Athena Base and go to whatever prison housed this particular criminal.

He couldn't just disappear from his practice, no matter how much he wanted to do this. Plus, any case that involved the Anniversary Day attacks would have to be approved through the partners. There were so many potential conflicts from so many different clients that everything needed approval.

He asked for a meeting with Rafael Salehi. Zhu figured Salehi would understand. After all, he was the one who had advised Zhu that at some point he would have to reconnect with his own personal sense of justice.

Although Zhu was wondering if he'd ever really had a personal sense of justice at all.

He expected to get his meeting with Salehi in a few days, but oddly, Salehi could see him within the hour.

Their offices were one floor apart, but they rarely saw each other. Once in a while they spoke in the firm's cafeteria—if, indeed, a restaurant of that quality could be called a cafeteria. Usually both men had been on the way to something else when they were grabbing a bite for lunch. After Zhu had become a full partner, neither man had time to talk with the other except for some cursory checking in.

Zhu took the stairs to Salehi's office rather than the elevator. Ever since Anniversary Day, Zhu had done a lot more exercising. He told himself he did it to keep in shape, but if he were honest with himself, he really did it because he had realized that day that he might need to run for his life at some point, and he was in no condition to do so.

He didn't want to use enhancements to improve his physical condition. He felt a deep-seated need to do it himself.

Salehi had half of the fifteenth floor for his office. The other half served some older partners, who weren't name partners. Salehi had promised Zhu an office on this floor when one of those partners retired.

The fifteenth floor had a hush that Zhu's floor did not. Many of Zhu's floor-mates liked music, and they liked sharing that music. He could close the door to his office, which sound-proofed it, but as he walked to that office every day, he heard a cacophony of sounds, from ancient Uscri tribal chants to modern Scree music, both of which sounded like screaming to Zhu. He preferred the melodic music of Old Earth, which fortunately many of his colleagues did as well.

No music played on Salehi's floor, not even overhead to "relax" clients. Salehi's office area had an almost religious hush.

He had no human assistant, preferring to use a data-based system that he claimed had a more personal touch. He monitored everything, because, he said, he was a control freak.

Zhu believed him; the desire for control was so strong that Salehi once admitted the real reason he didn't want a human assistant was because he couldn't control another person's expressions and tone every hour of every day.

As Zhu walked down the brown carpeted hallway, a door opened in the back. Salehi leaned against the door jamb. He was a slight man, with close-cropped dark hair and eyes that always seemed a bit too big for his face.

"You look too serious, Torkild," Salehi said. "The universe hasn't ended."

"Not yet," Zhu said.

He always felt overdressed when he went into Salehi's office. Salehi spent his days in white linen shirts, khaki pants, and sandals, unless he was going to court. Then he wore shiny brown suits that looked both expensive and tacky. His purpose, one of the other name partners said, was to stand out, and he certainly did that.

"Anniversary Day?" Salehi asked.

He didn't have to say more. He clearly understood that Zhu's response had come directly from his Anniversary Day experience.

"Yeah." Just answering the question made Zhu feel even heavier. It was as if he had gained twenty pounds since he had come back, even though his actual weight hadn't changed.

Salehi tilted his head toward the room behind him. "C'mon in."

He didn't wait for Zhu's response. Instead, Salehi went deep into the room, pulling back curtains to reveal a sunny desert covering the wall. The sunlight made Zhu's eyes hurt. He had forgotten that while everyone else in the firm seemed to prefer views of Athena Base and the space beyond, Salehi liked manipulating his wall screens so that it looked like he was anywhere but here.

Zhu had always thought it a strange habit from a man who claimed he didn't like to travel far from home.

"I suppose you want me to cool it down in here," Salehi said, and as he did, Zhu noticed that the temperature was several degrees warmer than he was used to. The floor had lost its carpet as well. It had some kind of covering that mimicked sand.

The lights on the ceiling were as bright as the sunlight emanating from the walls, and the air here smelled both dusty and spicy. Zhu frowned, and again, Salehi seemed almost like he could read minds.

"Sagebrush. I'm enjoying a high desert today, even though I do have the light properly filtered so that we won't get sunburned."

Or light-burned as the case might be. Zhu was about to lower himself onto one of the nearby chairs when Salehi stopped him.

"Not yet," Salehi said. "Let the sunlight fade a bit."

The brightness had eased, and a cool breeze came from the area of the wall. Storm clouds now covered the desert skyscape.

Zhu looked at it warily. "I hope that you're not going to make it rain in here."

Salehi grinned. "No. If I truly imitated a high desert cloudburst, we'd have to deal with flash flooding."

"Oh, fun," Zhu said.

"Ah," Salehi said, waving his hand dismissively, "if you can't control your environment, what's the point of living in space?"

Zhu decided that the question was meant rhetorically. Otherwise, his answer would depress both of them. People like them lived in space because that was where the jobs were. The court system had its own network of bases precisely so that it could remain neutral, and not be subject to any culture within the Alliance simply because it had its courts on that culture's property.

"You look morose, Torkild." Salehi put his hands on the arms of a nearby chair and eased himself down, as if testing the temperature. He finally sat all the way. "Temp's are back to normal."

Which was as good an invitation to sit as Zhu would get. He sat on the chair he'd been about to sit in before. Its smooth, leather-like surface was still a bit too warm, but not as hot as it probably had been a few minutes earlier.

"Lawyers aren't meant to see death and destruction up close," Salehi said. "Especially defense lawyers."

If Salehi had sent those words across a link, Zhu would have thought them flip. But Salehi's tone was serious, his expression more so.

"You hit the dark night of the soul, didn't you?" Salehi asked. "I told Schnabby you weren't the guy to handle our Moon-based clients, given their culpability—and you didn't hear that word from me."

Schnabby was Salehi's private nickname for one of the other name partners. Zhu wasn't sure Salehi had ever said it to Schnable's face.

"But," Salehi continued, "Schnabby was convinced that it wouldn't bother you. *Balls like rocks*, Schnabby had said. *Zhu always knows how to keep his emotions in check.* But I told Schnabby that guys like you—and me, for that matter—are the ones you got to watch out for. We do great until we don't."

Zhu managed a rueful smile. Balls like rocks, eh? That was the perception of him? It explained how he hit partner so fast. But those words didn't really describe him. Not after Anniversary Day, and maybe not before.

They actually described Berhane.

"So," Salehi said, "you want to drop everything and go to some prison somewhere to rescue somebody. I didn't get it all, but I assume this has something to do with Anniversary Day?"

"You told me once that I would need reminding—"

"About the difference between what's legal and what's right, and why our clients need defending." Salehi leaned back in the chair and placed one ankle on the opposite knee. "I give everyone that speech, you know."

"I know," Zhu said.

"Only the good ones listen," Salehi said.

Zhu really did smile now. "And you tell everyone that too so that they feel better, don't you?"

Salehi's grin had faded as Zhu spoke. "Actually, no. Most of the lawyers in this godforsaken place don't really care about the difference between what's right and what's legal. They care about billable hours and advancing to a bigger office and maybe handling a case in front of a Multicultural Tribunal. They're all about themselves."

Salehi tilted his head just a little, then rested a hand on his calf, bunching the leg of his pants.

"I was beginning to think you were one of them," he said. "I've been wondering for about a year now if I misjudged you."

"Maybe you did," Zhu said.

"And Anniversary Day shocked you into sense?" Salehi shook his head. "Those clowns who truly care only about the office or the job would've handled all the Moon-based cases without a qualm. You didn't have the stomach for them, did you?"

"No." Zhu's cheeks had grown warm.

"That's the guy I championed," Salehi said. "I knew there was a heart in there somewhere."

Zhu shook his head. "This isn't about heart. This is as self-focused as it gets. I gotta get back to what I do, to what I know, and you said this might work."

"I said that you would someday need to remember the difference between justice and what's right," Salehi said. "That's not you?"

"I was very proud of my office two months ago," Zhu said.

Salehi's mouth twitched, almost as if he were repressed a smile. Then he nodded, as if conceding a point. "Tell me about this case."

"I don't know anything about the case," Zhu said, "except that this guy claims he knows something about Anniversary Day, even though he's been in prison for years. He also looks something like the assassins."

"Which means he's a clone," Salehi said.

"We don't know that," Zhu said. "I can't get information."

Salehi nodded. "Probably just as well. I honestly thought clone law was the next frontier in the legal system. Discrimination and all that, those pesky definitions about what's human and if being human even matters in the Alliance. Then this tragedy happened, and it probably set clone law back a hundred years or more."

His gaze narrowed, and Zhu could almost feel the question. He answered it before Salehi asked it. "I don't care about making precedent."

"So you think this case will solve the mysteries of the Anniversary Day bombings," Salehi said.

"I think it might help," Zhu said.

"Whatever you figure out, it won't change what happened. All those people will still be dead. All those domes will still be damaged."

"I know," Zhu said.

"Yeah, that's right." Salehi's tone was dry, maybe even a bit sarcastic. "You would tell your clients the same thing."

"Actually, no," Zhu said. "I'd tell them there are no heroes."

Salehi crossed his arms and leaned back, studying Zhu. "Do you believe that now?"

Zhu had seen a lot of people act heroically that day. He'd seen others step up since. But did that make them heroes? He wasn't certain.

"I'm not sure what I believe in," he said.

Salehi sighed. "Would a rest be better? You know, a year off to regroup?"

And be alone with my thoughts? No. Zhu had to stop himself from blurting that. Instead, he managed to edit it to, "Let's reserve that as an option. Let me try this first."

Salehi frowned. He stared at Zhu for several minutes, then finally said, "You realize you're never going to be the man you were. And you can't solve the Anniversary Day cases all on your own."

"Yeah," Zhu said. "I know."

And he did. He knew both things. He didn't care. He still wanted this case.

"The case might be nothing, just some con trying to get out of a life sentence," Salehi said.

"I know that too," Zhu said.

Salehi raised his eyebrows. "And you still want to go."

"I still want to go," Zhu said.

Salehi nodded. "You realize a case like this, if it's what you imagine, might make you into someone else."

"I'm already someone else," Zhu said.

Salehi's expression vanished. It was as if he had no emotions at all. Zhu realized he shouldn't have responded so quickly.

"I'm sorry," Zhu said. "You had a point."

Salehi nodded, and the warmth returned to his face. "My point is that you might not want to continue with the law after this."

"Do you think that'll happen?" Zhu asked.

Salehi smiled. "I think anything's possible," he said. "That's why I build deserts in outer space."

Zhu grinned. "And I thought you built them to keep warm."

Salehi's smile faded. "That too, my friend," he said. "That too."

24

THE PRISON BASE WAS ACTUALLY DARK. GOMEZ HAD BEEN TO A DOZEN different prison bases throughout the Alliance, and most were unbelievably well-lit places, so well lit, in fact, that she had always thought they would drive her crazy. She liked a bit of darkness, particularly at night. She had trouble sleeping in the light.

But the lights on 8596 were dim at best. All the prison bases inside the Alliance had numerical designations, but they also had nicknames that developed over time. This one was called Clone Hell, and she was beginning to understand why.

No outside ships could dock on 8596 because it was a maximum-security prison for the very worst offenders. The ships had to dock on the habitat base, where the guards and administrators lived. Guests could stay there as well. Theoretically, guests would stay while waiting for approval to visit the prisoners.

Only, this place had almost no guests. The prison administration had responded with surprise when she requested a visit.

It had taken longer to get here than she expected. Not because of travel time, but because she had to finish the apology with the Cean. The humans did apologize, and theoretically all was well, but she had debrief interviews to conduct. She hated doing so while she had Anniversary Day on her mind.

Then she felt free to travel to Clone Hell.

She hadn't brought the *Stanley* to the habitat base. She had taken a shuttle, leaving the *Stanley* at a resort base so her crew could get some needed time off. She had docked at the habitat base, and she had stayed in a nearly empty hotel, courtesy of the Alliance, while she awaited the proper documentation.

The documentation had come through quickly, partly because she was listed as the arresting officer in the clone's file. It was impossible for her to distinguish which clone she was seeing. He was identified in the files only by his case and prisoner numbers.

Even if he had been called by his name, she wouldn't have known that either. The clones who had attacked Thirds hadn't identified themselves to her, and as far as she knew, Thirds hadn't identified them later.

All she knew was that this clone was one of the two who hadn't been near death when they were taken off Epriccom. His file—at least the one she could access—was very short on details. She had no idea how bad his injuries had been, if he had spoken to anyone, or even what exactly he had been charged with.

After all, he had killed clones on a non-affiliated planet. Epriccom or the Eaufasse might have had a law against clone murders, but she doubted it or the clone wouldn't have been here. In various places in the Alliance, clone murders were treated as major felonies, but in most places, human clone murders—governed by human law—were simply property crimes. Felonious property crimes, but property crimes nonetheless.

She had to take a prison shuttle to 8596. The shuttle was for guests and administration. 8596, like most places in the Alliance, ran by a 24-hour Earth clock. She was arriving in the middle of 8596's day, too early for shift-change. There were no other guests, and the shuttle was an automatic run.

She had been alone on the shuttle, which she found a bit unsettling, particularly when she realized that the cockpit wasn't just locked, it had been sealed closed. Even if there were a problem with the shuttle, she wouldn't have been able to resolve it. She had no access to the controls at all.

The docking port was relatively well lit, but she had entered on the administration side. After she had gone through all of the scans and decontamination units, she was allowed into the visitor center. It actually had windows that overlooked the prison proper. She saw rows and rows of units, some with tiny windows, and some with none at all.

About ten stories down, she saw what the guard who had led her into the visitor center called "the yard." There was no "yard"; they weren't on a planet, and the bare patch below her had no plants.

It was just a box with a more open skyline, a box that could probably fit fifty inmates. If the "yard" were anything like the other places she had visited around the Alliance, it could become whatever the administrators wanted it to be, from a sports arena to a garden-like spot to an uncomfortable vista that might punish the inmates more than give them a place for recreation.

Most of these places were standard holochambers with the controls in a completely different part of the base, so that the inmates couldn't break in and control the imagery they were seeing.

She shivered. She spent most of her life confined to a ship, but she was in control. She had freedom of movement; she could even choose many of the cases she worked on. She got to see entire parts of the universe that no one else did.

The idea of being in this dark and dingy place for the rest of her life unnerved her, just like it was supposed to do.

Clanging caught her attention. She turned. She expected a guard to get her from the visitor's center and take her to see the clone in a different part of the facility. Instead, clear walls dropped around various tables. A glowing arrow appeared on the floor, pointing toward a table and chair unit on the opposite side of the room from the window.

Four android guards entered. They were taller than the average human and made of a burnished black material. They didn't catch any light at all, which made them very difficult to see. They were lower-level androids—two arms, two legs, two eyes, but no nose and no mouth. They probably had built-in weapons as well, and some kind of recording device.

In the human part of the Alliance system, android guards worked in areas deemed too dangerous to risk an actual human presence. These androids were built with extra materials so that the inmates could not kidnap an android for its parts. It would be impossible to disassemble, at least with anything available to the inmates themselves.

And the androids were controlled through an off-site hub—what control they needed anyway. One reason to use androids instead of robots wasn't just the pseudo-human form, but also because of the androids' limited decision-making ability. While no one had yet perfected the art of human thought in an android system (or, if they had, someone or something had quashed the marketing), androids could make low-level decisions based on a set of parameters all on their own.

Each one looked at her as it entered. They had silver eyes. She studied the androids as they moved. In the dingy atmosphere of this particular prison, the android guards would be almost impossible to see. They could hide in plain sight.

An instruction menu dropped down over her left eye. It asked her if she wanted audio instructions or written instructions. Before she chose, it warned her, all emergency instructions would come in both forms.

She chose written instructions. She didn't want another voice coming through her links when she was going to concentrate on the clone.

After she chose, the instructions scrolled across her vision.

You will sit in the chair now glowing yellow.

As she looked, one of the chairs in the unit near the arrow lit up dimly. Obviously, the system was old. Only the back and legs of the chair were illuminated. The seat glowed faintly, as if it tried to light up, but couldn't.

A protective screen will drop around you. You will be able to see, hear, and speak through the screen, but you will not be able to touch the inmate. Nor will you be able to pass anything through the screen. Even gaseous and/or airborne matter will not penetrate the screen without going through nanofilters first. The screen will remain as long as you are in the chair and/or the inmate is in the room.

If these terms are acceptable to you, please take your seat.

This was a lower-class facility. Most places she had gone in recent years allowed her to have a private protective bubble that moved with her. She hadn't been in a prison that restricted her to a single chair in more than a decade.

She walked to the seat and touched the back. It was cool to her fingertips, which was good. She'd once sat in something like this when it was malfunctioning and had burned her skin.

She lowered herself slowly, and then heard more protective walls fall around her.

The inmate you requested will arrive in 2 minutes, 45 seconds....

The information over her left eye continued a countdown. She tried to shut it off, and found that she couldn't. But she could move the image to the side of her vision, so that she didn't see everything through the numbers.

Two more android guards arrived and took positions on the opposite side of the room from her. Then, precisely 2 minutes and 45 seconds from the notification, the inmate arrived.

He wore a bright yellow jumpsuit that stood out even in the dim lighting. He was smaller than she remembered. The clones who had bombed Armstrong had looked bigger, full-grown adults who had spent time working on their muscles and their athletic ability, not boys running through a wilderness with laser rifles.

As she studied the clone, though, she realized he walked with a limp. One arm was shorter than the other. He leaned toward his left, and something was off about his face.

He had received no reconstruction after the weapons' attack on Epriccom. The scars from those plantlike things remained visible on his body.

She should have been prepared for that, but she wasn't. Whenever she had sent injured human criminals into the system, they had received proper medical treatment, including enhancements that made the effects of the injury completely disappear.

She had never seen anyone this damaged before.

His gaze met hers directly, almost like a challenge. Had he seen her dismay? Had he pegged it to the more accurate term—disgust? She wasn't sure.

As he got closer, she realized what was wrong with his face. It was uneven. His right side had a large pucker, as if the skin had been pulled toward the ear. His mouth twisted slightly and his nostril was wider on that side. Ironically, his right eye was narrower, and his forehead smoother.

PierLuigi Frémont had been a handsome man, for all his paleness. This clone of him was not.

The clone sat down, slowly, not like he was worried that the chair would burn him the way that Gomez had been worried, but as if the movement hurt him.

The jumpsuit covered everything except his hands, neck, and head. His neck had scars all the way around, ropy indentations that looked like something was still strangling him. His right hand curled slightly, the fingers turned inward.

The right side was the one that had been truncated. He watched her assess his injuries—or what his injuries had wrought.

Still, she wasn't going to discuss them if she could at all avoid it.

"Did they tell you who I am?" she asked.

"Yes," he said. "You know, I never saw your face, but you changed my life."

She frowned slightly. She hadn't changed his life. She had saved it, by ordering him off the moon.

She wasn't going to correct him, though. She needed information from him, and she didn't want to have to threaten him to get it.

She let his comment slide. She would return to it when and if the time came.

"What do I call you?" she asked.

"You don't like the number system they have in the prison?" His smile only reached the left side of his face. "Or can't you choose between my case number and my prisoner number?"

"What do you call yourself?" she asked.

"One unlucky bastard," he said, the smile fading.

He wasn't going to make anything easy. Although, to be fair, she wasn't sure why he should.

"What did they call you back in that enclave on Eaufasse?"

He froze. Then he blinked, as if the question had surprised him. After a moment, he inclined his head toward her as if he were conceding a point.

She just wasn't sure what point he was conceding.

"They called me Twentieth of the Second," he said.

And the one who had escaped that day, the one who had brought her to Eaufasse in the first place, had been called Third of the Second, but he had also had a nickname.

"And your nickname was?"

He let out a small sound, almost like a laugh. This time, she suspected, the half smile on his face was intentional.

"TwoZero," he said. "Twenties was too confusing."

These questions made him relax; she wasn't sure why. His expression didn't soften—she wasn't sure it could—but his gaze seemed less challenging than it had before.

Before she had come, she had gone over the interview in her head several times. She wasn't certain how to approach it; she wasn't sure what, if anything, he knew about the event the Alliance was now calling Anniversary Day.

Now that she was here, she decided to mix honesty with a soft interrogation. If it looked like he was going to bolt, she'd push harder.

"Your case file is maddeningly empty," she said. "I was surprised to find you here."

He leaned back just a little. "Why? You put me here."

"Technically, I didn't," she said. "You left my custody on the hospital ship. From then on, the courts decided your fate."

"Really?" he asked. "Because that's not what I was told."

The chill in his tone made her wonder if she had taken the wrong tack. She didn't want as much current information from him as she did information about his childhood and life on Epriccom.

"What were you told?" she asked.

"That you claimed I was a murderer, that you put me here."

She frowned. "I barely saw you on Epriccom. I never spoke to you directly, and I had to send you to medical attention immediately. After you left, I wrote up the entire case, but did not testify in any court."

He blinked again. She was wondering if it was a nervous tick, or caused by his injuries. Or if he was simply reassessing her.

"I never went to court," he said.

"But you're here," she said.

"In Clone Hell," he said.

"Maximum security," she said, and because she couldn't help herself, she added this question. "For a murder of clones?"

"Those two words don't go together," he said. "Didn't they teach that to you in marshal's school?"

"'Murder' and 'clones'?" she asked, when it became clear that he wasn't going to elaborate.

He touched his left forefinger to his nose, then pointed at her. "You got it in one. Maybe you did go to marshal school."

"But you're in a maximum security prison," she said.

He tilted his head. The frown made his forehead red on the left side, but the right side remained pale, as if blood couldn't touch it. "You really don't know why?"

"I suppose I could ask the warden," she said. "I did research your case. As I said, there's very little in it."

"I'm here," he said with some heat, "because *I'm* illegal. And you said that I was dangerous. Therefore, I'm here for life."

She was holding her breath. She made herself exhale as she thought. *He* was illegal. And dangerous? Well, of course he was dangerous. He'd been trained in murder as a young man.

"You're not an authorized clone," she said slowly, as she figured out what he meant.

"Oh, you are brilliant, Marshal. They should put you in charge of a frontier ship or something." This time, his sarcasm was evident.

She ignored the sarcasm. "None of this is in your file."

"Does it have to be?" he asked.

"It should be, yes," she said. "And for the record, whatever that means, I did not recommend anything for you except hospitalization. I figured the system would treat you fairly."

"How can it treat me fairly?" he asked. "I'm not human."

She knew what he meant, but she believed him to be human. But to say that now would sound like she was pandering to him. And she wasn't.

"Please," she said. "Clarify for me. You've never been to court."

"Of course not," he said. "You sent me to a hospital ship along with the other injured from the Second, and they could see that we were clones. Then we were sent various places for treatment. My treatment included a search for a valid clone mark. There was none, and when I came to, I couldn't tell them where I was made or by whom, so I was stamped illegal. And because of your incident report, I was deemed violent, and unredeemable, and so I was sent here. For the rest of my natural—or unnatural—life."

Healed, but not repaired. Warehoused, because he was violent. And he had been violent. He had tried to kill Thirds. He *had* tracked down the other three to kill them as well, and had fired at them, at least according to the Eaufasse security records. Whether he had fired the deadly shot would never be determined.

Had anyone explained that part to him? Or had he simply rotted in here, stewing in his own resentment.

Oddly, she felt like she should apologize to him, primarily because she hadn't been aware of what happened. If someone had asked her what she thought would happen to him—if she had given it any thought at all, which she hadn't—she would have said that as a juvenile offender, he would have had extensive rehabilitation work, and maybe some nanotreatments to counteract the aggression trained into him from childhood.

He might never have been allowed free—he was the descendant of a mass murderer, and had been raised to kill—but he might have gone to a nicer place, somewhere that would have kept him on the fringes of society, using whatever skills he had and giving him a better life than he clearly enjoyed here, and maybe giving him a chance to contribute, in some small way, to the society that paid for his incarceration.

Plus, she would have thought that medical treatment would have included full repair.

"You should have had time in court," she said.

"As what?" he asked. "An illegal clone?"

"As a person," she said, and meant it. Even the worst alien offenders got time in court. The fact that a clone of a human being—who was, biologically, human as well—didn't have that automatic right seemed wrong to her.

His left eye narrowed, so that it was as slitted as his right eye. "Why didn't you say that fifteen years ago?"

"I had no idea what would happen to you," she said.

"As an officer of the law?" His question was snide.

"As an officer of frontier law," she said, "I go from crisis to crisis, resolving what I can and then moving to the next place, assuming that the system would work as intended."

"Well, it worked as intended for me," he said bitterly.

She sighed. "I had no idea you were an illegal clone."

That narrow-eyed look again. She could feel his disbelief.

"How could I?" she asked, and hoped it didn't sound too defensive. "I knew you were a clone. I didn't have time to look for a clone mark."

She almost added, *I saved your life by getting you out of there*, but she didn't. She knew that would sound defensive.

"Did they tell you what happened on Epriccom after you left?" she asked.

"Why would they do that?" he asked. "There was no trial."

"You didn't ask for one?"

"I didn't have the right to answers. I'm not anything, remember? Besides, who would I ask? You? I haven't seen anyone from the Frontier Security Service in fifteen years. I don't have a lawyer—I'm not entitled. And the prison officials believe that I'm just an inadequate laborer." He held up his bent hand. "They aren't even allowed to spend money to fix me. I'm surprised they can feed and clothe me, considering the fact that I can't really work at the level they want."

One of the androids disappeared out the door TwoZero had come in through. Gomez didn't see any instructions along her vision, so her time wasn't up yet. But she wondered if that movement marked the beginning of the end of this interview.

"So," TwoZero said, "what happened on Epriccom?"

"A couple of things," she said. "Five of you survived initially, but three died."

"I knew that," he said. "It happened fairly quickly. The others needed a full rebuild, which they weren't entitled to as clones. And the authorized medical treatment wasn't enough to save their lives. Thirty-Five of the Second, he survived too. And where he is, I have no idea."

She knew, but decided not to tell him. That clone—who also didn't have a name (at least according to the system)—was in a non-aligned prison on the Frontier, which probably made Clone Hell look like an upscale club.

TwoZero hadn't stopped talking in that bitter tone of his. "And Thirds, he disappeared into the system because you championed him."

She shook her head. "I didn't champion him. If anything, I failed him, at least from his perspective. He wanted asylum from humans, to stay with the Eaufasse, and we didn't allow that."

Thirds was in a different prison, and it was not maximum security. She had been relieved to discover that he was still imprisoned; she would have thought he would have gotten out by now, but maybe his illegal clone status had prevented him from leaving the system as well.

"It looks like I know everything, then," TwoZero said.

"Except what happened to the dome you were raised in," she said.

He froze again. That seemed to be his response when deeply startled. This time, he held the position only for a few seconds.

"Don't tell me," he said snidely. "You blew it up."

"*I* didn't," she said.

"The Frontier Security Service did," he said.

"No." She had to be careful here. He was just about to discover that everything he grew up with, every*one* he grew up with, was gone. "We observed laser fire inside, and then an explosion. Whoever ran the dome destroyed it from the inside."

He was frozen again, all except for his eyes. They had teared up, which surprised her. She somehow hadn't believed him capable of that kind of deep emotion.

Maybe she had been judging him by the same standards she had judged Thirds.

"You lie," TwoZero whispered.

"I can show you the images. I'll have to get them approved by the warden, but I can show them to you," she said.

TwoZero was silent. She could actually see him thinking about all she had said. Then he turned his head slowly, blinking, and raising his clawed hand to his cheek. Getting rid of the tears.

He believed her; she knew it. She wondered if that had been a part of the plan from the beginning—if all the clones inside that dome knew some would die there.

"Did you examine the wreckage then?" he asked, his voice wobbling a little.

"I didn't," she said. "The FSS did. No one survived."

He nodded almost dismissively, as if he didn't want her to tell him any more.

"Failures then," he said. "We were all failures."

That was a childish voice. A lost voice.

Thirds had emphasized failure too. He had sounded like failure was the worst thing of all. She had asked if everyone who failed died, at least according to the rules he grew up with.

She had never forgotten what he had said. *You can't have a failure in a unit.*

You can't have a failure.

Everyone died.

Like they had inside that dome.

TwoZero took a deep breath, wiped at his cheek on more time, and then faced her again. His eyes were red, but dry.

"You came all this way to tell me that?" he asked.

"No," she said. "I came all this way when I realized no one had ever talked to you."

He shook his head slightly. The movement seemed awkward. The skin on his neck didn't quite move right. "And you're going to—what? Heal me from within?"

She ignored that. "I want to find out what you know."

His gaze became sharp, and she saw Thirds in him. "You think I was trained to assassinate people on the Moon?"

So he knew about Anniversary Day. She hadn't been certain. She didn't know how much information prisoners got about the outside world.

"I don't know," she said. "Were you?"

"I don't know either," he said. "But I suppose I can help you find out."

25

THE TRIP FROM ATHENA BASE TO THE PRISON WHERE ZHU'S POTENTIAL client resided took three days. Zhu did not take public transport. He opted for a private ship, with the approval of Salehi, and loaded the ship with the legal library and files from S3.

Zhu decided to take the time to research potential problems with this client—real research, not AutoLearn. He wanted depth of knowledge, not a facile access to information.

Even though he had answered the request for an attorney, he still couldn't get information on the client. All he received was a summons to EAP 77743.

The first thing he did, after settling into the ship, was investigate that particular prison base. It was at the far reaches of the sector, medium security, and filled with human and clone prisoners, most of whom either did hard time at one point or who were classified as "unusual."

Even after three days of research, he still wasn't sure what "unusual" meant. There wasn't even anything listed on the various legal gossip sites, not even a nickname for this particular prison base, which he also found unusual.

His requests for information came back denied, which also told him something. He mentioned that to Salehi, who looked concerned.

They bury prisoners there, Salehi said. *You sure you want to go? Could be even worse than you think.*

Zhu wasn't sure how it could be worse: he already figured he was dealing with a clone who was probably an exact replica of the assassins on Anniversary Day. Which meant he was going to see someone with the same genetic makeup as PierLuigi Frémont, something that made him really nervous.

Apparently, it—or the lack of information—made Salehi nervous too, because that was when he offered one of his company space yachts, complete with pilot, copilot, and security detail. Zhu didn't really want that many people traveling with him, but they all came as a package. And one perk—or so Salehi claimed—was that the head of the security detail doubled as a chef.

It turned out that the yacht was huge and Zhu rarely saw the others, except during meals. Even then, he would have skipped the visiting, but he realized he wasn't changing positions enough. He was reading, listening, and watching information, buried in research, and if he didn't move around occasionally, he got so sore that his body made strange cracking noises whenever he stood.

On the second day, he had taken to using the exercise equipment in the captain's suite, continuing his research as he did so.

He learned next to nothing about EAP 77743, and of course he couldn't get information on his client, so he spent most of his time digging into clone law and the biography of PierLuigi Frémont.

The only place those two things intersected was the first place that had unnerved Zhu. Alliance law prevented the cloning of criminals, particularly criminals like PierLuigi Frémont. If the criminal was not rehabilitated or was deemed impossible to rehabilitate, the law clearly stated that he or his heirs could not sell his DNA or create clones. Any previously existing clones had to be destroyed upon conviction of the original.

Since clones had to be registered, tracking down the clones was easy. Theoretically. Unless the clones were made outside of the system. There were a lot of designer criminal clones, used as weapons, information, and most often as thieves. Those clones were unregistered and impossible to trace.

Zhu couldn't tell, from the information he had, where the clones of PierLuigi Frémont had come from. At this juncture, he wasn't sure if anyone knew. He had no idea if one of the coroners on the Moon had had a chance to examine the telomeres of the dead clones; that would at least reveal if they were clones of clones. Telomeres shortened with each replication, unless they were replaced through some kind of gene splicing thing he didn't understand. What he did understand, from his research, was that the gene splicing thing left a trace of itself no matter who was doing it.

So the secret of those clones—or at least one of the secrets—should have been in the clones' DNA.

From everything Zhu could tell about PierLuigi Frémont, the man wouldn't have tolerated being cloned. He was grandiose beyond belief, a cult leader who founded three different colonies, and destroyed two of them completely before starting the third. Every person—man, woman, and child—had died in those first two colonies, all at the command of Frémont.

The only reason the man got caught was that the people of Abbondiado, the third colony, staged an uprising and were smart enough to call in the Earth Alliance to help them. The Alliance arrested Frémont and destroyed anything he had touched. They called it "doing a full wipe," and they were, theoretically, good at it.

Zhu had even discussed the full-wipe technique one night over a spectacular dinner. He'd asked if the security detail he was traveling with had heard of PierLuigi Frémont. Of course they had—most humans had to study the bastard in school, mostly to see how both politics and biology could go wrong—but none of them had met him or anyone associated with him.

Still, one member of the security detail, a woman named Olivia, had been involved in more than one full wipe during her years in the Earth Alliance Police Force. She was of the belief that a full wipe worked.

Zhu had challenged her in his best courtroom manner. He'd been sitting across from her in the dining area, a small table surrounded by built-in bench seating. He had taken the corner with a view of both the doorway to the galley and a porthole looking out into space.

Olivia, a tiny woman with large eyes, downturned lips, and muscles that looked both strong and unenhanced, had sat directly across from him, tearing into the steak that the chef had served. Where he had gotten real beef this far out, Zhu had no idea, and he wasn't about to question it, because that meant he was also questioning his belief that what he was eating *was* real beef.

"I'm shedding DNA everywhere," Zhu had said to her. "A strand of hair here, skin cells there, and I can't keep track of them. You go to my cabin, you'll be able to get DNA off my unwashed clothes or the bed or the chair I sat in. It's impossible to wipe it all out."

She had smiled at him, a motion that, until that moment, he hadn't believed those lips capable of.

"A couple of points," she had said. "It doesn't take long for DNA to get contaminated. The skin cells in this room, for example, are going to be hard to isolate. They float, and they'll mix—yours and mine along with cells from everyone else who's been in this room since the last time it was cleaned."

"But they can be separated," Zhu said.

"Yes, they can," she said, "except that someone like you would complain about it in court. And scientists would worry that the cells were contaminated."

"Which reminds me," Zhu said. "Cleaning bots collect DNA all the time. It would be easy to get those cells. I'm sure the cleaning bots on this ship already have some of mine."

"And the bots' systems, if they are built to the Earth Alliance specifications, which have existed for centuries, automatically break up the tiniest cells. Instant contamination. Your bed is self-cleaning, at least on this ship, and in most places in the Alliance. Your clothing is also self-cleaning up to a point, though if you choose to wear it for five days straight you'll thwart that system. Pretty much anything you touch cannot store your DNA for long, by Alliance law."

"And outside the Alliance?" Zhu asked.

"Is like anything outside the Alliance. You're taking a huge risk any time you leave." She waved her fork around as she spoke. "When these criminals like your Frémont get arrested—"

"He's not *my* Frémont," Zhu said, offended even though he didn't want to be.

"You know what I mean," Olivia said. "When these criminals get arrested, not only is their DNA destroyed, but their whereabouts get tracked back decades. Mostly, we're looking to see if they lived or traveled outside of the Alliance. That's what you have to watch for. I'd look for it with your buddy Frémont."

That time she had done it to annoy him, and he realized it, so he didn't take the bait.

"What's to stop some Earth Alliance official from stealing the DNA?" Zhu asked.

"Besides the strict and somewhat nasty penalties for doing that?" Olivia asked. "Everything gets destroyed, usually by something really powerful. The preferred system is always fire, at a temperature high enough to melt bone. It's easiest in space, of course. We could destroy this yacht like that with the touch of a button."

That made him shiver. He tried not to think about those details. He hated realizing how vulnerable being in space made him.

"But domes or planetside," she said, "fire gets used a lot. No one wants these bad guys replicated, so we work hard to make sure it's impossible. Why else would the law call for preexisting clones to be destroyed?"

That detail had disturbed him the most. He'd already done a lot of research at that point, and knew that the science showed the clones were human in all ways except their creation. The fact that the law allowed them to be destroyed because the original had proven both criminal and irredeemable seemed wrong on a variety of levels.

"I don't understand that," Zhu said. "Why not destroy the legal biological children, then? And the killer's parents. After all, they passed on the DNA. All the relatives should be destroyed."

"Some cultures do that." Olivia didn't seem concerned. She had continued eating, while the conversation had destroyed Zhu's appetite. "Just not human ones. This is as close as we get to the 'sins of the fathers' thing that the Wygnin do."

Zhu hated it. He was also gaining an understanding of why Salehi thought clone law the next frontier in the legal system.

"Besides," Olivia had said, still focusing on her steak, "the parents, the children, their DNA isn't entirely from the original. The original is a combination in the case of the parents and a contributor in the case of the children."

"Can't you pull apart that DNA to get the original?" Zhu asked.

"All I know is that we were told it's been tried and hasn't worked." She set her utensils down and pushed her plate aside. "Hell, there's not even proof that the clones will have the same predilections as the original. In fact, the science says that they'll be different just due to how they're raised. But the science also postulates that with the right set of circumstances the clones will show the same tendencies as the original, and in the case of guys like Frémont, the Alliance thinks that risk of recreating a monster is too great to allow people like Frémont to reproduce in any way, once they're incarcerated. No biological children and certainly no clones. Hence the full wipe."

"Well, somehow Frémont got cloned anyway," Zhu had said.

"At least twenty times," Olivia said. "And if I were still in the Earth Alliance criminal justice system, I'd be making sure I knew how that happened to ensure that it wouldn't happen again."

"You don't think they're doing that?" Zhu asked.

"Haven't heard," she said.

"Do you expect to?" he asked.

She shrugged and got up, not even bothering to end the conversation. That had unnerved him almost as much as the discussion had. She had left him alone with his thoughts, which was where he had been too much these days.

Human systems were imperfect. Alliance systems were filled with cracks and mistakes. He knew: he manipulated them all the time to his clients' advantage.

So he went back to work, digging deep into clone law, and still look-ing up information about PierLuigi Frémont, who, so far as Zhu could tell, had never once left the Alliance.

Which was even more disturbing.

As if anything could be more disturbing than Frémont, who loved torture in big and small ways, who liked to experiment with various forms of murder, and who often used his charisma to charm people into doing exactly what he wanted—and then killed them as a reward.

By the second night, Zhu didn't sleep much.

By the time the space yacht arrived at the habitat near EAP 77743, he wasn't sure what his mission was any longer. He had no idea what he hoped to do when he saw the prisoner who had requested a lawyer.

Zhu promised himself that if he were too uncomfortable, he would just walk away.

After all, he wouldn't take on a client until all the documentation got filled out. And he would make sure the prisoner who had requested him knew that—and knew it when Zhu gave him the documentation.

If Zhu ever did give him the documentation.

Zhu reminded himself—repeatedly, it seemed—that he wasn't obli-gated to the client until Zhu decided to take the case. He'd never really acted on that before, but he planned to act on it this time.

He had to.

It was the only smart thing to do.

26

It couldn't be that easy, could it? TwoZero couldn't have the solutions to Anniversary Day.

Could he?

Gomez tried not to look pleased. She needed to remain calm.

TwoZero hadn't moved. He was still assessing her. His damaged hands rested on the tabletop, only a few meters from her. It looked like she could reach out and touch him—not that she wanted to do so—but she knew touching him would be impossible. The barrier between them would have captured her fingers.

"How would you help me find out what your training was for?" she asked. "The people who conducted it are dead. Thirds told me that no one knew what you were being trained for. Was he wrong?"

TwoZero looked down, and she felt a stab of disappointment. So he didn't know anything. He sighed.

"No one's contacted me," he said. "No one would want to contact me."

She thought he was going to hold up that ruined hand again, but he didn't.

"I can only tell you what I already know. What I remember. I think it might be enough." He looked up at her. His eyes seemed clear. She didn't believe he was lying, but then, she had thought Thirds was a different boy than he had been. This man had lived fifteen years in one of

175

the worst prisons in the Alliance System. Surely, he had learned how to dissemble.

"I'll be the judge of whether what you remember is enough or not," she said.

"Of course you will." That snide tone had returned. "What do I get if I help you?"

She almost shrugged. Then she realized he probably wouldn't talk to her any longer if she said she could do nothing for him.

"I can petition for you to go to a different prison," she said. "As your arresting officer, I will have some sway."

"What would that be? Medium security? Minimum security? A clone prison? Or would I get to mingle with real people?" His mouth had twisted even more, as if the words were hard for him to say.

"You know I am not the person who determines that," she said.

He frowned at her. She could see him debate what he wanted to do. He was weighing his options.

"You aren't the only one with this information," she said before he could speak. "The only reason I didn't go to the other clone who was injured or go see Thirds is because you were closer. That's all. I didn't come see you because I thought you would be more forthcoming."

"And if I'm not forthcoming, then you'll go to them," he said. "I get it. I also get that I shouldn't ask for much because you'll go to them if I do, and I get that I should be grateful for anything you give me."

He bowed his head, and braced his hands on the edge of the table.

"Thank you so much for conferring this great honor on me," he said. "And for telling me how all the failures died. It'll give me something to consider, as I mull your offer."

She welcomed his belligerence. It made her feel less sympathetic to him.

"So," she said as he stood. "This is all about what you're familiar with. You're comfortable. You really don't want to leave."

He froze, half standing and half sitting. Apparently, she had surprised him again. "I didn't say that."

"That's the net effect," she said. "*I* don't like it here, so I'm not coming back to see a recalcitrant prisoner. If I leave, the offer leaves with me."

"It's not much of an offer," he said, but he still hadn't moved.

"You don't have a lot to trade in return," she said. "Do you even know who your clone parent is?"

"I do now." He sat back down, although she got the sense he didn't want to. His limbs were shaking just a little, and she wondered if they would have been able to hold him up much longer. "Apparently, I was cloned from PierLuigi Frémont. If I had network access, I would have looked him up, but the media tells me that this Frémont killed a lot of people. They call him one of the most famous mass murderers of all time and, apparently, he killed people who were his…followers? Which means he led some kind of cult. Which means he had some kind of charisma or he knew how to manipulate something. Can you tell me more than that?"

"Only if it pertains to your past," she said.

He slapped his good hand on the table's surface. Her side of the table didn't even vibrate.

"How would I know what pertains and what doesn't?" he asked. "I don't know anything about him."

"Tell me what you do know," she said. "Tell me what you learned. Tell me about your training. Tell me who trained you, and what the procedures were. I'll tell you if that has anything to do with Frémont."

"No, you won't," he said, and even though it sounded like he was striving for bitterness, he couldn't quite manage it. He clearly did not want this opportunity to pass him by.

"You're right," she said, "I probably won't."

He sighed. "You can't guarantee that I will leave this place. You might not tell me about Frémont. What can you do for me really, Marshal?"

She smiled at him, happy that he had revealed this frustration, happy that he *was* similar to other criminals, despite his outward appearance.

"What can I do for you?" she asked. "It's pretty simple if you think about it."

His lopsided gaze met hers. He turned his head slightly, so that he could train his undamaged eye on her.

"I can distract you from this hell they have you in," she said. "For a few hours or a few days or maybe even a week. And that has to be worth something, doesn't it?"

He bowed his head. This time the movement didn't come from anger or reluctance. She could actually feel his sense of defeat. Underneath that bravado, this man was truly broken.

"Yeah," he said softly. "Sadly enough, that's worth a lot."

27

ZHU HAD BEEN TO DOZENS OF PRISONS IN HIS CAREER, BUT HE'D NEVER had an arrival like this one. Before he even left the habitat base, which was uncommonly small for a base that serviced friends, family, and staff of a medium-security prison, he had to submit to a variety of tests.

First, he had to provide all of his identification, including (surprisingly) access to his birth certificate. He hadn't needed that since he passed the Earth Alliance bar. He still had to provide all of his legal certifications, and then submit to several DNA tests.

Those tests took several hours, not because the tests themselves were time-consuming, but because the habitat base had to send away for his personal DNA profile. The administrator yelled at him for failing to prepare for this contingency.

Zhu apologized, knowing better than to justify his so-called failure. But he wanted to say that in all his years as a practicing defense attorney, he had never before had to prove that he was himself so that he could go into a prison.

He found it bizarre, and he'd mentioned that to one of the other diners at the habitat's main cafeteria. That diner, part of the prison's administrative staff, had laughed at Zhu.

You didn't know this was a clone facility? The diner asked. This is standard. You'd be surprised how many fake lawyers we get in places like this.

Finally, his clearance had come through. He boarded the VIP shuttle—made possible thanks to S3's connections—and headed to the prison proper.

Like all Alliance prisons in this sector, it had the same design he'd seen dozens of times. A large starbase with layers and warrens and all sorts of security measures, from decontamination chambers to isolated areas. It also had six different recreation areas for the prisoners that were designed to look like someplace else—a planetside garden, a sports arena, whatever the guards decided to program. It also had smaller recreational areas, and an excellent library that was not networked anywhere outside of the base itself.

What surprised him was that the prison was divided in half. One side was for offenders. The other was for lifers.

He was heading to the "lifer" section, which he only discovered when he put in the saved links he had received when he responded to the request for an attorney.

To get into the "lifer" section, he had to have all of his links except his emergency link shut down. Then his hands were sealed in an Alliance-approved wrap, to prevent easy transport of small chips and other materials out of the prison itself. He'd suffered through that part of the procedure before.

What he hadn't experienced before was a manual check of his links to make sure they were actually off. When that was over, he asked the guard who conducted the check who the lifer section housed.

The guard, a heavy-set older man, had looked at Zhu like he was crazy. "Illegals," he said.

Zhu hadn't understood. "As opposed to what?" he asked. They were all criminals. They had all done something illegal.

"Illegals, as opposed to criminals," the guard said. "The criminals done something bad. The illegals *are* bad."

The human side of the Alliance rejected that argument in the law. In fact, Zhu himself had prepared briefs for the Multicultural Tribunal that stated no non-human culture could consider a human bad *per se*, no matter what the non-human law required. The punishments would follow non-human law, but only humans got to define humans. And, by definition, humans were not born bad.

Then Zhu's breath caught as he realized what he'd been thinking. *Clones* were not human under the law.

"Clones," he breathed, "can be considered bad? Not defective? *Bad* by definition?"

"Yep," the guard said. "And you're about meet one. Feel like changing your mind now?"

"No," Zhu said. Oddly, he felt more resolved. The deeper he got into this side of the Alliance legal code, the less he liked it. And the more intrigued he became.

No wonder Salehi believed there was a future in clone law. Zhu was beginning to see it.

It would be hard to fight for, though, because the clients weren't human, but they weren't alien either. They were property. Or they were illegal. They weren't actual *beings* under the law.

At least as far as he could tell.

"Send me to him," Zhu said. "I want to meet my client."

"Good luck," the guard said. "He's not just bad, that one. He's evil."

Zhu frowned at the guard. "By whose definition?"

"The entire Alliance," the guard said.

"The Alliance has ruled this clone is evil?"

"Hell, no," the guard said. "It just showed what that creature's DNA is capable of. Evil, pure and simple. You should leave now, attorney. That clone don't need you."

Zhu straightened his spine. "It seems to me that that clone needs me now more than he ever has."

28

GOMEZ GATHERED THE TRUSTED MEMBERS OF HER TEAM AROUND HER. Two deputies, Simiaar, and a single researcher. They all looked confused about the reason for the meeting.

She hadn't told them, any more than she told them why she had opaqued the windows in the conference room of the *EAFS Stanley* and shut off the recording equipment. She also asked them to shut off all links except those they needed to monitor the ship. She monitored them silently, just to make sure that everyone had followed her request.

She didn't want any record of this meeting.

She'd been feeling paranoid ever since she left Clone Hell. The research she had done on the trip back to the *Stanley* had exacerbated that feeling.

It had taken her half a day to make the journey because of the regulations around Clone Hell and the fact that the shuttle simply wasn't built for speed.

She hadn't cared. She spent the time reviewing the file she had written about the incident on Epriccom fifteen years ago. In that report, she had focused on the diplomatic side of the incident, on the Frontier issues, and on the Eaufasse. She had given everything else, including Thirds and the clones, relative short shrift.

She didn't blame herself for that; she had been working on the Frontier after all, and her job was to stop problems, not analyze situations.

But in several places in the report, she had highlighted that these clones needed to be investigated in some way. She had even flagged the report for extensive review. She had felt, even then, that something was off about the entire setup.

But the review hadn't happened, and the report itself got buried in the mass of information filed about the Eaufasse as they continued to apply for acceptance in the Alliance. The report was excerpted, but not attached, to the files that accompanied the injured clones to the hospital. A full copy of the report went with Thirds on his journey into the system, but only because the damn Peyti translator had insisted that something had gone wrong with Thirds' treatment on Epriccom.

Uzven's complaint got attached to her report and sent with Thirds. As far as she could tell, that's as far as the information ever got.

She was researching what she had done fifteen years before because her sessions with TwoZero had completely unnerved her. The information he had given her—if true—should have been a warning to the Alliance.

She had known that he was the second clone of something known as twenty, which she assumed was the twentieth clone of PierLuigi Frémont, but she didn't know that for certain. He also told her that he knew a clone in that enclave named Sixteen of Two Hundred, a name that just scared her.

Two hundred was the highest second number that he could remember. He believed, but he wasn't certain, that he was "of Twenty," a fact that also unnerved her.

He had been in the enclave as long as he could remember. He also had been with a large group when he was very little, but that large group kept getting smaller and smaller over the years.

And he swore he had never seen anyone who looked different from him until he left Epriccom for good. The people who ran the enclave were much older, but their faces were familiar.

She had asked about his daily routine then, but he said it varied. He got vague on specifics on the way the enclave ran, and he claimed he couldn't remember what had happened on his outing to kill Thirds. She wanted to pin TwoZero down on that, but she wasn't certain how relevant it was.

Besides, she had learned enough to terrify her.

She had also learned enough to realize that he lacked a lot of crucial information.

He did not know where the clones had come from. He did not know who had created them. He hadn't realized he was created until he was in the hospital, trying to survive his hideous wounds. He had not realized that there was life outside of the enclave.

He had learned Standard and a few other languages. He had had a solid education in the classics, mathematics, and some science. He had also been tutored on the finer points of etiquette. But he had not been taught where those habits would be used.

And of course, he had learned to use every weapon known to the Alliance, plus how to make weapons out of pretty much anything. He had also learned how to turn weapons on the person who was trying to use that weapon against him, which made her think of Thirds and the way he had attacked the twelve chasing him.

He had been trained to do that.

Every description was difficult and chilling, and she had tried very hard not to show the disgust on her face.

She wasn't certain she had succeeded.

She had probably left before some trained Alliance interviewer would have, but she knew she could return to interview TwoZero any time. No one had spoken to him in more than a decade; she doubted anyone would talk to him until she returned.

Still, she asked the prison to notify her if anyone wanted to see him.

It greatly disturbed her that the Alliance hadn't treated him according to standard procedure. Standard procedure in cases like his involved interviews and re-interviews. Plus, the Alliance should have searched for his originator. *Someone* had created these clones. They had clearly been illegal, even to the hospital staff.

Standard procedure was simple: Illegal clones got investigated, their originators found and punished. None of that had happened.

All of TwoZero's information should have been investigated more than a decade before, and if it had been, she was beginning to believe that Anniversary Day might never have happened.

She couldn't shake the feeling that someone had deliberately buried the files. Someone or some*thing.* She wasn't entirely convinced it could all be blamed on carelessness, not with Uzven making such a fuss. She also couldn't blame the purity of hindsight. She had seen warning signs in her meeting with Thirds, in that damn enclave, in the death of the three boys, and with the attack of the twelve.

She had simply trusted her colleagues to do their jobs as well as she tried to do hers.

By the time she had returned to the *Stanley,* she had a plan in place. The plan made her stomach twist. She had never done anything like it before, and she couldn't do it alone.

Now, she faced the four people she had chosen to help her, and hoped she had chosen wisely.

She had asked them to return early from their off time, and they had all gotten back to the *Stanley* within the hour. Even though the ship only had a skeleton crew, she had darkened the conference area and shut off all access to it.

If anyone condemned her for making these plans, she would lie. She would say this meeting never took place.

The very idea of lying about this shook her. A few days ago, she had not been that kind of woman.

"You gonna tell us what this is about?" Simiaar asked. She sat at the head of the table, as if she had called the meeting. She was chewing on a long, hard strand of some kind of thin, pink, stick candy, something she tried to buy every time she had leave off the ship. Her diet was usually stringent—no sugar, no additives, as healthy as healthy could be on the Frontier—but she had a weakness for these things, and binged on them during her off time.

Apparently, she still considered herself off.

"Lashante," Gomez said, using her most no-nonsense voice, "you're the only one who remembers what happened on Epriccom. Can you tell the others?"

Simiaar narrowed her eyes at the tone, then broke the candy in half. She set most of it on the table in front of her, and sighed.

Gomez braced herself for Simiaar's next question—why didn't Gomez just assign the others the overall incident report, not the one she had written, but the official one that had gotten stored in the history of the Frontier network? Gomez had actually debated doing that, but she had decided she didn't even want that much information available to the rest of the crew.

She was so focused on her answer to the hypothetical question that she almost missed Simiaar's actual question. "How deep into detail do you want me to go?"

Gomez hadn't expected Simiaar to acquiesce so easily.

"Just the high points," Gomez said, "with this year's surprise as your ending."

Simiaar bit the end off the half-candy, crunching it loudly. Then she took a swig of water from the glass she had brought into the room and set the rest of the candy stick down.

She was now officially back to work.

She looked at the others in the room.

"Okay, kids," she said. "Back in the dark ages, long before you were baby deputies…"

She launched into the story of Epriccom as if it were a grand adventure. The others listened. Gomez watched them, assessing.

Nuuyoma's face remained impassive, but his eyes widened at some of the telling. Gomez was glad it distressed him. She wanted him on this team. She trusted him more than anyone on the ship with the exception of Simiaar, and Gomez wasn't sure she could go forward without him.

Chepi Verstraete listened with one hand over her mouth, her elbow braced on the table. She was small and slender, her tiny form disarming.

Most humans—most aliens for that matter—saw her as ineffectual, but she was both strong and intelligent.

The researcher, Neil Apaza, could find anything quickly. He also had enough basic knowledge of various scientific techniques that he could be a hands-on assistant to Simiaar.

He was the only one that Gomez couldn't entirely read. He was chewing on his thumbnail, a frown between his eyes, but as the story progressed, he didn't look shocked. He looked confused.

Was he already familiar with this material? If so, why?

Gomez made herself look away. Apaza was the only person in the room she didn't know very well. Whenever she saw him, he was hunched over a screen, tapping it, or mixing chemicals for Simiaar. He was heavy where Verstraete was slight, barely meeting the standard requirements for shipboard life and, Gomez would wager, no one had tested his fitness level since he qualified for the job two years ago.

He caught her looking at him, and then she remembered that he was the one who had tracked down TwoZero. He *had* known much of this material, just not why it had concerned Gomez.

Simiaar finished with her own reactions to the twenty clone assassins on Anniversary Day. Her tone had changed by then. The whole idea of a grand adventure was gone. Now, she admitted to something that even Gomez didn't know: Simiaar felt like the entire *Stanley* team had screwed up somehow.

That revelation relaxed Gomez a bit. Underneath everything, she felt the same way. She knew that she wasn't in charge of the others in the FSS nor did she have control over the things that others in the Alliance did, even in law enforcement.

Still, if she had followed up…

Her gaze met Simiaar's and she was surprised to see her old friend's eyes were just a bit moist. Simiaar tilted her head toward Gomez, and said, "All yours."

Gomez nodded, and gave Simiaar a small smile of thanks before taking over the meeting again.

"As Lashante and Neil know," she said, "I just visited one of the injured clones. He calls himself TwoZero, and he gave me a lot of information about his upbringing, the expectations he lived with, and what had led up to the incident on Epriccom. Since he's in Clone Hell and has been since he got out of the hospital, he has no direct knowledge of and no direct connection to Anniversary Day."

Verstraete kept her hand over her mouth. Apaza still chewed on his thumbnail. Nuuyoma leaned forward.

"But?" he asked.

Gomez could already see from his expression that the entire story disturbed him. He knew that someone had screwed up somewhere; he just didn't know where.

"But," Gomez said, trying to keep her voice level, "no one has ever spoken to him. No one has debriefed him. No one has investigated anything he had to say. No one even listened."

Apaza stopped biting his thumbnail and put his hand down. Verstraete frowned.

"The more I look, the more I wonder if this information was deliberately buried." It sounded dramatic, said like that, but Gomez didn't know how else to reveal what she knew.

Apaza nodded. "Makes sense. The information was awfully hard to find. Even this clone, this TwoZero, took a more-than-standard search to locate. He doesn't have a name, not an official one, and he's registered in the system under two different numbers, neither of which are linked together. And, for the record, neither of them have both a two and a zero."

Gomez wanted to thank him. She felt a stronger thread of relief than she should have, given how much she had already investigated. But she had been feeling paranoid, and the other side of that feeling was a sense of doubt, wondering if she had made everything up.

She gave him a small smile. "Normally, I would flag all the reports, send them through the chain of command, and insist that someone follow up on all of this. The problem is that I did so fifteen years ago, and the reports got buried, along with the clones. And then there's the difficulty we had finding TwoZero, not to mention the other two survivors. Something is off here."

Verstraete's hand formed a fist, then fell away from her face. "What are you saying? That the *Alliance* has something to do with Anniversary Day? That's crazy. Why would they do that?"

Nuuyoma shifted in his chair so that he faced Verstraete.

"The Alliance is composed of individuals," he said. "Some good, some bad."

"There are systems to weed out the bad ones," Verstraete said.

Simiaar snorted. "You're sure of that? Because I'd like to know those systems. Some of the deputy coroners I got assigned to the *Stanley* back in the day certainly needed weeding."

"But you're talking about incompetence," Verstraete said. "The marshal here is talking about something deliberate, something anti-Alliance."

"You've never encountered anyone who's anti-Alliance?" Nuuyoma asked.

"Not who works *for* the Alliance," Verstraete said.

"And youth triumphs over brains," Simiaar muttered.

For once, Gomez didn't chastise Simiaar for speaking her mind in a meeting. Gomez let that statement stand.

But she did add, "I'm not saying that the Alliance is connected at all. However, we're dealing with some delicate things in this instance. Illegal clones, who may or may not be related to PierLuigi Frémont—"

"How can you doubt that?" Simiaar asked.

"Lashante," Gomez said in her *shut-up-now* voice. "These could be some kind of designer criminal clone grouping made to look like Frémont for effect."

"I suppose," Simiaar said in a tone that actually meant *are you kidding?*

Nuuyoma was looking directly at Gomez. "Designer criminal clones can be weapons."

"Yes," Gomez said. "And we're already dealing with another kind of weapon. Those plant-like things the Eaufasse developed. Thirds proved that humans could control them."

No one in this group denied that Thirds was human, which she saw as a good thing.

"Then there's Uzven's behavior. I checked its records," Gomez said. "That incident on Epriccom is the only black mark in its file. The *only* one, and it didn't let the incident go for a long time. After the last time it tried to contact Thirds, Uzven went back to Peyla to teach Standard translators how to survive in human environments."

"If I were the paranoid type," Simiaar said, "I'd say that annoying Peyti got buried too."

Gomez nodded. She was convinced that Uzven had been forced into other work. But she didn't say that quite as bluntly as Simiaar. Instead, Gomez said, "For a translator with such a stellar record, the change in its career path *is* a bit sudden and unusual."

Apaza was biting his thumbnail again. Verstraete folded her hands together, then tapped her forefingers against her lips.

"If you're right," she said, "you're talking about some kind of conspiracy that extends from the Frontier to Peyla. With what kind of goal? Why go after the Moon?"

"You mean besides the fact that for most it's the only way to travel to Earth?" Simiaar asked. So she had thought of that as well.

"It makes no sense," Verstraete said. "The Earth Alliance is what keeps stability in the known universe. It prevents us from going to war."

"Yeah," Nuuyoma said. "And we're talking about weapons."

"So?" Apaza asked.

The pace of Verstraete's tapping increased. Then she swore. "They wouldn't do that."

"Do what?" Apaza asked. "What am I missing?"

"The Alliance wouldn't provoke an all-out war to jack up weapons prices," Verstraete said. "They wouldn't."

"That's your heart speaking, not your head," Simiaar said.

Gomez sank into a chair. She was suddenly exhausted.

"If that's what you're thinking," Apaza said, "then they're not trying to jack up prices."

"Oh?" Nuuyoma's tone was dismissive. "What are *they* trying to do?"

"Increase market share," Verstraete said softly. Then she looked at Simiaar. "Am I using my head now?"

"Yeah," Simiaar said softly.

"What do you mean?" Apaza said. He was clearly smart enough to understand this, but he seemed to have a block against it as well.

Gomez let Verstraete explain it. Gomez would correct Verstraete if she had to, but it was best for Verstraete to speak. That way she could think through the argument.

Besides, Gomez wanted to hear someone articulate this idea. She'd been batting it around inside her own head for too long.

"I just said that the Alliance stabilizes the known sector of space. Every group that joins has to agree to certain conditions," Verstraete said. "And one of them is to follow the Alliance's rules for warfare, which are, to be honest, pretty damn stringent. If you want to attack someone, you actually need Alliance approval. Then the entire Alliance will act with you or at least will be behind you."

Nuuyoma nodded. "That rule alone is why so many cultures never join the Alliance in the first place."

Simiaar made a disagreeing noise. "Eventually they do. The benefits outweigh the war rule. They make so much more money when they're allowed into the universe's biggest trading organization."

Gomez felt like the discussion was getting off-track. She raised a tired hand. "Let's not talk politics. It's—"

"Why not?" Verstraete said. "That's what we're facing here, isn't it? If this threat comes from the outside, it's because the market share for weapons makers, the ones that specialize in the truly nasty stuff, is decreasing, am I right?"

"They're probably buying administrators or lower-level bureaucrats," Apaza said. "Folks who can hide information easily and remove names from files, and lose the documentation so that these people stay in prison a long time."

"Let's not forget 'these people' are illegal clones," Simiaar said.

Gomez looked at her, unable to hide her shock. She thought Simiaar had no issues with clones.

Simiaar shrugged. "Illegal clones have no rights unless they're adopted and actually declared human. It takes *nothing* to hide illegal clones. Nothing, because the law doesn't consider them human."

She spoke with great passion, which was what Gomez would have expected from her. Gomez felt something akin to relief. For a moment, she had actually doubted her closest friend.

"Illegal clones…" Nuuyoma was musing aloud. "Aren't they generally used for identity theft and those kinds of crimes? They've never been considered weapons before."

"We don't know that," Gomez said.

"Even if they weren't," Verstraete said, "they will be now. That image of those twenty clones coming into Armstrong is pretty blatant, and nutcases around the universe are going to use that as inspiration."

"Wonderful," Apaza muttered.

Time to stop this part of the conversation.

"We have no idea what's actually going on," Gomez said. "Everything you've mentioned is speculation. But we actually can do the investigating that the Alliance refused to do. I have hours of interviews with TwoZero, and I think from those we can track down his originators, and maybe the reason for his existence."

"If he didn't lie to you," Simiaar said.

"If," Gomez agreed. "But he didn't have any reason to. And he holds the slim hope that things I find will be able to help him."

"That's why you brought us here?" Verstraete said. "You think we're going to be able to investigate the background of a group of clones made thirty years ago by some criminal organizations? We're not set up for that kind of investigation."

Gomez had had enough negativity. "You don't have to be on the team, Chepi."

Verstraete sighed, then leaned back in her chair. "I ask a lot of questions when I'm scared."

Gomez had noted that before, but she had forgotten it until now. "I won't put any black mark in your record or harm your career in any way—"

"What if we find something horrible?" Verstraete said. "I mean, we've got problems *inside* the Alliance, if what you're saying is true. What if those problems go way up?"

"You want us to ignore them?" Simiaar broke the candy into even smaller pieces, then piled the pieces on the edge of the table. "Just go on with our jobs like we haven't stumbled on anything here?"

Everyone looked at Gomez. She looked first at Nuuyoma. His eyes were narrower than usual, and his lips thin. He was clearly as worried about this as Verstraete. Apparently, he was just letting her run with the questioning.

He looked away before Gomez did. Then she looked at Apaza. He rubbed one thumb over the one he'd been chewing. He was studying the broken skin as if it were the most fascinating thing in the world.

Verstraete met Gomez's gaze. She sat up straight and her look was challenging.

"We're not going to be representing the FSS, are we?" she asked. "We will be completely on our own."

"Yes," Gomez said. "We're not even going to tell anyone what we're doing. I'm going to send the team on an extended leave, and hope we can gather information in a relatively short time."

"What do we do with that information?" Simiaar asked.

"I'm not sure yet," Gomez said. "Let's find out first if we're imagining this connection to the Alliance. What we're seeing might simply be apathy relating to illegal clones."

"You don't believe that," Verstraete said.

Gomez looked back at her. Verstraete might end up being her greatest ally or the biggest pain in the ass Gomez had ever worked with. She couldn't tell which it would be at the moment.

"What I believe doesn't matter," Gomez said. "All that matters is what I can prove."

"We might not find anything," Nuuyoma said. "The trail's thirty years old."

"Or fifteen, anyway," Simiaar said, using her left hand to push all of the candy into her cupped right palm.

"If that's the case, we've done what we can, and I, at least, will do my best to be satisfied with that," Gomez said.

Simiaar tossed the candy in the nearest recycler. "You're not satisfied with anything."

"Then let's try to solve this thing," Gomez said. "What can it hurt?"

"Besides our careers and maybe the Alliance," Verstraete said. "Not one whole hell of a lot."

Gomez liked the sarcasm. She smiled. "Are you all going to join me?"

They looked at each other. Finally, Nuuyoma nodded for all of them. "I guess you have a team, Marshal."

"Good," she said. "Now, let's get to work."

29

THE LIFER PART OF EAP 77743 DID NOT HAVE A PROPER LAWYER-CLIENT interview room. Instead, Zhu suspected he had been led to an interrogation room, and one that had been used for things not legal in the human part of the Alliance.

The room smelled faintly of urine and sweat, the kind of ground-in scent that not even nanobots could clean. Or maybe the prison actually piped in the stench of fear, just to make people who had to use this room uncomfortable.

The proportions were off as well. Not quite a box, barely a rectangle, it felt like the walls were at odd angles with each other. He supposed if he stepped it off, he would find that the measurements weren't the precise shapes he was used to.

And he would have to step it off because his links were down. The constant hum he let the links function under had gone away. He felt alone inside his head.

He paced, even though he should probably sit like a relaxed and comfortable attorney. Someone had put a table in the center of the room, but the table clearly wasn't part of the permanent décor. Neither were the chairs. They were all attached to the floor, but he could see the releases, even if he couldn't operate them himself.

The door clanged open and two android guards entered. They looked sturdier than the guards he had seen in other prisons, with extra layers over their internal workings. Their eyes were receded in their heads, and they had slits for mouths. Otherwise, they had very strong, almost rope-like arms and equally strong-looking legs. Their torsos were completely flat.

Zhu nodded at them. They did not acknowledge him in return.

Now that they were here, he couldn't sit at all. He really was nervous.

"I'm here to see a client," he said. "You may not stay in the room once he arrives."

"We will not record anything," said one of the guards in a flat monotone.

Zhu smiled. He'd played this game before. Young attorneys often lost cases because they didn't realize that any presence in the room other than the attorney and client would destroy attorney-client privilege under Alliance law.

"I don't care what you will and won't do," Zhu said. "I am an attorney. Under the law, I have the right to see my client in private."

"Your client is dangerous," the same guard said in the same flat voice. "We are here to protect you from harm."

"I will not waive protection, like you want me to. You can observe through the proper channels. I retain the right to see my client in private."

He was deliberately stating that *he* had the right to see *his* client in private. He had a hunch he would lose if he argued that his client had the right to privacy. He had no idea where clones stood in the laws governing attorney-client privilege, so he wasn't going to invoke his client's rights at all.

Zhu was only going to invoke his rights as an attorney. And on that, Alliance law was very clear. He had the right to see anyone or any sentient thing as a client, *alone,* if he wanted to. The prison (or jail) had to protect him from harm, by monitoring the proximity of the client and the attorney. Any touch and the guards could enter the room.

"We are here for your safety," the android guard repeated.

"Get out," Zhu said.

Their eyes flared. He couldn't tell if that was an acceptance from them or if someone else had made the flare occur. It didn't matter, because they left the room, one following the other.

And leaving him feeling even more nervous than he had a moment earlier.

He made himself sit at the table, then flatted his hands on its metallic surface. He was feeling paranoid enough that he thought he should search the table and chairs for recording and listening devices.

But he didn't have access to his links, so he couldn't really locate any devices. His hands were protected, so he couldn't feel much through his skin.

He would have to rely on his insistence to the androids that he needed time alone with his client. If the prison was recording this meeting, then it would have that request repeatedly on the footage. Not to mention the fact that the androids left after speaking to him. If somehow the prison deleted his conversation, then he would still be able to argue common sense, based on actions alone.

The door clanged open again. He looked up, glad he wasn't pacing anymore. If he had been, he would have startled visibly. As it were, his heart rate increased.

A broad-shouldered man slipped in, hands locked together and outstretched. He followed his arms like he was being pulled, and it took Zhu a moment to realize that he was. Whatever they had bound his wrists with was tugging him toward the table.

The man bent over, and his hands hit the table's edge. He would either have to stand while bent over like that, or he would have to sit down.

He sat.

He had piercing blue eyes. Zhu had never seen eyes like that, so clear, with such a deep blue color. They were riveting. His face was the face of the assassins, at least as they were presented in the Anniversary Day footage, except that his skin was mottled blue and yellow and purple.

He was bruised, badly bruised, and no nanoprobes had repaired his injuries. His nose looked wider than Zhu expected. The man's lips were thicker than they should have been as well, probably still swollen from whatever beating he had taken. A line of dried blood ran underneath his lower lip, and it took Zhu a second to understand that the dried blood was actually a scar. Something—the man's teeth?—had gone through the lower lip and damaged it.

Zhu had seen unrepaired humans before, but the extent of the damage, and the way it showed up on skin, always surprised him. He had no idea how humans had survived before medicine evolved to make such injuries disappear.

Yet this man—this clone—had those injuries, and he seemed mobile.

"You're the lawyer?" the man asked.

"My name is Torkild Zhu." Zhu spoke slowly. Even though the man's eyes radiated intelligence, Zhu had no idea how much he would understand. Some clones got no education at all. "I'm with one of the best defense firms in the Alliance: Schnable, Shishani, & Salehi."

The man's eyebrows went up. "What did I do to deserve S-three?"

Zhu knew better than to tell this man much. Zhu had learned long ago that saying anything about himself or his firm to the client, beyond the standard business information, was the wrong thing to do.

"You requested an attorney," Zhu said.

"And I'm your pro bono?" The man leaned his head back, then stopped when it clearly hurt him. "Because of Anniversary Day?"

Zhu didn't like the way the man tried to take control of the interview. In fact, he felt a strong antipathy toward the man, but couldn't tell if that was simply because of the Anniversary Day footage.

"I don't even know your name," Zhu said.

"I don't have a legal name," the man said. "I was called Third of the Second back in the day, and here I'm known as Trey. But according to prison records, all I have is an inmate number. You see, I lack a Day of Creation Document, and all of that lovely stuff legal clones have."

So that was what the guard had meant by *illegal*. Zhu frowned for just a moment as he thought through the law he had read.

"Are you a clone of PierLuigi Frémont?" Zhu asked.

Trey tugged on his restraints as if he were trying to find a more comfortable position. "Are you my lawyer?"

"What does that mean?" Zhu asked.

"PierLuigi Frémont was a mass murderer. Convicted, unrepentant. And now there are these Anniversary Day creatures that everyone says are related to him in some way." Trey stopped right there. He said nothing more, but he tilted his head slightly, as if inviting Zhu to answer his own question.

Zhu's breath caught. This man, this *clone*, knew the law. And under Alliance law, any known clone of PierLuigi Frémont could—*should*—be put to death.

"What do you want a lawyer for?" Zhu asked.

"Two things," Trey said. "I need a lawyer to help me challenge my illegal status."

"Do you have a clone mark?" Zhu asked.

"No," Trey said.

"And you lack a Day of Creation Document," Zhu said, "so how could a lawyer challenge your status?"

"Are you my lawyer?" Trey asked again. He seemed to prefer that question when he felt it wasn't in his own interest to answer Zhu's question.

"Not yet," Zhu said, although if he were honest with himself, he was leaning that way just for the challenge alone. "You mentioned two reasons, the first being to challenge your illegality. The second?"

"I have information the Earth Alliance wants. I'm willing to trade that information for my freedom." His gaze hadn't left Zhu's face.

"Looks like they already tried to beat it out of you," Zhu said.

Trey's swollen lips twisted slightly. "That happened in the yard right after we saw some Anniversary Day footage. You know, the one with the clones."

Zhu did know it.

"The beating went on too long. No one stepped in, even though I called for a lawyer. I suspect that outburst saved my life."

It probably had.

"I don't understand why clone prisoners would be upset that a group of clones tried to destroy the Moon," Zhu said.

"I'm not sure that's why they were upset," Trey said.

"You think it's coincidence?" Zhu asked.

"I don't know that either," Trey said.

They studied each other. Trey seemed quite calm for a man who had received a violent beating and who might lose his life because of whom he was related to.

"What kind of information do you have?" Zhu asked, then added, "And no, I am not your lawyer yet. I don't want to be attached to you in any way unless I know what I'm getting into."

"Because I look like the Anniversary Day suspects?" Trey asked.

"Because I have a massive caseload already," Zhu lied, "and I need to know if you're worth my time."

Trey's measuring gaze broke for just a millisecond, long enough for Zhu to note it. He realized then that no other lawyer had answered the summons. Zhu decided to gamble on that fact.

"I came to you," he said. "No other attorney has, even though your request has been out there for weeks. I suspect I'm the only possible lawyer you have, and given my history and the fact that I'm with S-three, I'm also the best lawyer you could hope to get. So think carefully about whether or not you'll answer my questions."

Trey's eyes narrowed, and he sighed. "Here's all I will tell you before you confirm that you're my lawyer. I was raised with more than a hundred other clones. We all came from the same source, known as the Second. I do not know what that means. We were raised in a dome on Epriccom, which was, then at least, on the Frontier. We were raised, from what I can tell, to kill. Whether we were designer criminal clones, weapons, or just someone's perverse idea of a joke, I have no idea. I do know how we were trained, and how the system worked. You may also check my background. I have been in this prison for fifteen years with no outside contact. Congratulations, Torkild Zhu. You are my first-ever visitor."

In other words, there was no way that Trey had known about the Anniversary Day attacks.

"So your information is very old and the Alliance probably has it all." Zhu started to stand. He didn't need this.

"If the Alliance knew what it had," Trey said, "do you think it would have let the attacks happen? Do you seriously believe it would have let clones of PierLuigi Frémont live?"

It was a very good point, and one that Zhu was unprepared to answer. He had half-expected to leave this place empty-handed. Now, he had to consider what he wanted.

"If you are what I think you are," Zhu said, "you're never getting out of here."

"Admitting defeat before even stepping onto the battlefield? Really, Torkild Zhu. Is that how they train defense lawyers these days? I thought you all wanted to get a hearing before one of the Multicultural Tribunals."

That would have worked a few months ago, but Trey misplayed his hand. Zhu didn't want that right now, nor did he want to save a possible mass murderer.

He did want to know what had happened on Anniversary Day, and this man had no idea.

"Think about this," Trey said. "I am the Third of the Second. That means there's a Third of the First out there. In fact, that means there's a First, period, and maybe several others. No one has that information— or at least, has thought through what information they have. There were at least one hundred clones my age in that dome."

"Where are they now?" Zhu asked.

"Dead," Trey said. "All of them except six of us. Or maybe less. I don't know. Six survived the day the marshals arrived. After that, I wasn't allowed to know. I got shuttled into the system, and ended up here."

There was a lot more to that story; Zhu could sense it. There was a lot more to Trey.

"I'll consider it," Zhu said.

"I'd like to sign on as your client now," Trey said.

And Zhu felt the pull of that. In that moment, he realized this man had inherited another side of PierLuigi Frémont. Trey had charisma.

Which made him dangerous.

"I said I'll consider it," Zhu said.

"What can I do to convince you?" Trey asked.

Zhu studied him, heart pounding. Zhu wasn't sure he was a match to this man, no matter how the law saw him.

"Nothing," Zhu said. "You can't do anything at all."

30

It took longer than Gomez expected to get the rest of the crew off the *EAFS Stanley*. She had to contact the FSS for approval for the extended time off, even though her crew was the hardest working crew in the system. Except for the few days she had just given them, several crew members had not had time off in more than a year—except the regulated downtime that any spacefaring large ship had.

Part of that was because the *Stanley* traveled constantly inside the Frontier. In order to take time away from work, the *Stanley* and ships like her had to be in Alliance space, and sometimes the *Stanley* didn't approach Alliance space for years. Gomez herself hadn't had more than a week's vacation in more than ten years.

Gomez tried not to get testy as she waited for some bureaucrat in the FSS to approve her crew's leave. She had to fill out more forms than she wanted, and she had to attest that the *Stanley* would receive a full overhaul before going back to standard duty.

She actually didn't mind attesting to that, since the *Stanley* would probably need an overhaul after she and her small team were through. If nothing else, she wanted to scrub some evidence of her private mission off the ship's records.

The ship would record several things whether she liked it or not, but she knew that after the trip, she could get rid of the record. She could easily shut down other parts of the ship's tracking capabilities before the team left on its new mission.

She shut down some external links, including all of the devices that actually pinged the Alliance with the *Stanley*'s location. She didn't tell any of the team she had done this. The by-the-book members of the crew—Nuuyoma and Verstraete—would probably argue with her about the wisdom of doing that. Apaza had already questioned the wisdom of taking the *Stanley*—and in some ways, he was right. It would have been easier to rent a ship or to buy one, since she had a long-stored-up salary that she never spent.

However, Gomez needed the *Stanley* for this trip. The *Stanley* was a fully-equipped law enforcement vehicle that had everything from a small restraining area to a full level with cells. And, most importantly, it had a science lab so extensive that Simiaar could work her magic, even in the far reaches of the known universe.

Gomez needed Simiaar, and she knew she needed Simiaar's equipment.

Which meant she had to keep the *Stanley*.

They moved out of Alliance space almost immediately, and found a stationary point behind an uninhabited moon. From there, the team split up into their various areas of research.

Gomez had brought back hours of interviews with TwoZero, as well as all of his prison records, including his biological data. She had taken fluids and skin cells from him, with his permission, so that Simiaar could confirm if the prison's biological materials and data actually belonged to TwoZero.

Gomez still felt extremely paranoid, and she was beginning to think that a good thing.

She put Verstraete to work building a map and a timeline. She wanted to know where TwoZero had been, where the other surviving clones went, and why Thirds had gone to a medium security prison while the others had gone to maximum security. She also had Verstraete compile a list of the various known places that provided Designer Criminal Clones.

She gave Nuuyoma the files provided fifteen years ago by the Eaufasse. A history of the colony as seen through the surveillance that the

Eaufasse set up. She wanted him to watch for anything that made the founders of that colony identifiable and she also wanted to know if there were other clone murders.

And she asked him to take a look at what was going on in that colony while she had been on Epriccom. At the time, two of her deputies were supposed to keep an eye on that enclave—and they had. But she had them looking for different things, because she had an active investigation.

Now, she wanted to know if anything had been hidden near there, if anyone else had escaped, or if the Eaufasse had approached the enclave as well.

Scanning that footage, even with the help of the excellent programs the *Stanley* had for such things, would take quite a bit of time.

Still, Nuuyoma had the patience and the eye for detail that she needed. Plus, he hadn't been involved in the earlier mission, so he wouldn't have the same prejudices Gomez or Simiaar had.

She had initially thought of putting Apaza on the footage. He could go through a lot of information quickly. But, she decided, he would be more useful doing other things.

She brought him her notes, and walked him through the things that TwoZero had told her about his childhood. She assigned Apaza to search for similar clone clusters and domed communities outside the Alliance—even if those clusters were not related to PierLuigi Frémont or were non-human clones.

Gomez figured they would be drowning in information, and she was all right with that. She figured the more information they had, the better they would be.

She was the one who investigated all of the information provided by the Eaufasse. She would not be able to hide the fact she looked at these records, and she wanted it all by the book.

The Eaufasse had joined the Alliance and were subject to Alliance laws. If she were to investigate current events happening with the Eaufasse, she would need their permission to see records not available to the public.

Fortunately for her, the information predated the Eaufasse's entrance into the Alliance by a decade. Plus, she was the one who had helped the

Eaufasse through the crisis with the clones. As one of the many Alliance first-contact providers who had facilitated the Eaufasse's entrance into the Alliance, she had a lot of leeway in accessing records, particularly records she was a part of.

She decided to do something she hadn't done when she was dealing with the Eaufasse and the clones. She was going to dig into the records of the history of that human colony.

Since she had to do this part by the book, she did her work on the screens in one of the most comfortable parts of the ship, a space that Simiaar had named the reference library. There were no paper books—Gomez hadn't seen a paper book outside of Alliance space, and even then they were collector's items, owned by people who could afford to spend money on silly things—but there were workstations that allowed easy access to various networks. Most of those networks provided entertainment of different kinds, uploaded or easily accessed through the FSS system and Alliance-approved.

The rest of the networks did provide a research library into all of the information that the Alliance had recorded during its existence. The problem was that there was too much information to access easily, and some of it wasn't even available outside of Alliance space. So, she had to download specific things before they left—or approve it for download.

She could then transfer that information into her office, but she didn't want to hang onto it. Besides, if someone did trace her research—and if someone were keeping track of PierLuigi Frémont clones, they might—then she wanted her search to look as cursory as possible.

Cursory happened in the research library. Not in the senior officer's cabin.

She loved the room. It got used a lot on long trips, particularly when the crew had nowhere to stop for weeks. Usually it was full, even though conversation was frowned on.

Now, with only a skeleton piloting crew—a few old timers who no longer had homes to go to and who weren't that fond of being away from the *Stanley*—and her four teammates, she could walk through corridor after corridor and fail to see a soul.

This room hadn't seen any activity since before the crew left for its initial leave.

Still, she took a screen behind the door, so whoever passed in the hall couldn't see what she was working on. Then she muted the sound, touching the command for non-aural presentations. Otherwise, she'd have to hook up a link so that she could hear privately, and she didn't even want that traced.

She downloaded the entire Epriccom file from that year, then logged off the network. It would take some research for someone to figure out what information she was actually looking for.

She would be honest about part of this if she were ever confronted: she would say that the images of the Anniversary Day assassins upset her and she wanted to make sure they had no connection to that incident on Epriccom.

Perfectly logical, and something a person in her position would do. She suspected that Simiaar had done some of that long before she ever contacted Gomez about Anniversary Day.

Gomez bent over the screen and started into the information, separating the files by timeline. She wanted to know what kind of communications the Eaufasse had with that domed community both before the principals arrived and afterward. She had received that information during the investigation—no one had thought it pertinent.

And if the entire incident were investigated by the Alliance later, which it was supposed to have been, then all of the information needed to be at the Alliance's fingertips.

Gomez knew she would have at least as much work as the others on the team. The Alliance always collected thousands of times more information than it actually needed on any matter. The key was extracting the tiny bit that related to the case.

Or cases, as in this instance.

Gomez separated everything according to the timelines she needed, then set to work. She had people dealing with the enclave's history and the things that happened after the enclave destroyed itself.

But so far, she was the only one who could work on its origins. Sometimes, in the beginnings of things, she found clarity. She hoped this was one of those times.

31

ZHU HAD TO USE THE PRISON'S RECORDS SYSTEM TO LOOK UP INFORMATION on Trey. The closed S3 system he had brought on the space yacht didn't include prison records, clone crime records, or alien crime records, and he didn't want to use any public system to investigate Trey's background.

Fortunately Zhu could access the prison system through his room in the habitat. The best hotel on the habitat, billed as a luxury hotel, was hardly good enough to be called a hotel. The rooms were sparsely furnished, and none were suites. The place lacked conference areas, and it barely had functional workspaces.

He was beginning to understand that the usual suspects who dealt with legal cases throughout the Alliance—lawyers, judges, politicians—rarely frequented prisons associated with clones. And of course, there was no family. Friends probably abandoned the relationship if the clone got arrested as well—and certainly would if the clone were imprisoned.

All of that should have made him more sympathetic to Trey, but Zhu had been a defense attorney long enough to know that relationships with his clients, particularly relationships based on empathy, were a big mistake.

He sat in his room—the Chancellor Suite, which wasn't designed for a chancellor and wasn't a suite—and did his research. Twice he'd left to get a meal in the habitat cafeteria, grateful for the walk and the diversion. The view from his hotel room window was depressing—the edge of the habitat, and then the prison itself, round and imposing against a glow of stars.

Ships had to avoid the area, landing on the far side of the habitat, obviously not the part that Zhu's room overlooked. The prison itself was far away from anything to prevent prison breaks—or at least attempted ones.

If there was a view that could make a man feel alone and isolated, make him believe that the universe was a cold and lonely place, this was it.

He could get out of here, he knew. He just had to give the crew an hour or two notice, and they could all head back to S3. He was tempted every single time he looked out that window except...

The research had him riveted.

Trey's file was more complete than Zhu had expected, partly because the frontier marshal, a woman named Gomez, had filed an extensive report. She had to—the incident Trey referred to could have caused a major problem in the diplomatic negotiations going on in that part of the Frontier.

Her report had a lot of documentation, including video of the bodies discovered on Epriccom, the autopsy, the recreations of the faces of the dead, and much of the communications with the boy who identified himself as Third of the Second.

Her interviews in the Eaufasse compound weren't on record and, unfortunately, there was no video of the attack on the compound by the twelve clones who had been pursuing Trey.

It didn't matter. No matter what Zhu read, he kept finding the same details.

Trey had been chased outside of the enclave by twelve attackers, who were determined to kill him. Trey had escaped through some cunning and careful planning. He tried to get protection for himself, first from the Eaufasse, then from the FSS. The FSS screwed things up—at least from Zhu's perspective, and also from the perspective of the Peyti translator who also contributed a report.

The translator was of the opinion that Trey had asked for asylum from the humans, not an unreasonable request, considering the way that human law in the Alliance treated clones.

From everything Zhu saw, Trey was the victim in this case.

Of course, Zhu read from a defense attorney's perspective, but still. If Trey had been considered human under the law, he might have been charged with manslaughter, only because the weapon he chose took some forethought to use.

But Zhu could have argued that Trey had planned to defend himself from the moment he learned how the culture inside the enclave worked, and that the attack outside the Eaufasse compound had simply been self-defense.

And, had Trey been human under the law, Zhu would more often than not have won that case. If anything, he would have pled it down to manslaughter and time served.

In fact, had he been on the case, he would have argued that Gomez and the FSS were responsible for the deaths of the eight clones, not Trey, and that both Gomez and the FSS might have had some criminal liability in the commission of those deaths.

It would have been a stretch, but had he argued in front of a jury or (more likely) a sympathetic judge, he would have created enough doubt to make sure his client got off.

The only reason Trey was imprisoned, the *only* reason, was because he himself was illegal. He was a clone without clone marks approved by the Alliance.

But that could work to Trey's advantage. Trey had been found outside of the Alliance. He had contacted the nearby culture for help, and it wasn't his fault that the culture was trying to join the Alliance. He clearly knew nothing about the Alliance at the time of his arrest.

Human clones created inside the Alliance were illegal if they were not made according to Alliance laws.

Human clones *created by non-Alliance humans* outside of the Alliance were subject to local laws.

The community that Trey had been raised in was gone, so its laws were not knowable.

Zhu let out a breath, then realized he already had an argument to get his client out of this hellhole. He wouldn't even need to talk with Trey about Anniversary Day.

Zhu ran a hand through his hair, then stared at that prison. It seemed so small from this vantage, yet he knew it was extremely large.

He leaned back in his chair and smiled.

Damn Salehi. He had been exactly right. Something had to rekindle Zhu's sense of right and wrong, of justice lived and justice denied. Anniversary Day had started the feeling—and it had begun out of fear—but he wasn't afraid any more.

In fact, Zhu had stumbled into something that challenged him, both mentally and ethically. He couldn't just fight this one by rote, and if he won the case, he might do good for thousands of people, many of them filling the illegals half of the prison he could see from his hotel room.

He smiled.

He felt alive for the first time in weeks. But more than that, he felt buoyant. He didn't know how else to describe it. He felt energetic and excited about the law and his place in it.

He might actually be able to bend it to his will or maybe even change how it would be interpreted.

Heady stuff for a man like him.

It no longer mattered how he felt about Trey.

It no longer mattered that Zhu wouldn't be able to solve Anniversary Day—not that he could have done it on his own anyway.

He had a mission and, in its own way, it was as important as Berhane's. Maybe more important. She was cleaning up after the dead.

He might make things better for the living.

All he had to do was try.

32

A WEEK'S WORTH OF WORK, AND THE TEAM HAD SOMETHING. SEVERAL somethings, in fact. Gomez met with them in the cafeteria, not because the food was better here. It wasn't. It was the same as the rest of the ship for as long as her personal chef had extended leave.

But the cafeteria felt homier. Besides, Simiaar actually tried her hand at cooking, something that made Apaza laugh.

"It makes sense," he whispered to Verstraete when he thought Gomez wasn't listening. "She's used to cutting up dead things already."

The very idea had upset Verstraete enough that she had moved away from Apaza, but Gomez had laughed, startling Apaza. He hadn't realized she was nearby.

"If you tell Lashante that," Gomez said, "she'll want to cook every night."

Verstraete made an *urp*ing sound, as if she had already eaten something that disagreed with her.

They were only using a small part of the cafeteria. The lights were down in the other sections, and the fresh food stations were shut down. Gomez had instructed the skeleton crew to begin a deep clean of the entire ship, overseeing bot work and sometimes doing some of the work by hand. She had excluded several parts of the ship—mostly where her team was working—and that included this part of the cafeteria.

Still, the work the skeleton crew had done had taken the food smells out of the cafeteria altogether. Before, it had smelled of fresh coffee and baking bread. Now it smelled like the rest of the ship.

Usually, anyway. On this night, someone had made coffee and it smelled heavenly. Real coffee, not the stuff that came out of the ship's cafeteria recipe. Gomez wasn't even sure the ship's recipe was made from coffee beans; she thought maybe it was just some chemical concoction with added caffeine. Although, if she thought about it, she knew that wasn't entirely true because Simiaar drank that stuff like it was water, and Simiaar was notoriously careful with her body.

Simiaar had enlisted Nuuyoma's help. They brought out plates of steaming pasta, with four different kinds of sauces—a red sauce, a white sauce, a meat sauce, and a garlic sauce. She also made or heated up trays of bread.

"Planning to feed an army?" Gomez asked.

"Figured we have a lot of planning to do," Simiaar said, "since you declared our research done."

Gomez noted the phrasing: *declared our research done*. Not entirely true. She had wanted a report on the research, although she had declared hers done and, unless everyone else had more pressing information, they would start with the leads she had found.

The group crowded around the food-laden table. The scents of garlic, roasted meat, tomatoes, and hot bread filled the air. Gomez's stomach growled. She hadn't been eating well while she researched. She had been too distracted. In fact, she had been so distracted that she just realized it now.

She grabbed a plate and piled it high with different kinds of pasta. Like the sauces, the pasta came in different colors, although she didn't know why that mattered. And she didn't care. She just took some whitish angel hair, green spaghetti, reddish twists, and multicolored hollow things that she couldn't name.

Then she piled on the red sauce. She'd had Simiaar's cooking before and knew that all of the sauces were good, although she didn't trust the meat sauce. Simiaar had once joked that she used leftovers from her office for her meat sauces and even though Gomez had laughed at the dark humor, she hadn't been able to eat any meat that Simiaar had cooked ever since.

Gomez grabbed a slice of bread, still warm from the oven, and sat down. The others had taken her lead and were filling their plates. Simiaar watched them, hands folded under her chin like a scaffold.

"Can you talk about what you found without ruining our appetites?" Gomez asked her.

"No fluids at dinner?" Simiaar asked, raising her eyebrows innocently.

"No *bodily* fluids at dinner," Gomez said.

"You take all the fun out of it," Simiaar said. "But, even with that restriction, I can talk about what I found while we're eating."

The others sat down, almost in unison, their plates piled as high as Gomez's. They probably hadn't eaten much either. The regulation stuff was barely edible; besides, they'd have to eat that most of this trip.

Simiaar's cooking was a rare treat.

Simiaar stood and served herself. She took a little of everything, and she talked as she dished up.

"Your clone friend," she said, nodding at Gomez, "is definitely a clone of PierLuigi Frémont. But I learned some interesting things about him as I investigated all of the biologicals you gave me."

"About Frémont or the clone?" Nuuyoma asked, his mouth filled with food. He nearly sprayed and covered his mouth with his left hand barely in time.

"The clone," Simiaar said. "Most of the clones, in fact. And a bit about record-keeping as well."

"All right." Gomez talked with her mouth full too. She had to remind herself to slow down. The meal was simply too good. The red sauce tasted like it had been made with fresh tomatoes and freshly picked oregano.

Simiaar sat down. She picked up her fork, but didn't dig in right away. Instead, she sat over the plate of food and watched the others eat.

"First, the clone," she said. "He's a copy of a copy of a copy."

"You can tell that?" Verstraete asked.

"Telomeres," Simiaar said. "They're really short, and somewhat damaged. His DNA is filled with breaks and errors that happen with imperfect cloning, especially imperfect cloning through generations."

"You mentioned something like that with the dead bodies." Gomez only remembered that because she had recently reread the file.

"I did," Simiaar said, "and the problems those bodies had are the same problems your friend has."

Gomez did not rise to the "friend" bait, much as she wanted to. Simiaar was trying to make a point, although what point, Gomez did not know.

"So they are, what's it called?" Verstraete asked. "Siblings?"

"They were cloned from the same source." Simiaar took a delicate bite of some tube pasta covered in garlic sauce. She moaned with quiet pleasure. Apparently Gomez wasn't the only one who had missed real food.

"All of them?" Gomez asked.

"What I have access to," Simiaar said. "That's the three dead bodies, and your friend TwoZero."

"Not the other injured clones?" Gomez asked. "Or Thirds?"

"Nope," Simiaar said. "The other survivor doesn't have DNA on record. The injured clones that died, well, their DNA and biologicals got trashed because they were, in the words of the files, 'tainted, possibly hazardous.'"

"Because of what?" Gomez asked. "The plant weapons?"

"Presumably," Simiaar said. "But that would mean that TwoZero's DNA or his biologicals would have been contaminated from the start, and I have all of his records. He was nearly dead—it's amazing he's alive—but he wasn't contaminated with anything. He's just a bad copy of a bad copy, and he doesn't have the same ability to recover that the average human has."

"He also doesn't have access to normal medical procedures," Gomez said.

"Why?" Nuuyoma asked.

"He's an accused murderer and a clone," Verstraete said. "You figure it out."

"I thought we have to treat prisoners humanely," Nuuyoma said.

"Sometimes I forget how stuck you are in the human branch of the FSS," Gomez said. "We have to treat *human* prisoners humanely. We have to treat other species according to their customs. Clones are neither human nor another species."

Nuuyoma shook his head. "How are these laws able to stand?"

Apaza looked at Gomez in disbelief. "He doesn't know the history of the sector, does he?"

She ignored that because she didn't want the discussion to go sideways.

"So we don't have anything from the other injured clones?" she asked.

"No, we don't." During their little discussion, Simiaar had managed to eat half the food on her plate.

Gomez suddenly felt like she was behind. "And Thirds?"

"Ah, Thirds." Simiaar said. "We have some information, but I don't trust it."

"Why?" Gomez asked.

Simiaar set her fork down and looked at everyone for effect. "Because," she said, when she was done meeting their gazes. "The information provided about TwoZero from the prison itself is incorrect."

"Incorrect how?" Gomez asked.

"You want to tell them?" Simiaar asked Apaza. "After all, you're the one who found him."

"I found him by tracing records," Apaza said, his face red. "What exactly are you accusing me of?"

"She's accusing you of tracking faulty DNA," Verstraete said. She was picking at the green pasta covered with garlic sauce.

"I didn't track the DNA." Apaza sounded offended. "I tracked the arrest records. And it was damn hard because the names—"

"We know about the names," Nuuyoma said, "even if we might not know the history of the sector."

Apparently Apaza's dig had stung.

"Why didn't you track the DNA?" Gomez asked Apaza. That point caught her attention. It clearly caught Simiaar's too, because she was frowning at Apaza.

"I figured clones, you know? I could be led down a false trail, especially since we didn't know the names. I figured several people had the same DNA, but only one had his history. That's how I tracked him." Apaza's gaze met Gomez's. It appeared as if he expected her to chastise him.

"No wonder he found them," Simiaar muttered. She picked up her fork.

"Oh, no," Gomez said. "You can't go all cryptic on me. What does that mean?"

"If he'd tried to track by DNA, he would never have found TwoZero, that's what I'm saying."

"I got that," Gomez said. "But why wouldn't he?"

Simiaar took a large bite of pasta and chewed. Everyone waited for her to finish. "His biologicals claim he's had a lot of nanowork, and that his DNA isn't available because it's clearly been tampered with."

Gomez let out an involuntary sigh of exasperation. "I asked specifically for his DNA files."

"And you got them," Simiaar said, "along with an apology that there was no DNA inside it."

"But there was a lot of material in those files," Gomez said.

"Mostly about procedures done at the prison to keep him alive. I can't quite figure that out either, since he's a clone. They shouldn't have made any extra efforts. They wasted the money on him."

"You're so cynical," Nuuyoma said.

"No," Verstraete said. "She's just reporting the facts. I've been looking into some of the laws. There's no requirement for a prison to maintain the health of a clone."

Simiaar shrugged. "It is at their discretion. Maybe they just found it too hard not to follow the rules."

"Or maybe they weren't aware of the rules," Nuuyoma said. "I wasn't, and I've been in the field for years, and I had years of training."

"It doesn't matter," Gomez said. She needed them to focus. "What we do know—what I could see just by looking at him—was that he's clearly had no nanorepair procedures. He still has scars so bad from his injuries on Epriccom that I can't see how he's of any use to the prison at all. He said he wasn't."

"Maybe he's their pet," Simiaar said.

"Are you saying that the files imply that he looks like a clone of Pier-Luigi Frémont because of a nanoprocedure?" Nuuyoma asked Simiaar.

Simiaar nodded. "It's not said outright, but that's what I would have expected if I had a body on my table along with his file. Because the prison-provided materials say he's a unique individual with a lot of nanorepairs, when the truth is something different. If I hadn't known the truth, I would not have been able to identify him as TwoZero from that file, since his DNA definitely shows that he's a clone of PierLuigi Frémont."

"That's so odd," Gomez said. "Because he doesn't look like PierLuigi Frémont any more. He's too damaged. In fact, he was that damaged when the file was made."

"I know," Simiaar said. "The files don't reflect the reality. Fascinating, isn't it? I suspect if we look for the other injured clone, we'd find the same thing."

Gomez frowned. She toyed with her food for a moment. She could understand doctoring the files to make TwoZero seem like he had chosen to remake himself in the image of a mass murderer. But there was no reason for that, not if TwoZero looked different. So someone was doing this to hide who he actually was.

"What about Thirds?" Gomez asked Apaza. "You found him the same way, right? Through his history?"

"Yeah." Apaza had a frown that was probably deeper than Gomez's. "Here's what's bothering me. If what Dr. Simiaar says is true, then I wouldn't have found these clones at all."

Gomez could read the thought that everyone suddenly shared. No one had known that the twenty men who looked alike but dressed differently as they arrived at Armstrong's port were going to do their best to assassinate leaders all over the Moon.

No one had known that from looking at them, and they had been grown, created, and deployed, after years of work. The reports that

Gomez had read stated that these clones were not fast-grow clones, which meant that they were as individual as TwoZero or Thirds.

They could have hidden in plain sight for years, if someone wanted the mission to work that way. They didn't have to arrive on the Moon on the same day.

"I don't like this," Nuuyoma said.

Gomez didn't either. None of them did.

"Then you won't like this either," Simiaar said. "TwoZero's DNA does not match that of the Armstrong assassins' DNA."

Gomez felt her breath catch.

Nuuyoma lifted up one of his hands, palm out, as if he were blocking that piece of information. "But you found the assassins' DNA in the records, right? And we should assume those records were tampered with, right?"

Simiaar was shaking her head before he had even finished. "I'm not going to assume that. The reports on the assassins' DNA were filed by twenty-five different sources, twenty of them on the Moon itself, at least one only an hour after the assassination of Mayor Arek Soseki. That would take a lot of planning, in my opinion, for someone to handle tampering throughout the system so quickly that it would cover any sign of tampering."

"It could be done, I suppose," Apaza said. "But I wouldn't want to try. Plus, a couple of these guys failed, right? And a few got caught—or their bodies got found or something? Wasn't the timing off?"

"It certainly wasn't a smooth operation," Gomez said. "If it had gone smoothly, we would have had a lot more dead. It had been designed to let the assassination trigger a panic, and then first responders and other emergency personnel would show up just as the bomb went off, destroying not just them but the dome as well—and an unprotected dome. If this had gone right, the main domes on the Moon would be completely obliterated."

"But they weren't," Simiaar said, "and the Moon shares information among its domes, or they started to when poor Celia Alfreda decided to found the United Domes of the Moon. It was her director of security—what's her name?"

"DeRicci, I think," Apaza said.

"Who insisted on the sharing of information, which means that someone would have found that footage of the clones arriving at the Port of Armstrong, even if the damn port got obliterated." Simiaar grabbed her half-full plate like a lifeline. "Which is all a long way of saying that, in this instance, I think someone *wanted* to blame PierLuigi Frémont, or at least his crazed followers. They wanted us to find those clones. So, back to Elián's very good original question, the files would not have been tampered with."

"That's a long way to go without facts," Verstraete said. "You're asking us to assume that whoever is doing this is hiding information on the one hand and revealing it on the other."

"And you're assuming that the same person, persons, or organization is behind those attacks and the warehousing of TwoZero and Thirds," Simiaar snapped.

"And neither thing is relevant to us at the moment," Gomez said, "although your point about different organizations is well taken."

Simiaar inclined her head in acknowledgement, although she kept her gaze on Verstraete.

"Does the different DNA point to that as well?" Gomez asked. "I'm afraid I'm not entirely clear on that. Are you saying that the assassins weren't clones of PierLuigi Frémont?"

"No, that's not what I'm saying," Simiaar said. "They're of a purer line. Maybe first generation clones, rather than clones of clones of clones."

"Great," Nuuyoma said softly.

Gomez shook her head. She'd spent her career studying non-human life, not clones. She knew very little about the intricacies of cloning because she didn't have to know it. She had more work looking at the universe outside of the Alliance rather than the worlds inside of it—including the cloned worlds.

"I'm still unclear on what that means, exactly. They're closer to Frémont? They're less damaged? They're more malleable? What, exactly?" Gomez asked.

"Nothing, exactly," Simiaar said. "It could be all of the above and none of the above. We don't know. Clones are as different from each other as siblings, no matter what the propagandists say."

"Some things are similar," Verstraete said. "Like a propensity for left-handedness or eye color."

"Although even the basic appearance stuff can be different from clone sibling to clone sibling," Simiaar said. "They can have enhancements like anyone else."

"So…?" Gomez didn't want to repeat the question, so she let that single syllable serve as the entire question itself.

"So," Simiaar said. "I'm thinking they're not made by the same group, person, ideologue, whomever. I'm thinking there's lots of Frémont DNA loose in the universe."

"There are supposed to be procedures to prevent that for mass murderers and other undesirables," Nuuyoma said.

"And there are supposed to be procedures for accurate logging of DNA for prisoners," Verstraete said. "We're seeing right now how well that's working."

Apaza shook his head in disbelief. "This is such a mess."

"It might not be as big a mess as you think," Simiaar said. "It doesn't take a lot of DNA to clone someone. So if you have any from the original source, and someone steals a little bit of it, that someone is going to make that little bit stretch."

"And maybe sell it to someone else," Nuuyoma said.

"So, you're saying we've stumbled on someone with a different agenda than taking on the Moon," Gomez said.

"We don't know that either," Simiaar said. "What we do know was that colony was really far away from the Alliance, at least at the time of the colony's founding. They were out there for a reason."

"Yeah, I think I know what that is," Nuuyoma said.

Everyone looked at him.

He pushed his plate away, his mouth twisted in disgust. "Someone was training those clones to be killers."

"I figured that," Gomez said. "That's why they hunted."

"Yeah," he said softly. "But that wasn't the first training session or the first deaths. It was just the oldest group of clones."

"They sent out children?" Verstraete asked.

"Yeah," he said, looking down. "And it wasn't pretty."

33

Z HU HAD ALREADY TAKEN THE SHUTTLE TO E ARTH A LLIANCE I NTRA S PECIES Court Special Circumstances Region 625 before he notified Trey that they were now lawyer and client. Zhu did not want Trey to convince some guard to allow him to come to the hearing.

The Special Circumstances courts had cropped up near the major prisons for hearings just like this. Most of the courts had several lower level magistrates who were on a career track. They had to serve their time here, shuffling documents and okaying standard procedure, before moving up to more interesting work in a "real" court.

Most of the judges he'd met who had worked in a Special Circumstances court let that fact remain in their personal histories, but never mentioned it in public and tried to downplay it. Zhu suspected that the judges who had worked in Earth Alliance IntraSpecies Court Special Circumstances Region 625 really downplayed their involvement here, because this court's nickname was Clone Court Primary.

The major clone cases came through here. The fact that Clone Court Primary wasn't near any of the maximum security clone prisons spoke to the lack of power that clones had, not the frequency of requests for a case review.

Only a few judges presided over these courts, and generally prevented the cases from moving to a district court or a Multicultural Tribunal. No one wanted these cases reviewed. No one wanted to think about what happened here. Most just followed the law, and stuck with what they knew.

Which was why, unlike the magistrates, the judges here were in their last years on the bench. The judges never had the careers they wanted, but if they served their time in Clone Court, they could retire on a head judge's pay with their title intact. Most head judges spent two or three years in places like Clone Court or some other special circumstances court, and then went back to the center of the Alliance, as if they'd truly achieved something, rather than being shunted off to the bottom of the legal system.

Zhu was counting on all of this as he put together his case. He had even contacted Salehi to find out which judge was the least risk-averse in Clone Court Primary. Salehi had thought the request amusing.

Got your spirit back, huh? he asked.

I feel like fighting again, yes, Zhu said. *When I return, I'd like to talk about some of your ideas regarding clone law.*

Salehi had laughed. *I'll be here.*

And then, a little while later, he had contacted Zhu with a name.

It hadn't been hard to get placement in that judge's court. Zhu had thought he'd have to sweet-talk someone in the courthouse. There was no court "house," just wings and sections of the base that operated as a unit. Zhu actually hated it when he had to use antiquated terms to describe something modern. But that was the law.

Fortunately, he didn't have to sweet-talk anyone. He got a hearing the very next day.

Which was why he had focused so hard to finish the presentation, but not why he had contacted Trey at the very last minute.

The shuttle arrivals in Clone Court Primary looked nothing like shuttle arrivals in the two courts where Zhu had spent most of his time—the Impossibles and the courts of the Tenth District. In those two courts, the arrivals area was filled with disoriented people and, in the case of the Impossibles, disoriented species. A lot of lawyers threaded their way through the arrivals, ushering families about, gathering witnesses, finding assistants.

Families came to watch proceedings, friends brought bail money—which had to be presented in person—and there were all kinds of security personnel everywhere, obvious and not so obvious.

Most everyone in shuttle arrivals in the other two courts had a reason for being there, even if they didn't know how to find their way to the proper courtroom.

But when Zhu stepped off the nearly empty shuttle at the Arrival Area listed for Judge Bruchac's court, he found himself the only person on the platform. The air smelled faintly metallic, probably from the shuttle's operating system.

As he turned to ask if he was in the right place, he discovered the shuttle's doors had closed and it was already gliding down the path to the next shuttle stop.

This Arrivals area at least had the right number. But the area itself was tiny. The walls were covered with grime, and Zhu saw no security personnel at all. Just one of the mouthless androids like the ones he'd seen in the prison, leaning up against the faux brick wall.

Zhu's stomach clenched, and for a moment, he felt out of his depth. But he'd been out of his depth in court hundreds of times; he couldn't worry about that. He was all Trey had, and more importantly, he was all Trey would *ever* have.

Zhu took a step forward. Glowing signs appeared in front of his links, instructing him on how to get to Judge Bruchac's court. For Zhu's viewing pleasure, the instructions came with a three-dimensional map that overlaid his eyes and that, he knew from experience, would take some effort to shut off. And the instructions also came with a lovely timer, telling him how many minutes he had until he had to start his argument.

Fortunately, he had arrived early enough to get lost twice, just in case the map overlay was confusing.

He followed the red arrows that led out a side door. As he walked, he nodded at the android, mostly because Zhu had always nodded at security people and he was just superstitious enough not to want to blow this.

The nerves were because he was in a new place and in a new court, not because he lacked faith in his argument. He'd been there before; he'd lacked faith in both the argument and the client more times than he wanted to think about. When he defended cases at the Impossibles, he lost, but when he defended corporate clients in the Tenth, he won more often than not.

Money had talked throughout human history, and it still talked.

Which explained the sheer emptiness of this place. Not only were the clients indigent, they weren't even human under the law. If a lawyer decided to defend some of these clones, he'd be taking on the rich, who either owned or created them.

But that was an argument for another time. This time, Zhu would simply discuss Trey—without Trey's presence. Because Zhu worried that if Trey arrived, he would destroy the entire argument.

Zhu's biggest worry was that Trey looking like the Anniversary Day assassins would count against him in court, no matter how fair the judge thought she was. Zhu himself had problems with it, which was another reason he did not want to see Trey during the argument.

Zhu wasn't going to mention who Trey's clone parent was. Zhu wasn't going to say much about Trey at all.

The key thing for a lawyer in any situation was to focus on the facts he could use, not the facts that would harm his case. Since he wasn't arguing *against* anyone—there was no prosecutor here—he didn't have to worry about hiding information.

Still, Zhu's heart pounded as he made his way through the maze of corridors leading to the judge's chambers.

Zhu had sent the message to Trey by the slowest route possible, sending it not only with a packet of other materials for the prison itself, but also sending it directly to the warden. The warden's office would funnel the announcement to some secretary who would examine it to make sure that the warden actually had to see everything in the packet. The warden (or most likely the secretary) would make note of Trey's representation for his file, then send the notification to the correct wing.

Someone there would send it to the cell block, and eventually, the notification would get to Trey.

Legally, all Zhu had to do was contact Trey before the arguments began. Zhu had to be the attorney of record the moment he walked into court—and Trey had to know that. Or, at least, Zhu had to have used best efforts to inform him.

If Trey later tried to argue that he didn't want Zhu representing him, well, Zhu had footage of that moment Trey begged him to take the case. That would work.

Zhu had represented people on less.

The judge's fiefdom was less of a slog than Zhu expected. He pulled open the doors and let himself in. The chambers contained a courtroom, a private conference area, and a private office for the judge. The visuals told Zhu that he was going to argue his case in the courtroom.

Which was empty.

He expected an audience. In the Tenth, the cases always had an audience—friends, family, reporters, historians, and hangers-on. Someone always cared about the outcome.

Judges never had an empty courtroom, because a judge's decision was often the first step in a march to the Multicultural Tribunal. The cases judges saw dealt with complexities in the law, complexities that the lower level magistrates never even thought of.

But of course this courtroom would be empty. It had very few spectator seats—only two rows. There were two large witness stands, floating next to the judge's bench, and two huge podiums where lawyers could argue their sides of the case.

Still, the courtroom was smaller than he expected.

At least the lights were on. He found that a little comforting.

A door on his left led to the judge's personal chambers. A door on his right obviously led to the conference area. The lights were off there.

Zhu was about to contact someone on his links to make sure he hadn't been given the wrong courtroom when another of those creepy security androids walked into the room, followed by two gigantic triangular robot units.

One of the robots had *court reporter* written on its side in Standard.

Then Zhu blinked and realized that the writing was yet another feature of that stupid map. Apparently, he wasn't supposed to understand how a courtroom worked.

It truly was amateur hour here.

The second triangular robot stopped beside the entrance they had used. *Reporter backup* was written along its sides, at least in Zhu's links.

He blinked hard, trying to shut off the stupid map. It would distract him.

He finally managed to shut it down, just as the door to the judge's chamber opened.

A short, round woman entered, clutching a tablet and adjusting her black robe. Her hair was dark, her skin unlined. Zhu would have thought her young if it weren't for the world-weariness in her eyes.

She mounted the steps to the bench, set the tablet down, and peered at Zhu. "I take it you're Torkild Zhu?"

"Yes, sir," he said.

"What the hell is someone from a firm like S-three doing here?"

"It's a long story, sir," he said.

"I have time," she said, as if her life were the most boring life in the history of the universe.

He didn't want her to have time. He wanted her to be harried and inattentive, like all the other judges and magistrates he had known.

"Are we on the record?" he asked.

She rolled her eyes and sighed dramatically. "Oh, you're one of those."

He didn't like that characterization, but he wasn't going to have a conversation that harmed his client if he was on the record. Not to mention the fact that he really didn't want to have the conversation in the first place.

"Just tell me this before we turn on all the official recording data," she said. "Who is paying for your services? Because my file says this clone has no resources."

She had a file. That was one step forward at least.

"That is correct, Judge," he said. "Prisoner Number 99373 has no resources. I'm handling this case pro bono."

"How the hell did a clone get someone from a place as prestigious as S-three?" she asked.

"Honestly, sir, he petitioned for a lawyer and I was looking for something outside of my normal routine." All of it true. None of it The Truth.

She narrowed her eyes and studied Zhu for a moment. Then she grunted.

"All right," she said after a moment. "And now we're on the record. Happy, counselor?"

"I'm pleased to be standing in your court, sir," he said, and hoped it wasn't a lie.

"All right," she said again, a little sarcastically, peering over her bench again as if she were making sure the robot court reporter was actually recording the proceedings. "Now you can argue whatever the hell this clone thought he should bother me with."

This was the best judge that Salehi knew in Clone Court Primary? Zhu would have hated to have drawn the worst judge.

"Begging your pardon, sir," Zhu said. "The clone—"

And how he hated to refer to Trey that way. It dehumanized him. But Zhu was going to go with the judge's language. It was better not to antagonize her.

"—wants me to argue a somewhat different case. I looked at it, and realized that since he—" Should Zhu have said "it" to square with the judge's prejudices? He didn't know, so he continued "—has no legal training and barely has an education at all, I figured I'd handle this my way."

"Which is why he is not here beside you," the judge said, answering his mental question with her pronoun.

"Yes, sir."

"Cagey, Mr. S-three."

"Thank you, sir," he said, even though he wasn't sure it was a compliment.

"What's *your* argument?"

"Well, sir, this clone is imprisoned for being an illegal. He has no identifying marks and no Day of Creation Document, as required by Alliance law. He has no idea who made him."

"Yeah, I saw that," the judge said.

"The problem, judge, and I detail it in the brief I sent you just now, is that this clone was found through the Eaufasse. They contacted the Frontier Security Service because the clone made a request they didn't understand. All of this occurred before the Eaufasse joined the Alliance."

The judge's mouth twisted in a wry smile. "Really, Mr. Zhu? You're going to argue that he's not illegal?"

"Yes, sir," Zhu said. "The record clearly shows that he was raised on Epriccom in an isolated settlement. It also shows through a series of interviews that occurred at the time of the FSS's first encounter with the clone that he had no idea that the Alliance existed. Nor had he encountered a human outside of his enclave before. Maybe not even then. The evidence suggests he was made on Epriccom, inside a domed enclave, along with dozens of other clones."

"To what purpose?" The judge asked.

"I don't know," Zhu said honestly. "It wasn't in the record. I'll be frank, Judge. I met with him, wasn't sure I wanted to take his case, and promised to read his file. That's when I realized that his imprisonment is not strictly legal within the Alliance. If he was manufactured—"

"—outside of the Alliance, he doesn't need Alliance identification, and if he's not owned by someone inside the Alliance—or wasn't at the time of his arrest—then he's not illegal in anyway. That's what you're going to argue, Counselor?"

"Yes, sir." Zhu felt warm. He was relieved no one else was in the courtroom. He couldn't tell if her sarcasm came from the law itself or was directed at him.

"I assume a big-shot attorney from S-three has all his facts straight? You've made sure there's no proof that this clone was made inside the Alliance?"

He was relieved to hear the question. It meant that she was taking him seriously. "Sir, I think the preponderance of evidence shows that

this enclave was trying to make clones *outside* of the Alliance, on purpose. The enclave got destroyed shortly after the FSS arrived, and the
destruction came from within. Someone was getting rid of evidence."

"Of what?"

He shrugged. "We don't know, and no one investigated. Apparently
everyone was more concerned with the Eaufasse's entry into the Alliance
than they were with solving the mystery of the enclave."

"And that's in the file too," she said.

"Yes, sir."

"And this file, how long will it take me to go over the evidence and
to read your brief?"

He didn't know how to answer that. Was she asking him if he was
thorough or was she asking him if he had been *too* thorough?

"It depends, sir," he said. "If you want to review the footage of the
initial interviews, it could take eight to ten hours. If you just want to read
the brief and scan the evidence, maybe two hours…?"

"Sounds like a waste of time," she said, and his heart skipped. He
didn't want her to rule against him, but it sounded like she was going to
do just that.

He tried not to look too upset.

"And," she added, "imprisoning clones costs money, especially in
medium-security facilities. We can't work the critters like we can in the
maximum security."

He was holding his breath. He made himself exhale.

"So I'm inclined to rule in your favor, Counselor. Does S-three need
a judge on the payroll?"

Oh, crap. Was this a quid pro quo? "I'm just a junior partner, sir. I
could check with the senior partners. I know they're always looking for…"

He let his voice trail off when he realized he was about to say "leverage."

"Well, we can't have a junior partner dictating things to the senior
partners, now can we?" she said, and he felt his case dry up and vanish.

Then her gaze met his and she grinned. *Grinned.* He'd never seen a
judge do that in court, at least with an attorney arguing in front of her.

"But you will put in a good word, right?" she asked.

"Yes, sir," he said.

"That's all I can ask." She nodded, the grin fading. "I will, of course, review everything. But unless I find something glaring, you'll have your order for release within the normal three weeks."

Three weeks? In all the other courts, motions for release could take place the same day.

"Make sure someone from your office is here to shepherd this clone out of the area. I don't care what happens to him," the judge said, "so long as he gets out of the sector. He really shouldn't even be in the Alliance. Is that clear?"

"Yes, sir," Zhu said, wondering how he could get her to gavel this down today. He didn't want to come back, even for a technicality. And he really didn't want her to see that Trey was related to Frémont. It might make her change her mind.

"Record off," she said.

That was when Zhu realized she didn't care if the quid pro quo was on the transcript. Was that as a possible escape in case someone questioned her ruling? Did that give one of the higher courts grounds to overturn something if Trey did something wrong?

Or did she really not care about anything anymore?

The robot powered down. Then it left the court room.

She watched it go. The android remained, but the other robot left too.

Zhu felt a little dizzy. That had gone better and stranger than he had imagined it would.

She watched them leave. When the door closed, she grinned again.

"You talk to your partners," she said, "and I'll have your clone ready for deportation. Deal?"

"Yes, sir," he said, and then because he couldn't do otherwise, he asked, "You're not going to review—?"

"Would you?" she asked. "Clone law is about as dry as it gets. I'll see you—or one of your staff—in three weeks."

Then she stood and stomped back to her office. The android left through a different door.

Zhu remained rooted in place for a moment. He was committed to helping her at S3 now. He'd have to tell Salehi. And if she hated work as much she intimated, she didn't belong in the firm's culture. Still, a former head judge on their roster would only help the firm, and she knew it.

It wouldn't be his decision. All he would ask Salehi was to postpone the decision until Trey was free.

Zhu let out a sigh, then packed up. He debated telling Trey that it had all gone well, and decided against it.

He didn't want to see that face again. He didn't want to think about what, if anything, he had just loosed on the universe.

At least, as a condition of his release, Trey would be banned from Alliance space. That was good.

Zhu stared at the bench. Maybe clone law wasn't for him after all. Or maybe he could argue theory somewhere else.

Or maybe this was Zhu's last hurrah. It certainly wasn't as much fun as he had hoped. Nor had he changed anything for anyone else.

He gathered his things and walked out of the courtroom. He tried to call the map back up on his links, but he had somehow erased it.

At least he was in no hurry to find his way back to the shuttle. Although he did want to get to that company space yacht. He wanted to indulge in comfort all the way home.

The one thing he did know: he wasn't coming back here ever again.

34

GOMEZ FELT THE PASTA SIT HEAVILY ON HER STOMACH. SHE'D SEEN TOO much over the course of her career to be completely shocked. "You saw children killing each other in the footage from Epriccom?"

Everyone in the cafeteria was watching Nuuyoma. He stirred his pasta with a spoon, but had stopped eating a while ago.

When he didn't clarify, she took that as a yes. She had known he wasn't lying. He *couldn't* be lying, not about this. Yet, it felt odd.

"I had previous deputies look at this footage fifteen years ago," she said. "How could they miss this?"

He set his spoon down. "I searched for laser fire. I didn't just eyeball it. Considering how much time they had, they were probably eyeballing."

She remembered. She had felt confused in those few days, like she often did with a case on the Frontier, pulled in many directions at once. Her mandate was to smooth over difficulties with any alien culture, to make sure that they knew about the Alliance in a positive manner, and of course, to make sure that she served justice for the humans who had somehow ventured deep into the Frontier.

"The computer helped me," Nuuyoma was saying. "I couldn't have eyeballed the laser fire. I wouldn't have been able to see most of it. I had to enhance a lot of what I saw."

He kept his gaze down, but she could see how haunted his eyes were. He would never forget what he had seen.

"So," Simiaar said to Gomez, "your friend TwoZero didn't tell you that, did he?"

Gomez hated the needling, but she wasn't going to rise to it. She wasn't sure what she would say. She finally understood why TwoZero had been so vague about his routines inside the enclave.

He had given her clues. He had stressed that they were being trained. He had said there were more clones when he was young than there were when she found the enclave. But he had never tied those together.

"No," Gomez said. "He didn't say a word about that. In fact, he led me to believe this was the first time the clones inside that compound had gone after each other."

Her words hung in the air for a moment. Then Verstraete shifted in her chair so that she was looking directly at Nuuyoma.

"Could that be true?" she asked him. "Could only some of the colony have been involved in the earlier attacks against the clones?"

Nuuyoma looked at Gomez first, maybe asking her to save him. But she wanted the answers as well.

Then he looked tiredly at Verstraete. "I don't see how only some of the colony could have been involved. It seemed to me that they were weeding down the kids, looking for…something. The most murderous? The most pliable? I don't know. And remember, I was just looking at visuals, and these kids really do look the same."

"God," Apaza said. Gomez didn't know if that was a comment, a prayer, or just a sound that Apaza hadn't even realized he was making.

"Well, we stumbled on something charming way back when," Simiaar said. "And now we have a lot of information that apparently we can't give to the Alliance. So what're we doing, Marshal Gomez?"

"Well, that's what we have to figure out," Gomez said. "I have some ideas, but I don't think we're entirely done briefing each other. I know I'm not. Have you finished, Elián?"

"No," he said, and then to Gomez's surprise, he smiled just a little. "A ship did leave the enclave before the enclave destroyed itself."

Gomez shook her head. Now she was feeling uncomfortable. Was he watching the wrong footage? Because she had had scanned through the footage of that enclave herself when she had been on Epriccom. When she had gotten the news that the enclave had destroyed itself, she watched the footage to make sure no one had escaped.

She had wanted so desperately to catch someone, anyone, whom she could blame for the horrors.

"We didn't see that," she said to Nuuyoma now. "And we were watching for it."

"You wouldn't have seen it," Nuuyoma said. "Near as I can figure, it left when Thirds asked for asylum."

"He didn't ask for asylum," Gomez said through gritted teeth.

"I'm sorry," Nuuyoma said. "When he asked the Eaufasse for protection."

Gomez stopped focusing on his words, and realized what he had just told her. Thirds had asked for protection *before* the *Stanley* had arrived. Even though the Eaufasse hadn't properly communicated it, that request was what had brought the *Stanley* to Epriccom in the first place.

Simiaar stood, then picked up her plate. She set it on the recycler, then grabbed some of the others. She had her back to the table when she said, "So let me get this straight. Thirds asks for protection. Then the Eaufasse contact the crazies inside that enclave?"

"They told me they hadn't," Gomez said, "and I don't think they could. I've been looking through the history of the relationship between the Eaufasse and the enclave, and to call it a 'relationship' is truly an overstatement. The people who wanted to start the enclave contacted the Eaufasse to figure out what it would take to acquire the land, and if the Eaufasse had any complaints about human usage of that land. When the Eaufasse said they did not, then that's when the enclave got started. I didn't see much after that, after all of the regulations got followed, not that there were a lot. The Eaufasse are pretty live and let live."

"The reports on them from the diplomats and scholarly teams that facilitated their admission into the Alliance say that they fight among themselves, and have so many tribes that it's not fair to call them the Eaufasse at all," Verstraete said. "So maybe they didn't have time to pay attention to what some small group of humans did."

"That's the impression I got," Gomez said. "If the human enclave had just taken care of itself and had no real impact on Epriccom, then we would never have known about it."

"Apparently, they didn't care about the deaths of the clones as much as Thirds' request," Nuuyoma said.

"Had those bodies you talked about appeared outside before?" Simiaar asked.

"Yes and no," Nuuyoma said. "They were killed outside of the enclave, then dragged back into the enclave. But from what I can tell, no one had ever escaped one of those hunting missions before. The twelve were still chasing Thirds. If they had caught and killed him, then they would have dragged all the bodies back to the enclave."

"Lovely," Apaza said. Now Gomez knew that these comments of his were deliberate. And she agreed with his sarcasm. This was horrible.

"I don't get it then." Simiaar had grabbed Gomez's plate, and held it just to her left. "You said the ship left *before* we arrived, but the Eaufasse and the enclave had no communications. How could both be true?"

There was still a lot of good food on that plate. Gomez took the plate back. "Most likely, the enclave tapped into the communications between the Eaufasse and the Alliance."

"It wouldn't have been hard," Apaza said. "Particularly if the Eaufasse weren't aware that they needed to encode messages."

"So someone or someones fled before you arrived," Verstraete said.

"It looks that way." Gomez hated this feeling of the floor slipping away beneath her, and yet she had chosen a job where that feeling happened all the time. It was almost like she was someone who loathed zero-g and decided to go into space anyway.

"So…what…? If the twelve didn't come back, the colony would destroy itself?" Simiaar returned to her chair. She had lost the protection of sarcasm. She was clearly disturbed by this, and didn't know how to comprehend it.

"I don't think so," Gomez said. "I would wager the colony was supposed to destroy itself at a specific time. If what you surmise is correct, Elián, then the most pliable and the most deadly clones were the ones who were left. And they were following orders."

"There's no way to know," Verstraete said.

"No, there isn't," Gomez said, "not without catching the initial perpetrators. And they fled Epriccom fifteen years ago."

"Yes," Nuuyoma said. "But I identified the ship."

Everyone looked at him. Simiaar leaned forward. "You *found* it?"

"Nope," he said. "I just have the name and the registration. I was tracking all of that when the marshal here called the meeting."

"Well, let's send you back to it," Simiaar said.

"Not yet," Gomez said, "because we have two other ships to deal with as well."

Nuuyoma took another slice of bread. Verstraete picked up her coffee mug. It looked like they were settling in.

"Another ship?" Apaza asked. "Like some other alien or something?"

"As in the ship that first established the enclave and the ship that brought its inhabitants," Gomez said. "Neither ship, by the way, stayed on Epriccom."

"You have the registrations for the ships?" Apaza asked.

"I do," Gomez said, "but remember, the information I have is thirty-one years old. I have no idea what's happened to those ships since."

"This information was in the files you examined from the Eaufasse?" Simiaar asked.

"The reports had everything detailed," Gomez said. "The Eaufasse had to provide information, after we showed up, to the Alliance teams working on the Alliance application. The Eaufasse provided a lot of information, most of it useless. But I'm hoping that the ships and their registrations aren't useless at all."

"You want me to trace them?" Apaza asked.

"I don't know yet," Gomez said, then looked at Verstraete. "Did you bring your map and timeline?"

"I did," she said, "but I need a clear table to show it to you."

Apaza and Nuuyoma took their plates off the table. Simiaar grabbed the food bowls. Gomez ate a few more bites of pasta, which tasted just as delicious at room temperature as it had hot, then set the plate on the table behind her.

Verstraete tapped the table's screen, which blinked into life. "Flat or hologram?" she asked Gomez.

"Flat at the moment," Gomez said. She wanted to see if the surviving clones had been anywhere near the part of space where the ships had originally been registered.

The map was multicolored, with each clone a different color and line. The timelines were detailed out. Verstraete tapped on one, and information rose in three dimensions.

"I had to ask Neil to help me set up the search," she said. "But once I had it, I was able to get a lot done. Thirds, for instance—"

"Let's not discuss Thirds yet," Gomez said, studying everything. She felt a surge of disappointment. She had hoped to see places she recognized from her investigation of the ships, but she didn't. There didn't seem to be any overlap between the travel the clones had done after they were captured and the ships that brought them (or the people who cloned them) to Epriccom.

She had hoped for that. Sometimes investigations were easy in that way. No one believed that anyone would take the time to trace information over the vast distances in Alliance space. In fact, she found those kinds of errors in her investigations more often than not.

But not this time. This time, either the arrest and imprisonment of the surviving clones were separate from the registration of those ships—meaning that someone else had taken the time to hide the clones—or the information was so old as to be meaningless. It could have been either thing, and she wouldn't know which—or if it was a third thing—without more investigation.

She studied the map for a long moment, knowing that there was information here she couldn't yet comprehend. She lifted her head slightly, and looked at Nuuyoma.

"Is there anything on this map that ties to the ship you found?" she asked him.

"No," he said. "I wish there was."

Probably not as much as she did. She could feel the clock ticking. She knew that she only had so much time to look for this before she had to report back to the Frontier. She wanted this investigation to go quickly— and it wasn't going to be quick or easy.

"All right then." She stood up and stretched, realizing in that movement that she had overeaten. She felt a little stuffed. "I want one more cross-comparison, and I want Neil to do it."

Apaza sat up as if she had told him to salute her.

"Neil, cross-check the registrations on these ships with places known to harbor companies that specialize in Designer Criminal Clones. It's going to require some digging in the legal archives, but you should find what I mean."

He nodded.

"I think he should look for suspected locations as well," Verstraete said.

"Good thought," Gomez said. "Let me know immediately if there's crossover."

She tried not to sigh. She didn't want the others to know how disappointed she was.

"You all did good work," she said. "Let's keep digging. I think we're on the right track."

They picked up their plates and their tablets, and slowly filed out of the cafeteria.

She watched them go. Then she watched the cleaning bots slide into place. The cleaning bots would obliterate any trace of this meal and this meeting.

Her heart skipped a beat. There was one more thing she needed to investigate.

Maybe the answers she was seeking were in the mess left by the destroyed enclave. The Alliance would have insisted on an orderly gathering of the data and materials from the remains of that enclave, and all that information had to be filed somewhere, probably in codes that Gomez wouldn't entirely understand.

But Simiaar would.

35

THREE DAYS. THREE DAMN DAYS SINCE THAT STINKING LAWYER HAD TALKED to him. Trey sat in the prison library, where he'd managed to find work, such as it was, and tapped at the computer screen on the wall beside him.

All information here was restricted. Each prisoner had to submit to a fingerprint and eyeball scan every time he tried to access information. In the case of Trey, who apparently shared a fingerprint and a retina pattern with at least two other prisoners in different cell blocks, he also had to type in his prisoner identification number.

Correctly. On the first try, or he'd be locked out for two days. He'd gotten to the point that he could type that information in his sleep.

As one of the librarians, he had access to most of the files here. But he couldn't hack his way into the message system. He didn't have the education, the training, or the willingness to spend time in solitary for disobeying the rules. He'd been in this prison—this cell block—long enough to appreciate all he'd earned.

It was, apparently, all he would ever earn.

He sighed. He checked the court records, but they still hadn't been updated. It was all last month's information. He couldn't find out if the lawyer had even registered with this particular court system. Without that, Trey couldn't even find out if someone named Torkild Zhu had tried to access information about Trey himself.

A month ago, Trey hadn't even contacted attorneys.

Not that he'd heard from any others either.

Not that he would know if he had heard.

The only reason he knew about Torkild Zhu from the very famous law firm with the stupid name was because the man had come to visit him. If others had just sent a message or something, Trey wasn't even sure it would reach him.

Sometimes the laws in the Alliance really defeated him. He wasn't anything, not property, not an existing being. Just a number, and a bunch of different numbers at that.

He had been trying for years to send a request to an attorney, and it had taken bombings on a massive scale and a threat to his life in the yard before anyone allowed him to send a message.

Mostly, he got to send that message so that the prison's legal ass was covered if he ended up dead in his cell after the whole airing of the Anniversary Day footage.

Or so he had believed at the time.

Now, he was beginning to wonder if the doctor had actually assisted him in sending that message. The doc was there when he'd cried out for a lawyer, and much as the doc hated the prisoners, he hated the rules here almost as much as Trey did.

The doc wanted to repair people like he could on the outside. Trey kinda suspected the doc wanted to do it to improve his medical skills, not because he actually cared about his patients, but it didn't really matter. The result would have been the same.

The doc couldn't really practice his craft on clones. He could patch them up, but he couldn't make them pretty. He couldn't use extraordinary measures to save their lives. He couldn't do a lot of things, and that frustrated him.

Maybe in the middle of that frustration, he had tried to help Trey.

Not that Trey would ever find that out either. It wasn't like the doc respected him or anything. The doc was probably just doing his job.

Or maybe some idiot in the prison administration was new, and was doing his job the way he would have done it at a "human" prison. Maybe Trey slipped through those proverbial cracks.

He rubbed a hand over his eyes. He tried not to feel discouraged, but it was hard. Because he was.

And he was angry and frustrated and sad.

Damn that lawyer, giving him hope.

Trey had survived for years without hope. He didn't know how to survive with it.

And he knew how it felt to have hope taken away.

He stood up, trying not to look too agitated. Becoming agitated might cause someone to take his privileges away.

He took a deep breath, then made himself sit back down.

He couldn't give up. Giving up would turn him into one of the pathetic prisoners he dealt with each and every day.

Maybe he should try finding those other clones. Maybe if the three of them banded together and pooled what information they had about their origins, they could try to get an attorney who wanted to help with the whole Anniversary Day investigation.

Or maybe Trey would be better off contacting some investigator on the Moon, someone who actually *wanted* his information rather than going through an attorney first.

Maybe Trey's links to the Moon, which was in the Alliance, wouldn't be blocked.

He had no idea, of course, but it might be worth pursuing.

He had resisted contacting the other clones of PierLuigi Frémont before. Trey had felt they had nothing in common. They weren't from the same batch—he had checked that much at least. Two of them had been in the system longer than Trey had. Their knowledge was even older than Trey's.

But maybe they were raised similarly. Maybe they had gone through similar training. Maybe they, as a group, had something to offer the investigation.

Maybe, if Trey figured all that out, he would be able to talk some law enforcement idiot into getting him a lawyer, rather than starting with the lawyer first.

He needed something. Because clearly that Zhu guy turned out to be a bust.

Trey couldn't even figure out why such a big name lawyer had contacted him in the first place—except maybe the Anniversary Day connection. When the Zhu guy found out that Trey knew nothing of true value, the guy just vanished.

Trey sighed and called up the prison records.

He would see what he could find about the others—if the system even let him search for them. If he could figure out who they were.

It would take him time.

Which, apparently, was something he still had a lot of.

36

THE MAP FLOATING BEFORE GOMEZ HAD SIX DIFFERENT COLOR LINES AND many different color dots. Apaza stood beside her, hands in his pockets, slouching. They were in her office, although they could have been anywhere on the ship for all she noticed.

Her gaze was focused on those lines. A bright red line ran from a starbase in a sector that Gomez had never seen before to Epriccom. A bright blue line ran from Epriccom to another moon near Epriccom, orbiting the same huge planet. A pale pink line ran from another starbase deeper in the sector where Epriccom was.

Those lines represented the ships. The red and pink lines were the ships that founded the enclave on Epriccom; the bright blue line marked the escape route for the ship that left the enclave.

None of the multicolored dots scattered around both sectors and inside Alliance space connected to the lines.

The tan, beige, and white lines left Epriccom and went either to a prison or to a hospital. In the case of the beige and tan lines, they went to a hospital first, and then to a prison.

Those locations were where the Epriccom clones ended up. None of these three lines crossed the first three lines, and none were in areas where designer criminal clones got made. None linked areas known for criminal activities at the time, and none were in areas known for criminal activities now.

Even the areas that PierLuigi Frémont had inhabited in his violent life were nowhere near these lines, and areas known for supporting his memory even now weren't near the lines either.

"Okay," Gomez said. "What's on that moon?"

"At the time the ship went there," Apaza said, "the moon was uninhabited."

"Now?" Gomez asked.

"Part of it is used for some mining operation," he said.

"See if there's a connection—"

"I'm looking into it, but I have no way of knowing," he said. "The corporation running the mining operation is only five years old. And, yes, I'm investigating its registrations and its ties to any conglomerates, but I'm turning up nothing so far."

Gomez frowned at it all. Lots of information, and none of it enlightening.

"And that base?" she asked. "Where the ships originated?"

"I can't find any information about it," he said. "At least in our databases."

She studied it all for another few minutes. She saw nothing that surprised her, nothing that helped her either.

"Thank you," she said to Apaza, dismissing him.

"You want me to shut the map down?" he asked.

She shook her head. "I'm going to stare at it for a while."

"Okay." He let himself out of the office.

She stared until the lines blurred, but it didn't help. The connections were tenuous, and they were old. Nothing TwoZero had told her helped either.

She had one more thing to try.

She used her private links to contact the *Stanley's* pilot.

Hey, Charlie, she sent, making certain that the link she used was secure. *I have some coordinates. I don't like what I'm seeing in the Alliance's database. You want to tell me what's in other databases?*

The star maps FSS pilots used had to come from a variety of sources, partly because the Alliance didn't map every non-Alliance sector, and partly because corporations and native groups often used their maps for misinformation. If a corporation didn't want the Alliance to know a starbase existed on the Frontier, then the corporation simply did not list it.

Such misinformation meant using Alliance maps outside of the Alliance was often a dangerous proposition. Ships could go into hostile areas without knowing it, or actually be on a collision course with an existing (but small) starbase.

Give the coordinates to me, Charlie sent. *You know I have to give you the usual caveats.*

He said that as if this were an official mission. On an official mission, he had to inform her every single time that the maps were simply of places, and often not much more. Occasionally they would show ownership or the name of a native group. Sometimes the maps would contain warnings specific to other groups which were not always human-focused.

In other words, the maps were "use at your own risk."

Consider the caveats understood, Gomez sent. And then she added the coordinates. She knew he could just input them into his navigation system with a little less than the speed of thought. *Got anything?*

The moon near Epriccom has a mining operation, he sent. *We'd need permission to land on that part of the moon.*

She nodded, even though she didn't have him on visual. *And the other?*

Hang on, he sent, which got her interest up right away.

She waited, staring at that little base, with the red line attached to it. Nothing in that part of the sector looked familiar to her. While she waited, she overlaid another map on top of the one Apaza had made. The overlay showed her travels throughout her career, something she kept just for her. If she were a different kind of woman, she would have had that map displayed on the wall of this very room.

But mostly, she liked to move forward, not back. She looked at the map with its overlay, and saw that it confirmed what she had already sensed.

Even though she'd spent decades traveling all over the Frontier, she had never gone to that part of it. She hadn't even been close.

She overlaid a third map on it, showing human-oriented FSS investigations in that part of known space.

The FSS had never officially gone that far out.

Okay, sorry to take so long, Charlie sent. *I was trying to confirm.*

Confirm what? she sent.

That base only shows up on Alliance maps, he sent.

That surprised her. Secret Alliance bases were on special maps, which she had used here. But this base was on *all* Alliance maps, which meant that no one inside the Alliance was trying to hide it.

She touched the holographic map, and watched the little base grow in size as everything else decreased. *What do you mean? Is someone else hiding the base? Are certain groups in the Frontier unwilling to go there?*

That's what I thought, he sent, *but that's not what I'm finding.*

What are you finding? she asked.

It's on some of the oldest maps from outside the Alliance, he sent. *It's got a dozen names, but it's there.*

Her heart was pounding. *But?*

But it's not on any of the new maps. Not at all.

Who's hiding it? She asked.

That's what I was trying to confirm, he sent, *and what I got were a bunch of net vids from twenty-some years ago.*

She felt chilled. Why would information make her feel chilled?

So something happened there, she sent. She didn't want to guess. A murder? A lot of murders? Some kind of criminal conspiracy? Maybe the ones her team had been looking for?

Yeah, something happened there, he sent. *Something huge.*

What? she sent, because it sounded like he needed prompting.

It blew up. And she heard something in his voice, although she might have imagined it. After all, the voice was filtered through a dozen systems before it went directly inside her head.

All of it? She sent.

She peered at that base in relation to other things in that part of space. The base didn't seem huge, but it wasn't small. Not like a ship. It would take a lot of coordinated effort to destroy an entire base.

Yeah, he sent. *Dozens of explosions, mostly at the same time. The dome was compromised and the ships on its rings were destroyed, and oh my God, would you like to see the footage?*

I would, she sent. Even though she had a feeling she had seen such footage before. Only that footage had been on Earth's Moon, decades later.

She rubbed her arms, feeling goose bumps along her skin. She wasn't just chilled now. She was *cold*. Ice-cold.

Clones of PierLuigi Frémont. A series of explosions. Destruction on a massive scale.

It was Anniversary Day. Twenty years before. On a base that no longer existed.

Except on maps, put out by the Alliance.

37

THE RELEASE ORDER ARRIVED IN ZHU'S MAIL EXACTLY TWO WEEKS after he left Clone Court Primary. He grinned to himself as he examined the document.

He had been right about one thing: that judge really wanted to leave the bench and join S3. She didn't know, of course, that Zhu hadn't even discussed her request with the partners. On the way back to S3, he decided he didn't want any appearance of impropriety on his side, so he wasn't even going to bring up her inappropriate request until the case was decided.

And even then, he would approach it all gingerly.

For a moment, he fought the urge to see Salehi. They really hadn't talked much since Zhu got back, and all of that was because of Zhu. He wasn't sure what he was going to do. He felt queasy whenever he thought of this case.

He remembered his excitement before he argued it, and then the judge's snide comments about clone law, the fact that she was aware of the arguments as if dozens of others had pursued it all before as well, and she usually turned them down.

Maybe that was why he kept silent about her desire to work at S3. Because she was so willing to trade one life for her career. He wasn't naïve—he'd seen that sort of thing before—but he'd never experienced it, and certainly not on a case he'd been passionate about.

And then there was the entire problem of Trey himself.

Zhu ran a hand through his hair and stood up. He sent for his assistant, but didn't want to be sitting down when she came into the room.

He'd been restless since he got back—hell, he'd been restless since he left Armstrong—and it wasn't abating. If anything, the trip to Clone Court had made the feeling worse.

His assistant Louise came inside the office, clutching a tablet like a lifeline. She looked ten years younger than he was, but she was as old as his grandmother. Louise's job here marked the beginning of her third "life-long" career, and she was using this legal assistant position as a stepping stone into one of the best law schools in the region.

She'd probably be working long after Zhu was dead.

Still, he couldn't get by without her.

"The prisoner release came through," Zhu said. His words echoed in the large space, and he realized the release hasn't felt real until just now.

Trey would be free to do whatever he wanted, provided he got out of the Alliance.

Zhu shivered. He hoped Louise hadn't seen that.

She was staring at him, her chocolate brown eyes never leaving his. She had never let her opinions be known about any of his cases, at least not aloud, but he had the sense that when she got her license, she wouldn't become a practicing defense attorney.

"It's our job to make sure he leaves the Alliance," Zhu said. "We have people for that, right?"

"We have several services," she said, "but we only use them for difficult cases. Usually the lawyer or an assistant handles the release."

He raised his eyebrows at her. "You want to go to that prison and lead a clone who has never been unsupervised to some distant place outside of the Alliance?"

Her lips thinned. "That's not my job, sir."

He almost smiled. He knew he could get her on that.

"However, we do have someone in-house, if you feel the need—"

"No," he said. "I need one of the services, and one that can handle a dangerous client."

"All right," she said, "but most of those insist on a couple things. Half the payment up front, money for the client to get started elsewhere, and expenses."

He nodded. He didn't care, but knew better than to say that.

Apparently, she could read him. "It should matter to you. This is a pro bono case, which means the firm spends a fixed amount. On a case like this, you'll be thousands out of pocket."

He suppressed a sigh. Thousands out of pocket sometimes made other attorneys travel with their clients. It was called *incentive*. Want to save money? Travel outside the sector on the law firm's money. Want to lose money? Hire someone else to do the dirty work.

Maybe if he had liked Trey, Zhu would have supervised Trey's release on his own. But Trey scared him, more so now. Trey had sent a video through Zhu's link, composed before Trey found out that Zhu represented him. The prison system either automatically or accidentally sent it to him. That video was filled with invective and a kind of anger that Zhu usually saw in the scariest of his criminal clients.

The out-of-control ones weren't the scary ones. It was the cold ones, the ones who eyed him like they could see into his soul, like they knew exactly what terrified him, and how to achieve that.

He had no doubt that Trey could see into his soul. Zhu even felt it through that vid. The only difference between Trey and all those other scary clients was that Trey probably didn't know how to terrorize Zhu.

At least, not yet.

Zhu hadn't heard from Trey since Trey received notification that Zhu was his attorney. Zhu had no idea how Trey reacted to the release information if, indeed, he knew it. Some prisons liked to keep that information confidential until just an hour or so before release. Doing that solved several problems. It prevented the newly freed former prisoner from carrying information to the outside, and it also prevented some disgruntled current prisoners from killing the new release in the days before he got out.

"Out of pocket, right," Zhu said. "Let's get the best service we got for this. I don't want trouble. This is the kind of case in which trouble would bounce back on us."

Louise's gaze stayed on his for a long moment. It almost felt like she had sent him a message through the links. *You should have thought of that before defending this creature.* That's what she would have said. But of course, she hadn't.

This time.

She had asked sideways if he considered what he was doing. But of course, that had been after he returned, after she realized that he had helped a clone of PierLuigi Frémont go free.

"Is that all?" he asked her.

"I suppose," she said.

He hated her tone. Maybe he would ask for a different assistant. Maybe he'd make a note in her file that she wasn't suited to defending anyone. Maybe he would let the partners know she wasn't worth recommending to any law school.

Of course, if they did that, then he might be stuck with her. And he couldn't face that judgmental gaze for much longer.

"Get this done," he said.

"Yes, sir." She let herself out of his office.

Maybe the problem wasn't that she was judgmental. Maybe it was that he felt guilty for getting this man out of prison.

He walked to the windows and looked out into space. He was doing exactly what he hated in others. He was prejudging someone. Trey clearly had been unjustly imprisoned. Trey had also defended himself. He could have unleashed those plant weapon things on the twelve clones at any point; he waited until they tried to attack him again.

Zhu leaned his forehead against the coolness of the window.

Maybe he did need time away from the law. Maybe he needed some counseling. After all, it was pretty clear that those Anniversary Day bombings affected him deeply, and he hadn't dealt with it.

The firm covered psychological services.

Time to take advantage of them.

Because trying to solve this one on his own simply wasn't working.

38

THE FOOTAGE LOOKED EERILY FAMILIAR, EVEN THOUGH IT WAS decades-old. An explosion, followed by another, and then another, in rapid succession.

Gomez remained standing while she watched all of it. Charlie could only provide two-dimensional imagery, so she watched it on the wall in front of her, the holographic map of the clone travels floating almost forgotten behind her.

Her office felt small and close, and it took her a while to realize that she was rocking from side to side as she watched. She didn't make herself stop; she needed to get some of the distress out somehow.

Much of the narration of the footage was in a language she did not understand. The translation into Standard was poorly done—the original narrator would speak for a minute, and then the translator would speak for maybe three seconds—but she gleaned enough.

Only the last part of that gigantic base attack completely mimicked the attack on Anniversary Day. In that part of the base, security personnel had run to find the bureaucrat in charge, some person with a name she couldn't quite decipher—a man, by the looks of the official portrait—and as they reached him, someone near him shot him with a laser pistol.

The security guards had shot that person, and then, as others were trying to get help for those wounded in the cross fire, the rest of the base blew up.

The vids she had watched were among the last transmitted off base.

Her stomach turned again. Instead of freezing the vid, she shut it off, and stared at the blank wall for a long time. Her arms were folded over her torso, her back aching from the awkward position. Slowly, eventually, she managed to stop herself from rocking.

All of this happened ten years after the ship that would take the clones to Epriccom left the area. Ten years.

A sample attack. Or maybe the real inspiration.

All the reports about Anniversary Day listed the bombing in Armstrong four years before as the practice event and/or as the inspiration, but what if it wasn't? What if it became part of the Anniversary Day attacks only because the leaders all over the Moon commemorated the survivors of that bombing, and the choices it led to on the Moon.

After all, the leaders on the Moon were working on unifying the Moon, and they had used that initial bombing to seize more power—in the words of some—and to solidify the Moon as a base around Earth—in the words of others.

She usually didn't pay attention to controversies that came from the center of the Alliance. There were hundreds, maybe thousands of them each day. But she kept a hand in, just in case she would find some of the disaffected political types out on the Frontier. She had to be able to talk to them.

Worse, she had to be able to talk to them as if they were rational, which most of them were not.

She finally sat down at her desk. She had to find a few things. First, she had to see if she could find even more explosions, to see if these bombers practiced elsewhere.

That she could do on her own. She didn't want her crew to dig in that area.

Besides, she had a set way she wanted to work. She wanted to see how the Alliance continued its fiction that this starbase still existed. If she found the same language or the same kind of data uploads elsewhere in the Alliance database, then she might have coordinates to hand to Charlie for his other databases.

She let the system search.

And while she did, she contacted Apaza through a secure link.

I know I had you search the ships' registrations to see if you could find the ships, she sent. *But did you find who owned them? Not the legal title information, but who the title actually traced to?*

His answer was immediate. *I looked at the registrations, but I didn't dig deep because they were old, and because I knew that old information wouldn't lead me immediately to the ships. You want me to dig?*

Yes, she sent. *I want to know the names of all the shell owners, the corporations, everything. If there is an "everything."*

With your permission, he sent back, *I'd like to investigate the payment records for those ships. It's easy to come up with a name to register ships in some places on the Frontier, but it's harder to hide who bought the ship. Even out in the wilds, it's hard to hide who buys something. Universal funds are rare, and the local currency—*

I know, she sent. She did, too. She understood that local currency could change from culture to culture, but almost every group near the Alliance took Alliance funds in one way or another. It was one of the few leverages the Alliance had to encourage membership.

Search for it all, she sent. *The more we know, the better.*

Then she signed off. She glanced at the Alliance databases now that her searches were done. She found nothing about the explosions, the destroyed base, or the causes of the violence.

The language about the base seemed pretty normal for something that far away from the Alliance. The only thing she found that was suspicious was an entry about the base from five years before. The entry sounded like someone had traveled there recently. But the posting was anonymous, one of those ubiquitous reviews that showed up about every corner of the universe.

As if the base still existed.

She would have Apaza investigate the listing as well.

She rubbed her hands over her arms. The chill hadn't gone away. Neither had the goose bumps.

She started to contact Charlie, to have him search his outside maps for more locations like this one—destroyed cities, destroyed bases, destroyed domes.

Then she stopped herself just before activating her link.

Everything on the *Stanley* was monitored. She'd shut off most of it, but not all of it. Even though she thought she had gotten everything, she wasn't certain about the cockpit. There might have been some really deep fail safes that she had missed. Maybe the cockpit couldn't entirely shut off its connection to the Alliance.

She would be alerting someone that she was on their trail.

If there was a someone within the Alliance whom she should worry about.

If there was a trail.

She moved the holographic map back into place.

She needed to go to the second moon.

But she would do it under the guise of something else entirely.

No one would blame her for investigating the clones she had discovered on Epriccom. Everyone would assume she was looking into the connections with Anniversary Day.

After all, who wouldn't look?

They would simply think her oblivious to the links to the Alliance.

If she played this right.

She needed to play it right.

She needed to talk to the Eaufasse first.

39

RAFIK FUJITA HATED THESE JOBS THE MOST. TRANSPORTING FORMER prisoners always entailed some kind of problem, usually caused by the prisoner himself. The prisoner expected freedom, expected that he could order Fujita around, expected that he would be able to do whatever he wanted from the moment he boarded Fujita's ship.

Fujita carried a full crew on cases like this, and the crew knew how to handle former prisoners and troublemakers.

Usually, though, Fujita carried former prisoners with enough clout to hire S3 and to get out of prison, whether the charge was just or not. He'd never dealt with a clone prisoner before, and certainly not one like this.

Zhu had warned him that the clone would look like the clones that harmed the Moon. Zhu also paid a little extra so that the clone—whom Zhu said to call Trey—would be as far from Alliance space as possible.

Fujita loved working for S3, so he would follow orders. Even if he had to imprison that deadly clone all over again.

He'd been reading the file that Zhu provided. The clone seemed harmless enough. But Fujita had dealt with enough so-called harmless prisoners to know that what a former prisoner seemed like and what he actually was were often two different things.

But Fujita was as prepared as a man could be. He owned five different ships, and he was using the Alus 15, the most complex, for this mission. The Alus 15 had a double-reinforced frame, so that it would survive most standard weapons attacks. It had a sophisticated internal security system that could determine if a marked passenger acted strange or out of line—and Fujita would certainly mark this clone.

The internal security system would also detect common bomb manufacturing and standard weaponry, and isolate anyone not authorized to use such things on a ship.

All of the weaponry that Fujita's people had—and he had two dozen highly trained warriors on the Alus 15—was keyed to their DNA, so if they lost a grip on their weapons, then those weapons went out of commission. No stealing anything.

Fujita didn't have back-up weaponry anywhere that wasn't tied to his staff, although he did have some additional firepower built into the Alus 15 itself.

If, somehow, someone was able to take over the Alus 15, then that person could, in theory, use the ship to attack another ship.

But that would take a lot of work, and many, many things would have to go right for the attacker.

In fact, almost everything would have to go right.

Everyone on this ship could pilot it, just like everyone could man the external weaponry, and everyone could defend the interior. The crew that Fujita had chosen for this mission had worked together off and on for more than thirty years.

He figured they'd do all right.

Fujita had been to clone prisons before, but never to pick up a clone. He'd dropped off guards, and picked up Salehi back when the man was practicing a lot more law than he'd been doing of late.

Fujita missed Salehi. He liked working with the man. Salehi was a bit of an idealist, but he was a risk-taker too. He'd gotten disillusioned during some major cases. Fujita had actually tried to talk him down, to make him feel better, but to no avail.

So Fujita continued to work for S3, hoping Salehi would come back. But Fujita had a feeling he might not. Fujita didn't really like the other partners, and he hadn't liked Zhu at all.

They'd had an uncomfortable meeting. Zhu had apparently done a good job for his client, and then regretted it. Fujita thought it a strange attitude for a high-level defense attorney.

So Fujita tried to have the right attitude, the attitude that Zhu clearly didn't have. Fujita told himself that it didn't matter what the former prisoner had done or what he would do in the future. What mattered was that for this short window of time, the former prisoner was a man who needed transport and maybe a bit of coaching on life on the outside.

Fujita had coached dozens of people on how to make it after a lifetime in prison. He'd try to do the same—with compassion—for this Trey, no matter what the guy looked like, no matter who his DNA said he was.

None of that stopped Fujita from reading up on PierLuigi Frémont or preparing for the worst. He suspected that if Trey was going to be bad, he'd be bad in his own way. Fujita would be prepared for all of it.

S3 paid him to anticipate, not to be surprised.

As much research as he had done on the way to EAP 77743, he better not be surprised.

The prison expected him in exactly twelve hours. He would arrive within eleven.

He'd learned the hard way that being on time was often too late. Some guards took advantage of that last hour to ensure that a prisoner wouldn't get his release. Arriving early was the best thing.

Early and unannounced.

He prepared his identification, his court orders, and his arguments. He prepared the maximum security cell in the bowels of the Alus 15 in case this Trey turned out to be a raving lunatic. Fujita prepared the minimum security cell two levels above the max cell in case this Trey didn't want to leave the Alliance.

Fujita prepared for every contingency, including the one he couldn't foresee—whatever that was.

He knew something might go awry here.

That's the one thing the file told him. The release had been too easy. That judge had cooperated on the record, clearly saying she would take a bribe. But she never received that bribe because Zhu was too cowardly to tell his companions at S3.

Although Zhu had said he didn't want to seem like he was taking advantage of the "quid pro quo" the judge had offered.

Fujita always kept his own counsel with delusional lawyers. And Zhu seemed more delusional than most. He didn't seem to understand that by getting this Trey released, he had already taken the quid pro quo. He just had to provide his pro quo or quid or whatever the proper terminology was.

If that judge ever got a job at S3, then Zhu would forever be on the hot seat.

The man seemed to have convinced himself otherwise.

Not that it was Fujita's business.

Fujita had done his due diligence—except for the interview with Trey.

And that would happen shortly after Trey arrived on board.

It wasn't fair to say that Fujita was looking forward to that moment. But he was anticipating it. Because, his experience had taught him, once he'd acquired the prisoner, his work was 95% complete.

40

EPRICCOM LOOKED NOTHING LIKE IT HAD FIFTEEN YEARS BEFORE. DOZENS of small bases orbited the moon, all of them affiliated with some Alliance corporation. The *Stanley* got through the beefed-up space traffic control regulations easily because it was an Earth Alliance ship, but Gomez could see how hard it would be for non-aligned ships to enter Epriccom's space.

The Eaufasse appeared to be in charge of all of the contacts, even though there were fifteen other sentient species on Epriccom. Gomez hadn't really studied the changes—she didn't expect to be on Epriccom long—but she hoped Simiaar had.

They landed in an actual Alliance-approved port, with the standard regulations that all Alliance ports had. The port was small, but the small crew Gomez had brought with her had to go through everything from document check to decontamination to the hiring of a certified Eaufasse guide, none of which she'd had to go through fifteen years before.

This is creepy, Simiaar sent Gomez privately.

We rarely see what we've wrought, Gomez sent back, hoping the wry tone made it through her linked communication.

No kidding, Simiaar sent back.

They were walking side by side through the port's main arrival area. Nuuyoma and Verstraete walked behind them. Apaza had stayed on the

Stanley, ostensibly to help facilitate any research that they needed from the surface, but primarily because he hadn't finished searching the financials yet. The ship registrations had led to nothing, but the financials, he said, were "promising."

The walls of the port depicted scenes that Gomez's links told her came from Eaufasse history. Most of the scenes looked like battles, but she couldn't tell, really.

The Eaufasse certainly seemed less alien than they had at that first encounter. Some of the Eaufasse now wore robes instead of tight material over their torsos. The robes hid a lot of their differences, from the length of the arms and legs to the sexless characteristics of that torso.

Only their liquid eyes and small size made them seem obviously different.

The guide walked quickly, taking the team to a building attached to the port. On the maps of the area drawn up in Standard, the building was called The Alliance Center for Harmonious Relations. Gomez had no idea what the actual name of the place really was.

The corridors leading from the port to the Alliance Center were wider than the average Eaufasse corridor—at least the ones that Gomez remembered. She remembered weird window-shaped things, inexplicable doors, ceilings just a bit too low, and the buzz of a language she did not understand.

Instead, this place looked like it could be dropped anywhere in the Alliance, with corridors wide enough to accommodate the Rev. She understood most of the conversations, but then most everyone in the port was human, Peyti, Gyonnese, or LaBotian. She hardly saw any Eaufasse either, although she realized halfway to the Alliance Center that she simply had taken many of the ones she had seen for human, because of the robes.

Other natives from Epriccom hugged the walls or didn't seem to appear at all. They often watched from restricted areas.

She usually prepared before she arrived at a new place, but she hadn't considered Epriccom new, considering what she had gone through here.

Now she realized that her entire attitude toward this trip here was a mistake.

She sent to Simiaar on their private link, *You want to abort this one?*
Getting cold feet? Simiaar sent back.

I wasn't prepared for all the changes, Gomez sent.

No worries, Simiaar sent back. *I was. I'll go head-to-head with them.*
You handle the other thing.

She hadn't referred to the trip that Gomez really wanted to take because both of them had learned that in places like this, sometimes the
most secure link could get hacked.

Gomez nodded and followed their guide up a flight of human-sized
stairs and into a brownish-beige corridor. Some of those rectangular
window coverings decorated the walls here, and the net effect was just a
bit more like that outpost where she had first interviewed Thirds.

A nearly invisible door slid open, filling the corridor with the scent
of dried mud and chocolate.

An Eaufasse wearing something that looked like the uniforms of old
opened its long arms wide.

"Mar-shal Gomez," it said with what she took to be joy. "Wel-come.
It be long years."

Gomez compared the old memories she had downloaded into
her current data stream with a recognition program that should have
worked for Eaufasse.

This was the Eaufasse who had led them to Thirds. Gomez couldn't
pronounce the Eaufasse's name. She wasn't sure she had even known it
back then.

"I learn Stan-dard bad," the Eaufasse said proudly.

"I think you learned it well," Gomez said. "Would I offend you if I
give you a standard Earth handshake?"

"Hon-or-ed would be I," the Eaufasse said, and extended its hand.

Gomez couldn't remember touching an Eaufasse before. As her
hand hit its skin, she was pleased to discover that the texture was as soft
as fine silk. Still, Gomez was careful to grip lightly, shake once gently,
and disengage.

"I am honored that you came to see us," Gomez said.

"Un-fin-i-sh-ed bus-i-ness we," the Eaufasse said, then peered at the other three members of her team. "New?"

It took Gomez a minute. "Two of them have not been to Epriccom before. But Doctor Simiaar was with me the last time."

"I don't think I ever left the ship," Simiaar said, then bowed slightly. "Meeting you is my pleasure."

"My yes," the Eaufasse said, bowing back.

Simiaar looked at Gomez, as if she didn't really understand. *It's okay,* Gomez sent.

"Talk us a-lone?" the Eaufasse asked Gomez.

"I'd like Dr. Simiaar to come with us, if possible," Gomez said. "She's very familiar with your culture. And she's the one who encouraged me to come here again."

The Eaufasse's gaze shifted to Simiaar. The Eaufasse's eyes seemed even more liquid for a moment. Then it nodded.

"Yes," it said. "No Pey-ti?"

Gomez smiled as she understood. "That's right. I didn't bring my own translator. I can send for one if you think I need one."

"No, I have trans-late," the Eaufasse said. "Right all?"

"Yes, that will work." Gomez turned to the other two. "You two can probably get something to eat or just look around. We'll send for you when we need you."

As she said that, she sent, *It'll take maybe an hour, so stay close.*

Nuuyoma nodded. Verstraete looked like she didn't need to be told twice. She was already looking down the corridor.

The Eaufasse ushered Gomez and Simiaar into a room that was as bland as the corridor. Gomez's links didn't detect any unusual recording devices. She assumed everything in this Alliance-built building would be up to Alliance standards, so she should be able to find something out of the ordinary.

She wasn't sure if that was a safe assumption, but she wanted it to be.

Another Eaufasse stood near the back of the room, wearing a light blue robe, its hands clasped together. It was younger. Gomez only knew that because she had just compared the fifteen-year-old images of the first Eaufasse to that Eaufasse now, and realized that its skin had become grayer and more elastic.

This Eaufasse had skin that was taut, at least around its face.

"Marshal," it said with no decipherable accent at all. Standard spoken as—well, as standard as possible. "I am Oaupheau. I will act as your translator, with your permission."

"Thank you," Gomez said. "You have my permission."

She was recording everything. She hoped Simiaar was doing the same.

There were four chairs in the room, two normal human chairs with a flat seat and a flat back, and two Eaufasse chairs that looked like mushrooms growing out of the floor.

"I have been chosen for my discretion," Oaupheau said. "Mir Munshi trusts me with his life and now yours. In return, I give you my oath that I will not reveal anything said here on pain of death."

In the early years of her command, Gomez would have politely stated that such extremes weren't necessary. Now, she had learned to respect cultures that insisted on such things.

So she acknowledged Oaupheau's statement with a polite response, while pondering what else it (he?) had told her. He had used an old Earth title for someone who ran a foreign office. She had had to learn most Earth forms of address, old and new, because different cultures translated the names of their leaders using words they found in Earth histories, for accuracy.

She wasn't sure how accurate this title was, but considering the precision with which Oaupheau spoke Standard, she had a hunch the title was as accurate as the Eaufasse could make it. That title made sense. She wondered how much work it had taken to find the proper title to translate into Standard.

Oaupheau had also given the Mir Munshi's gender as male. Gomez had never been able to tell gender with the Eaufasse before, so she appreciated that.

Mir Munshi spoke Fasse to Oaupheau, while keeping his gaze on Gomez.

"With your permission, Mir Munshi would like to begin the important conversation now," Oaupheau said.

"That would be good," Gomez said.

Simiaar remained seated quietly beside her, watching everything and listening as Mir Munshi spoke.

"Mir Munshi says since you last met, he has learned much about your people. Before you met, he thought that your people looked very similar. It was because of the enclave, as you recall."

"I remember," Gomez said. "We had figured as much."

Oaupheau spoke slowly as it translated. The only thing she wished was that she could somehow monitor what it said so that she knew if it were a good translator or not.

"Not long ago, Mir Munshi saw the images of the destroyers of your moon."

Gomez was about to correct Oaupheau, to say that the Moon hadn't been destroyed, but Oaupheau didn't pause long enough for her to add that.

"Mir Munshi recognized the faces, but confirmed with our technology the look of those evil ones is the look that we saw daily on Eaufasse fifteen years ago and more."

"Yes," Gomez said.

"Mir Munshi believes this is why you are here."

"Yes, it is." Gomez spoke to Mir Munshi, not to Oaupheau. "We have reviewed the information from our first encounter and believe that somehow what happened on Epriccom is related to what happened on Earth's Moon fifteen years later."

"Mir Munshi believes that such an attack strikes at the heart of the Earth Alliance, which we are now part of. He wishes to know if his belief is correct."

Mir Munshi sat with his hands at his side. He swayed slightly on that mushroom-like chair, but his gaze never left Gomez's.

"It is correct." Gomez knew that, even with a translator, she had to choose her words wisely.

"Mir Munshi says there is much material that we need to share with you. It is investigative and very old, but might prove of value."

Gomez felt her heart jump. Simiaar shifted slightly beside her, and Gomez wanted to caution her not to look too enthusiastic. But she didn't communicate with Simiaar. Gomez didn't even want to look at Simiaar at the moment.

"We would appreciate that," Gomez said.

"Mir Munshi would like to be candid." Oaupheau paused for what seemed like effect. It glanced at Mir Munshi, almost as if confirming this next part. Mir Munshi waved a finger. Oaupheau waved the same finger in return.

If Gomez hadn't been trained to watch for the smallest of movements, she would have missed that.

"Mir Munshi tried to reach his contact at the Alliance, but was told what occurred fifteen years ago has no bearing on today."

Simiaar became rigid, obviously thinking that if she moved, she would give something away.

Gomez wasn't sure how to respond either.

"Mir Munshi believes you are not here because that representative sent you, but because of your own ethics, morals, and desire to do the proper thing. Mir Munshi says that even the Alliance has factions as the Eaufasse do."

Gomez remembered being told that the Eaufasse tribes had different ways of functioning from each other. She also remembered their difficulty with the Standard word "justice" as applied to a force like the marshals. She wondered if that was because of the primitive translations of the time or if it had to do with the differences in their cultures.

Now, she wished she had prepared more for this meeting. She had believed she would have a perfunctory discussion and go to the second moon of Q-Teril, the planet below. She had not expected this.

"Mir Munshi is correct," Gomez said carefully. "Despite its rules, the Alliance sometimes deals with factions within its ranks, which causes the occasional problem."

Oaupheau glanced at Mir Munshi again. Mir Munshi continued to watch Gomez, but he moved a second finger. Oaupheau moved the same finger, then said, "Mir Munshi must apologize. When you first came to Epriccom, the Eaufasse gave you only the information you requested. We were concerned that you would not allow us to join your Alliance, which has greatly benefitted our people. We are grateful to you and your people for all we have received from the Alliance."

"Thank you," Gomez said, not sure where this was going.

"We have much information on the enclave that arrived. We have even more on its predecessors."

Gomez felt the blood drain from her face. She hadn't realized there were other enclaves.

Simiaar hadn't moved at all, but Gomez could feel the tension she was radiating.

"We weren't aware there were predecessors," Gomez said, wondering if she should have admitted that.

"Mir Munshi thought that might be so," Oaupheau said. "He tried to inform your Alliance, but they believed that old cases did not matter to new problems. We believe the problems are not new, but old."

"May we have the name of your contact in the Alliance?" Gomez asked.

"Our contact is not the difficulty," Oaupheau said. "Our contact is the ambassador to Eaufasse. The ambassador has done all she could, even traveling into the Alliance to speak with her superiors. She is there now. She has told the Emir repeatedly that she believes such information is important, and she will get someone to come to Epriccom. At first Mir Munshi thought you were that someone, but we received a message just this morning from the ambassador saying she is still doing what she can. That is when we realized that you are not here to investigate for the Alliance."

Gomez actually heard Simiaar swallow. She tried not to let her friend's nerves infect her.

"Well," Gomez said, "that is not entirely the case. We believe that some faction in the Alliance is blocking the information from reaching its proper destination."

Mir Munshi made a peeping noise that Gomez hadn't heard since she'd last been to Epriccom. It was so high pitched and strong that Simiaar scooted her chair backwards. Gomez caught Simiaar's arm and sent, *That's a normal sound for them.*

Lovely, Simiaar sent. *Tell that to my ears.*

"Mir Munshi believed that to be the case. He had hoped to contact you but did not know how to find you. He is relieved that you have found us."

Gomez smiled and nodded. "I am relieved as well. I am grateful that you are willing to talk with me."

"Mir Munshi would have asked for you if the ambassador had been successful. After you left Epriccom, Mir Munshi spent years studying your concept of justice. We are amazed that you have many organizations dedicated to justice. Mir Munshi is amazed that some of these organizations disagree as to what justice is. He did not understand the reason for the differences until he tried to help with justice for the victims on your Moon."

Gomez didn't know what to say. She knew better than to try to justify what happened within the Alliance. It was too big and too complicated. Usually, when she talked to groups outside of the Alliance, she told them that the Alliance was unified in its goals, but sometimes disagreed on how to achieve those goals, and that such disagreement was healthy within the Alliance.

But the Eaufasse had gone beyond such platitudes. At least Mir Munshi had.

He had continued to speak, his liquid gaze remaining on hers.

Oaupheau waited just a moment, as if he expected Gomez to say something, and then nodded before launching into the translation.

"Mir Munshi will help in any way you believe useful. We have a great deal of information, all of it old, on the humans who first decided to set up the enclave. We have financial records and vid histories, some badly done interviews, and histories of their ships. Mir Munshi believes you will want this."

"Thank you," Gomez said. "I didn't realize you had it, or I would have asked for it. We've spent days trying to find that information on our own."

"Our people were concerned that these humans wanted to build on our soil. They promised that they would not interfere with our lives here or our businesses. They also promised that the moment such interference became inevitable, they would leave."

Mir Munshi made another peeping sound, although not as loud or as piercing. "It would seem leave what they do," he said directly to Gomez.

"Yes, you're right," she said. "We're beginning to believe that they left when they realized that you had contacted the Alliance to seek help for the boy who had asked to be protected from the enclave."

Mir Munshi nodded, a movement that looked odd, so Gomez knew he had done it deliberately for her. "The same," he said.

Strange how she could understand someone even when he wasn't speaking clearly.

He just told her he believed the same thing.

Then he looked directly at Oaupheau before saying something else in Fasse.

"Mir Munshi says we have reviewed our records. Originally, the humans did not mention the Alliance at all. The second group of humans told us that they would not bring the Alliance to Epriccom, as if it were a promise that we would value."

Oaupheau raised all of its fingers, then threw an arm over its shoulder.

Ew, Simiaar sent. Gomez didn't look at Simiaar, but she hoped that Simiaar wasn't grimacing. Gomez remembered the first time she had seen that movement. It looked like the shoulder shattered. She had been disgusted by it then.

Truth be told, she was still disgusted by it, but it no longer surprised her.

Mir Munshi spoke directly to Oaupheau, and then tossed both arms over his shoulders.

Oaupheau bowed its head and let its arm drop.

It said, "Mir Munshi would like you to know that we had not heard of an Alliance before that mention. Our people then began the research into the Alliance. We liked what we saw. Those interactions were the first that made us worry about the enclaves. We worried that they might be wrong-doers of some kind, but we did not know what kind. By then, they had been on Epriccom for many years, and had not harmed or even interacted with our people."

"So you decided to leave them alone," Gomez said, as a statement to get it to continue, not as a question.

"Yes," Oaupheau said. "We thought perhaps it was a faction against this Alliance we had not heard of, and thought maybe it wanted to be isolated."

Then Oaupheau seemed to realize that it had spoken for Mir Munshi. It tossed both arms over its shoulders, bowed its head, and spoke softly.

Mir Munshi replied, but Oaupheau did not translate.

"Strange this after," Mir Munshi said directly to Gomez. She guessed he meant that things became strange after they started contacting the Alliance. Then Mir Munshi made a thwapping sound and spoke harshly to Oaupheau.

Oaupheau kept its arms back and head down. "I have spoken for myself, although I am correct," it said. "I must apologize."

"We accept your apology," Gomez said.

Oaupheau dropped its arms. "Mir Munshi says that things changed after we discovered this Alliance and started communicating with it. It had been our understanding that the enclaves would grow, but they did not."

Gomez met Mir Munshi's gaze. He nodded slowly. Simiaar shifted slightly beside her.

"Mir Munshi says you had asked if there were other deaths. There had been, but none that we witnessed up close."

Gomez frowned. She hadn't asked about other deaths. And then she remembered. She had asked when she had come the first time.

"We did not believe those deaths were what you meant, but Mir Munshi believes it now. We have footage, but no longer keep what you would call, I believe, 'evidence'?"

"Footage is helpful," Gomez said, trying not to sound too eager.

Ask about that last enclave. What did they do with that evidence? Simiaar asked.

Gomez wasn't going to do any such thing. She was going to let this conversation evolve.

"Mir Munshi believes that the enclave monitored our external communications. When we started talks with your Alliance, the enclave retreated farther. Mir Munshi believes that these talks may have triggered those initial deaths which brought you."

"With due respect," Gomez said, facing Mir Munshi directly. "I have recently interviewed one of the surviving clones. He says that such killings were part of their hideous training rituals. You should not take any blame for those deaths."

Mir Munshi nodded and swayed.

Oaupheau waited until Mir Munshi was done. "Mir Munshi says we are not taking 'blame.' We do not have the same concept of guilt that humans do. But Mir Munshi believes there is a cause and effect. He has studied the footage we will give you. He sees no releases like that in previous enclaves. But he admits that such things might have their own timetable, and he is unaware of what that might be. His core message to you is simple: he would like to help."

It took Gomez this long to realize that never once did Oaupheau say that the Eaufasse wanted to help. In fact, at times, Oaupheau very clearly said that Mir Munshi had determined something, believed something, or wanted something. A few others times, Oaupheau had said "we" when referring to the Eaufasse.

She wished she knew just a little Fasse so that she could ask Mir Munshi if he was acting alone.

But, she supposed, that did not matter. What mattered was that Mir Munshi wanted to help, and she needed his help. The *Alliance* needed his help, whether it realized that or not.

"We greatly appreciate your willingness to assist us," she said to Mir Munshi.

He bowed his head, looking like he might topple over.

"We would love to review the materials you have for us. We would prefer to take them with us, if that is possible. If not, we understand."

We do? Simiaar sent. Gomez ignored that, like she ignored all the other comments Simiaar had made in this interaction.

Mir Munshi spoke for a moment. Oaupheau replied in Fasse, then flung its arms back again.

Mir Munshi leaned toward Gomez. "Take you may," Mir Munshi said. "Honored to help."

"Thank you," she said. "We are honored as well."

Ask about the damn site, Simiaar sent, as if Gomez had forgotten the reason for coming here.

"I do have two other requests," Gomez said. "If it is not possible to fulfill those requests, we understand. You will not offend us by saying no to any of our requests, and I hope we do not offend by asking."

"Ask no me offend," Mir Munshi said.

Oaupheau had bowed its head. Gomez didn't want to think about what might be happening here diplomatically.

"We have traced the ship that left the enclave just before it got destroyed to Ohksmyte," she said, hoping she pronounced the name of the second moon correctly. "We were wondering if you know anything about why it landed there."

Mir Munshi spoke harshly and rapidly in Fasse. Oaupheau kept its head down, but moved its arms. It said, "We do not know why it landed, but we know where it is. Mir Munshi believes it might tell you something."

"Forgive me," Gomez said, as she interrupted. "Is he saying that you know where the ship *is*?"

"Yes," Oaupheau said. "It did not leave Ohksmyte."

"Did the occupants transfer ships?" she asked.

Oaupheau spoke to Mir Munshi. Mir Munshi answered in rapid Fasse again.

"No one investigated that. We located the ship. It has remained in the same place for fifteen years."

Wow, Simiaar sent.

Wow, indeed. Gomez tried not to look thrilled at the news.

Oaupheau continued, "We will give you coordinates, but you must exercise caution. The mining operation on Ohksmyte is protective of the dome they have built there."

"How old is that dome?" Gomez asked Oaupheau.

"It did not exist when the ship landed," Oaupheau said.

She nodded, then realized it had not answered her question. She didn't need to press. She could find the answer to that question in some other way.

"My last question has two parts," Gomez said, "and I ask them for my friend, Doctor Simiaar. She would like to inspect the enclave's grounds, if they have not been built upon or excavated."

Oaupheau made a small peep as if the request startled it. Then it spoke, as if it were translating.

It paused and looked at Gomez. Mir Munshi was watching her as well. Apparently, they were waiting for the other part of the question.

"And," she said, "if the Eaufasse collected materials from the destroyed enclave or conducted some kind of investigation, we would like that information as well."

"What do you think you will find?" Oaupheau asked Simiaar so quickly that Gomez knew it had not had a chance to speak to Mir Munshi.

"The way that humans practice investigative science," Simiaar said slowly, "is to go into an area without preconceptions. I do not believe I will find anything. But I would like the opportunity to look at what is there, and see if it means anything to me."

Oaupheau eyed her for a long moment, then looked at Gomez, maybe wondering if she disapproved of what Simiaar said. Gomez remained quiet. Simiaar had handled that well.

Finally, Oaupheau translated that (she hoped) into Fasse.

Mir Munshi answered. Oaupheau dropped its arms.

"We do not know if the gathered materials still exist, but Mir Munshi said he would make sure that whatever we have is added to the material he would give you. The enclave itself is long abandoned, the land destroyed, and now is part of the nearby city. We cannot allow you to visit without a discussion between our ambassadors."

"There is no need at this time," Gomez said. "I think the materials you provide will be more than enough. Thank you."

Mir Munshi spoke again. Oaupheau bent almost in half, before it said, "Mir Munshi will have a friend talk with your pilot about how to land on Ohksmyte undetected. He does not say, but I will. It is dangerous. I do not think you will learn anything."

"Have you seen the ship?" Gomez asked it.

"I have not. Mir Munshi has not. It is in an isolated part of Ohksmyte. I suggest that you do not visit. Mir Munshi believes you should do what is best for your investigation."

Fascinating. Gomez felt her heart rate increase. She had not expected Epriccom to be such a wealth of information.

She turned to Mir Munshi. "You have assisted us greatly. I cannot speak for the Alliance, but I can speak for myself. I am in your debt."

Mir Munshi made that peeping sound again. Then he said, "No, me debt you," shook his head, and said something rapidly to Oaupheau.

"Mir Munshi says that without you, your help, and your discretion, the Eaufasse would not be part of the Alliance. The Alliance has been extremely beneficial to us. It has changed life here on Epriccom. Mir Munshi says that we are in your debt and we cannot ever repay you. He is honored to assist."

Gomez actually felt moved. "Thank you," she said, thinking that the words—even doubly translated—were extremely inadequate. "Thank you so much."

41

TREY'S HEART POUNDED, BUT HE TRIED NOT TO LOOK FRIGHTENED. FOR THE first time since he'd come to this horrible place, he had been summoned to the warden's office unexpectedly.

Trey had gone to see the warden before, usually after some incident that Trey had stopped or to corroborate some problem that someone else caused. Trey had worked hard not to be considered a suck-up, and he'd worked hard to keep himself clean.

He hadn't quite kept his head down, but he hadn't voluntarily raised it either.

All he had managed to do was get himself a cushy job within the system and a single cell. It had taken years to get both.

And now, for some reason, they were probably threatened. No one got called to the warden's office for a good reason.

The stupid android guards had their fake hands on his shoulders. Four of those gigantic things surrounded him, with small robot units patching the holes.

Someone was afraid that Trey would die on the way. Trey had seen this kind of protection before, usually for some prisoner that everyone hated or who was going to rat out someone else in court. A lot of times, those prisoners never returned.

The ones who did return often didn't make it through the week.

Trey tried to make himself small. He kept his face hidden behind the android guard in front of him, and hoped no one could see the number on his jumpsuit in the back. For the first time in years, he felt happy about the fact he looked like a few of the other inmates.

The farther he got away from his cell block, the more likely it was that someone would mistake him for them.

The administrators had sent the android guards that had no mouths. They were probably linked to the system, but he'd never been able to break in. He'd always felt that trying was probably stupid on his part, and would call attention to himself.

Now he wished he had. He wanted to know what the hell was going on.

All he'd received was a message through his prison-installed links: *Warden's Office*, and the time he was due there.

The guards had shown up exactly thirty minutes before his appointment, and now they led him at a leisurely pace through the corridors. The inmates all got silent when they saw the little troupe. They wanted to know what was going on too.

All Trey could hear were murmurs, and he didn't even have to hear the words to know what the murmurs were: *Who is that? What's he done? Who's he ratting out?*

If they didn't know, the inmates would make something up, and in some ways, that was worse.

His skin prickled, almost as if it had received some kind of charge. His throat had closed up. He hadn't been this terrified in years.

Usually because he had a plan. Hell, even getting beat up in the yard hadn't been a surprise, not after he saw those images. He'd known some of the other clones would get him in trouble one day, and he'd had a plan.

Not that it had worked. He felt a twinge of anger, which he'd tried to bury. Damn lawyer. Trey had never heard from the bastard again.

Of course.

Finally their little marching unit swerved into the administration corridors. The lighting was better here, the air fresher, the temperature just about perfect. It was always cold in the cellblocks—apparently to keep the inmates a little on edge. Heat somehow made them angrier, or so the theories went.

Most of the doors in the corridor were closed and dark, but a bright orange light surrounded the doors to the warden's office.

Trey's stomach clenched. He wasn't just going to some assistant's office so that he could be told what the warden thought. He was going to see the warden proper.

That never happened.

At least that he knew of. He had no idea what had happened to all of those other prisoners who never came back.

What had he done? How had he gotten this kind of attention?

He hated it here, but he wasn't ready to die for some reason he didn't understand. And he also didn't want to go to another prison. He'd learned the systems here.

He knew what every sound meant, what every gesture could do.

He knew everything about this prison except what happened to prisoners in the position he was in now.

The robot guards peeled off and wheeled their way down a side corridor.

Three other androids joined the grouping. These androids had mouths. Their coloring was dark gray, their bodies sleeker than the androids that had led him out of the cell block.

The warden's special guards.

Trey didn't think his heart could pound harder, but it did. He probably stank of fear. He was sweating, and he couldn't stop it.

Those damn machines around him probably picked up every nuance— the increased heart rate, the shallow breathing. They had probably already informed the warden—or whoever Trey was meeting—just how terrified he was.

He wasn't sure he could bluff through any of it. He wasn't sure he wanted to.

The door slid back, and the androids led him through the orange light. It coated him, and that was when he realized it was searching him for hidden weapons and probably other things he hadn't even thought about. Someone clearly had thought about those things, once upon a time, and probably used them on a warden somewhere, so the protections were in place.

For all he knew, this orange light was a small decontamination unit too.

His mouth tasted metallic, and he wasn't sure if that was because he had bit his lip and drawn blood without realizing it, or if the very thought of a decontamination unit made him react like he always did when he went through one.

Then he was on the other side of the light. The android guards in front of him moved to the left and right of him. The guards with their hands on his shoulders tightened their grip.

The door swooshed shut behind him.

He'd never been in this room before. It was smaller than he expected. Then he blinked, his vision cleared, and he realized he was in some kind of antechamber. The warden didn't work here; she met with prisoners and/or undesirables here, and didn't let them go any farther.

The room was probably well defended. Circles and squares jutted out of the walls, and there were small shadowy circles on the floor as well. He didn't know if he wasn't allowed to see some of the items in the room—he had no real links, except those the prison system installed—or if each circle and square marked some kind of hidden camera or weapon.

He expected there were a lot of ways to control an angry prisoner in this small room. He also guessed that some part of the room might be able to kill him.

The warden stood in the very center of the room. She had a lined face, grayish in color, and her hair, tied back in a bun, was as black as the walls. He knew that was not exactly what she looked like. Wardens never allowed an inmate to know precisely what they looked like; too many inmates got out and might go after the wardens.

It would be easy to track the face, the eyes, the look, on a simple link. A lot of the inmates here had illegal links. A few of those inmates had even offered some to Trey. He hadn't taken anyone up on it; he didn't want to be beholden to anyone—and he didn't want a possibility of them in his head.

"99373," the warden said, using Trey's prison number. Her voice had been altered as well. He wasn't even sure if it was her voice. It sounded as metallic as the taste in his mouth. "Judge Bruchac ruled on your petition. You are being released in ninety minutes into the custody of your attorney's representative. You may return to your cell to collect your things or you may go through the orientation we have prepared for you."

Whatever he had expected, it wasn't that. He felt his mouth drop open.

"Forgive me, sir," he said. "I—my attorney? I didn't know I had one."

"According to the record, your attorney is Torkild Zhu. He visited you here three weeks ago."

So the bastard *had* become his attorney. "No one notified me that he had taken my case," Trey said.

As that sentence was halfway out of his mouth, he realized he sounded ungrateful.

"Would you like to return to your cell?" the warden asked.

He thought for a moment. He was *leaving*? Had she said *released*?

"Forgive me, sir," Trey said, "this is surprising me. Does this mean that I'm in my attorney's custody? That I'm going to another prison?"

"No, 99373. Judge Bruchac has invalidated your imprisonment. Apparently you are not an illegal under Alliance law. You are free to go, provided you leave the Alliance immediately. Since inmates rarely have the resources to hire a ship to take them anywhere, it is the Earth Alliance Prison System's policy to have the attorney of record take responsibility for the client upon release. The attorney will be in charge of getting you to your destination. After that, you will be on your own. A free…creature…without any notice of this imprisonment on your record. As far as the Alliance is concerned, you have not been here."

All those years did not exist? He felt dizzy. What had Zhu done?

"Am I supposed to talk to some Alliance representative?" Trey asked.

"You are to leave the Alliance, and you are not to return unless you have the proper documentation, including a Day of Creation Document and other information proving you are who you say you are. If you return to the Alliance without those documents, you will be subject to imprisonment again as a possible illegal. Do you understand this?"

He understood her words, but he could barely process them.

"You now have eighty-five minutes. Would you like to return to your cell to collect your possessions?"

His possessions. All of them acquired after long and hard negotiations with other prisoners, with difficult work through the system, with a lot of saved money from his tiny allowance given to him through the EAPS regulations.

Everything he had in that room, that *cell*, he had acquired to ease his life inside.

"No, sir," he said. "I don't need anything. Except maybe real clothes."

"Those are the responsibility of your attorney's representative," the warden said.

"My attorney—" and he was startled to think he had one "—he's not coming?"

"Most attorneys do not handle this phase of client release. They hire a service. I can give you the name of the service if you like," the warden said. Her voice sounded eerily formal.

It finally dawned on Trey that the person standing in front of him wasn't in this room at all. It was some kind of projection.

The warden was probably somewhere else in this office suite, talking with him via some network or something.

"For the record," the warden said, "I do not approve of this release. We know who you are here, and what created you. We know how deeply evil your kind can be."

He felt a chill. He couldn't really see her eyes. Was she going to do something to him? Was that really the purpose behind his visit here?

"In my opinion, you should remain locked up. But the court does not share in that opinion, and I do the court's bidding. Still, I will make sure that you leave this place. If I discover that you're in the Alliance, I will ensure that you are confined for the rest of your unnatural life. Is that clear?"

A MURDER OF CLONES

He had to swallow hard. "Yes, sir, it is."

"Good," she said. "Now, get out of my sight. I have trouble looking at your face."

He felt his cheeks warm. He wanted to say that he had nothing to do with the bombings, but he knew it would make no difference.

The guards spun him around and led him to the door.

"Where are we going now?" he asked.

One of the androids with a mouth actually answered him. "There is a holding area," it said. "You will wait there until your representative appears in…seventy-three-point-two… minutes Earth time."

"Thank you," Trey said, then bit his lower lip. He was shaken enough that he was thanking a nonliving guard.

He was getting out of here in a little more than an hour. Then he would leave the Alliance with people he had never met before. People he had to trust.

Without a plan, without even an idea of what to do next.

He had always imagined getting out of this prison—it had been his goal for years. But he had doubted he would ever achieve it.

Even if he had achieved it, he'd thought he would have weeks, maybe months, maybe even a year to prepare. He would research where he could comfortably live, what kind of work he might get, how he would survive.

He hadn't done any of that. He knew nothing of the worlds outside of the Alliance. He had always thought he would remain within the Alliance.

He had no friends, no family, no one to help him. He didn't even know who this representative was.

And it sounded like he wasn't needed to testify on the Anniversary Day bombings. Apparently, Zhu had gotten him out without even mentioning that.

Which was weird, since he never heard from Zhu.

Trey rubbed his palms against the jumpsuit. He was terrified. He didn't want to be terrified, but he was. What if this was a plot to kill him? What if it was all a ruse?

What if it wasn't?

285

How would he live? What could he do? He had no formal education, no training in any sort of real job, no active skills. And, in the Alliance at least, he wasn't a person. He had no idea what the worlds outside of the Alliance thought of people like him.

They couldn't have thought too kindly of him. Could they? He'd talked to others in the prison, some of whom were known as designer criminal clones. They too had been made outside the Alliance, usually for an express purpose. Most of them wanted to get back to that purpose.

Very few of them wanted to become something else.

He had about an hour to figure out how he would live the next few years of his life. He had no weapons, no money, no possessions, no real identity.

He had nothing.

Except, apparently, something he had never had before in his entire life.

He would have freedom.

And he had no idea what to do with it.

42

THE INFORMATION ON OHKSMYTE WAS SPARSE. BEFORE GOMEZ LEFT, she had Charlie, the pilot, check other star maps for outside-of-the-Alliance specs on Ohksmyte. She also had Apaza find what information he could in the data that Mir Munshi had sent.

There wasn't much, and what existed differed from Alliance information only in the rules and regulations for arrivals. Apparently Eaufasse, with the proper clearance, could visit the mining site, but it took months, sometimes years, to get that clearance.

The mining site had heavy security and could not be approached from the ground or from space, at least by unknown outsiders. Since the corporation running the site was registered in the Alliance, Gomez could approach the site without difficulty.

Not that she planned to.

She was going to one spot on the farthest side of Ohksmyte from Epriccom. She had had Charlie double-check the coordinates that Mir Munshi had given her, and see what was nearby.

Apparently nothing was. No cities, no settlements, no outsiders, and most importantly, no domed communities, like the enclave that had been built on Epriccom.

Gomez had half expected to find one or the remains of one.

But the remains should have been visible to the *Stanley's* sensors.

And there was nothing—at least in the non-mining side of the moon.

Ohksmyte wasn't as big as Epriccom, and its atmosphere was thin. It had no real plant life, and very little water. Part of the area secured by the mining operation included some ice fields that went thirty meters deep into Ohksmyte's soil. The ice fields were probably providing some of the operation's water supply. And, Gomez suspected, might also be the source of some of the moon's mineral richness.

The area she was going to was often used by smugglers back in the day, at least according to some of the information Apaza had found. The smugglers would land, change ships, and leave before anyone could catch them.

Apaza had found that information in Mir Munshi's records. *It wasn't hard*, Apaza had said, *almost like he wanted us to find this*.

Mir Munshi was good at making his suspicions known without saying a word.

Gomez did not notify the mining operation that she was coming. She had taken a fully loaded security shuttle, which everyone in the EAFSS called a "gunboat." It was sleek and maneuverable. It would allow her to pursue anyone who tried to take off in a fast-moving ship—at least until the *Stanley* could take over the pursuit.

It also had every weapon known to the service, and more security protocols than any other ship outside of the military arms of the Alliance. She could start a war herself with this thing, or at least fight a serious and prolonged battle.

Not that she wanted to. She'd done that before, and it hadn't ended well.

The gunboat, named *Stanley Security One*, was the top-of-the-line model. She had had dozens of gunboats named *Stanley Security One* over the years. The *Security One* was always the best gunboat on the *Stanley*. This particular *Security One* would be replaced when she took the *Stanley* in at the end of this sojourn, or at least demoted to a lower-level security ship. It saddened her to lose this one; she liked this incarnation.

It was easy to pilot, so she didn't need to bring anyone with specialized skills. She could handle everything in the cockpit herself, from the weaponry to the cells to the flight.

Since this side of the moon was dead, and since she didn't expect to find any serious trouble near the remains of a fifteen-year-old ship, she did not bring the pilots along. She brought Nuuyoma and Verstraete. Simiaar muscled her way in as well.

Gomez had tried to argue Simiaar out of coming—the amount of forensic material that Mir Munshi had given them was astonishing—but Simiaar insisted. She wanted to collect the evidence from the ship herself, even though she fully admitted that Gomez could probably handle it. From Simiaar's tone, however, it was clear she believed that Gomez wouldn't do the best possible job.

Gomez flew in. She went directly to the coordinates, having decided long before that she was not going to orbit Ohksmyte even once. She didn't want to attract any attention from the mining operation.

Nuuyoma sat in the cockpit beside her. Gomez was monitoring the flight on a holographic screen, showing the area of space around Ohksmyte. Nuuyoma was monitoring the landing area, on both instruments and according to the visuals *Security One* was picking up.

As they got closer, it became pretty clear that the area near the abandoned ship was littered with other ship bits. Not quite a ship graveyard, because that implied intact ships, and nothing here was intact.

That trade-off the smugglers used to do probably involved repairing ships as well. Or stealing better ships.

Everything near the site seemed to be covered with dust from the flakey soil. Gomez had warned Simiaar that might be the case, but Simiaar claimed she didn't care.

All the better that I'm going, she had said.

The presence of the ship debris made it harder to find a good landing location than Gomez had thought. She had to scan the surface, find something relatively flat, and choose that, not worrying what the bottom of her ship might rest on.

Gunboats were designed to land on pretty much anything, so she wasn't really worried about harming the ship. She was actually worried about exiting the ship. She'd once had a deputy get injured when he disembarked on a bad landing site, and she really didn't want to repeat that here, especially with such a small team.

No one from the mining operation pinged her as she entered the space around Ohksmyte. She didn't receive any warnings from the operation, which she found odd.

Usually in places like this, heavily guarded by a proprietary corporation, incoming ships would receive ads or warnings or little messages, often in the form of holograms that just appeared in the cockpit. Such things were hard to filter out and, to be honest, on this trip, Gomez hadn't even tried. She wanted to see what the corporation warned against.

Apparently, it didn't see any Alliance ship as a threat. Or it didn't give warnings.

She wasn't sure which was the case.

She brought the *Security One* down ten meters away from the coordinates Mir Munshi had given her. As the *Security One* landed, a puff of dust or sand or whatever this part of the moon was made of wafted over the ship.

The ship warned that too long at this site unprotected and its systems would get filled with fine particles that would make it nearly impossible to take off.

She linked the ship to her external chips, told Nuuyoma to do the same, and then got into an environmental suit. Even though the atmosphere here was good enough to sustain human life, according to the information she had found, she didn't want to risk getting whatever this soil was made of in her system. She didn't want to go through the detox.

Through her links, she ordered everyone who was going out onto the moon to wear their suits as well.

She rather hoped that would discourage Simiaar, since Simiaar loathed the things, but as Gomez and Nuuyoma approached the airlock, Simiaar was waiting for them.

"This kind of place is a nightmare for evidence collection," Simiaar said, her voice sounding hollow through her helmet's speaker. "So I'm going with you."

In other words, her tone said, you can't get rid of me that easily.

Gomez tried not to sigh. The environmental suits they had on the *Security One* were better suited toward military and police operations than simple exploration. The suits were heavy and bulky, their helmets the only good thing about them. They were completely clear, so that the wearer's face was easily visible.

Simiaar's eyebrows had risen in a challenge to Gomez, as if she expected Gomez to tell her to stay.

"Your choice," Gomez said. "It's not going to be fun out there. And you know, what you're calling evidence is meaningless. The site is—"

"Fifteen years old," Simiaar said. "I got it, Chief."

The "chief" was sarcasm. Nuuyoma looked at Gomez to see if she would challenge Simiaar's disrespectful attitude, but Gomez wasn't going to. They were all taking risks here. If Simiaar wanted to explore the site, then Gomez was willing to let her.

Verstraete was the only one who wasn't going to join them. She had seen the landing site and decided to be the one to stay inside the *Security One*. She was going to maintain a private encoded link with each member of the landing team, and make an automatic back-up of the information they collected.

Gomez nodded at Simiaar and Nuuyoma. Then she put her gloved hand on the airlock controls.

"Here we go," she said.

She went through the airlock first. Protocol was different for marshals. They were the ones who generally made first contact, who needed to know what the dangers were and how they were encountered. Unlike the military vessels, on FSS ships, the marshals were often the only ones who had any planetary or alien contact at all.

The *Security One*'s exterior door opened, and she stepped into what seemed like a sand storm. Wind blew at a steady rate of ten kilometers per hour, at least according to Gomez's suit.

The particles were primarily composed of silica, zircon, and feldspar, but mixed in were all kinds of other materials, from bits of permaplastic to metals used in shipbuilding to biogenic fragments. The suit asked Gomez if she wanted to know more, and she didn't. She would leave that sort of information filtering to Simiaar.

Gomez had to use two different maps to find the coordinates because the air was so thick with particulates that she could barely see. Her breath was ragged, partly because she'd been in real sandstorms without protection, and she knew how they felt.

The map she ran along her left eye, in bright red, showed a direct line from the *Security One* to the coordinates. The other map she ran came through her environmental suit sensors. It was a topological map—adjusted for items in the sand, so that she could put her feet down safely and not damage her suit.

She also sent the information from that particular map to Simiaar and Nuuyoma. Then she slowly walked the ten meters to the coordinates.

The sky was a gray-brown, but she couldn't tell if that was from the constantly moving particles or if it was from the actual atmosphere itself. A separate visual, with the sand storm filtered out, showed mounds in the dirt, constantly shifting as the sand moved over them. Sometimes she could tell what the item was—a control panel, a chair—and sometimes it looked like nothing she had ever seen before.

A few ships' hulls loomed beside her, but the only one she cared about was the one that rose in front of her.

The ship that had left Epriccom just before she arrived the first time was smaller than she had expected, little more than a short-distance speed ship, designed to travel between moons, from a moon to a planet, or from a larger ship to a landing site.

Whoever had that ship on Epriccom had not expected to use it to get out of the sector. That someone had planned to travel to Ohksmyte all along.

She opened a file in yet another link and recorded her observations. She did not make these observations available to the rest of her team.

She did not want to influence them; if they made different assumptions, that would help rather than hurt.

She also made a list of items to review when she returned to the *Stanley*. She needed to know the timing between the request for her presence from the Eaufasse and the moment when this ship left Epriccom. Had another ship arrived on Ohksmyte? And if not, were there ships in the area? Did the Eaufasse and/or one of the other cultures on Epriccom keep track of those kinds of things or did she need to ask the mining operation?

The wind buffeted her, and the sand pelted her suit. She left the exterior audio on. She heard the constant suss of particles scraping her suit, plus the crunch of her feet on the surface.

She only turned around once, to make absolutely certain that Nuuyoma and Simiaar were following her. Nuuyoma walked in Gomez's footprints, but Simiaar toddled on her own, arms extended for balance, as if she were afraid she was going to fall at any moment.

It took longer to reach the ship than Gomez would have predicted. The wind hampered her, and she moved slower than she had thought she would because she didn't want to trip.

It seemed like the ground was composed of ship parts. She wasn't paying a lot of attention to the sand components on the lower part of her visor, but she could see that the particulate composition kept changing, and sometimes the particles listed were in an alarming red, which she did not read.

As long as whatever it was did not penetrate her suit, she was happy; she wouldn't be here long enough to suffer much damage. She did commend herself for deciding on the environmental suit even before she knew about the sandstorm.

She reached the ship a few moments ahead of Nuuyoma and Simiaar. The ship was a half-enclosed shell. The back area, where the galley and the bathroom would have been, had no casing at all, just ship frame suggesting where the pieces had been.

But the front, where the bullet-shaped cockpit was, still had a bubble-like enclosure over the seats. The actual roof was gone here too, and so were the controls, but other pieces remained. The bubble-like enclosure was sand-scored and cloudy. She suspected that damage had happened shortly after the ship arrived in this place, provided the wind blew constantly. She hadn't checked, but she would wager that it did.

Nuuyoma joined her first. *What a surprise,* he sent through his links. *There's nothing here.*

The ship's tiny, Gomez sent back.

He nodded. *I see why smugglers use this place for an exchange. No one would want to be here permanently, and building a dome is probably prohibitively costly.*

I wonder how the mining operation works, Gomez sent as she watched Simiaar nearly topple, catch herself, and then finish walking the last meter to the ship.

This ship is so uninteresting you're talking about mining? Simiaar sent.

It was a long shot, Gomez sent. *We'll search it for additional identifying marks, but I doubt we'll find anything.*

Oh, ye of little faith, Simiaar said, quoting some old religious text like she was prone to do when she was feeling particularly sarcastic. *There is a lot of information here. Especially now that I see part of the cockpit is actually preserved.*

What's here? Nuuyoma asked.

Simiaar grinned. *Lots of DNA and, I'll wager, all of the cockpit information from the last trip this little baby took.*

How can you be so sure of that? Gomez asked.

I had a gigantic hunch after I saw the model description, Simiaar sent. *These babies were designed as information gatherers. The Alliance released them into the wild as "stolen" ships so that criminals would trade them and we could gather information.*

How come I didn't know about that? Gomez sent.

Because it happened twenty years ago, my friend, Simiaar sent. *And only the folks in forensics really cared. Or do you remember every memo that crossed your screen during the course of your career?*

Of course she didn't. But Gomez still felt a little odd. *You're positive you'll get information from this thing.*

Oh, yeah, Simiaar sent. *My sensors are already beeping. We can get lots of information here. But it'll take some work.*

What kind of work? Nuuyoma asked.

Simiaar didn't answer. Instead, she bent at the waist, her gloved hand searching for something under the enclosure.

Gomez looked at Nuuyoma and shrugged. *I have a hunch,* she sent him privately, *we're about to find out.*

43

THE DOCKING RING ON THE MOST PROTECTED SIDE OF EAP 77743 GAVE Fujita the creeps. Prison docking rings always bothered him. They were always on the protected side of a prison, near the guard rings and all of the weaponry. The exterior docking ring was one of any prison's most vulnerable spots, and so the show of force was always dramatic.

But the design bothered him. It was hard to land here, hard to maneuver, and hard to unhook the *Alus 15* from the ring. He knew that was on purpose, but when he saw this design, it made him feel trapped.

No matter how much he investigated, no matter how he tried to change his own ship's procedures, he couldn't control this part of the situation.

If there was some kind of prison riot, if someone attacked the prison itself, he would be stuck here, just like the prisoners. He wouldn't be able to get his ship out quickly.

He docked his ship in what looked like the narrowest part of the ring. But he knew from experience that this section of the ring was where prison employees docked their ships. The materials surrounding the *Alus 15* weren't as sturdily made here, and often dropped away in a crisis so that the employees could leave fast.

Plus, his crew was ready for anything. They were armed and they were on alert.

Two of his best men accompanied him into the prison. Fujita would have brought more, but prison regulations only allowed three people to pick up a prisoner. To bring more, he would either need permission or he would have to show that the prisoner might be dangerous to transport.

He'd only done that once, early on, and learned that his opinion of danger then influenced prison officials. The prisoner didn't get his release, and Fujita had lost the business of that particular law firm.

From that moment on, he had always followed the prison rules to the letter. He just made certain that the security team he brought with him included the most highly trained (and trustworthy) people on his staff.

The docking ring was empty except for the ubiquitous mouthless android guards that these places seemed to favor. Lights glimmered from the walls and ceiling. The lights weren't designed to illuminate; they were designed to show whoever was entering the prison that they were being watched.

He noted that the walls themselves weren't really walls, not from his waist down. What looked like wall pieces were actually guard bots that would attack if anyone unauthorized entered the docking ring.

Despite himself, he felt a thread of nerves. He tried to talk himself down. This prison, even though it specialized in clones, was no different than any other prison he had dealt with. He had to remind himself that he always got nervous at this moment because he never quite knew both what and who he was facing.

Faint lavender lights lit the way to the holding area and this prisoner that the system called 99373 and Zhu called "Trey." The guard bots still blended into the walls of the corridors, and four android guards followed Fujita's team as if the team were the bad guys.

Fujita had camera chips mounted on the back of his neck as well as on his clothing. He monitored what was happening behind him as well as what was in front of him. His security team did the same.

The lights took him to the prisoner release area, and he felt a small thread of relief. At least he wouldn't have to meet with the warden.

Whenever the prison warden got involved in the release of a prisoner, procedures slowed down and the transfer became awkward.

Either the warden didn't want her name on any of this except the release order, or everything was going according to plan.

He had a code he needed to send to the doors that allowed him access. He sent it, along with all of his identifying information. The doors swung open, revealing a narrow corridor with obvious weaponry built in, and a series of doors that extended into the distance.

These areas were designed for massive prisoner releases. Most prisons tried to coordinate release times, so very few ships had to dock on the ring.

Single pick-ups were unusual, except for the S3 clients he usually dealt with. At first, when he'd come to large areas like this to pick up one client, he got even more nervous.

Now, he relaxed slightly. There was always a lesser chance of an incident when he was on his own than when others arrived to pick up their released prisoners.

He sent a reminder to his team: *In, out, gone.*

He got an affirmative from both of them.

The doors closed behind them, and for a moment, they stood in a square part of the corridor, doors on all sides.

He took a deep breath to shed the rest of the nerves, then concentrated. He would retrieve the client, and then he would leave.

If the client didn't want to get out fast, the client would be picked up and carried out of this place.

If the client fought too hard, then one of the security team would knock the idiot out and drag him out of here, put him in the minimum security cell on the *Alus 15*, and take him to his brand-new home.

And leave him there.

Fujita had an obligation to S3, but the obligation only went so far. If S3 wanted more out of him, they would have to pay him more.

The door on Fujita's left swung open. As it did, identification documentation downloaded into Fujita's chips. It was the documentation Fujita would need to get this Trey character out of the Alliance. The documentation certified that 99373 had been held as an illegal clone when it was discovered that he was a non-Alliance clone.

He did not have Alliance identification. The prison hoped the Alliance would accept their word that 99373 was both legal and free to go.

The documentation was the bare minimum needed by the Alliance. Fujita was glad he'd had the presence of mind to bring Trey's entire file, including the whole court case (such as it was). That way, if he got stopped, he could prove he wasn't transporting an illegal clone.

He stepped inside the room. The security team flanked him. The android guards remained at the door.

A too-thin man stood near the back wall. He'd clearly been sitting on the bench seat not a moment before. He was taller than Fujita expected and he looked frailer.

He was also unbelievably pale, from his hair to his skin to his eyes.

Those eyes met Fujita's. They were alive with intelligence. Fujita hadn't expected that. Nor had he expected the force of this man's personality.

A voice overhead identified him:

Prisoner 99373, you are being released into the custody of Rafik Fujita, a representative of the law firm Schnable, Shishani, & Salehi. He will transport you out of the Alliance. Until you leave Alliance space, you are legal only if you remain in his custody. Do you understand?

The clone swallowed hard. He actually appeared nervous, but Fujita wasn't sure if that was an act. "I do understand," the clone said.

Rafik Fujita, do you accept responsibility for 99373?

"Yes," Fujita said.

You will take him out of the Alliance and will not stop for anything except emergencies listed in the Clone Prisoner Release section of the Earth Alliance Criminal Code regarding Prison Rules and Regulations, identification number...

Fujita tuned out the legalese, allowing his own automated system to answer questions. The system was designed to notify him if the wording was different than the wording required by law.

As the voice droned on, he and the clone stared at each other. The clone was still wearing his prison garb. He had no satchel, and no personal items.

He looked older than Fujita expected.

"Do you have everything?" Fujita asked when the droning was done.

The clone actually bit his lower lip. Was the nervousness an act? Fujita couldn't tell.

"Yes," the clone said.

"No personal items at all?" Fujita asked.

The clone glanced around the room. "I only had ninety minutes notice, and that wasn't time to go back to my cell."

"My team can accompany you there if need be." Fujita had to make the offer because it was required by law, but he was hoping that the clone would say no.

The clone gave him a slight smile. "I...everything...there's nothing of value. Not even to me."

Fujita felt a tug of compassion, then dismissed it. For every venal criminal he'd met, he'd met a dozen others who were good at empathy, good at compassion, and good at making others like them. Apparently, this clone could do it as well.

"Can we leave before they change their mind?" the clone asked.

Fujita almost smiled, but stopped himself just in time. Great question, also designed to evoke an emotional response. He'd had his emotional response. He wouldn't allow himself to feel any more.

"Before we do," Fujita said, "you heard the rules. I'm in charge. If you have a problem with that, we will imprison you until we get you out of the Alliance."

"Where am I going?" the clone asked.

"To my ship," Fujita said.

The clone nodded, as if he believed he did not deserve more information. Then he swept his hands down his torso. "I have to wear this?"

"Yep," Fujita said. "We'll find you something shipboard. Unless you want to stay...?"

"No." The clone's voice trembled. "I'm ready to leave. And I'll follow your rules."

"Good," Fujita said. "Because the truth is, you really don't have much of a choice."

44

THE WIND REMAINED STEADY. GOMEZ COULDN'T FEEL IT, BUT IT ANNOYED her all the same. Mostly, the continual *shurr-shurr* of sand across her suit annoyed her. As did the warnings the suit gave about the tiny particulates burrowing into its systems.

Nothing seemed to last long on this part of Ohksmyte, unless it was designed for that purpose.

Not that she had a lot of time to think about this. Simiaar kept her and Nuuyoma busy. It almost felt like they were disassembling the little ship.

First, Simiaar lifted the enclosure. It rose with an audible squeal. She slipped inside the old cockpit, but wouldn't let Gomez or Nuuyoma join her. Instead, she pulled the enclosure back down, then removed the gloves she had been wearing and put on a new pair that she had kept inside her suit. With those gloves, she disassembled the remains of that cockpit, pouring the interiors of the remaining equipment into little bags that she then secreted inside her suit.

When she was done, she bagged the remaining equipment pieces and handed them, one by one, to Gomez.

Get them to Security One, Simiaar sent. *Then come back for more.*

Gomez did. She kept her head down against the constant wind and sand, and made her way back along the path she and the other two had created. Not that she could see the path any longer. The blowing sand had smoothed out their steps, hiding the little things they had uncovered, and making the landscape look as barren as it had before.

Security One was now coated with the sand, even though Verstraete had kept the shields up.

Verstraete lowered the shields when Gomez contacted her. The actual ship hull seemed cleaner and clearer than it had a moment before. But as Gomez opened the airlock, particulates started to cling to the metal surface.

You nearly done? Verstraete sent as Gomez deposited items in the airlock.

Looks like we're just getting started, Gomez sent.

The ship doesn't like it here, Verstraete sent. *It's not the sand. It's the low-level radiation. It's worried that we don't have the right gear for this kind of work.*

They didn't really, but this was the only gear they had.

I'll let Simiaar know we need to hurry, Gomez sent, even though she knew Verstraete could have let Simiaar know that herself. Verstraete did everything she could to avoid Simiaar. It wasn't that they disliked each other; it was almost as if they couldn't communicate well because they were too similar.

As Gomez returned, she passed Nuuyoma, who was carrying even more bagged items.

We should just bag the whole damn ship, he sent her on a private link.

Gomez smiled but didn't respond. Simiaar had warned her this would happen, and Gomez hadn't believed her. Of course, Simiaar hadn't told her these marked ships even existed.

As Gomez staggered back to the skeletal remains of that ship, she checked the wind speed. It hadn't increased, but moving in this environment was tiring her. In space, she didn't have to push against wind as she moved. The gravity was Earth normal here, but the wind made it seem heavier.

We almost done? she sent Simiaar as she returned.

There were two people on this ship when it left Epriccom, Simiaar sent her, ignoring the question. *Only one of them left this little ship alive.*

What? Gomez stopped outside the enclosure. Simiaar was hunched in front of a floor panel. Gomez couldn't see what she was doing. Simiaar did not look up.

You heard me. One of the people who escaped Epriccom died in this ship.

Before it landed? Gomez asked.

Dunno, Simiaar sent. *We'll find out when I get this stuff back to the* Stanley.

She poked her head up and peered through the enclosure. She was frowning, but she wasn't looking at Gomez. Simiaar was looking—or trying to look—for Nuuyoma.

"Listen," Simiaar said out loud, through the message system in their suits. "This is just for you. Double-check me. Are we on a secure channel?"

Gomez double-checked. They were. "I'll encode," she said.

"Good." Simiaar pulled off her gloves and bagged them. Then she grabbed yet one more pair of gloves from those magic pockets in her suit. "We got an issue here."

"An issue? In a ship this old?"

"Yeah," Simiaar said. "Remember I told you that the Alliance seeded these things throughout the various sectors so that they could track criminals?"

"Of course," Gomez said, a bit annoyed that Simiaar had to check. It had only been an hour or so since she had dropped that piece of information.

"This thing wasn't seeded," Simiaar said.

"What does that mean?" Gomez asked.

"It means this thing only had one owner."

Gomez blinked, trying to figure out what Simiaar meant. "The Alliance would be the first owner, right?"

"Yeah," Simiaar said.

"You're telling me that the Alliance gave this ship to whoever flew this thing?"

"I'm not sure how the person who flew it got it, but this thing was never abandoned, never stolen, never given to anyone else. The first person who flew it was the last person who flew it."

"How can you be sure?" Gomez asked.

"I can't exactly. Not without a bunch of testing. But that's what it looks like."

"In the middle of a sandstorm after sitting for fifteen years," Gomez said.

"Some of this stuff was designed to download immediately with the right access code," Simiaar said. "The idea was that operatives would have maybe five minutes to get the information and leave the site."

Gomez swore. At that moment, Nuuyoma joined them.

What new torture do you have for us now? he sent on the joint links.

A few more items to carry back, Simiaar sent. *Judita, I'm going to need you to help me get back.*

What does that mean? Gomez sent.

I'm going to wrap myself in a protective covering, Simiaar sent. *I won't be able to see anything. You're going to guide me back.*

Gomez grinned. *Such trust.*

Screw you, Simiaar sent. *You ready to carry a few things, Elián?*

I guess, he sent, then gave Gomez a confused look that basically asked, *weren't we carrying things already?*

Gomez tilted her head just a little and shrugged.

I'm lifting this enclosure thing and handing you bags fast. You take them even faster. Then I'm closing the lid. Got that? Apparently, Simiaar was still talking to Nuuyoma.

How many bags? He asked.

Five. Think you can handle that?

I had ten the last time, he sent.

Okay, then. She didn't seem to see the irony. *Here goes.*

He bent over the enclosure, gloved hands extended. Simiaar opened the enclosure just a little, shoving bags at him. Gomez helped him take them, holding three of them while he adjusted the first two.

Simiaar had already shut the enclosure. She had removed some kind of sheeting. Gomez recognized it. Simiaar usually used it at a crime scene to wrap a body or a crucial piece of evidence. Apparently, she considered herself that crucial piece of evidence.

I don't have to come back, right? Nuuyoma sent both of them, but he was looking at Gomez.

Put the items in the airlock, then wait outside it, Gomez sent. *I might need your help.*

Okay, he sent. He adjusted the last of the bags, and then walked slowly toward *Security One.*

"How are we doing?" Simiaar asked on that secure channel.

"I haven't had this much fun in years," Gomez said.

"Cute."

Simiaar had wrapped the sheet around her suit. The sheet adhered, coating everything. It took some special process to remove the thing in the lab. Simiaar would probably have to wear her environmental suit all the way to the *Stanley.*

"I'm ready," Simiaar said. "You're going to have to lift the damn enclosure."

"Okay," Gomez said. It wasn't as easy as it sounded. The enclosure was latched in five different places, and the latches had to release in a particular order.

Gomez thought it odd that Simiaar had known that order.

That order also explained why more materials hadn't been taken from that cockpit. No one wanted to stay on this part of the moon long enough to break into the ship, not when there were so many other ship pieces around to steal from.

The enclosure opened. Gomez put her gloved hands under Simiaar's arms and pulled her out, then staggered backwards. Simiaar seemed to weigh five times what she normally did.

Gomez couldn't quite process how much material Simiaar had taken from the ship. Or maybe it was the weight of the equipment Simiaar had brought with her.

"You ready?" Gomez asked.

"Go slow," Simiaar said. "I got two different maps and real-time imagery, but I still feel blind."

Gomez could understand. She held Simiaar in place, then paused, and lowered the enclosure. It clicked closed.

It just felt wrong to leave it open, after its secrets had been intact for so long. Gomez didn't defend her actions. She wrapped her arm around Simiaar's waist. Simiaar put her arm around Gomez's.

Together they walked slowly back to *Security One*.

Nuuyoma stood outside it. His environmental suit was black with the sand. He looked like part of the landscape.

Security One had become a mountain of sand, even though every time the shields lowered, the sand sloughed off.

Lower shields, Gomez sent Verstraete. *We're coming in.*

Not a moment too soon, Verstraete sent. *This stuff is insidious. I'm checking it for nanoparticles. It wouldn't surprise me if we pick up hitchhikers.*

If we do, we do, Gomez sent. *We're not getting everything off Doctor Simiaar's suit until we get to the* Stanley.

Oh, yes, we are, Simiaar sent. *You'll help me into the cargo hold of this thing. We can decontaminate me there.*

Won't it ruin the evidence? Gomez asked.

You think I didn't plan for this? I read the specs on Ohksmyte. Did you?

Apparently not in the same kind of detail. The shields went down, and sand poured from the air to the ground. The airlock opened. Nuuyoma helped Gomez shove Simiaar into the airlock.

Gomez climbed in next, followed by Nuuyoma. The airlock's floor was clean, even though they'd been dumping bags into it. Verstraete had done her job.

More sand fell off them. Cleansing air brushed off their suits. Only Simiaar's remained covered.

Gomez blinked hard, realizing just how exhausted she was. She didn't like living in atmosphere. She'd been in space too long. And she could do without wind.

The interior door opened. Verstraete stood in the corridor, also wearing an environmental suit. Cleaning bots made their way into the airlock, and Gomez felt cramped.

"So?" Verstraete asked. "Was it worthwhile?"

"We won't know for some time," Gomez lied.

Simiaar looked blindly at her. "Oh, hell," Simiaar said. "Don't listen to her. Adventure is always fun."

I never took her to be an optimist, Nuuyoma sent Gomez on a secure link.

I never knew she could have fun, Gomez sent back. Then they grinned at each other, and joined Verstraete in the corridor.

Then she helped Simiaar out of the airlock. Together, they made their way to the lower level and the decontamination chamber, where the real evidence collection would begin.

45

So far, the clone wasn't trouble. Fujita put him in a heavily guarded wing, in an actual suite with its own sitting area, bedroom, and bathroom. Everything in the guarded wing suites was bolted down. Anything that could possibly be a weapon was either made of a bendable material or hadn't been put in the room at all.

The clone's suite was heavily monitored. He stood for the longest time in the center of the suite, as if he hadn't known what to do. Then he looked at the clothes that the crew had placed on the bed, grabbed some items, and headed to the bathroom. He opted for a real water shower, and stayed in it until the water shut off after the required eight minutes.

They had two days of travel before leaving Alliance space, then five days of travel after that. Fujita didn't mind. The hardest part was over, based on his experience.

He also knew from experience not to let the long-time incarcerated alone for long. So he invited the clone to a captain's dinner.

It sounded grand and elegant, but really it was just a meal with Fujita and his senior staff. His most *qualified* staff for any kind of physical emergency. Even here, in the presence of five strong security personnel, the clone wouldn't be allowed sharp utensils.

They didn't use the main dining area, but a small room off one of the VIP suites. Fujita didn't want former prisoners anywhere near the actual living quarters, although this level had been done up to look like living quarters. The clone was blocked from all network access and the prison had removed all of his links, so he had no way to check any information that Fujita had told him.

Angela Tamberlane, the head of Fujita's security detail, brought the clone to the dining area. Fujita's rules dictated that whoever was with the so-called client had two other crew members along. Tamberlane left those two crew members outside the door. The other four inside the room were the two who had gone to the prison with Fujita and the man Fujita called his ringer, a psychiatrist he always had on these transports in case the client became difficult.

Tamberlane let the clone—whom Fujita would have to force himself to call Trey—into the dining area first. The clone—Trey—came in, moving his head around as he took in everything. He walked slowly, hunched so that his torso was protected, his hands in loose fists.

Fujita recognized the posture: it was both defensive and protective, as if he expected to be attacked at any moment.

On occasions like this, Fujita always played the expansive host. "Welcome to the captain's dining room," he said. "I figured you needed to celebrate on your first night of freedom."

Trey lifted his head and those eyes met Fujita's with such force that Fujita almost felt like he needed to step backwards. But he held his ground.

Trey studied him for a moment, as if trying to see if Fujita was fooling him in some way. Then Trey said solemnly, "Thank you."

"You'll be sitting here." Fujita indicated a chair on the far side of the table. Trey's back would be to the wall, and he would be sitting between two members of the security team.

Most prisoners liked that enclosed feeling, not that Fujita really cared. He was more concerned that Trey couldn't do something impulsive and then easily escape the room.

Trey looked at the seat, swallowed hard, and then nodded. He made his way around the table as if movement hurt him.

Fujita's gaze met Tamberlane's. *He all right?* he sent on a secure link.

310

I think he's terrified and not willing to admit it, she sent. *This is more free space than he's seen in decades.*

Fujita swept an arm over the table, indicating the other empty seats. "Sit down, everyone. Let's get started."

There were no wine glasses on the table. In fact, there was no alcohol on the *Alus 15* at all. His staff didn't need it, and early on, Fujita had learned that former prisoners had a great instinct for finding the mood-altering substances on board any ship. The best thing to do was to make sure there were no mood-altering substances at all.

At the moment, the only liquid on the table was water. There were two gigantic plates of cured meats from all over the Alliance, and another gigantic plate of sliced breads and crackers.

Nothing that would be served tonight would take a knife to make the portion size correct, and all of it could be eaten with spoons or weakly constructed forks.

Fujita wasn't sure Trey even noticed. He ran his finger around the edge of the unbreakable plate, then touched the glass as Tamberlane filled it with water.

"Thank you," Trey said. "Forgive me if I seem…odd. I've never eaten like this."

"This kind of food?" one of the security staff asked.

They had all been instructed to talk to him like he was a friend, to try to relax him.

"At a table. Formal, you know. Not after someone served some slop and you sat down, but where people converse. I've seen vids, though." Trey sounded both nervous and eager at the same time.

He's good at vulnerable, Tamberlane sent Fujita.

Yeah, I noticed that earlier, Fujita sent back. He sat down. "Just ask. We'll help you figure out what to do. Mostly, though, it's common sense."

Trey nodded. He waited until someone else started a plate of meat, then watched as each person selected their favorite slices. He took exactly the median number of slices that everyone else had taken so far.

Smart. He had a gift for observation.

Fujita would remember that.

"Is it okay if I ask questions?" Trey said to Fujita. "Or do I have to meet alone with you?"

"The team is briefed on everything," Fujita said. "I have no secrets from them."

And they were very practiced at pretending not to hear things—and at recalling it should it become important.

"I...don't mean to be rude," Trey said as he handed the dish of cured meats to Tamberlane. "I was only told everything this morning."

Then he looked around the table, looked at the tray of breads going around, looked at the various condiments available to spread on the breads, and paused.

Everyone knew what he was thinking. To him, this level of food—which was just the first course—was a luxury. Fujita had planned this meal so that the courses came out slowly, giving Trey's stomach time to adjust.

"I didn't even know that..." Trey shook his head, as if censoring himself. "Sorry. Um, I was just wondering. Where's Torkild Zhu? He's the one who got me off, right? You guys aren't lawyers, right?"

Fujita had expected this question sooner. "We work for the firm," he said. "This is our job."

"You've done it before?" Trey asked. "Taken people out of the Alliance?"

"We pick up newly released clients and take them to their destinations," Fujita said.

Trey made a small sandwich out of his bread and ham, just like Tamberlane had done beside him.

"What is my destination?" Trey asked, clearly trying to make the question sound casual.

"You're heading to a small city in the Irr Sector. It's at the edge of the Frontier." Fujita wasn't sure how to make this place sound palatable to Trey. He had no idea who Trey really was, what he would like, what he wanted.

"I don't have any money or job skills or—"

"We're taking you to an organization that trains people for jobs in return for some work. You'll do things like cook and clean, and they'll provide you with a room, food, and training. The law firm has a fund for this sort of thing. Your stay is paid for the next six months, but you can extend that through work and good behavior."

"Good behavior," Trey repeated, and Fujita knew why. It sounded like a prison term. It *was* a prison term. "So I'm trapped there?"

"You can leave at any time," Fujita said. "But you won't have any money. You can't get a refund if you refuse to stay for the entire six months."

Trey nodded. Then he took a bite out of the small sandwich.

Fujita placed some salami on rye bread. He'd brought a lot of his favorites for the first part of this trip. They'd be out of the fresh food in a few days, so he planned to enjoy all of it now.

He was about to take a bite when the *Alus 15* shuddered. The lights dimmed.

"What the hell?" Tamberlane asked.

Trey wrapped his arms around his torso and hunched in his chair.

Fujita's links lit up with emergency warnings. Some blared inside his head. Others coated his vision red.

Someone had fired on the *Alus 15*.

They were under attack.

Fujita remained calm. Attacks on private prisoner transport ships happened at least fifty percent of the time. The attacks were annoying, but they were little more than that with a ship as prepared as this one was.

He stood, pointed at Trey, and said, "Secure him. Angela, you stay here. The rest of you, stations."

Every single member of his crew had been through this before. They stood and moved as a unit. They each had a job to do and they were all ready to do it.

Fujita let himself out of the dining room and hurried down the corridor. He needed to be on the bridge. He took the most direct route, up a service elevator two levels to command center.

Had Trey lied to him? Had Trey somehow contacted someone on the outside to rescue him from Fujita's ship?

Because rescues like that were the most common form of attack on transports like Fujita's. That, or someone did not want Trey to go free. Those things happened too.

Even that, though, required contact with the outside, and according to Trey's file, he had no friends, no family, no contacts at all. And no one had visited him, except for Zhu, in the entire time he was imprisoned.

So what the hell?

What have we got? Fujita sent as he ran through the upper level corridor.

Something big, sent this evening's pilot, Abid Stone. *We've got two battle cruisers.*

Fujita nearly tripped. He'd never been attacked by battle cruisers. Ever. Big prisoners, political prisoners, folks who required battle cruisers, they never got out of prison. Or if they did, they had a military escort.

Battleships? He sent.

Yeah, Stone sent. *These things are* huge. *And good God, do they have firepower.*

Fujita couldn't run any faster. He was having trouble drawing breath, not because he was out of shape, but because he was worried. Startled.

Frightened.

The only thing he could hope for was that Stone was wrong.

Shields okay? Fujita sent.

For now, Stone sent. *We've never been up against anything like this, though. It looks like they might be getting reinforcements, and if they do, we're screwed.*

The few bites Fujita had taken of his food threatened to come back up. *Are we firing back?*

Um, no, Stone sent. *We don't know who these things belong to.*

You said they were old, Fujita sent. *I thought that meant you recognized them.*

I do, Stone sent. *They're Alliance made. But that doesn't mean they're Alliance owned. They're old.*

Fujita wanted to ask how old, if they dated from the days of PierLuigi Frémont. But he didn't. He needed to get to the bridge.

He hurried through a tight corridor, and wished he could somehow levitate himself up to the most protected part of the ship.

So they're just randomly firing on us? He sent.

It's not random. They're targeting engines, shields, and weapons.

Tell me you're not firing back, Fujita sent. He didn't want these things pissed off at him worse than they already were. Besides, the shields worked better when they devoured most of the ship's energy.

I'm not stupid, Stone sent. *I gotta tell you. I'm not sure firing is an option. I don't think anything we use on those cruisers would make a difference.*

Fujita felt chilled. His ship was one of the most powerful private ships he'd ever seen inside the Alliance. But Stone did say *battle cruiser.* That implied big. Huge. Able to take on warships, not dinky private vessels like his.

He turned a corner, and ran up the half level to the bridge.

He palmed the controls to the bridge entrance, let the system do its DNA and retinal scans, and watched as the doors slid open.

The bridge wasn't huge, but it seemed big. Fujita had designed it himself, so that everything was within reach. It was shaped like a triangle. Screens and holographic information appeared in the point.

At the moment, Abid Stone stood at the controls, and his co-pilot, Kavi Maddix, hunched over the navigation system. In the triangle, two gigantic ships menaced a ship the size of Fujita's thumb. It took him a moment to realize that tiny ship was his.

"They're firing on us." Maddix sounded breathless. She also sounded panicked. She tucked a strand of her long, copper hair behind one ear, her hand shaking. "And I'm seeing two more ships on the edge of my screen—this is awful."

"Whose are they?" Fujita asked as he went to the third console. He called up every bit of information he could in a 3-D screen—their location, the cruisers, the fire power, and the status of his shields.

"I have no idea," Stone said.

"What do they want?" Fujita asked.

"Like I said, no idea."

One of the battle cruisers fired again, and the *Alus 15* shuddered. The shields cut out for less than a second, but if the battle cruisers noticed that flaw, then this ship wasn't just screwed.

It—and everyone on it—was dead.

Fujita hit the command override and sent his ship careening out of the area. The only thing he had was speed, especially against behemoths like that.

He used it.

"You didn't chart a course," Maddix screamed at him.

"Chart one now." He didn't defend himself. He didn't have to defend himself. This was his crew.

Besides, when she calmed down, Maddix would realize that had he charted, the behemoths would have anticipated his arrival somewhere. At the moment, they had no idea where he was going or what he was going to do.

"To the Irr Sector?" Maddix asked.

"I don't know," Fujita snapped. "Just make sure we don't run into something."

He ran his hands through his hair, and looked at the navigation screen. The behemoths were turning, even as they faded from his ability to track them. In a moment, they'd be hot on his trail.

"Find out what the hell those ships are," he said to Stone. "And figure out what they want from us."

"How the hell am I supposed to do that?" Stone asked.

"I don't know," Fujita snapped. "That's your job."

"What's yours?" Stone asked.

"Keeping us alive," Fujita said, and went to work.

46

GOMEZ STOOD INSIDE SIMIAAR'S LAB ON THE *STANLEY*. THE EVIDENCE spread before her. The packages that Simiaar had collected on Ohksmyte ranged from miniscule to huge, but they weren't sorted that way. In fact, Gomez couldn't tell how Simiaar was sorting them. It all looked haphazard, as if someone had thrown pieces of junk throughout the room.

Simiaar leaned against one of the tables. Behind her, screens reported information in multi-colored charts and graphs. Some moved so fast that Gomez couldn't even tell what they were measuring. Of course, on the ones that Gomez could read, she couldn't quite understand what the measurements meant.

She was tired. She'd gone through decontamination, had something to eat, and even took a short nap, but it didn't get rid of the feeling of sheer exhaustion that walking on Ohksmyte had given her. The wind, the dust, the lifting, all left her drained.

Simiaar didn't look exhausted at all. She seemed energized, if serious. She'd apparently worked steadily since they came back.

"We got decisions to make," she said to Gomez, which was exactly what she had sent on Gomez's links not half an hour ago.

"That's why I'm here in the middle of the night," Gomez said. The others had bunked down hours ago. She had told them she'd let them know the next day's plans as soon as she knew what they would be.

She didn't have to go back to Epriccom, and she needed to get the *Stanley* away from Ohksmyte. She really only had two choices: she could take the *Stanley* in for its scheduled maintenance or she could continue to pursue this investigation.

And right now, it looked like the investigation was all in Simiaar's hands.

"I take it you found something," Gomez said.

"I found a lot of somethings," Simiaar said. "None of it conclusive."

Gomez suppressed a sigh. She needed conclusive.

"Remember what I told you on Ohksmyte? That the ship had one owner?"

Gomez nodded.

"The first thing I did was double-check that." Simiaar paused, her gaze meeting Gomez's. "It's worse than I thought."

"How can it be worse?" Gomez asked. Simiaar had already made a link to the Alliance.

Simiaar tapped the screen on the table behind her. A navigation panel rose between them. It was clear. Gomez could still see Simiaar standing on the other side.

"I found the back-up of the distances traveled by this little craft," Simiaar said. "It includes navigation logs, and time to transverse one area to the next, and a lot more."

"Okay," Gomez said, not sure she believed something that old would hold up on those conditions. But she was saving her questions until Simiaar was done.

"This ship hardly went anywhere," Simiaar said. "It went from the Alliance to Epriccom to Ohksmyte."

Gomez couldn't keep quiet any longer. "So it went from a fringe place in the Alliance to the Frontier. That's not a surprise is it?"

"It wasn't a fringe part of the Alliance," Simiaar said. "It left the factory and went directly to Epriccom."

"The factory—where it was made?" Gomez asked, because she honestly wasn't certain if Simiaar was talking about a clone factory or not.

"Yeah," Simiaar said. "These ships get pilots who then dump the ships somewhere so that they appear stolen or abandoned. And I would have thought that's what happened except for two things."

Gomez braced herself, and waited.

"First, the ship went directly to the enclave," Simiaar said. "And second, the only people who ever piloted this thing were clones of PierLuigi Frémont."

Gomez put up her hands as if she could physically block the information. "That's not possible. There's something wrong with the data."

"That's what I thought, and I'll check again," Simiaar said, "but there's a lot of information that the system tracks, including DNA from pilots. The pilot's DNA came from a clone of PierLuigi Frémont."

Gomez sat down. Her legs wouldn't hold her any longer.

"So here's the thing we have to decide," Simiaar said. "We have to decide if it's worth our careers to keep looking at this."

Gomez studied her. "We made that decision already. What's different?"

"Judita," Simiaar said, leaning forward. "Assume I'm right here, because I am. But you don't think so yet, so just assume I am. This ship came from the Alliance. The ship had clones in it, and those clones went to the enclave. Then, as the enclave was about to be invaded by law enforcement from the Alliance, the ship left. One of the clones died, and the other went somewhere else."

"That makes no sense," Gomez said. "Why flee the Alliance if you're part of it?"

Simiaar stared at her.

Gomez felt a flush building. Simiaar only used that look if Gomez was missing something obvious.

"The Alliance wouldn't try to destroy the Alliance," Gomez said.

"No," Simiaar said. "It wouldn't. But a faction inside the Alliance might. How better to destroy something than attack it from within?"

Gomez bit her lower lip. It made a curious kind of sense. The attacks on the Moon were *inside* the Alliance, deep inside the Alliance, as close to Earth as possible. Without the Moon, the Earth would either have to change its access policies or it would no longer be the center of the Alliance.

And then there was the part that had bothered her the most—cloning a known villain to make the attacks obvious. Humans inside the Alliance knew who PierLuigi Frémont was. Maybe people from Abbondiado did as well. But people on the Frontier? Not at all. And most aliens didn't know either, which spoke to a human connection for all of this.

Simiaar was talking about a vast conspiracy, and that was where Gomez had her problem. She didn't believe in conspiracies. They were hard; they were complicated; they fell apart before long-term plans became viable.

"You're guessing," Gomez said, even though she knew it sounded weak.

"Informed guesses," Simiaar said.

"Based on ancient information on an old spaceship that could have been planted just for an event like this."

"Don't you remember Thirds?" Simiaar asked. "He said he'd never seen anyone like us. The Eaufasse thought all humans looked the same. Because the humans in the enclave—adult and child—were the same."

Gomez sighed. She wasn't going to get Simiaar off this without evidence of her own.

"So what do you want to do?" Gomez asked.

"Pretend we never found this. Go back to doing our jobs. Let someone else worry about it all."

Gomez raised her eyebrows. "You're usually not one to give up."

"I don't fight wars," Simiaar said. "I capture criminals."

"You think this is a war?" Gomez asked.

"You don't?" Simiaar said.

Gomez threaded her fingers together. The attacks were seen as an act of terrorism, but often when historians revisited the events leading up to a major war, the initial act of terrorism became the first volley in a protracted conflict.

She needed to think. She stood.

"Get me all the information you can from this stuff," Gomez said.

"And then what?" Simiaar asked.

Gomez looked at her. Simiaar was frightened. Gomez wasn't sure she'd ever seen her friend this terrified.

"Then we'll take the *Stanley* in for its maintenance," Gomez said.

"And nothing else?" Simiaar asked.

"And nothing else," Gomez lied.

47

MADDIX MANAGED TO GET THEM AWAY FROM THE BATTLE CRUISERS without hitting anything. Fujita had no idea how; the *Alus 15* didn't have the best remote guidance system at its top speeds. But she'd managed, and he blessed her for it.

They hadn't followed a pre-plotted course either. Fujita had never done that before, just hit some buttons that basically mean *Get The Hell Out Of Here!*, but he was relieved to know it worked.

At least it had worked kinda. The *Alus 15* did have escape modes programmed in, and theoretically, those modes plotted random courses that were harder to follow and track.

He would find out if the theory now actually worked in practice.

The problem was that the *Alus 15* was now light years away from the course it had planned to take.

He wasn't even sure he could go to the Irr Sector now. What did the people on those battle cruisers know? How had they found him? Were they searching for Trey or was this about something else?

The image of those gigantic ships menacing the *Alus 15* still hovered in the point of the triangle. Star maps that Fujita didn't recognize floated on flat holoscreens above it all. The one star map he did recognize had to keep readjusting itself as the *Alus 15* flew farther from its desired path.

Behind him, Stone swore.

"What?" Fujita asked.

"You should thank me, Rafik," Stone said.

"Thank you," Fujita snapped. "Now tell me what's going on."

"If we'd fired on those things, we would have become enemies of the Alliance."

Fujita craned his head sideways and looked at Stone. Stone had gone gray. "What the hell?"

"I told you before, those were old Alliance battle cruisers. But I figured they were so old they'd been decommissioned."

That chill that Fujita had been fighting got worse. "They weren't?"

"No," Stone said. "According to what I've got from their names and registration numbers, they're still active. They're used to patrol the far reaches of Alliance territory."

"We were attacked by the *Alliance*?" Maddix's voice shivered. "But we're an Alliance vessel."

With all the documentation, all the notifications and warnings and everything that Alliance vessels were required to carry. The *Alus 15* broadcast all of that stuff to nearby Alliance ships all the time. That information essentially said, *We're on the same side; leave us alone.*

"Did the prison somehow shut off our notifications?" Fujita asked Stone.

"No," Stone said. "It was the first thing I checked."

Fujita's hands were shaking. If those were Alliance vessels, then they knew what his mission was. They knew who he had on board.

"Any word that these ships were rogue?" he asked, hoping against hope that some captains had taken it on themselves to get rid of someone with the Anniversary Day assassins' DNA.

"Not from a cursory search," Stone said. "And you'd think if someone stole battle cruisers or was misusing them or something, there'd be notifications."

There would be.

Fujita felt like an idiot. He'd never taken political jobs before, and somehow Zhu had convinced him this one wasn't political. Zhu hadn't thought so, and Fujita really hadn't either. After all, Trey just shared DNA with the assassins. He wasn't one of them.

"What do we do now?" Maddix asked.

Good question. Because they were screwed. If they left the Alliance, then it would actually be easier to attack them and kill them. They could be considered hostile and not be subject to Alliance law.

But if they remained here, they'd be easy to find.

"I need you to shut down all our identifiers," Fujita said to Maddix. "*All* of them."

"But then we can't—"

"We're being targeted by the damn *Alliance*," he said. "We're constantly sending our identification throughout the Alliance."

She swore. Usually Fujita liked her long creative curses, but right now, she was just being annoying.

"I've shut down the identifiers," she said.

"Okay," he said. "Get us out of here, fast, like you did before."

"But—"

"Stop arguing with me!" he snapped. "*Get us out of here.*"

She nodded, slammed her hands on the controls, and the ship lurched. For one brief moment, Fujita worried that they'd been disabled. Then the systems engaged and the ship moved quickly.

"How bad's the damage?" he asked Stone.

"Worse than I thought," Stone said. "And I was just monitoring our former position. You got us out just in time. Two more battle cruisers were on the way."

"Not the ones that found us earlier?"

"No," Stone said.

Fujita felt his heart sink. That meant they were truly being targeted.

He turned toward Maddix. "I want you to have the ship chart some random courses. In between, you chart something, in case this is a program and it's not as random as we thought. I want to zigzag all over the sector for the next few hours."

She nodded, subdued after he had yelled at her.

"And for the next ten minutes, you guys are not to talk unless I ask you to. You got that?"

Stone frowned at him, and didn't say anything. Maddix didn't raise her head, but she nodded.

Fujita activated a private encoded link, and hoped to hell that no one from the Alliance was monitoring it.

A tiny holographic image of Rafael Salehi appeared in front of Fujita's right eye.

"Rafik?" Salehi asked, his voice sounding tinny through the faint connection. "You're not supposed to use this except in an emergency."

"Yeah," Fujita said aloud. He didn't care if the team heard him. "I think it's an emergency when Alliance battle cruisers are trying to destroy my ship, don't you?"

"What?" Salehi asked.

"You heard me," Fujita said. "You call them off, now. I don't care what you threaten, but do something. Because I can't. Even if I kill this passenger you saddled us with or turn him over, the Alliance is going to target my ship for years."

Maddix looked up, startled. Stone ran a hand over his mouth.

"What passenger?" Salehi asked.

"The clone that Zhu set free," Fujita said. "Do something. Or I swear every member of my family will come gunning for you. Because I will make sure that they know the person responsible for my death is you."

He severed the connection, then fell into the command chair.

"Is that true?" Maddix asked. "We're going to be targeted?"

"That's true," Fujita said.

"Then get me off this thing. No job's worth this."

"I'd love to kick you free," Fujita said. "I'd love to return this clone to the Alliance. But we can't stop anywhere without being blown up. And our life pods are all stamped with information from the *Alus 15*. We're stuck."

"What are we going to do?" Maddix asked.

"Hope to hell that S-three has the kinds of connections they say they do," Fujita said. "Because if they don't, we're not getting out of this one alive."

48

GOMEZ COULDN'T SLEEP.

She sat in the office in her suite on the *Stanley*, going over everything. She watched the Anniversary Day explosions again, the footage of the clones in Armstrong's port, the images she had of the clones she'd discovered on Eaufasse, and the destruction of that faraway base.

She made a list of all the contradictions: the clones buried in the penal system; the incorrect maps; the ship that went from the Alliance to Epriccom; the use of PierLuigi Frémont's DNA in the first place.

Then she got up and paced. Conspiracies were easy to believe. The evidence built on itself, provided the investigator took a paranoid view. Rather than believing in coincidences, the investigator always linked pieces that shouldn't have been linked.

And yet, pieces nagged at her.

Simiaar's fear nagged at her.

Gomez had asked a lot of her team. She didn't dare ask them to investigate a trail that could lead into the Alliance.

She sat at the computer where she had stored most of the information that her team had collated. She searched through her discussions with TwoZero. She knew he hadn't mentioned the ship, but had he mentioned the people running the enclave?

She didn't remember it. And no matter how hard she searched, she couldn't find it.

Maybe if she talked with him one more time, then she would be able to put this all to rest.

She ran a hand through her hair, and started the process that would take her back to Clone Hell. She would ask just a few questions, and then she would leave.

She was figuring out the travel schedule when her links got pinged.

She looked up at the screen, startled. Why had someone from the prison system pinged her links when she was working through the net?

With her right hand, she touched a chip on the back of her hand. A small holoimage rose. A standard avatar—genderless, but human-looking—stared forward with an expression that someone considered emotionally neutral.

We are sorry to inform you that the party you seek is no longer incarcerated in the Earth Alliance Prison System. The prisoner you seek is deceased. If you feel that you are entitled to an explanation of the death and/ or entitled to benefits that might accrue to you under the Alliance Familial Leave and Benefits Act, then please use Release Form 3241025. We will respond to your request within the next six weeks.

The avatar vanished.

Gomez stared at the spot on the back of her hand where the avatar had stood. Deceased? But she had just seen TwoZero. Granted, he wasn't in the best of health, but...

Then she took a deep breath. She decided to be the paranoid investigator.

She looked for information on the other clone. She got no response. She started to look for news when her links pinged.

She swallowed hard. That same avatar appeared, and gave the same speech.

"Oh, God," she whispered. Had she done this? Had her inquiries brought the Epriccom clones to the attention of the Alliance? Or to the attention of those inside the Alliance who were trying to bring down the Alliance?

That couldn't be possible. Could it?

She opened the files that Apaza had given her, and scanned them. She found the prisoner numbers for the other PierLuigi Frémont clones and she inputted them one by one.

Fifteen minutes after each input, the avatar appeared, reciting the death of the clones.

The only one that came back differently was Thirds.

When she inputted his prisoner number, she was told that particular number did not exist.

She stood. Maybe it was her system. Maybe she had done something wrong.

She sent a message to Apaza. *Do me a favor. See if you can set up a new appointment with TwoZero for two days from now.*

His response seemed a bit puzzled in tone. *Oooo-kay.*

She knew it was an invitation to explain, but she didn't take the bait. She checked her network, but found nothing wrong.

She was about to send a message to the warden of Clone Hell when Apaza got back to her.

He used a holographic image rather than an audio message. His image was just a floating head, which looked odd in her small office.

I just got the weirdest message, he sent. *I was told that TwoZero is dead.*

Gomez nodded. *I got that message too. That's why I wanted you to try it. Can you see if it's legit?*

I already did, Apaza said. *And I compared against other clones of Pier-Luigi Frémont. They're all dead.*

Even Thirds? She sent.

Apaza shook his head. *They say he doesn't exist.*

She sighed. Then she thanked Apaza, and signed off.

She didn't want to talk about this with him. She didn't want to talk to Simiaar either.

Sometimes it was hard to ignore evidence, even when it was faint. The clones were dead. The maps lied. The ship had come from the Alliance.

Maybe she was paranoid.

But what if she wasn't? What if there was a conspiracy?
What if a group was trying to dismantle the Alliance from within?
What could she do?
She had no idea. But she knew she had to do something.

49

RAFAEL SALEHI PUT HIS HANDS OVER HIS FACE AND CLOSED HIS EYES FOR just a moment. His stomach twisted.

He had broken the link with Rafik Fujita, then checked the case log from Torkild Zhu. The bastard had defended a clone—of PierLuigi Frémont. But a clone that had been incarcerated during the Anniversary Day attacks.

Zhu had asked for the best transport captain, and Salehi had given him Fujita. Salehi and Fujita went back decades. Salehi had had an idea that this trip would be difficult, but not this difficult.

Had he known that, he would have—what? Sent an army? He had no idea.

He sent a message through his links to Torkild Zhu. *Get your ass to my office. Now.*

Then Salehi mentally sorted through his contacts at the Alliance. He knew council presidents and heads of departments. But he didn't know anyone who could call off battle cruisers.

He sent another message, this one to one of the named partners in S3, Debra Shishani.

We have an emergency situation. You in the building? If so, my office, please.

He only added "please" because if he didn't, Shishani wouldn't show up.

My office, Shishani sent back.

No, Salehi sent. *I have others already here.*

Or other, anyway. If Zhu arrived before Shishani, which Salehi hoped he would. Because right now, Salehi didn't need a pissing contest. He needed to do something fast.

Salehi reset his entire office, getting rid of the desert sequence. He set up panels everywhere, mostly showing space, but also with one star map of Fujita's proposed trip, the trip that S3 had hired him for. Obviously, that trip wasn't happening, but Salehi found illustrations so much better than any attempted explanation.

He also cooled the room down, so that it didn't feel like a desert any longer. He wasn't dressed for standard temperatures, but at the moment, he didn't care if he got a chill. Shishani would complain about how hot it was, and that was the last thing he wanted.

He needed her to focus.

Then he opened the door to his office and made his desk disappear into the floor. He also had the chairs slide under the floor as well, so that no one could be comfortable.

"Hey." Zhu leaned in, as if he were afraid to enter. He looked thinner than Salehi remembered, or maybe he was just noticing for the first time. "What's going on?"

"That's what I want to know," Salehi snapped. "Who did you tell about your Anniversary Day clone?'

"He's not an Anniversary Day clone," Zhu said. "He was in prison—"

"Who did you tell?" Salehi asked again.

"Why?"

Salehi wasn't in the mood for legal games. "You told me and who else?"

Zhu blinked, clearly beginning to understand that he wasn't going to hold the upper hand in this conversation. "Um, I told you and my clerk, and I'm sure the warden knew, and so did the judge…."

His voice trailed off, as his face flushed. He knew something.

"What about the judge?" Salehi asked.

"It's not important right now," Zhu said. "I'll tell you—"

"Now," Salehi said. "You'll tell me now."

Zhu looked down. "She would only free Trey if I promised to recommend her for a position in this law firm."

Salehi stomped to one side as anger filled him. He'd championed this idiot. "And you're only telling me now?"

"I—figured—you know, it wasn't important. We—"

"You think she knew when this clone was being released?"

Zhu shrugged. "What's going on?"

"Did you tell the people who were going to rehabilitate this clone who they were about to take in?"

"No," Zhu said. "I told them exactly what you told me. That they'd be getting a former prisoner, and that his room and board would be paid for six months, nonrefundable, and—"

"Nonrefundable," Salehi muttered. "Marvelous."

Someone knocked on the door. Salehi looked up. Debra Shishani walked inside, looking at the screens. She was taller than both men, angular and busty at the same time, her brown hair piled on top of her head.

"I love what you've done with the place," she said with that sarcasm that had once attracted Salehi, when he'd been a lot younger and a lot stupider.

"We don't have a lot of time," he said to her. "I just heard from Rafik Fujita. He's under attack from, of all things, Alliance battle cruisers. He—"

"Battle cruisers?" she asked. "You're kidding."

"I am not kidding," Salehi said. "He's transporting a clone that Torkild here managed to get released. This clone's been illegally held for fifteen years. But—and here's the kicker—he's a clone of PierLuigi Frémont."

"Like the Anniversary Day killers?" Shishani asked, sarcasm gone.

"Yeah," Salehi said.

"And he had nothing to do with the killings," Zhu said. "He's had no visitors, no nothing the entire time he's been in prison. He wasn't even made in the Alliance—"

Shishani turned away from Zhu as if he didn't matter at all. Maybe he didn't. "So the clone's been released, he's heading—?"

"To the Irr Sector, that halfway house we use."

"And now there's an attack?" Shishani glanced at the screens as if they had an answer. "From the Alliance? Why didn't they just kill this guy in prison?"

"I'm not sure they knew what they had," Zhu said.

Despite himself Salehi felt a bit of admiration for Zhu, standing up for himself however he could.

"And then you pointed right to him." Shishani shook her head. "Did anyone stop to consider this was a stupid idea?"

"Initially Torkild went to find out what the clone knew about other Frémont clones," Salehi said. "I have no idea how it evolved into a release."

Zhu started to say something, but Salehi wouldn't let him.

"The problem is that we're about to lose one of our best transport operatives. He can't leave the Alliance, but he can't stay, not with this clone on his ship. I don't know anyone who can stop this attack. Do you? And if you don't, do you think Schnable does?"

"Yeah, I got someone," Shishani said. "Let me handle this. Where are they?"

"I don't know exactly. I think that's by design. They started here." Salehi went to the screen with Fujita's route on it. "He sent me the registration of the initial attacking ships. I'll send that on your links."

"Thanks." Shishani waggled her fingers at him, and left the room.

Zhu watched her go. Then he turned to Salehi. "What went wrong?"

"You tell me," Salehi said.

"I don't know," Zhu said. "It took weeks for this to go through. It would've been easier to kill Trey in prison."

Salehi stared at the screens. They told him nothing. But he played Zhu's words over and over in his head.

They could have killed the clone in prison.

But they hadn't.

They were killing him in a visible and dramatic fashion.

As a lesson to S3?

To all lawyers who wanted to represent the Anniversary Day clones?

Or was something else going on here?

"Did you ever find out what this clone knew?" Salehi asked.

"I don't think he knew anything," Zhu said. "He was in prison long before the attacks. I checked all of his documentation. He went from wherever he was created to some enclave on Epriccom to prison after some other clones tried to kill him. He killed them in self-defense."

"He committed murder."

"No," Zhu said. "It wasn't murder. It was self-defense."

Salehi cursed. "This is all tied together somehow."

"They should have killed him in prison," Zhu repeated.

"And we wouldn't have noticed," Salehi snapped. "But we're paying attention now, aren't we?"

Zhu looked terrified. "Are they going to come after us?"

Salehi rolled his eyes. He couldn't help it.

"Don't you get it, Torkild?" he said. "They already have."

50

TWENTY MANEUVERS LATER, FUJITA WONDERED IF HE COULD SIMPLY HIDE the *Alus 15*. Go behind a moon, mirror the ship against an asteroid. Something.

But he didn't know how to do any of that.

He'd fought off pirate ships, criminal vessels, a few stolen law enforcement vehicles, but never in his entire career had he faced battle cruisers.

Certainly not Alliance battle cruisers.

"Maybe we should give him up," Stone said.

It was too late for that. They'd been running. Besides, Fujita hadn't given up any prisoner, ever. It wouldn't help his reputation, although in this instance, he wasn't sure what would help him.

Maddix looked at him over her console. She seemed to think that giving up Trey was a good idea as well.

Five ships suddenly appeared in the holoimage at the tip of the triangle.

Five ships, surrounding the dot that was *Alus 15*.

Fujita tapped the screen in front of him. It showed the same image. Somehow it seemed more alarming to him when he saw the ships displayed as numbers and dots.

He tapped his encoded secure link to S3 on. *You got something for me, Rafael?*

Shishani's in touch with someone in the Alliance. She thinks they'll stop this.

Thinks? Fujita sent. *We don't have time for thinks. We're surrounded. They're going to fire on us.*

What have they said?

Nothing, Fujita sent. *They don't answer our hails.*

"They're firing," Maddix said.

The ship shuddered as the shots hit.

All five ships had fired at the same time.

We're not going to survive this, Fujita sent. *They hit us a few more times, and we're done. Make them stop, Salehi.*

We're doing what we can, Salehi sent.

"Screw it," Fujita said to Stone. "Tell them they can have Trey. Tell them that now."

"I'm doing it," Stone said. "I already had the message ready. I'm sending it to all of them on all channels. I hope—"

The ship shuddered again, then the power blinked down.

"Shields are gone," Maddix said. Her gaze met Fujita's. "Do you think they'll listen? I mean, we're willing to give him up."

"I know," Fujita said, because he couldn't say anything else. He looked at Stone. "Keep sending the message."

"Yeah," Stone said, but he was staring at his screen.

Fujita was staring at his too. Five points of light. Shots, coming from all five battle cruisers. Not small weapons fire either. Big laser weapons. Weapons of war.

I don't know what the hell you got us into, Fujita sent to Salehi, *but it's bad. We're—*

The shots hit. For a moment, the *Alus 15* lit up, exterior, interior, all blurred into red light, before evaporating. Fujita had one moment to notice how beautiful it was, and then he stopped noticing anything at all.

51

Rafik? Salehi sent along his links. Rafik?

He looked at Zhu, who seemed panicked. Shishani hadn't even returned to the room yet.

"Get her," Salehi said to Zhu.

Then Salehi put a hand to his ear, even though he knew it meant nothing. He stared at the screens, at the useless map.

Rafik, answer me. You got cut off—

LINK CONNECTION SEVERED. IMPOSSIBLE TO RE-ESTABLISH. LINKS EITHER NO LONGER EXIST OR NETWORK NO LONGER EXISTS.

Salehi played the message a second time. He'd never seen anything like that before. His heart was pounding.

He walked around the screens, leaned out the door, saw Shishani waving Zhu off.

Salehi pushed past Zhu.

"You want to tell me what's going on, Debra?" Salehi said. "Because your damn delay just cost us our best transport captain."

"What?" Zhu asked.

Shishani frowned at Salehi. "I just told the head of the Earth Alliance Military Human Unit that there was some mistake. He promised me he'd stop this. I was double-checking with one of our councilors."

"He's gone," Salehi said to her. "Fujita's gone. I got a severed link notice."

337

"Try some other channel," Zhu said. "He's got to be there."

"Yes, try," Shishani said.

Salehi swallowed hard. He tried every link he could think of. He finally tried Fujita again.

LINK CONNECTION SEVERED. IMPOSSIBLE TO RE-ESTABLISH. LINKS EITHER NO LONGER EXIST OR NETWORK NO LONGER EXISTS.

"He's gone," Salehi said. "*They're* gone. They killed your clone, Zhu."

Zhu turned even grayer. He put a hand to his mouth and stumbled off.

Shishani watched him go. "Are we in trouble?"

"If we fight this, yes, we probably are," Salehi said. "Something's happening here. Something bigger than us."

"You're usually our idealist," Shishani said. "You're the one who fights for lost causes."

Salehi nodded. A clone that looked like the Anniversary Day killers. An Alliance connection to his death.

"We should never have gotten involved in this one," Salehi said.

Their involvement cost them a great working relationship. Hell, he needed to be honest. It had cost him Fujita.

A friend.

Salehi didn't have a lot of friends.

"Hold on," Shishani said, and turned away from him. Her body hunched forward, the way some people did when they were conducting a private conversation on a link.

He watched her. His entire body felt jittery, as if he were about to bounce out of the corridor and into another wing of the law firm.

She turned, hand down, expression bleak.

"They'd been told that Fujita was transporting terrorists," she said. "They scanned his ship, and found the clone's signature. Standard procedure is to destroy any ship transporting designer criminal clones. Particularly those with mass murderer DNA."

"Who told them?" Salehi said.

She shook her head. "That's classified."

"That's convenient," Salehi said.

"Yeah." She reached up, as if she were going to run a hand through her hair, and then remembered that she wore it up. "He warned me away. They warned me away. They said we shouldn't have done anything."

Salehi nodded. He got that message loud and clear.

"He sounded shaken," Shishani said. "Like he was surprised by all of this."

"Does he know who classified this operation?" Salehi said.

"I don't know," she said. "I didn't ask. We have to let go, Rafael."

Easy for her to say. She hadn't lost a friend.

But he understood.

She was scared.

He was too.

"It was a clone," she said. "Of a mass murderer."

"And a group we had hired to transport him," Salehi said.

"We didn't hire them," she said. "Zhu did."

Salehi's stomach clenched. Zhu. His career was over now, even if he didn't realize it.

"That doesn't make me feel any better," Salehi said.

"I wasn't trying to make you feel better," Shishani said. "I was just telling you the truth."

She didn't know the truth. Neither did he.

But he wasn't sure he wanted to.

He needed to go sit down. He needed to think.

He needed to apologize to Fujita's family.

Sometimes the law was so simple.

And sometimes, it was so very hard.

52

THE SHIP WAS FAST, ESPECIALLY FOR SOMETHING OF ITS SIZE. IT WAS larger than the main crew quarters on the *Stanley*. But it felt small to Gomez. She was used to commanding a ship the size of a small battle cruiser.

Still, this one would be hers. Just hers.

She stood inside the model, looking at the traditional galley. It had replicated food, like so many ships, but it also had a space for a personal chef. She had walked through, stunned at the ship's three levels: a large cargo area below, the main floor for cabins, food, and recreation, and the upper level for ship administration.

"You don't want it." The voice was familiar.

Gomez turned. Simiaar stood behind her, arms crossed.

"You'd be a damn sitting duck in that cockpit. Besides, the kind of weapons that come with this thing *I* could dismantle, and I know nothing about dismantling weapons."

Gomez's mouth opened. She hadn't expected to see Simiaar here. Gomez had told her crew to take the weekend off when they arrived at Jezzen Base. She hadn't told them she would be taking a leave of absence, even though she had put in for it. She would be gone at least a year.

Gomez knew why she was leaving the *Stanley*. She just wasn't sure it would add up if she explained it to someone else.

She didn't believe in a conspiracy, but she didn't believe that there *wasn't* one either. She needed to know. Because if someone was conspiring to bring down the Alliance, she couldn't sit back and let it happen.

She wasn't sure how to stop it, but in the long sleepless nights that she'd had on the way to this Jezzen Base, she had realized one thing: she had a particular skill.

She could investigate. Maybe she wasn't as good with data retrieval as Apaza or as good at forensics as Simiaar, but she was good at putting things together. She was also good at reading people, and dealing with aliens. She was uniquely suited to asking stupid questions for all the right reasons, and leaving those she questioned without any suspicion of her motives at all.

And she couldn't ignore all that she'd learned. Anniversary Day happened on the Moon in part because she hadn't followed up on the clones she'd found at Epriccom. It didn't matter what anyone else said; if she had done more than flag the file, then maybe hundreds of thousands (millions?) of people would still be alive.

She couldn't live with that, particularly after discovering there might be something bad going on in the Alliance. She needed to resolve it.

"I thought you needed beer," she said to Simiaar. Simiaar had said that when they arrived: *I need good beer and bad food,* she'd said as she toddled off the *Stanley.*

Simiaar shrugged. "I was on my way to getting a great buzz when Apaza showed up. The bastard asked me why you were taking a leave. I didn't know you were taking a leave, and then I thought about it. I decided I was wrong. Still, I tried to locate you and I found you were in a dealership, looking at fast, weaponized vessels. Turns out I wasn't wrong after all."

Gomez's back and shoulders were so stiff they ached. "Wrong about what?"

"You're going off to find out what happened with the damn clones. You're going to do the investigation the Alliance was going to do, and you somehow think you can do it alone."

"I can't take the *Stanley*," Gomez said.

Simiaar crossed her arms. "And those are your only choices? Good God, woman, I thought you had an imagination."

Gomez's cheeks warmed. "You said you didn't want anything to do with a war."

"And yet, somehow, I'm part of the precipitating event. Imagine if you could have prevented—wait! You know how that feels. You need me, Judita. I find out things, and I'm smarter than you."

She just said that to anger Gomez. Gomez shook her head slightly.

"I *am*," Simiaar said. "I know that anyone who pilots a ship with its controls on the outer edges of that ship is asking for someone to attack them—whether that's pirates or personal enemies or, gosh, maybe someone who wants secrets to remain secret."

"I was just looking," Gomez said defensively.

"You moved money from your stash," Simiaar said.

"You *looked* at my accounts?" Gomez asked.

"To be fair," Simiaar said, "Apaza did. He's worried about you. And me. And us. He thinks this isn't over. I think he's right. Is he right?"

Gomez let out a sigh. She leaned against a wall and felt it give a little in the pressure. The wall was awfully cheaply made, considering how much this ship cost.

"I can't keep doing my job if I think no one follows up on the important stuff," she said quietly.

"So you think this is an isolated incident," Simiaar said.

Gomez shrugged. "I don't know. And because I don't know, I can't head back to the Frontier as someone who works for the Alliance. I really believe all that—"

"Truth and justice crap. I know," Simiaar said. "Sometimes enjoying the purity of science is so much better. I get to do work I wouldn't normally do. I don't need to believe in right and wrong."

"But you do," Gomez said softly.

"Sadly," Simiaar said. "Which is why I'm willing to pool my resources with yours. We buy a ship—a good one, not an expensive piece of hype like this thing—and we replicate my lab in it, get a few crew members who can help out, and ask Apaza what he wants—"

"He's leaving?"

"He's got qualifying tests coming up, Judita. He's not willing to get enhancements, nor is he willing to lose weight. He's going to physical out of the service, and he knows it."

"So he'd come because he has nowhere else to go?"

"He'd come because he's scared, like you are. Judita, there might be hundreds of those clones—"

"I know," she said, cutting off Simiaar. Gomez didn't want to have the discussion in the middle of some model in a dealership.

"We find a couple of other people who can help and who aren't afraid of what you want to do, and we head off into the unknown. Unless you know what you want to do."

Gomez let out a sigh. She looked at the area around them, and knew they were being watched. They had to be, because they could just walk off with some of the expensive doodads that would lull people into thinking the ship was well made. (Like they had almost lulled her.)

There are three things I need to investigate, Gomez sent on an encoded link. *I need to find out where those clones came from. I need to find out what happened to that starbase in the Frontier, and I need to find out who got rid of TwoZero and the others.*

All by your lonesome you were planning to do that? Simiaar sent back.

I was thinking I'd go to the Moon first, visit that security chief, see if she had some people who could help me.

Simiaar shook her head. *And spend half your year off getting there and back. Seems relatively worthless to me. Do it my way.*

I usually do, Gomez thought but didn't send. Or maybe she did, given the sideways glance Simiaar suddenly gave her.

Better to go to her with information in hand. Besides, they're probably overwhelmed on the Moon at the moment anyway. Think of that level of destruction. No one's investigating anything.

What Simiaar didn't send, and what Gomez suddenly realized, was that some of the natural investigators from the Moon were probably dead. Or in mourning. Or injured.

Her plan had been flawed. She'd been reacting out of guilt, not because she was thinking clearly.

She needed to investigate, yes, and she had to do it outside of the aegis of the Alliance. But she couldn't do it alone.

She needed Simiaar. Apaza would make things so much easier as well. With the right pilot (or pilots), and a few others, she would be able to travel much more safely.

And Simiaar was right: she needed a ship with good weaponry.

"Okay," Gomez said out loud. "You're right. I need help."

Simiaar opened her hands and looked up, as if some higher power had assisted her in convincing Gomez.

"This could be dangerous," Gomez said.

"And our day job isn't?" Simiaar asked. "Please, don't insult me."

Gomez grinned.

Simiaar put an arm around her. "We are leaving this expensive piece of crap, and we're heading to the bar for good beer and bad food. There we will research the type of vessel we actually need. Deal?"

Gomez's stomach growled. She hadn't realized she was hungry. Or maybe she hadn't been hungry until she made this decision.

"Deal," she said, and let Simiaar lead her out of the ship.

They would find out all the information the Alliance had missed. They would take whatever they learned to the Moon. By then, the security chief and the survivors would be ready to hear it.

By then, they would be looking for answers.

And Gomez might just be able to provide them.

The thrilling adventure continues with the fourth book
in the Anniversary Day Saga, *Search & Recovery*.

Amid the ruin, heroes emerge from the unlikeliest places...

The Anniversary Day bombings devastated the Moon, killing thousands. While survivors search for missing loved ones and the rich and powerful set plans in motion to capitalize on the Moon's misfortune, one ruthless man vows to uncover those responsible for the attacks on the Moon.

Luc Deshin, the most feared man in Armstrong, knows all too well the bombings could have killed the wife and son he loves more than life itself. To protect his family, Deshin immerses himself in a criminal network he fought long and hard to leave behind. Deshin doesn't scare easy, but what he finds in the black market underbelly of the Moon will chill him to the bone.

Turn the page for the first chapter of *Search & Recovery*.

FOUR YEARS AGO

1

BERHANE MAGALHÃES'S MOTHER PUT HER ARM AROUND BERHANE'S shoulder, pulled her close, and kissed the top of her head. Berhane flushed, but refrained from looking around the *Armstrong Express* car at the other passengers to see if they noticed her mother's inappropriate display of affection. Berhane used to glance at others guiltily when she was younger, and all it would do was make her mother's trilling laugh echo through whatever compartment they were in.

This compartment was large and wide, with silver built-in seats that accommodated most two-legged species, and some sideways booths for wider aliens. There was even a flat tabletop area for the Disty. A Disty sat cross-legged on it now, its tiny childlike shape belying its ferocity.

Berhane had grown up fearing the Disty. Apparently, her father had lost business associates to them, and he loved to talk about how awful the Disty were and how they murdered indiscriminately. *Earth Alliance law allowed for it*, he would say, and then he would add, *That's such a travesty.*

She tried not to look at the Disty—and found herself looking at a wide variety of humans instead. They were standing, sitting, watching vids on their links, swaying to the train's movement. Scattered among them, a few Peyti—gray aliens so thin that they looked like they would shatter with a tap to their twig-like arms. They wore masks over much of their faces, which she had grown used to in her time at the university.

Berhane hadn't had a lot of contact with aliens before she graduated from the Armstrong Wing of the Aristotle Academy two years ago. Now, aliens filled her classes, and the hallway, and the public transportation she took daily to get to Dome University's Armstrong campus.

Apparently, Berhane's mother noted her discomfort with the aliens and pulled Berhane even closer. Berhane didn't move away, although she wanted to. Her mother—and probably most of the humans in the car—would have found the movement rude.

And whatever she thought of her mother, Berhane didn't want to be rude to her. She knew they just misunderstood each other most of the time.

Madeline Magalhães believed in laughter and affection and warmth; for some reason, she had married a man who believed in none of those things, leaving her children confused about the very nature of love and proper behavior.

None more than Berhane, who adored her father. He seemed to approve of her, although he rarely said so. But of all the family members, the only one he talked to about business and the future was Berhane.

Her mother grinned at everyone else in the compartment. Most of them looked away. Her mother rarely rode public transportation, but this morning, she was accommodating Berhane—sort of.

Berhane had mentioned that they'd be taking the five a.m. inner dome train in an effort to dissuade her mother from accompanying her. Predictably, her mother had mentioned bringing their own car, but Berhane had vetoed that.

She hated parking in the university lots. Not only was it difficult to find a space, but she found that having a car—particularly one of the most expensive models on the Moon—made her feel less like a student and more like a wealthy dilettante.

"You really need to listen to me," her mother said softly, after she had kissed Berhane's head.

"I do listen," Berhane said a little too loudly. The big man near her looked over. She glared at him, wondering if his size was a conscious choice. He looked wealthy enough to afford thinness enhancements.

"My darling," her mother said, laughter in her voice, "you have never listened to me. But you need to, now."

"Mom," Berhane said. "I have finals this week. I don't have time to think about any big life changes."

Whenever her mother got this tone, she wanted Berhane to do something. Change her major, be nicer to her father, talk to her brother about something he was doing wrong.

Given the timing, her mother probably wanted her to break up with her boyfriend. Her mother had never liked Torkild Zhu, believing him to be a cold-hearted bastard like her father. At least, those were her mother's words.

And maybe her mother was right on some level. Torkild wanted to be a lawyer, not because he cared about people, per se, but because he found the law intellectually challenging—and because he thought being a lawyer would be a great way to make money. Not Bernard Magalhães kind of money (one of the richest men on the Moon money), but out-earning your own parents kind of money.

Torkild had said that if he were a lawyer, he would have to answer to himself, the courts, and no one else.

He seemed to think that a good idea. Berhane had not found a way to argue with him.

And she hadn't felt like it. He had his passions; she wished she had hers. She was still looking for her place in the universe. Right now, she was that Magalhães girl, or Torkild's girlfriend, or a Dome University student.

No one knew who Berhane was because Berhane didn't know who Berhane was either.

Her mother's smile vanished. "You need to make time to talk with me. I don't think this can wait any longer."

Drama. Her mother was all about drama—happy drama, but drama nonetheless.

Her mother must have seen the reluctance on Berhane's face. She patted Berhane on the leg.

"Tell you what," her mother said. "I'll stop at the Shenandoah Café and get that cinnamon coffee you like. I'll bring it to your favorite table in the quad in, what? An hour?"

Berhane resisted the urge to roll her eyes. That was what she got for telling her mother her exam schedule. She could almost hear herself blithely nattering last night:

I'm not worried about the first exam, even if it is at 6:30 in the morning. It's Poetry of the New Worlds, which is going to be an essay exam, graded on creativity, which just means repeating the lectures the professor gave that he obviously thought were brilliant...

"I thought you had a meeting," Berhane said, trying not to sound desperate. She hated heart-to-hearts with her mother. "That was what you told me last night."

Her mother's smile was wide and warm, deepening the creases around her eyes and making her seem even more cheerful than usual.

"I do have a meeting," her mother said. "It's with you."

Berhane felt a surge of irritation. Her mother always manipulated her like that. But before Berhane could say anything, her mother stood. The train was slowing. Her mother headed to the nearest exit, along with two Peyti, three Imme, and a short woman who didn't quite block Berhane's view of her mother's face.

Her mother smiled at Berhane, then waggled her fingers. Berhane gave her a reluctant shake of the head. Her mother knew that Berhane was annoyed at her—and in typical fashion, her mother didn't really care.

The train stopped, the door eased open, and the group of seven from this part of the car stepped onto the outdoor platform—although nowhere in Armstrong's dome was really outside. Outside was the Moon itself, with its own gravity and lack of oxygen. Berhane had gone out there several times in an environmental suit, generally with her father on business, and it had always freaked her out.

The platform glowed golden in light from Dome Dawn. Her mother's hair had reddish highlights from the fake sunlight, and her matching black pantsuit glowed reddish as well. She walked to the side of the platform, heading toward the stairs, as the train eased forward.

Berhane felt a longing for cinnamon coffee. The Shenandoah Café made the best in Armstrong. Her mother definitely knew how to bribe her. And after this stupid final, Berhane would want some kind of refreshment, even if it meant letting her mother harangue her.

The train sped up, heading across the famed University shopping district with its funky stores and fantastic restaurants (including the Shenandoah Café), before it reached the first of five University stops. Berhane didn't settle in. She would get off on the second stop and walk less than a block to get to her exam.

Berhane felt annoyed. Instead of focusing on the exam (which was going to count for 75% of her grade), she was thinking about whatever it was that her mother wanted. And it had to be something important (life-changing, her mother had said) to merit cinnamon coffee and a forced meeting.

The train slid sideways.

Berhane's heart rose and her breath caught.

Trains weren't supposed to slide sideways. They couldn't slide sideways.

Berhane felt a surge of alarm.

Then the train car toppled backwards, and the people near the door flew toward her.

A big man landed on her, knocking the wind from her. Screams echoed around her. Beside her, a Peyti—its face grotesque and strange—gasped. It had no mask. It was on its side, groping for its mask with its twig-like fingers. Somehow Berhane managed to grab the mask and give it to the Peyti, all without dislodging the big man on top of her.

More people had landed on him, and the screaming continued.

Then another *thump* occurred, making the car jolt upward as if nothing held it down, not even the weight of the people inside. The car had gone dark.

She managed to catch a thin breath, although it hurt. Then she realized that the air tasted of chemicals. Burned chemicals. She peered through the window, which was now above her, and saw a blackened dome.

The car hadn't gone dark—or maybe it had—but the dome had gone dark too. Domes didn't go dark. That meant the power was off, the environment was no longer being filtered, and everyone would die.

They would all die.

She gasped for air again, her chest aching. The air burned its way down her throat.

She willed herself to think—not about dying, but about surviving. She needed to survive. She needed to live. If she thought about dying, she would, underneath the big man who smelled of sweat, in a closed car filled with screamers, and near a Peyti clutching its mask to its bony little face. Its eyes met hers, and in their liquid depths, she thought she saw panic.

She wouldn't panic. She couldn't.

The car hadn't shifted any more. Whatever had happened was over—at least for the moment.

She moved her arms under the big man, finding his back or his shoulders or some solid part of him, and she shoved.

"We have to move," she said.

She could barely hear herself in all the screaming. The Peyti was still staring at her.

She shoved again.

"Move!" she shouted at the big man, and he did, somehow, sliding toward the seat behind her.

A tangle of people and a Disty tumbled on top of her and she kept shoving.

"Move!" she yelled again, and this time, her voice cut through the screams. The fact that someone (she) had taken charge seemed to galvanize everyone.

People started picking themselves up, rolling away from each other, asking questions instead of screaming.

"Anything broken?"

"You okay?"

"Can you slide this way?"

Berhane tuned out the words and managed to pull herself upright. She was now standing on the window of the car, her back against the ceiling. The train had derailed, something she hadn't thought possible. Weren't they built so that they couldn't derail? She remembered hearing about that in one of her classes. Something about magnetized couplings and nanobots and—

She wiped a hand over her face, and took another deep breath of the chemical-laden air. She was in shock, or sliding into shock, and she didn't dare, because they were trapped in this car. Judging from the smells around her—those chemicals, the stench of burning—something had gone very wrong somewhere, and she couldn't know if it was the train itself or if it was the dome.

The Peyti grabbed her leg. She looked down at the thin gray fingers wrapped around her pants.

"Please," it said.

She reached down, and helped it up. Its other arm dangled at its side, clearly broken. She'd always thought the twig-like Peyti looked fragile. Now she knew that they were.

"Thank you," it said.

"There's something in the air," she said because she knew the Peyti, with its mask, couldn't smell what had gone wrong. "Something bad."

The Peyti nodded and surveyed the area around them. Other survivors were moving, shuffling toward the side of the car.

The Peyti said something in its native language and looked back at her.

"What?" she asked.

It shook its head, a movement that looked very unnatural. It clearly worked among humans and had learned their movements.

"The dome sectioned," it said.

She frowned. "How do you know that?"

"Do not look north," it said.

She didn't even know where north was. She was completely disoriented.

"Oh, my God." The big guy was standing on the seat back beside her. "We got cut in half."

Berhane didn't understand him at first. She was fine. Except for broken bones and bleeding, everyone else seemed fine too. She glanced at the big man, then started to turn toward the direction he was looking in, but the Peyti grabbed her arm.

"Do not look," it said. "The dome bisected the train."

Her breath caught. "It can't do that."

"Not under regular circumstances, no," the Peyti said. "The trains must stop when the dome sections, but clearly this is not a regular circumstance."

The dome only dropped its sections when the mayor ordered the dome to get segmented off. He had done so during the crisis surrounding the Moon marathon. He had sectioned off one part of the dome, so the disease running through the marathon didn't infect the rest of the city.

But that was the only time in her memory that the dome had sectioned.

And that sectioning had been *ordered*. Trains had stopped in time. Cars hadn't been able to get through the area. People had been instructed to move away from the section before it came down.

Not this time.

"What happened?" she whispered.

"Something bad," the Peyti said.

The something bad had happened in the forward compartments.

Then Berhane realized she was turned around. The sectioning had occurred behind her.

Where her mother had been.

"No," Berhane said.

She scrambled past the people still picking themselves up, and climbed toward the door. It was half open, something that shouldn't have happened either, or maybe that was a fail-safe when the train derailed (only it wasn't supposed to derail).

Somehow she pried the doors open and squeezed through.

The air was thick with the smell of burnt rubber and fried circuits. Her eyes watered.

She could see the dome behind her, set against the famed university shopping district, but it looked wrong.

Black. Rubble. Smoke, billowing everywhere. Some of it near the sectioned dome, but most of it behind the protective barrier.

She climbed on top of the car. The train was twisted too. Cut in half. Sort of. Because in the back, past the section, she couldn't see a train at all.

She couldn't see anything she recognized.

"Mother," she whispered. And then she shouted, "Mother!"

Her mother never shouted back.

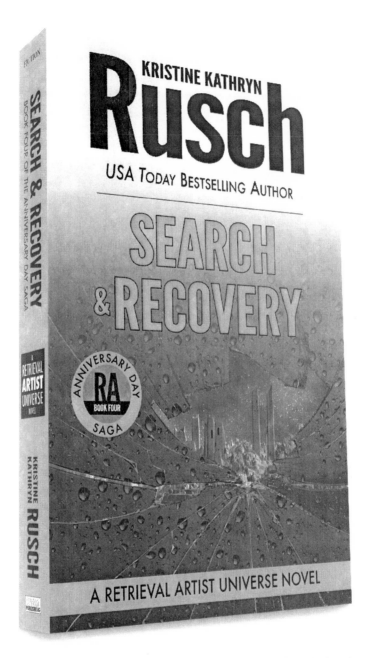

The thrilling adventure continues with the fourth book
in the Anniversary Day Saga, *Search & Recovery,*
available now from your favorite bookseller.

ABOUT THE AUTHOR

USA Today bestselling author Kristine Kathryn Rusch writes in almost every genre. Generally, she uses her real name (Rusch) for most of her writing. Under that name, she publishes bestselling science fiction and fantasy, award-winning mysteries, acclaimed mainstream fiction, controversial nonfiction, and the occasional romance. Her novels have made bestseller lists around the world and her short fiction has appeared in eighteen best of the year collections. She has won more than twenty-five awards for her fiction, including the Hugo, *Le Prix Imaginales,* the *Asimov's* Readers Choice award, and the *Ellery Queen Mystery Magazine* Readers Choice Award.

To keep up with everything she does, go to kriswrites.com. To track her many pen names and series, see their individual websites (krisnelscott.com, kristinegrayson.com, krisdelake.com, retrievalartist.com, divingintothewreck. com, fictionriver.com). She lives and occasionally sleeps in Oregon.

CPSIA information can be obtained at www.ICGtesting.com
Printed in the USA
LVOW09s2135190215

427631LV00001B/235/P